With Pleasure, Ms. Rathbone

Sierra Prynne

Book Two in the *Revenge & Riches Billionaire Series*

"A girl should be two things:
Who and what she wants."
-   Coco Chanel

CHAPTER 1

LULU

"Please, Mr. Malbec, I just want to talk with you!"

"Go away!"

There must be something wrong with me. I mean, there's something wrong with all of us, I think, on a primal level. We're all just trying to mess up in ways that take us forward rather than backward, but...

My heartrate spiked the second Kaden Malbec slammed his cabin door in my face. Not because I got one glimpse of the most reclusive, exceptional artist of our time in person, but because he completely dismissed me in the blink of an eye. Left me out here on his porch in the freezing, snowy cold, like I wasn't worth talking to.

Maybe I'm not. Even though he has a notorious reputation for hating people, I had convinced myself on the helicopter ride up here that my interaction with him would be different. Special. It would be the exception that proved the rule. He would hear my paint-splattered soul call to his and rejoice that he finally found somebody who understood.

I don't know why I do this to myself. I don't know why I set myself up for failure. Malbec spoke to Mr. King when he came out here, so there must be something about me that turned Malbec off. Something that lumped me in with the rest of humanity in his eyes the moment he saw me.

I know the shame that settles in my heart at the thought isn't rational, but it's there all the same. Mr. King sent me out here to talk to him, to vet him as a potential client, but maybe he should have picked someone else.

I completely froze when Malbec opened the door. Like a fangirl. Like I haven't been a private art advisor *my entire adult life*. Like I don't have Bharti Kher and Jerry Saltz on speed dial!

It's so embarrassing. I just stared at him. It probably wasn't even a cute stare, either; everybody knows natural reactions to awe and wonder rarely look sexy. But I couldn't help it. I never expected the man, the mind, the visionary I've admired from afar would look so…empty.

Hollow.

Malbec looked so lifeless that for a long second I thought I was looking at a ghost.

Beautiful, of course, with his mass of curly dark hair and ice blue eyes, that dimple on his chin and the two I could see framing his mouth. But in his current state, the combination just made him look deader. More evocative. Fascinating.

If he opens the door again, I'll probably try to take a picture of him so I can sketch him later. Hell, forget the photo, I already know I'm drawing him from memory the second I get home.

Which means I am *absolutely* not the person Malbec needs in his life right now. I'm treating him like the idea of a person rather than a person. I should definitely leave, call Cara, and see if she can send someone for a wellness check. And I will…right after I ensure I don't leave empty handed. Kindred spirit nonsense aside, I'm a professional. I came here with a job to do and, dammit, I want to do it.

I bang on the door again, a little harder this time, ignoring the sting in my hand.

"I can stay out here all day!" I sing, pulling my coat tighter against the biting wind.

"Enjoy freezing to death then!" he sings back.

"Come on, man! I'll go away faster if you just hear me out."

He doesn't respond right away. I hear some bulky piece of furniture rattle as he stomps closer to the door. He yanks it open like it's been keeping him hostage and sneers at me.

"I told the last two guys who came here that I already have an agent," he says. "I'm not interested in switching. I don't care who you know or what vision you have for my career. If you want something from me, direct everything to Ethan King at the Star-King Agency, all right?"

He almost shuts the door again before I can yelp, "Mr. King is the one who sent me!"

That stops him, but only barely. "Why?"

"A few reasons," I say. "Reasons that would be much easier to discuss *inside*, in the warmth. Please?"

Malbec sighs like I just asked him to save the world. Considering I can't feel my toes anymore, maybe that's exactly what I'm asking him to do.

"You're shaking like a chihuahua," he grumbles after a moment. "I hate chihuahuas."

With that, he's gone. His heavy footfalls pound across the wood floor as he retreats deeper into the cabin, but…he left the door open. It's all the invitation I need.

I step inside and lock the door behind me, as a gesture to the universe not to send me out into the bitter cold again until I've done what I came here to do. I slip my coat off for good measure; it's so warm in here I don't need it anyway. Then I take off my icy heels and rub my feet against the nearest carpet I can find, trying to warm them up through friction.

Calling this place a cabin is a little disingenuous. This is a lodge. A hoarder's lodge. Large and dark and overcrowded with a thousand and one pieces of junk I never expected to see. Mannequins and rolls of fabric, birdcages, and antiques stacked on antiques. Paintings, too, of course. So many paintings lean against the walls and in racks and shelves, there's more art than air in here.

"I'm in the middle of something."

I turn at the sound of his low, impatient voice. He's standing in the hallway by the stairs, leaning against the bottom post, leering at me with eyes so bright in the dim light they look like they're made out of glass.

"If you want to yap, you'll have to do it back here."

He disappears before I can say anything, but who cares? I'll go wherever he wants if he's willing to talk to me—

The thought dies as I hustle after him and realize there's paint on his clothing. Handprints in red hug the ass of his pants, like someone gripped him hard and pulled him in. There are also red scratch marks across the entire back of his shirt, ending in thick, pressing, wrinkled handprints on either side of his waist. There are also two angled paint lines along the back of his thighs. For a moment, I think he was in a fight...but that's not it. My mind floods with images of what *I* would have to do to make those marks. The angles I would need to achieve. For starters, I'd have to be underneath him with my arms and legs wrapped around him. Heat rises to my cheeks. My heart leaps inside me as a theory of what they are begins to form.

Sure enough, as we reach a large back room lit by skylights, he turns and confirms what I'm thinking. There's a red imprint of a face along the shirt's neckline; whoever she was, she pressed her head to his shirt in a moment of exquisite ecstasy. And the crotch of his pants...well...there's an imprint there too.

The paint has long dried, but it's making me wet all the same. These aren't marks of violence; they're marks of lust. Not just lust, but *lust in action*.

I step closer wondering how long ago they were made. By whom. I wonder how she made him feel, how he washes it, if he does this with every sexual partner or if she was special. There's a scrunched splatter right in the center of his abdomen, like she twisted her fist into the fabric of the shirt and tugged. It's beautiful.

"Ahem."

It isn't until he clears his throat that I realize I'm staring. I jerk my gaze away, but looking elsewhere doesn't quench the fire in my belly; it only flames it further. I'm standing in a cathedral of canvas and color. Every square inch of wall and gable space wears his artwork. Most are pieces I've only ever seen in the corners of photographs he's taken of this studio.

There's even a barely started new piece on a massive easel nearby. I can just see the outline of someone—a ballerina en pointe, maybe—starting to take shape.

Just like the artwork on his shirt, almost every piece in the room is the human body in motion. Each body is blurred and distorted, as if you're peering through a veil, voyeuristically watching the goings-on within. Just like the artist himself, they look haunted.

"This is…" I murmur. "This is…"

"A place almost no one else has ever seen," he says quietly. "So be respectful, please."

Respectful? He's misread me totally. I'm not going to say anything critical; if anything, I have the sudden aching desire to find a witch, medium, or god in human form who can let me live inside one.

"What did I just say!" Malbec suddenly barks.

His voice snaps me out of my reverent haze to find my hand hovering between me and the closest painting, of a contortionist bent over themselves. Jesus, I was seconds from touching it.

"I'm sorry!" I say, because I genuinely am. "Fuck, I'm sorry. I just—"

"Why that painting?" he interrupts.

"What?"

Malbec moves like a sleepwalker, a few inches at a time, through the maze of supplies to stand beside me.

"There are a hundred paintings in this room. That isn't the one closest to the door or the easiest to reach. You were drawn to that one specifically. Why?"

"The light," I answer honestly. "You can see through her clothes there and there. It's a detail not a lot of people would have cared about capturing, but it adds beautiful texture and dimension. I feel like I could reach in and pull the curtain back."

"Would you?" he asks. "Would you pull the curtain back if given the chance?"

I answer without hesitation. "Absolutely."

He doesn't respond. Instead, he stares at his own work with a bitter scowl on his face. When he *does* speak, his voice is almost as hollow as he is. But even in the hollowness, there's something lovely about him. Lovely and broken.

The words leave his mouth slowly. "What do you want from me?"

It takes every ounce of self-control I possess to lie to him. Well, not *lie*, but to disguise the deeper truth I really wish I knew him well enough to say.

"Mr. King has sent me to get to know you," I tell him. "But I personally wanted to thank you for the painting you gave him."

His sea-glass eyes slide to me, giving nothing away. "You're Louise Rathbone?"

Hearing him say my name makes me shiver.

"I am. Please, call me Lulu."

"Lulu." He sighs like a nor'easter, and I shiver again. "What did you do with the painting, Lulu?"

"I placed it with the Russo Trust after I..."

I cut myself off a second before disaster, absolutely *mortified* about what I was about to say to this man. This stranger who doesn't want me here invading his space.

"After you what?"

"After I received it." My voice comes out clipped and quick. I glance back at the painting of the contortionist just to give myself something to focus on.

"After you what, Ms. Rathbone?" His voice is soft, but curious. "Tell me the truth and I'll answer any questions you want."

"It's nothing," I try.

"You had a beautiful expression on your face for a moment. You grimaced with anticipation, like a memory struck you and you pulled away from it. Why?"

"Because it's private," I admit.

"Good." When I glance at him, he adds, "You've come to pry into my personal life. It's only fair you let me pry into yours."

He's staring. *Staring*. And he's only a few inches away; I can smell the coffee he drank this morning on his breath.

"Tell me?" His voice travels as softly as a passed message on a bit of paper between us. He doesn't blink or glance away, but the tip of his tongue darts out of his mouth, wagging a little with curiosity. He doesn't even know he's doing it.

I shouldn't tell him. I know I shouldn't tell him. But I want to. I want him to know.

So I take a deep breath and tell him the raw, unvarnished truth he asked for.

Holding his gaze, I whisper, "I placed the painting in the Russo Trust after I slept with it and touched myself to thoughts of you painting it."

CHAPTER 2

KADEN

The words, "touched myself to thoughts of you painting it," escape her mouth like a prayer. One she knows only I can answer. One I *would* have answered once upon a time. In a heartbeat. I would have fisted my hand in her hair, pulled her into me, into my lips, and drank nectar from her until I felt her hands go to my waist, heard her whimper of desire. I would have lifted her into my arms, found any flat surface in the studio and fucked her until our voices rang out in the gables overhead like some exalted hymn.

That used to be my favorite sound in the world. Better than a paintbrush against an easel leg. Better than rain on the porch. Better than *The Strokes*.

Now, I just feel numb to it. Maybe I've been alone too long. Maybe I've lost my spark. The numbness nullifies everything else. All I feel is a clinical attempt by my mind to interpret her words as a lie and her presence as a threat. The exact type of threat I tried to escape by leaving the city and locking myself away up here at the estate.

All that artificial admiration.

All that parasitic schmoozing.

All those lies people told because they wanted something from me.

It was my fault I believed any of it, I know, but...once I knew how phony it all was, I couldn't...pretend anymore. Which made me feel like such a hypocrite; I'm a hypocrite for playing the game until I won and grew tired of it, and then punishing others who play it too.

But I just…

Louise begins to turn in a circle, gazing up at my work. Her movement forces me from the doom-spiral of my own bullshit for half a second.

Louise—*Lulu*—is a vision. She was when I first saw her on the porch, completely swallowed in that ridiculous parka, and she still is, standing three feet from me. It's not just the outfit she's wearing, although the layered look has me wanting to peel each piece off her slowly just to see how many there are. It's not the ridiculously lush dark hair, or her hazel eyes that look like crystallized honey. It's her. Something in her.

Something which leaves an acrid bitter taste on my tongue. Her eyes peer around at the art on the walls with an inspired awe I haven't felt in *years*. Not since I last saw Van Gogh's *Starry Night* in person. His and my art styles couldn't be more different, but his masterwork awed me in a way few other pieces have.

Eh, that's underselling it.

Looking at his art made me feel like I was having an out-of-body experience; I was both lucky and cursed that I realized it *while* admiring his painting. I knew I'd never get another moment like it.

That's how Louise looks now. Beautiful bowed lips parted. Expressive eyes wide and bright. Neck tilted as she turns in a circle, studying pieces I haven't thought about in years. She's almost dancing; the sway of her body and the flutter of her fingers tell me she's holding back from being as excited as she truly is.

I want to tell her not to hide.

Hell, I *want* to gather together half a dozen blankets, lay her down on them and tell her to touch herself while I watch. Of course, I'd never do that—it's creepy as fuck—but I don't even mean it that way. Not entirely. I just…

I *crave* her life force…even though I know I only want it to use as inspiration for my own work. To witness joy and capture it in a still frame of art, one that looks like it's moving out of the corner of your eye.

Louise's lips curve suddenly into a secret smile while admiring a painting of a bird seen through a thin linen curtain and I realize this moment is like my epiphany with Van Gogh, only I'm witnessing it from the outside looking in. It should make me happy, the fact that my work affects people like this, but I'm not in the right headspace for it. Her smile only reminds me I can't feel that anymore.

I need to take a picture of her before the look disappears so I can use it later—

Fuck, I feel like a damned emotional vampire. But how could I not want to capture that look and keep it for myself? Her eyes are *glowing* with wonder. When's the last time my eyes glowed with anything that wasn't self-induced sleep deprivation?

The shine in her eyes dies the moment she turns back to me, though. "Are you okay?"

I tear my gaze away when I realize I've been staring. "Of course, yeah."

But when I look back, something has changed. Her body's tighter, withdrawn. She's shifting her weight nervously like the floor is sticking to her feet. "I hope what I said didn't freak you out."

My eyes widen. "No, that's the nicest thing anybody's said to me in a while."

I don't admit it's also the *only* thing anybody's said to me since Mr. King left a few days ago. Before that, it'd been almost three years since I spoke to another human, aside from sending emails. Even when the cleaners come, I stay in here where they aren't allowed and—

"Would you mind if I ask you some questions, then?" she asks, teasing her fingers together. "I don't have to stay long. It could be just an hour."

"Fine."

The fact that she came here for a reason snaps me out of my self-pity. I wipe my hands on a cloth, scrounge up two metal stools for us and motion her onto the one across from me. But the moment we both sit down, she pulls a little black book from her jacket. Then a pen.

"Uh, could you…not?" I ask, taking her off guard again. "Sorry, no recording of any kind. Not even on paper. I'm…" How the hell am I supposed to explain my problems to a normal person? "It's not something I usually allow."

Louise nods kindly and sets the notebook and pen down on a nearby table. Then she puts her phone and a pair of glasses aside too. "Of course, I totally understand."

I highly doubt that. I'm not sure *I* even really understand. But the sight of those things away from us sets me at ease anyway. And the fact that she just…did it…without asking why; my shoulders literally drop away from my ears with relief.

With as much normalcy as I can muster, I offer, "Thanks. Please, fire away."

CHAPTER 3

LULU

It's funny. Artistic types always seem surprised when they meet someone else who doesn't judge the habits they consider weird, the little idiosyncrasies they fret over. I mean...to me, it's just basic empathy. And common sense where Malbec is concerned; his whole schtick, his whole public image, is being a ghost. *Of course*, he doesn't want notes taken. Aside from a couple photos of him as a teenager and one of him playing lacrosse, there are no recent photographs of him, no information about his people, nothing. Everything I know about him I know because he volunteered those pieces of information for articles and profiles written about him. And it's done more good for his legacy than two dozen PR campaigns could ever do. People love mystery. They also love the idea of a larger-than-life mysterious painter who drops masterpieces out of thin air and then disappears in a puff of smoke.

It's why it's okay that he didn't bat an eye at my naughty confession. Really. Really, it's okay. I'd rather he keeps what he thinks of me to himself than open his mouth and kill the fantasy in my head that I have of him.

Ha, as if asking him a thousand and one personal questions won't do that. But that's the sacrifice I accepted by coming here. With that in mind, I settle into professional mode.

"So," I begin. "Mr. Malbec."

"Kaden," he offers.

I blink at that. Everyone in the art world knows him as *Malbec*.

That's the name on his paintings, it's his signature in magazine articles—just Malbec, like Madonna or Cher. It wasn't until this morning when Mr. King called him Kaden, that I knew his first name, and hearing him just offer it to me freely makes my heart flutter.

"Kaden, okay," I say. "I know a bit about you. Well, I should say, I know what you've written about yourself. I've studied your work, of course, and heard all the theories about you, but obviously none of that is *you*. I don't presume I'm going to know you from coming here either. Although…"

My eyes wander. It's hard to rein them in in this space. The paintings on the walls, the tarps and canvases and easels and tools scattered everywhere—it's like walking around in somebody else's brain.

"Although what?"

"I wish I could just sit in here and watch you work," I confess.

He studies me for a long moment with an unreadable expression on his face before he asks, "You think you'd know me from just observing?"

"No, not *you*. But I'd know your work better," I say.

His gaze darts sideways at that to the canvas currently on his easel; it's massive, three by six. The ballerina en pointe—at least, I think that's what it is, it's still early stages—is life-sized, just like most of his work.

Kaden rises to his feet and motions me up too.

"Come on, then," he says. "Watch me work and ask me questions."

He doesn't wait for me; he maneuvers a path through the junk crowding the room until he reaches the canvas. I follow his lead slower. And I ask the obvious question, "Is that a ballerina?"

"It's supposed to be," he says, rapping the outline of the figure with his knuckles. "But it's lifeless."

"What do you mean lifeless?" I ask, coming to stand alongside him. "You've only just started."

"Sure, but usually there's a breath of life at the beginning," he says, crossing his arms. "The subject is alive before I'm ever involved."

"Who is she?"

"I don't know. My family took me to the ballet when I was a kid and she's the memory I have of that night. My mom was a Prima ballerina when she was younger so throughout the performance, she had me on her lap while she explained things to me."

I don't say anything. I'm not really sure I should. It's not just a ballerina at all; it's a core memory, a sacred one to him, it seems.

"But she's *not really there*," he says after a moment of silence. "She's not talking to me."

"Maybe because she's not..."

"Not what?"

I grimace at him, hoping what I'm about to say won't insult him. "She's not the ballerina you saw when you were little."

"She is," he insists. "This is the pose I remember most vividly from that night."

"But you haven't even started sketching the face," I point out. "Maybe she's somebody else."

Kaden's body tightens a little. I wish I knew him well enough to ask why. Just as quickly, though, the tension is gone.

"I don't know," he says. "I might just burn it and move on to a different subject."

"What do you mean burn?" I almost recoil from the thought.

"Anything I don't finish," he shrugs.

"How often don't you finish something?" I ask, trying—and failing—to keep the indignation out of my voice.

Turning to me, his lips curl a little in rebellion. "Would it shock you if I said I don't finish most pieces, Ms. Rathbone?"

That revelation *does* shock me; my mouth drops open in surprise and his eyes dart to them, then back up, bright with mischief.

"Would you like to watch me burn this one?"

He's teasing me, I know it, but it hits like a gut-punch anyway. The thought that the world will never see pieces of his work because they don't exist anymore—that there are pieces *I* will never get to see because they're already gone—saddens me on a primal level. Which is ridiculous. I don't have any say in what this man does with his work, even if the thought of him destroying it grates on my soul like nails on a chalkboard.

"N-No," I say quietly. "I wanted to watch you work."

"That's part of the process," he says. "C'mon, we'll burn it now."

He snaps the canvas off its perch without a second thought, and I reach for it before I can stop myself. I don't even know where he *would* burn it, but my body seems to think so long as I'm standing in the way, he can't.

"Wait," I say.

"Why?"

That's a question I don't want to answer. One I can't answer without turning this into some sort of silly therapy session...and I didn't come here to talk about me.

"Could you just wait until I'm gone to do that?" I ask instead. "I would really feel more comfortable if you waited."

He stops trying to get around me, but his voice still teases as he asks again, "Why?"

That tone is the second reason I can't answer him for real. The honest answer would bum us both the fuck out and dredge up shit I haven't talked about, or even thought about, in years.

I shouldn't have said anything. I shouldn't be getting between him and whatever he's trying to do anyway.

"Sorry," I say, forcing myself to hold still for half a second and calm down. "I shouldn't have interrupted. Go burn it and I'll stay right here until you get back. I promise I won't touch anything."

Trying to be magnanimous—hell, trying to be *normal*—I take a wide step backward, gesturing to the narrow path between me and what I assume is the way out of the junk maze.

Kaden's eyes go wide a split second before he shouts, "Stop!"

But it's too late. I'm already mid-step when my back hits a bulky thing behind me, shifting it out of place, and something hard and metallic lands square on the top of my head.

CHAPTER 4

KADEN

"Owww."

"Oh fuck." I absolutely did *not* mean for that to happen. Tossing the canvas aside, I rush to Louise where she sits on the floor absolutely coated from head to toe in blue paint, holding her head where the full gallon can hit her as it fell off the ladder. "Louise, don't...don't open your eyes. Stay still."

"Am I blind?" Her voice catches me off-guard. She sounds...annoyed by the possibility that she's blind, rather than horrified by it. It's funny. The tone is funny.

Especially since she's *not* blind—holy fucking thank God—there's just so much blue on her face I can barely see her features.

"No," I tell her. "Grab my hands right-right here, there you go. I'm going to help you stand up. Keep your eyes shut."

"What'd I hit?"

"A ladder. Paint can came down on you."

The moment she's on her feet, I sweep her into my arms and aim us for the deep sink in the far corner of the room. She wouldn't be able to find her way like this and she hardly weighs anything; carrying her is the least I could do. But a few steps in, I realize something embarrassing. This is the first time I've touched a human being since squirreling myself away in this house three years ago.

Her warmth.

The way she sinks into me, so trusting.

Fuck.

Touch starvation wriggles through my body like ice crystals thawing. And when I reach the sink and set her down on her feet, I hate the loss of her.

"Is it at least a good color?" she asks.

"Blue ruin," I tell her, turning on the water and letting it run a bit.

"That's me," she giggles. "A mess in the shape of a woman."

"Here, tilt forward. I'm going to guide you into the water to flush out your eyes, okay? Fair warning, this sink only has one temperature and in the winter, that temperature is arctic blast, so just be prepared."

I don't know what I expected when she leaned in, but I freeze when one of her hands grabs the sink rim and the other feels for…me. Her hand grabs my waist and holds on as she leans her beautiful face down and waits for me to guide her. I leap at the chance to touch her again, placing my hand just below her ear and maneuvering her toward the stream of water.

"Here it comes."

"Okay. Oh! Holy moly, you weren't kidding!"

"I know."

"That's *freezing*!"

"I promise I'll warm you up afterward."

I genuinely meant that I would get her a towel, throw another log in the woodstove, give her a change of warmer clothes, but her eyes pop open in surprise and heat. Her hand tightens on my waist with what I think is excitement. Hope, maybe? Or maybe I'm reading too much into it.

"Do your eyes sting at all?" I ask, guiding her under the faucet a little more until she looks like a reverse raccoon with an area cleared of paint around her eyes.

"No. Thank you," she says, standing up. Instinctively, she reaches up to wipe the water away.

"Wait! Your hands are covered in paint too."

I take her hands in mine and wash them carefully. And quickly as she begins to shiver.

"You're all right," I assure her.

"S-Sorry," she almost vibrates, her lips chattering. "I've never been very g-g-good with cold."

And I've never been very good about keeping clean cloth in here. Literally every rag I can see around us is caked in old paint.

"Here." I shove my hand behind my neck and grip the collar of my shirt, pulling it off quickly for her. "Dry with this."

"Oh," she mewls sadly, studying the shirt. "I don't want to ruin this too."

"It's fine," I say.

"But, won't she be angry I got blue on her red?"

It takes me a long second to realize what she's talking about—the marks on the shirt. I smile at her, "No, it was just a gag. I went to an artist's retreat in Quebec a while back and this mixed media artist gave this to me as a joke. She said I was too serious for my own good."

Her shoulders fall. She seems disappointed. Is that right? "Oh. Okay."

"What?"

"It's nothing," she says, wiping some of the paint off her mouth, slopping a bit more off the top of her head. "I just hoped she meant something to you."

Oh. *Oh.* "You mean, did she and I have sex?"

"Passionate, hot, painty sex hopefully," she teases.

I don't know why the way she says it has me blushing. I'm a grown man, way too old to be embarrassed by old lovers, but I can feel the heat rise to my cheeks all the same. I step behind Louise and gently place my hand on the back of her head.

"Tell me if this hurts," I say, softly nudging at her scalp with my fingers.

"That—that right there, is tender," she says.

I part her blue hair as carefully as I can. There's no bruise or bump that I can see. "I'm going to call a doctor."

"It's okay," she says. "I feel fine."

"Just because you *feel* fine doesn't mean you are," I say, stepping back and pulling out my cell phone. "There's a doc just up the road, she can come."

"Really, I can just get it checked when I return to the city."

A flicker of irritation sparks in me. "Louise. You're not leaving now. You could have a concussion. Don't be ridiculous."

I shoot off the text message to the doctor in seconds, but when I return the cell to my pocket, I realize Louise has gone quiet. She's sort of wringing my shirt between her hands.

Guilt twinges in my chest. I've forgotten how to talk to people. Maybe my voice was off-putting?

"If it helps," I say quietly, tapping the shirt, "I would have thoroughly disappointed her if she'd let me. Absolutely stunning older woman. She had her pick among the other artists that week."

Louise's amber eyes quirk with disbelief. "And she didn't pick you?"

"I was too serious, remember? Too in my head all the time." I don't know if I should admit it to her, but… "That painting over there. That's her."

I point to a little tucked away canvas on the wall. It's partially obscured by a studio lamp and dusty after so long unattended, but it's hard to miss once you notice it.

"She's beautiful!" Louise whispers. "And it's before your veil period. A straight portrait."

"I was just playing around then, hadn't found my style yet," I admit. "Took a long time to realize I should paint the way I interact with the world."

Her eyes dart my way suddenly. She just considers me and hums before she says, "So that's why you asked if I would pull the veil back from your painting?"

I…suppose it was. But I don't want to talk about that. It's too personal for the first time meeting someone, especially someone sent to do a wellness check on me; that is absolutely why Mr. King sent her here. And now she's going to go back to him with a concussion looking like I converted her to the Blue Man Group.

I have made a stellar first impression…and I'm making an even more awkward one as we stand in silence just sort of staring at one another.

But then her nose crinkles. "Not to pry—"

I smirk. "I thought that's what you were sent here to do."

A dazzling smile sprints across her painted face. "Okay then, *prying deeply*, can I ask about the veil in your artwork?"

Thinking there's no way she could ever guess what it actually is, I say, "Shoot."

"From your perspective, are you spying on your subjects or are you hiding from them?"

CHAPTER 5

LULU

The veil is a key element in his work. All his pieces that have gone to auction in the last three years have featured it; every figure, every animal, they've all been obscured by impossibly thin curtains, webs, and fogs he draws across them, as if he's standing outside the scene peering in.

Leering in, more like.

People in our world have been theorizing about the significance of the veil in his art ever since it appeared a few years ago. To me, there are only two possibilities—it's a technique he learned to do and became obsessed with *or* it's a glimpse of who he really is. I have and would wager money on the latter. *No other artist* has captured the intrusive gaze so well as he has. Every painting feels like we're intruding on some intimate moment, no matter the subject. A dog with a bone. A kid tying his shoes. Lovers hiding under the same poncho during a rainstorm. Every piece of art openly and loudly accuses the viewer of being a spectator. A busybody. A creeper. In most, the subject of the painting isn't even aware they're being painted, but in some, the person is looking straight at us, like they know we're there watching them from behind the veil. Sometimes their expression suggests they like that we're there, others not so much. And one of his most famous pieces is of a furious man staring at us through the curtain, with his hand gripping it, preparing to rip it away.

I've wondered forever which he's doing—spying or hiding. And now I'm wondering even more. He's standing in front of me now half-naked, towering over me, gorgeous and chiseled, as if someone took a Roman statue and put jeans on it. He literally gave me the shirt off his back, so it doesn't feel like he's hiding.

And if he likes spying, well, let's just say I'd be happy to give him something to watch.

"Aren't those the same things?" he asks.

"Not to me," I say. "Different perspective. Spying suggests the person you're painting is the subject of your work—you sought them out and are exposing their life to us. Hiding suggests that *you* are the actual subject of your work, even though we can't see you. Active versus passive. Either way you're on the outside peering in. I just don't know if you're watching because you like to or watching because you have to."

"We all like watching, Ms. Rathbone," Kaden says after a moment. "That's human nature. If you're asking *me* specifically, I definitely enjoy watching. Even if—"

Kaden hisses suddenly and his full lips disappear between his teeth, like he caught himself before spilling some secret he'd rather keep close to his beautifully muscular chest.

I can't help it; my curiosity gets the better of me. "Even if what?"

"It's not relevant to why you came out here for Mr. King," he chides.

If only he knew how relevant it is to *me*. But I don't want to push, and given how far removed from the world he seems, I think I have my answer anyway. So instead, I take a slippery step and say, "Do you have another can I could squeeze some of this paint into? Seems a shame to waste it."

"Don't worry about the paint, I'll grab you something to change into," he says.

He slips from the room silently and the moment he's gone, I realize just how cold and weird the paint feels against my skin. It's not just in my hair or drying across my face. It's inside my clothes, sliding down my spine, dripping into my underwear, trickling between my toes.

Tossing his t-shirt aside in a tragic attempt not to ruin it any more than I already have, I shed my top layer like old skin. The shirt underneath is dappled with blue too, but it doesn't feel as...gropey. Unfortunately, the leather bustier under that is all but destroyed, I can already tell. The paint slid right down my neckline in a wave and the bustier is absolutely sopping with it. I always loved that piece too.

Suppose it's a fair exchange for the mess I've made. The floor is lined in tarps, so the halo of blue I can see around the ladder shouldn't be too tough to clean up, but I still feel bad about it.

Following the blue bootprints he left across the floor to carry me to this spot, I hopscotch back over to where the can fell and stand it upright. But the second I bend over, the shirt I thought wasn't too full of paint falls against my back, icy cold and grossly wet.

I don't mean to, but I yelp and lurch upright, tearing at the buttons to take the goopy thing off—

"Freeze." Kaden's voice drifts in like a whisper across a wooded valley, almost ghostly, but I hear him and pause where I stand.

"Why?"

"Just stay like that."

My elbows are bent sharply backward in an awkward stretch, almost like wings, my chest is pushed out a little, my shoulder blades are almost touching, and one leg is carrying the majority of my weight. I was halfway through removing the shirt when he stopped me and it is *not* a comfortable position to be in...

Until I hear a soft sound I would recognize anywhere—the *shuck-slide* of canvas against canvas as it's removed from a shelf.

"Is that—"

"Yes."

"Are you going to paint me?"

Heavy silence fills the space between us until he asks, "May I, Ms. Rathbone?"

I shiver at the way he says my name, so low and dulcet. As for the question, "God yes."

Kaden steps into view, partially dragging a massive blank framed canvas. He moves around me in a semi-circle—as far as he can with the junk in his way—looking for an angle. His sea-eyes never meet mine, they only skim across me, my face, my curves, never lingering for long…and my heart begins to race. I'm suddenly aware of every part of my body, wondering what I must look like in this position, what he must see.

I hear him set the canvas down and shift the massive easel, scraping, across the floor. But I can't see him. For a moment I think it's the back he wants…until I feel him move closer, then closer again.

"May I touch you, Ms. Rathbone?" He's not right against my ear, but he might as well be. "I need to turn you around, but only a little bit."

"Sure."

I expect a moment of hesitation, or maybe a warning, but there isn't one. One of his massive, warm hands slides along my waist, the other along the opposite thigh; he grips my body so reverently and I'm suddenly moving as if I weigh nothing at all.

And when I yelp nervously, he coos, "It's all right. I've got you."

He turns me maybe thirty degrees toward him. Once he has me in the position he wants, he takes his time making micro-adjustments. He grabs one of my feet and exaggerates the arch. Moves one of my hands so it's farther from my ribs. Tilts my chin just a little further up…as if to look at him.

And I *am* looking. It's hard not to. He's haloed by the winter white pouring in through the skylight. It brightens his dark hair to chocolate, darkens his eyes to midnight lagoon. I hadn't noticed how *beautifully long* his eyelashes were before—Elizabeth Taylor eyelashes that look like they're caked in mascara when they're au naturel.

But then he moves aside and points up. "You see that bird painting you loved so much?"

"Yes." The painting of a sparrow outside a farmhouse window is angled on the gabled ceiling.

"Focus on that," he says.

Then he disappears behind the canvas. This one is a six-by-eight-foot surface, so I can only see the top couple of inches of his head, that wavy mass of darkness splattered with blue ruin.

"The bird, Ms. Rathbone." He's not even looking at me; he *sensed* I wasn't looking where I should. My stomach squeezes at the thought.

I force my gaze skyward as the sound of a moving pencil fills the air like the hum of an incessant insect. For a long time—until my arms *ache* and the paint has more or less sealed me to the tarp under my feet—I just listen to that symphony of scratches and study the sparrow while he sketches.

But then questions leap to mind that I've always wanted to know. "Are you classically trained?"

"Yes."

"Where did you study?"

"Not at an art school, that's for sure."

"But then—"

"You'd think less of me if I told you." My brow furrows instinctively, but he adds, "Relax your face."

I do, reluctantly, as I wonder what he means. The only way he could have classically trained without a school is if he had private tutors or worked under a master. Neither would make me think less of him. If he were anyone else, I could just look up the information, but he's *Malbec*—even his true identity is a mystery.

"Why did you choose the name Malbec?" I ask.

A chuckle escapes him low and slow. "Ooh, do you *want* me to disappoint you?"

"Well, considering what you said about the older woman from the artists' retreat…it depends on what sort of disappointment you have in mind."

I hear a scratch…then his pencil clatters to the floor.

My heart flutters… "Did I shock you, Mr. Malbec?"

He recovers his pencil without saying anything…and embarrassment trickles in. Just a little. "Sorry. Didn't mean to make you uncomfortable. Again."

"You didn't," he lies.

"Really. Show me your face, let me see if you're blushing," I tease.

He grumbles, "Eyes to the sky, Ms. Rathbone," as I hear the pencil start moving on the canvas again. But the grumble is more playful purr than territorial growl.

"Don't tell me," I tease. "You named yourself after the grape."

"All right, I won't tell you."

It takes everything in me to keep my face from twisting with amusement. Honestly, I sort of love the possibility that he *did* name himself after the grape. It makes sense, the fruit is a beautiful color, especially when the sunlight shines through it, like an inky blueberry.

But…I really want to know the truth, for my own personal reasons. People who choose their names often give a lot of thought to it, to who they want to be. How they want to be perceived by the world. I have no doubt his story would reveal a lot. Just like mine does about me.

"If it helps, my given name isn't Louise Rathbone eith—"

CLICK!

A mechanical noise catches me off guard. My neck snaps in his direction before I even think about it, and I find Malbec with a camera pressed to his eye. I hear another click before he takes it away.

"Sorry, I just wanted to make sure I had a photo reference for this position and lighting," he says.

"I'm not upset," I say, because I'm not. He should have asked, but I'm not surprised he'll need it if he *actually* plans to finish this painting. "Can I move?"

"Yeah, of course."

I finally toss off the shirt I've been awkwardly holding away from myself for the last half hour, and walk across the space to join him, ignoring the *stick-stick-stick* of my blue feet against the tarp. Rounding the canvas, I'm surprised to find he's sketched me *thoroughly*. My face, sure, my pose, of course. But also every silken curve exactly as I think it is on my body. It's as if I could walk up and fit in the lines he's drawn.

Strangely, he's put me on the far left quarter of the canvas as if I'm walking into frame.

"Are you going to draw something else?" I ask. I'm curious, regardless of whether the answer is yes or no.

"I'd like to," he says cryptically.

"Better use blue ruin," I joke, motioning to myself.

But he doesn't laugh or smile. Instead, he sets his camera aside and reaches for me, for my neck. His fingers slide along my skin, almost caressing, scattering sensation, before they pull away coated in paint. Then he turns and applies it to the canvas, right where he's sketched my neck. He leaves his finger strokes intact, creating a beautiful fingerpainted texture.

For a moment, excitement lances through me, wondering if he'll pick another spot on my still-slick body to take paint from, but that's not what he does. Instead, he studies what he's done, then studies me again with that same piercing eye. Back and forth.

Like he's trying to decide something.

Like some idea is clouding his mind with blue.

Excitement strains in his neck muscles, riling the same excitement in me.

"Tell me what you need," I say quietly, taking a tiny step forward. "Another pose?"

His eyes meet mine, brighter than I've seen to this point. It's a look I know well; he's in his head, slipping quickly into intense creative concentration. Before I lose him to it, I just need a nod.

And he gives me one right before he picks up his camera again.

I back away to where I was before and pause to think. I was in the process of taking off the shirt when my positioning caught his attention.

So, careful to keep my angles beautiful, I reach for the buttons on my pants. Lower the zipper—CLICK!

He takes several more pictures as I lower my pants to the floor slowly.

Then again when I shake them off my ankles.

But it's the sound he makes when I stand upright again that surprises me. He groans. It's a tiny sound, as sweet as cherry candy. When I meet his eye, I realize he's lowered his camera just a little, caught at the sight of me. There's a delicious expression on his face—like he's just woken up. Who knew bikini briefs could do that to a fella.

I'm joking, of course I knew, but…it still makes me giddy. I don't seek out the male gaze—not intentionally, anyway. When I was much younger, men looked all the time, but it was for…inappropriate reasons. Reasons that led me to nurture my invisibility as I got older and began my professional life.

Invisibility is safety.

It's peaceful.

But…I sometimes miss the attention, even though I know I shouldn't.

I miss feeling seen.

When people notice me, I feel like I actually exist.

There's no point lamenting how sad that is; not when you come from my background. When you grow up like I did—when you escape what I did—you cement the cracked parts of yourself as they are, so you don't risk them shattering completely.

But at least in this moment, I meet Kaden's gaze and let the giddiness out. I stretch my arms up and behind my head the way I would after getting home from a long day and removing my pants for real in my own apartment.

CLICK-CLICK-CLICK!

"Hold there," he says, and I do.

My back is arched a little, my arms are tucked behind my head, I'm on tiptoe. Honestly, it's a *great* stretch. And I hold it as I hear him pick up his pencil again.

"Turn toward me, two inches," he says. As I do, his beautiful blue eyes catch on me. When he finally tears his gaze away, a strained murmur escapes him, "*O for a muse of fire…*"

They're such simple words, said apart from me. And yet, they heat me from within. In my thirty-three years on this planet, I've probably visited a thousand art museums and the private art collections of half the world's billionaires. I've seen paintings in person that haven't been seen in public in centuries. I've watched the restorations of paintings I would literally die to save in a fire.

Art isn't just my job, my life, my obsession. It's me. If you asked me who I am, I'd tell you with a painting like *La Femme Damnée* or *The Two*

Fridas, not with words. But I suppose it's more than that.

I've always wanted to be a work of art. Not just *in* art, but the true embodiment of it. I'm convinced it must be possible. If it's not, then what's the point of anything?

"Would you like to see it?" he asks after a few minutes.

I tiptoe over on bated breath—and the soreness on my scalp and the slight discomfort in my arms from holding them over my head so long was *so worth it*!

I creep around the canvas to find motion. Movement. Far more than you'd ever expect a sketch to have. It's *alive*. The piece is *alive*. Aside from the blue slick of paint he applied on the far left, it's still just black pencil against white, and there's no veil yet, but he could still stop now and it'd be art all the same. The figure of me is a stream of movement, a blur of vitality, across the canvas from left to right, sloughing off clothing as if I've just arrived home and desperately needed to free myself from the uniform of life. The costume I'm forced to wear *out there*.

My heart swells to bursting. I can feel his penetrating stare against the side of my face as he waits for my reaction, but my reaction is too big—he wouldn't understand it.

"Kaden, it's…" Before I can finish, something catches my eye, twisting what I was going to say. "Unfinished."

The right half of the canvas is blank. He left room for something else.

"Yeah," he said, sighing. "I'm not sure what you're doing. You could walk out of frame. You could crawl into bed…"

My eyes jerk in his direction involuntarily, wondering if he means it the way it sounds. But he's still in his head, thinking like a painter, not like a man.

So I point out the obvious to him, "Well, after taking off my shirt and pants, I'd take off my bra."

It's his turn to snap his head in my direction. I meet his gaze head on and step back into position, reaching behind my back to undo the laces on the bustier. The paint-sticky leather doesn't slide away easily, but once it's gone I realize the paint has left an accidental imprint against my skin of the bustier's structure. It's sort of beautiful. Especially when my nipples peak as the warm studio air sighs against the parts of me where the paint is still wet.

I step into a walking pose, holding the corner of my bustier in my fingertips behind me as if I'm about to discard it on the floor. Then I pause.

And I wait.

It's several minutes before I realize Malbec's not making any sounds. No camera clicks, no pencil skating across the canvas. I turn my head just enough to look at him. He's frozen by the canvas, watching, but I can't quite tell if he's studying me professionally...or personally.

But as our eyes connect, I realize which it is very quickly. Canvas forgotten, Kaden strides toward me, blue eyes unblinking, absorbing the sight with a hunger that tightens my stomach and kicks my heart into overdrive. I realize I'm holding my breath about the same time he sighs, blowing warm air across my shoulders, raising goosebumps.

"May I touch you, Ms. Rathbone?" he asks again.

"Yes," escapes me, breathless and needy.

I wish I could split focus. I wish I could both watch his hands as they land against my waist on either side *and* watch his face, but as I feel his fire-hot skin against mine I keep my focus on his eyes, his lips, the tip of his tongue as it peeks between them.

He turns me an inch before his hands trail slowly down to my hips and turn them too, just a little. Barely anything. Then his hands are in my messy hair, delicately removing the hairband before coaxing the once-bun into a waterfall wave of blue over my shoulders. And when I shiver from the still-wet cold paint, he whispers, "This is what I meant when I said the art is alive before I'm ever involved. You're the sort of alive I wish I could be."

I dry swallow. "You could always put yourself in the painting too."

He groans at that. His hands return to my waist and his forehead lands gently against my shoulder for a moment, as if he's fighting his desire to do exactly that. The three points of contact and that energy I can feel in him fill me with…*aching need*. A thirst unquenchable. He can feel my raging heart, he's watching my heaving naked chest as my peaked nipples sway in and out of his line of sight. I know he is because with each sway of me, his hands are flexing against my skin in tiny squeezes like he only needs some sign of consent to reach for less appropriate but more excitable handholds. And I want to give him my consent to touch more of me. I have the desperate urge to tilt my head against his and press my lips to his ear. To break my pose and reach for him.

"Louise?"

He growls the name low in his throat, and I can hardly wait a second to whisper, "Yes?"

"May I—"

DINGALINGALING!

In the nearly silent room, the jangle of my cell phone might as well be the rip-start of a chainsaw. It tears us both out of the moment, like neither of us had realized we were in one.

"Sorry," he says.

"Sorry for what?"

"I don't know," he says. "You should get that."

I wish I didn't have to. Even though the moment has ended, it really hasn't. Not for me. His hands still grip my body. And he has blue on his face where he pressed it to my shoulder. I left my mark on him and my gaze skates across the glory of his face trying to memorize exactly where the paint is so I can add it to my sketch of him later.

He knows what I'm doing. After a moment, the tiniest smile curls the corners of his lips before he steps away, motioning to the phone. "Louise."

I rush over to the phone, hoping to find the Caller ID of someone I like on the screen—maybe one of my friends, Ivy or Cara—but a kaleidoscopic bomb of emotions go off inside me when I see my boss *Mrs. Russo* is calling. In the early days of working for her family, I used to get excited whenever she called, mostly because a call from the Russo matriarch felt like a rare treat. A gift that often came with high praise for sourcing some rare piece of art. Now, those eight tiny letters fill me with a dread so intense it sours my stomach instantly.

She's the only person I know who treats a missed phone call like a slap to the face.

"Hi, Mrs. Russo," I say, trying to keep my voice steady.

"I need you here in an hour." In the ten years I've worked for her family, she's never started a phone call any other way. Never "hi," never "good morning." Always with a demand.

"I'm actually with an artist upstate, but I'll get there as soon as I can, *signora*."

She *tsks* under her breath. It's a sound I've come to loath…that and, "*Uffa*," which is her way of telling me she's *deeply disappointed*. Spoken with her Italian accent, it has some power over me; guilt always comes rushing in. "Well, if that's the best you can do."

"I'm leaving right now, Mrs. Russo, I promise," I say.

"I just don't understand, Lulu," she continues. "You tell me you love this job, that it's the most important thing in your life, and yet you're never where you're supposed to be. We have been meeting *every Friday for weeks* in preparation for the auction in January and you pick today to go out of state."

"Upstate," I say gently. "And we've been meeting on *Thursdays* every week. I met with Lorenzo, Bianca, and Emilio at the gallery yesterday. I was sorry you couldn't attend."

I try to be gentle when I remind her of things. I really do. I try to remember she's going through something no mother should ever have to experience…but it's hard when she takes her scatter-brained-ness out on me.

"*Then where are the notes for the meeting, eh?*" She barks this in Italian…a language I've absorbed through osmosis in the ten years I've worked for them. She also barks it so loudly, my shoulders rise almost to my ears as I flinch against the sound.

"They should be in your inbox, *signora*, but I'll send them again right now."

"*Mi hai rotto i coglioni!* Don't make excuses. Just do things right the first time. See you *in one hour!*"

She ends the call cold, and I take my first breath since it started. I close my eyes and count to three, reminding myself of all the perks that come along with my job. It's that, or give into the intrusive thought that's grown unignorable in recent months that my position with the Russos might have to change.

I've thought about quitting so many times, as much for her temper as for how this job has changed in the ten years I've had it. And for other reasons, which I've tried to ignore.

But then I chide myself for being so ungrateful.

I'm the highest paid and respected art advisor in NYC, two things which are only possible because I work for the Russos. This is a job so many others in my field would figuratively kill for...and maybe literally kill for, if given the chance. They don't care that it's a gilded cage and I'd be so fucked if I tried to leave and start over now.

Ping.

I'm saved from my spiraling thoughts by a text notification. As I raise my phone to look, I expect to see another demand from Mrs. Russo...but I don't.

Bright relief shines through me as I see a string of texts, all from my friend Ivy asking where I've disappeared to. I completely forgot I was in the middle of a text chat with her when I arrived at Malbec's door.

As I swipe open the phone, I ignore Ivy's playful string of accusations that I've been abducted by aliens or gotten into some stranger's van because they swore they had a Rembrandt in there.

Her last messages read, *You and Cara have both disappeared and it's too much for my fragile heart. Earth to Lulu, Are. You. Alive? I'll take a winky emoji.*

My eye catches on a large mirror nearby and I choose to reply with a photo instead. Snapping open my camera app, I aim my phone and capture the whole landscape of this room, me in all my painted naked glory, and the very edge of Malbec in the background by the canvas. You can only see his hair...his luscious crown of dark curls.

I send it off without a second thought—

Malbec's voice catches with indignation. "Did you just take a picture of me?"

"N-No!" I swear, rushing to his side to show him. "You're barely there, see? You can't even see your face. It's just me."

But it doesn't seem to reassure him. He winces at the photo, then me, before he turns away.

"What? What is it?" I ask.

"You sent that to a friend?"

"Yeah, my best friends, Ivy and Cara."

"But...you're naked." The tone isn't rude, but it's playing chicken with judgment. "Little weird, don't you think?"

I almost laugh. "This isn't even in the top ten weirdest things I've done that they know about."

To my surprise, he grows colder. A little dismissive. "So, going over to strangers' houses and stripping for them is a normal thing that you do?"

That was judgment. And it bites harder at my heart than I anticipated. Maybe because I thought we were getting along. Maybe because I *don't* feel shame for it; art modeling is an incredibly personal, but empowering experience.

Or it should be. He, of all people, should know it is.

All at once, I realize the intimate moment we shared is over, if that's what it even was. The bubble bursts, releasing anger through me like a camera flash. I didn't expect *him* to shame me. Others, sure, but him?

I am so disappointed. Heartbroken. Which is as inappropriate as his judgment.

It's my fault, though. I presumed an understanding between us that clearly doesn't exist, and the epiphany stings with embarrassment. I am an *idiot*!

Quickly, I press my ruined bustier back in place around my chest and lace it up. Then I shove my ankles through my paint-stiff pants and yank them up my still-drying legs as quickly as I can.

"What are you doing?" he asks.

"I'm leaving."

"What? Why?"

"My boss needs me. Besides, I have the information Mr. King wanted, so. Thank you for speaking with me, really. I'm sure he'll be in touch shortly."

"Could you just stay long enough to get the sketch done?" he asks obliviously. It only infuriates me more. *Fuck* his judgment *and* his expectations. What an *asshole*.

"Why? You'll probably just burn it anyway."

My shoes. My Coat. They're still by the front door.

I scoop up my phone and notepad and begin making my way through the junk maze.

"Louise." His voice booms as I turn the corner into the hallway and make my way toward the foyer. "Just stop. You have a concussion. At least wait for the doctor."

He barrels into the hallway behind me with his arms spread wide in confusion. He's carrying the shirt I ruined, which he shoves back over his head as I start to put on my shoes. I'm saddened to see that my blue has all but destroyed one of the woman's handprints along his waist.

But I suppose it is what it is. He doesn't give a shit about it anyway.

I fish my coat off the hook and open a rideshare app on my phone; I just need a lift to the airfield where the helicopter landed.

"I'm calling a taxi, it's fine," I say, staring at my phone as he steps closer. "You don't have to stay here while I wait. I can let myself out."

"Of course I'll wait with you."

"Okay." I keep my voice light and unconcerned. The rideshare app *pings* as a driver connects. I ignore my own frustration when I see the twenty-minute wait, even though I know I should be grateful considering how isolated this place is and the snow on the roads outside.

In the silence after, his feet shift nervously. "Look, I didn't mean anything by what I said."

"Right," I offer, just as light as before. "It was totally my misunderstanding. I overstepped. Don't worry, it won't happen again."

"Would you just look at me?" His fingers curl under my chin, coaxing me to look up.

I do, but I also reach for the door handle to open it. Ignoring his obnoxious handsomeness—and the soft, imploring concern I find in his eyes—I force myself to see him as the random stranger he is. He might be an exceptional painter, but he's also just some guy.

"I do hope we can stay friendly acquaintances, Mr. Malbec."

"I'm sorry," he says.

"Okay," I echo.

I turn the handle, desperate to leave, but as the icy chill of the frozen world outside breaks through the inch gap, his hand lands flat against the wood, shoving it closed again.

"Stop saying 'okay,'" he says. "Just...go back to being normal."

"This *is* normal," I say. "We're strangers. I feel embarrassed. I'd like to leave."

I'm fucking mortified honestly.

I open the door again, only for him to shut it again.

"Why are you embarrassed?"

My eyebrow arches at him. "I thought modeling for you was a nice thing to do but I didn't realize you'd think less of me for it."

"That isn't what I said."

"That's how it came across," I point out.

His shoulders sink, but he doesn't say anything, and the silence stales quickly as he keeps his hand on the door. It's still there when a tepid knock sounds against the wood from the other side. He knows, just like I do, that this moment ends the moment that door opens.

And I'm ready for it to end, so I twist the handle and force the door wide open this time, revealing a pretty woman with red hair wearing a Michelin-man-oversized parka on the porch.

Her eyes spark with excitement as they land on Malbec; she's not even paying attention to the woman bathed in blue standing beside him.

"Hi! I know you usually see my dad, Dr. Garber, but he's sick, so he sent me," she says. "You texted?"

But his eyes are still on me for some reason. So I turn to her, "Yeah, he did. You're the doctor?" Off her nod, I add, "I accidentally got clobbered by a paint can. Landed right on my head. Do you think I might have a concussion?"

"Err...you might," she stammers. "I can come in and have a look...?"

Her vehicle, a truck with one of those little snowplows attached to the nose, sits at the end of the front walk, so I shake my head politely at her. "Nah, let's do it at your office, if that's okay."

"O-Oh. Okay."

I turn to Malbec, once more completely in control of my professional demeanor, and offer him my hand. "It was nice to meet you. I'm sure you'll be hearing from Mr. King shortly."

He stares at the appendage between us like it's a snake seconds from biting, but eventually, his warm, painted hand slides into mine and squeezes, holding for half a beat longer after I let go.

"It was nice to meet you as well, Ms. Rathbone."

And with that, I walk out into the snow.

***

The one benefit of working for the same family for a decade is that I know all their weak spots, their sweet-tooths.

Two and a half hours after leaving Malbec's compound, when I walk into the Russos' preferred New York residence—their ostentatious Long Island estate the size of a small village—I come bearing sweets from their favorite Italian bakery in the city.

I already know the sound I'll hear as I step into their living room; their shrill sound of disapproval for being late morphs mid-yell into excitement and appreciation as they swarm the large box in my hands.

They don't even notice I'm covered in blue paint for several seconds. Even then, the only one concerned enough to ask what happened is the patriarch's consigliere, Matteo.

"You're looking a little blue, Lu," Matteo says. "Need a therapist, or what?"

I smirk at him. "Had a fight with a smurf."

"Oh yeah? Who won?"

"Me every day," I almost sing, matching his smile with one of my own.

"That'a girl."

I like Matteo. He's like an uncle to me now…a very dangerous uncle who has ordered the "disposal" of at least three people that I know of. But he respects me, which is more than I can say for the rest of the Russos.

Especially the son, Emilio, who overhears my banter with Matteo and loudly adds, "You blue a smurf?"

A laugh escapes him, like the hack of an axe into wood, at his own inappropriate pun. The fact that neither Matteo nor I laugh is irrelevant. Emilio adds, "Must've been a blu-kkake party. Don't worry, doll, my shower's always open to you."

Lorenzo seems to have heard what his son said. *"What is this you're talking about, amore?"*

"Nothing, Pops," Emilio says.

"Then let it be nothing, faccia tosta," he chides.

Even though this is the living room where there isn't a 'head of the table,' Lorenzo still looms over the family from his high-backed leather armchair as he bites into his *bomboloni*. It's all aura, though. The Russo patriarch is only a few inches taller than me, just as slender, and surprisingly unassuming—his vibe is more mortuary accountant than Boss with a capital B—but that's by design. His mind is a bear trap, his pockets are bottomless, and I know for a fact that he always carries a switchblade somewhere on his body, just in case.

He doesn't mind me. I think he thinks of me like a…truffle pig. We're not close, but he admires my utility and the tasty art morsels I find for him.

His wife, Giulietta, on the other hand… *Mrs. Russo* is an enigma even to me. She didn't used to involve herself in her husband's business, at least not when I started working for him. She was a model, a trendsetter, a force to be reckoned with in her own spheres, who spent most of her time in Italy and came and went at odd times. Being summoned by her felt like a rare treat; even though she was always a massive C-U-Next-Tuesday, I put up with it to learn from her. But that all changed last year. Since then, she's here constantly, breathing down my neck, questioning every decision I had free reign over before, making extraordinary demands at every turn. Now, watching her stand off by herself while she scowls at me feels like a punishment I don't deserve.

And then there are the twins. Bianca and Emilio. They're like a yin and yang of awful, spiraling in opposite directions yet complementary in all the worst ways. Bianca is beautiful, clever, and vicious. A poisonous flower who, thankfully, is so wrapped up in family business, she couldn't care less about me. And Emilio is like a reverse Dorian Gray; I know there's a handsome portrait of him locked away somewhere growing younger and more beautiful while he grows grosser and weirder. He's not unattractive. With his thick dark hair, medium complexion, and piercing black eyes and the fact that he's a pretty decent artist in his own right, plenty of women can't seem to get enough of him. But the inside is rotten; the brain, the heart, the creativity—he let it all fester. He's basically a bog beast wearing a human suit.

Okay, that's harsh. True…but harsh.

They didn't use to be like this. Or not this bad, anyway. I have to remember that this is what tragedy made of them. I don't dislike *them*, I just miss who they used to be.

It's impossible not to when we're in a room with a *giant shrine* in one of the corners dedicated to a man they all love more than each other. Carlo. The oldest son. A blown-up funerary portrait of him sits in the shrine surrounded by weeping candle wax from the candles that are left *constantly* burning for him. The waterfall of colorful wax drapes down around the shrine table like a tablecloth.

The crazy thing is, he's not even dead.

Carlo's very alive.

But you don't disown the Russo family without consequence.

Before the events of last summer, they were all much happier people. And that's why I have to remind myself not to be so mean, or to give up on them. If I stay strong for them, if I keep up my end of our relationship, eventually those versions of them will come back, I just know it.

But it's hard when they're...well...when they're like this.

"Let us get on with this, Lorenzo," Mrs. Russo snaps after everyone's taken a bite of the food—food she refuses to touch herself. Before he can speak, she snaps at me, "The Curris painting is unacceptable."

I blink, and wait to speak, knowing they have more to say.

"Yes, *passerotta*," Lorenzo says to me. "It is too explicit. Too modern as well."

I keep careful control of my facial features, because I know Mrs. Russo is watching me for "signs of insolence" as she likes to call *any* facial expression that isn't a happy smile or blind respect.

"I see." I bite my tongue to keep from saying what I actually want to say, which is, *"You mean the Curris piece your wife threatened to fire me over if I couldn't add it to the collection? That piece?"*

She showed me *that specific piece* and told me to go fetch it if I wanted to keep my job. Her narrowed eyes are all the reminder I need of that little fact, which she keeps to herself.

"It was highly inappropriate," Mrs. Russo says. "We cannot have naked women featured so prominently during the auction. We expected better of you."

"My apologies, Mr. and Mrs. Russo," I say. "I can return it to the artist. Although he may not be willing to part with the six million you paid him for it."

Usually, a reminder like that is all it takes to have them change their minds, but Mrs. Russo seems to be *on one* today.

"Nobody said that, you spoiled girl!" she hisses, surprising me.

My eyes glide to Matteo in question, but even he seems surprised by her tone. So does Lorenzo.

"*Be nice, my love*," Lorenzo croons, before turning to me. "That won't be necessary. We just need to find a replacement for the auction

40

in January. We will keep the painting in our collection as an investment piece, that's no problem. It is the replacement we must find."

"Yes sir, I understand," I say. "I can put together a selection of twenty pieces for you to choose from. Should only take a few hours."

"You cannot possibly find anything of value in two hours," Mrs. Russo scoffs.

Since that's literally my job, I bristle.

"*Signora*, I keep a record of every new piece that hits the private markets, just like I have for the last ten years," I say gently. "The final decision will, of course, be up to you. I just wanted to save you some time and offer a curated list of possib—"

"*You see how she talks back?*" she snaps at her husband. "*Is this what you want in this family?*"

They argue between each other for a few seconds in Italian and the bristling along my back intensifies as I stare at the Persian carpet under my feet—the one I sourced for them from a prince's palace in Saudi Arabia nearly five years ago. Back when I loved this job. Back when I loved being able to buy masterpieces on somebody else's dime, thinking they'd be treasured and properly taken care of.

I count half a dozen stains and frays on the carpet before Emilio pipes in, "Ma, it isn't a problem. I'm working on another piece anyway. We can replace the Curris with that."

Mrs. Russo smiles at him in that saccharine "little prince" way I've come to loath ever since the Carlo fiasco last summer.

"That settles it," she says, her voice high and pleased, before adding, "Oh, and Ms. Rathbone, gallery meetings will be *on Fridays* from now on."

"Yes, *signora*," I say, right before I make a silent wish to the universe for better days ahead. I need something—anything—*anyone*—to make life a little more bearable. To give me something to get excited about again.

Life's disappointing enough without it being boring too…and this game they like to play with me…it's so boring it makes me want to scream.

But of course, the moment a thought like that pops into my head, the universe seems determined to prove me wrong.

Emilio looks to his dad and whispers, "Pops, do it now," like a child.

"Yes, *amore*," Lorenzo says, rising from his chair. "*Passerotta*, please walk with me."

I'm not scared of Lorenzo Russo, even though objectively I should be. He's the most powerful man in the city, but he's never given me reason to fear him and he once saved my life in a way I'll never be able to pay back.

But as I walk down a long hallway by his side, with Matteo and Mrs. Russo following a few paces behind, I get the sense that they're plotting something. That plus Emilio's nudging words raise my hackles.

Sorrow streaks through me wondering if it's finally happening. If they're finally going to fire me and throw me away.

"Is everything okay, *signore*?" I ask. "I really *am* sorry about the Curris painting."

"No-No, you are a good girl." That's always been his throw-away compliment to me. "You do very good work for us. But I have…something delicate to discuss with you and I do not want you to be uncomfortable."

"Oh."

When we come to his office door, he opens it for me—a gesture he's only made to me once before when I first came to work for them. Usually, I'm the one opening the door for him. I try not to let it go to my head as I step inside, and he moves to his preferred armchair. Matteo and Mrs. Russo remain standing on either side and slightly behind him. Standing, cold and sticky with paint, I suddenly feel like a kid about to be suspended by a school principal.

"Louise, our family has always trusted you," Mr. Russo finally says. "Carlo *always* trusted you."

That is an even greater compliment; again, I try not to let it go to my head.

"Thank you, *signore*."

"And of course Emilio has always adored you."

But that one, while true, isn't the compliment he thinks it is, so I smile politely.

"Emilio is preparing to take over for me, now that Carlo has...moved on...and he has made a special request of his mother and me. A request that we speak with you on his behalf. He...uh...he would like to...uh..."

My intuition has always been a little...broken, due to things out of my control, but it revs to life now, splattering my insides with dread as Lorenzo turns to Mrs. Russo.

"He would like to make you his wife," she says, slicing to the chase like a knife through butter.

It hits me the way any piece of insane information would—softly at first and then all at once like a shockwave. I don't even know what to say to that. I've turned down Emilio's propositions maybe a hundred times in the decade I've worked for them. At first it was just wink-nudges to meet him in coat closets or to wear shorter skirts, which I pretended never happened. Then it was "accidental" grazes on my legs and hips and chest when they invited me to family dinners. There was that one time in Sicily at their family estate when Emilio "mistakenly" locked us in the wine cellar and breathed down my neck for half an hour while I pounded on the door for someone to let us out. Then Lorenzo started asking me if I'd ever thought about marriage, how his son "needed to find a good girl and you are a good girl, *passerotta*," but I thought it was just nonsense talk. Never in a million years did I think this powerful family would see me as anything other than a truffle pig employee.

"Oh?"

At least I'm not the only one who's shocked. Surprise registers on Matteo's face too...but he doesn't say anything.

"It would make us very happy to have you as part of the family." Mr. Russo has a much easier time saying those words, and I think he actually means them.

Mrs. Russo, on the other hand, sounds like she's pulling teeth when she echoes, "Whatever makes our little prince happy."

And I struggle to form words *in my mind* let alone my mouth when they stop speaking altogether and wait for my response.

The silence stretches like old taffy.

Until we all seem frozen.

Until I can hear the near-silent *tick-tick-tick* of the room's grandfather clock.

Until I know I have to say something or risk offending the Russos.

But I have no idea what to say. What *can* I say? I literally referred to Emilio as a bog beast in my own head not ten minutes ago *because that's what he is*. I have no idea where this proposal is even coming from. I mean, yes I'm well aware he's attracted to me. Yes, he's hit on me enough times to make a pick-me girl uncomfortable…but not once has he ever asked me on a date. Despite the inappropriate behavior, we've had *maybe* two dozen real conversations in the last decade, all of which ended with innuendos I had to ignore for fear of losing my job.

"This is quite sudden," I try. "I didn't think he liked me that way."

"Of course he does, *passerotta*," Lorenzo swears, as if he thinks that's what I need to hear.

"But Mrs. Russo, you don't seem to like the idea. I wouldn't want to overstep," I try next.

"Yes, well…as I said, whatever my little prince wants, he gets."

Shit! Shit-shit-shitty-shit-shit!

"You would insult us by not considering it," she adds, almost like a kiss of death.

And it might be.

But I…just…can't…say yes. Even if I wanted to, my intuition is screaming too loudly in my head to ignore.

It's impossible. Impossible! Without a lobotomy, there'd be no future with Emilio.

My mind reaches for the only thing it thinks might save me, "Oh! Mr. and Mrs. Russo, I love working for you, and I am honored you would even consider me for this. B-But I'm seeing someone."

"Seeing someone?" Lorenzo's voice lilts with disappointment.

"Yes, *signore*," I blurt. "I have a b-boyfriend. I couldn't do that to him. I'm a v-very loyal person and he m-means the world to me."

The room stills again, this time with too many unspoken thoughts.

So I double down. "I-If Emilio had asked me out sooner, I would have been very flattered, of course, b-but...he didn't, *signore*. I didn't know he cared for me. I'm sorry, I didn't know."

"It's all right, *passerotta*," Lorenzo finally says. "If your heart is already taken, it is already taken. We will break this sorrow to our son. For now, go home, continue your good work for us and we can revisit this in the future if you're ever free again."

"Thank you, *signore*," I say, beelining for the door like I'm running out of air.

Because I am.

I don't care why they tried to push for this now.

I don't care why the universe decided to make a plaything of me.

All I know is that today was the weirdest day of my life, and I feel like I was lucky to make it out alive.

CHAPTER 6

KADEN

I am nothing more than a block tower of idiocy toppling day by day—that's the lesson I learned in the moments after Louise left me standing there at my front door. She walked right to the doctor's truck and climbed in before the doctor had even left the porch.

I didn't mean what I said. I just thought it was odd that she would feel so comfortable sharing something like the naked picture of herself with her friends. That was it. I've just never had friends like that. It also felt like a pin bursting the bubble we were sharing. An intrusion from an outside world I left behind years ago.

But I've been replaying the moment over in my head and I can hear the crassness of what I said to her now, about modeling. How it must have sounded.

Fuck, I didn't mean to make her feel small *at all*.

I didn't think I even could. She tore in and out of this cabin like the smog of my bullshit—the clutter, my Eeyore-ness—didn't bother her in the slightest. Like *I* wasn't one of the top ten weirdest people she'd ever met. Like I was just another one of her friends. She lured me into 'human mode' again so easily I didn't realize it until she'd already left.

And I didn't hate it. I missed it after she was gone. Her. Something about her.

Which is insane, considering she was only here a couple hours at most.

The thought tightens my chest with anxiety.

I'm just...not used to people anymore. I forgot what they're like, especially when you meet a real one. But for a brief moment there, I remembered. When she was on tiptoe, stretching, eyes on fire, smile so content, I remembered what it was like to feel human.

It's been nearly 72 hours since she left and the tiny gif of that moment has been replaying in my mind nonstop. So has the touch of her warm softness. The scent of her. It's a special sort of torture to know she smells like fruit. Even through the sharp paint smell, she was all yuzu and pineapple. Salivating.

Mr. King left Louise's number behind when he came here and I've texted her about four hundred times since she walked away. She read the first twenty or so but never responded. Then, she just didn't open the rest of them.

I don't know if I can fix this...or even why I'm trying to. She was the first person beside the cleaning staff that I let into the house in three years. Hell, I didn't even let Mr. King come inside. I left his corporate ass on the porch while I went and got a painting off the wall just to make him go away.

I don't even really know why I *did* let her in, aside from the obvious. She's a gorgeous woman and I'm a man who's been voluntarily celibate for way, *way* too long. Especially considering I used to be a very proud member of the 'man-heaux' community. I would've slept with any pretty face that glanced my way.

Not to mention, as far as my art is concerned, my spark abandoned me years ago—at this point, the veil in my work is more shroud than motif. Working with her was the first glimpse of that spark I've had in ages.

But it's not Louise's beauty that has me staring at the unfinished painting of her, pining as if something has been lost. It's the way she reached for my painting. It's the way she tried to open up to me.

It's the fact that after she left, I dove down a rabbit hole online discovering things about her. Louise went to RISD. Both *ArtForum* and *Apollo* magazines did profile pieces on her when she was barely twenty years old. And she sold pieces of her own work to international buyers while she was still an art student.

What the hell inspired her to become an art advisor? More than that, how the hell didn't I recognize that she was an artist when she was here?

Of course, she's an artist herself. *Of course*, my bullshit didn't bother her. *Of course*, she laid herself out before me.

I thought she was just like everybody else who's tried to come here. All those fakes who hang around hoping I'll rub off on them or let my guard down long enough to rob me of my peace for their own personal gain. Moochers. Dilettantes. Sure, Louise wanted information, but I got the sense after a few questions that they were mostly asked out of curiosity. She wanted to know *me*.

And I punished her for it. I really am a dumb fucker.

Joke's on me, though; she robbed me of my peace without even trying.

I haven't been able to paint since she left.

I haven't gone a day without painting in *years* and it's been three fucking days now.

It makes me want to claw my own hands off. What fucking use do they have if they're not painting?

You need them to touch her. The dark intrusive thought flies by like a bat in the night. It's followed by a crueler one, *like she's ever going to let you do that again.*

I need Louise back here. Now. I need her life force, the raw intrusion of her, the way she clutched my side.

That spot at my waist has been *burning* since Friday.

I don't care what I have to do to get her back.

So, around midnight, I send her one more text, spilling my proverbial guts at her feet so she can either stomp all over them or, hopefully, bring them back to me.

CHAPTER 7

LULU

Ping!

I am on my couch, dead asleep with a facemask on and a plate of Brooklyn's best fried chicken perched on my lap about to slide off onto the floor, when a text message wakes me.

It's from Cara and all it says is, *S.O.S. I need your help. Can you meet me at the 7th Ave Central Park entrance asap?*

The last mists of sleep abandon me instantly. Cara never asks for help, even when *she absolutely should*. It's the most infuriating thing about being her friend, the fear she has that she's asking for too much when Ivy and I both know she's one of the loveliest people in the world and we'd move mountains for her.

I text back immediately, *Is something wrong? Is it Troy?*

I'd never tell her this, but leaving her was the only good thing that dipshit loser ex of hers ever did. I'll never understand how she gave so much time to him or why she put up with his shit for so long, but if helping her *keeps her away from him*, she can always sign me right up.

She texts back, *No, nothing to do with Troy. I need help with Mr. King.*

Well, I owe him too so, I respond, *I'll be there in 90. I'll let you know when I'm close.*

Almost 90 minutes to the second, I step off the subway in Central Manhattan and scurry to the park entrance, where I find her waiting. She's wearing clothing I've never seen before, but which I can only assume Mr. King bought for her. The outfit doesn't just fit her like a glove, it makes her look like the light, free Cara I always thought she could be…once she purged her parasitic husband from her life.

She's turned away from me as I approach and, given the urgency in her message, I half expect her to turn around with tears in her eyes.

But there are no tears in sight. Her brown eyes shine like polished agate and her smile is so wide I can't help but shoot her one in return as we hug, "Hey babe!"

"Thank you so much for coming, Lulu, I…" she says, shivering. "I need your help."

"Of course, what is it?"

"I'm…doomed."

I blink at her for a moment. The words escape her in a high tone, hopeful and excited. As if it's a *good* thing to be doomed. Then she giggles in a bright burst of joy, and I'm caught off guard again.

"Okay?" I say.

"He's wonderful," she says, as if that explains anything. "He's good. And he's kind. And he likes me, Lu."

"Mr. King?" I ask. Off her nervous nod, I add, "Of course he does. He should. Have you seen yourself lately? You're the smoking-hot catch of a lifetime, babe."

But she shakes her head. "Come on, we've got to go rob his house."

"Sure, why not," I say. "Let's do that."

I mean, if your best friend says you're robbing somebody, what else are you gonna do?

We cross the street and plunge into a Christmas-crowded Nordstrom's; she pulls me along like she's been here enough times to know the quickest path to his apartment. When we reach the cavernous private residential lobby, a security guard spots us immediately but doesn't even bother to step away from his place by the far wall.

Cara doesn't pause either. She waves at him, "Hi Frank!"

"Good evening, Ms. Miramontes."

We slip into a specific elevator using a key card she must have stolen from Mr. King at some point…unless he's already given her a key to his place.

"We have to be quick here," she says. "I don't know when he'll be back."

"What are we stealin', honey?" It seems like the sensible question to ask.

"A picture. A very important picture."

My heart skips a beat in warning. "...A *painting*?"

"No-No-No. No," she says. "A photo of Ethan's mom."

"Oh, okay." That's definitely better. I mean, I'm pretty sure it's still a felony, but it seems like a...less dicey one? Maybe?

"I need you to help me find someone to paint it for me, though," she adds as the elevator reaches a height that belongs to airplanes and King Kong and pulls me out into the gargantuan, empty penthouse.

"Why paint?" I ask. "And why do you need me? You know as many people as I do."

Cara pauses us in the foyer and takes a breath. "I need you because he showed me the photo when we were absolutely drunk as skunks and I don't know where it is now. Also, I need you to take it to someone you think can paint it before Christmas and bring it back so he won't realize it's gone. Okay?"

It hits me a second before she tugs me toward the kitchen what she's trying to do and it warms my heart like nothing else.

"Babe, are you...trying to get him a Christmas gift?"

Her body spikes with panic; it rolls through her slender body like an adorable little shockwave. "*What do you get a man who has* everything, Lulu?!"

"Oh honey, that's a great idea for a gift," I assure her. "But why are you so bent out of shape about it?"

"It's not important," she claims as she starts opening drawers and motions for me to do the same, which I do.

Of course, I realize the answer to my own question twenty seconds into the search. Cara likes Mr. King. *Really* likes him. She might even love him. I've only ever seen her like this once before—for her tenth wedding anniversary to Troy. Back then, I felt a sour sort of pity for her, watching her rush around to bend over backward for a man who treated her like a servant. The same fear rolls through me now, wondering if I should intervene earlier this time. It was torturous to see how sad she was after Troy put in absolutely *zero* effort on the day. And I hated listening to her make excuses for him later.

She hasn't known Ethan very long. I don't want her to start bending herself into a pretzel again so soon. It's too early to give her joy away to another guy who won't appreciate it.

"Honey, can I ask something?"

"Yeah."

"You know I love you, and I want to like Ethan enough to be okay with you doing all this for him...but...can you tell me one nice thing he's done for you, beyond the job and sex, that I can root for?"

To my surprise, Cara's face flushes red and a smile curves up her round cheek. In a quiet voice I can barely hear over the sound of drawers opening, she says, "He said he's proud of me."

That stops me. "Just, like, apropos of nothing? What was the context?"

"Troy was being an asshole and I snapped back at him—*I snapped back at him, Lu!*—and when I told Ethan, he said he was so proud of me for standing up to my worthless ex. And then he said it again when I signed my first clients."

"Oh," escapes me like a breath. "Now *that* is something I can get behind."

Because it's sentiments like that that Cara deserves more than anything. Somebody who's going to go to bat for her, in small ways and large, and champion her otherwise. Hell, we *all* deserve a partner who will do that.

"Yeah," she agrees, pointing at drawers. "Help me look."

We find the photo about ten minutes later, delicately tucked away in the desk in Mr. King's office. It's framed, which surprises me, considering there are a million shelves and ledges in this ginormous house to display it on, but he keeps it in the desk.

But there's another photo tucked under it that makes me think he's a bit sentimental. It's as if he didn't want to keep them separate, but also didn't want to frame the second one.

I can't imagine why. The photo shows three college-age guys with their arms around each other, smiling and happy, preening a little for the camera.

"Is that Mr. King?" I ask, of the middle guy.

Cara smiles, admiring him. The look in her eye and subtle bite of her lip is unmistakable; she's smitten. It's so cute on her.

"That, I think is Ethan's friend, Valerian Fox." She points to the narrow arrow of a guy on Mr. King's left before sliding her finger over to the third guy. "And I think that's Ethan's brother, Nero."

It's strange. I'm sure Nero looks very different from how he did at twenty, but my throat actually tightens a tiny bit when my eyes catch on him. Déjà vu. He seems familiar, even though I know I've never met him before.

I abandon that thought as quickly as it comes to me. My mistake with Malbec over the weekend leaps to the forefront of my mind as some sort of warning—a reminder that I'm a friggen moron with laughable instincts when it comes to men.

Mr. King's brother was a hot college student. That's all. Plus, I think Cara said he's in prison?

But a couple hours later when I arrive back at my apartment in Brooklyn with the framed photo of Mr. King's mom tucked protectively inside my coat, I find myself wondering if it was *my* laughable instincts that went wrong with Malbec or if he's just a weirdo with social issues.

He's been sending me almost non-stop text messages since I walked out of his house on Friday, which would normally freak me out a little, except that he spent most of the texts I read simply apologizing for what he said.

They were real apologies too. Not once did he write *I'm sorry but...* They were all just *I'm sorry*.

I want to believe he means it. And I don't want to alienate an artist like him. I would genuinely appreciate the chance to see him work, just like I've watched countless others.

As if Malbec can hear me arguing with myself about him, my phone *pings* with a text message around midnight.

He makes me an offer I can't refuse: *Louise, I've felt dead for years. It's not an excuse for my terrible choice of words, I'm just learning how to be human again. Anything I can do to make my mistake up to you, just tell me.*

CHAPTER 8

KADEN

I re-read the text message, wallowing a little in my own self-pity. It's…pathetic, what I wrote to Louise. True, but pathetic. It's selfish too. The unfinished painting of her is still trapped in purgatory where she left it, hogging the big studio easel, screaming at me to complete it every time I enter the room.

I can't finish it without her here.

I can't burn it alive either.

She's holding me hostage by not answering. Holding the *art* hostage. And that half-full paint can of blue ruin belongs to her now, I can't use it for any other piece until hers is finished.

But I can't sit here staring at my phone forever either.

I've just convinced myself to finally set the phone down when I see the little 'read' notification appear below my text. Honestly, it stops my heart. I freeze for half a millennium, waiting to see how she'll respond. If she will at all.

And then, like a lifesaver, three dots appear on the screen.

I'm so happy for a second, there's an actual physical pain in my chest…until I remember there's no guarantee her message will be good.

But with a few simple words from her, the pain in my chest winks out.

Would you paint me something if I asked you to?

Well, she's not telling me to fuck off, which I consider a win. But I need to make my misstep up to her.

So after a pathetically short pause, I write back, *If you sit with me while I paint it, yes.*

Three dots appear again and I hold my breath until...*Okay. Are you free tomorrow?*

It's a small mercy that she's not here to witness my awkward one-man celebration.

Yes, I text back. *I'll leave the door open for you.*

CHAPTER 9

LULU

"Friendly and professional. Friendly. And. Professional," I repeat this to myself as I walk up Malbec's stairs for the second time in less than a week. I'm wearing better shoes this time. A thicker coat, too, just in case I have to flee again.

When I turn the handle, I half expect it to be locked despite what Malbec texted. But it's not. It turns under my hand easily, invitingly. Weirder still, when it swings open, I discover Malbec has...cleaned?

Eh, I wouldn't go that far. But he's tidied up. A lot. Antiques previously crowding the rooms to either side of the front hall seem to have shifted position and been covered by giant drop cloths. Maybe he's planning a trip? I mean, all I know of him is that his reclusive nature has given way to a legend that precedes his artwork wherever it's sold, but...that just means he keeps his life private. For all I know, he travels extensively.

I hang my coat again and walk deeper into Malbec's house carrying the framed photo of Mr. King's mom in my arms like an unwieldy pet that really wants to be put down.

"Mr. Malbec?"

"In the studio!" he calls out, and I ignore the depth of his voice, how it makes my entire body perk up.

"He's just some guy," I whisper to myself.

But I know that's a lie the second I turn the corner into his studio and see him standing in front of...my piece of art.

The piece modeled off me.

The barely started canvas sits where it sat before, in the giant easel behind him like an offensive white hole in the middle of a room full of color. It steals focus immediately, almost yelling at me in its incompleteness.

It matches Malbec's energy. He's showered since I last visited, and put on a dark undershirt devoid of paint, but his face still holds that haunted desperation that it did before. I hate that it makes me want to touch him again. That, more than the unfinished canvas, makes me take a tentative step forward.

"You didn't burn it," I say, when neither of us speaks.

"I won't," he says, almost promising. Walking toward me, he adds, "Not until my model tells me to."

My head shakes lightly, of its own accord. "I'm not doing that for you again. I think it's best if we just respect each other as profess—"

But he doesn't let me finish before he closes the distance between us, drawing to a soft stop inches from me, peering down at me with some mixture of remorse and disbelief on his face.

"I *do* respect you, Ms. Rathbone," he says in that strong but dulcet tone that scatters shivers across my body. "As I said in my messages, I *know* I put my foot in my mouth last time you were here, and I'm sorry. As penance, that canvas will sit on that easel untouched, staring at me every time I come in, until you forgive me."

I open my mouth to tell him none of that is necessary, that what happened was just a mistake I've already put behind me, but he continues before I can.

"When you forgive me, Ms. Rathbone, we'll pick up where we left off last time. With you as a work of art inviting me into the canvas with you."

I don't know what to say to that. My heart squeezes inside me at the thought, and the solemn vow shining brightly in his eyes, but my brain knows better. Pretty words do not a changed man make.

"We'll see," is all I say.

"Yes, you will." A tiny smile—but a real one—suddenly plays at the corners of his lips, tugging on my heartstrings in the process. Fuck he's beautiful. But it's gone in the blink of an eye as he points to the picture frame in my hand and his brows rise. "Did you bring me something?"

"Uh, I did," I say, turning the frame around so he can see the photo of Ethan's mother—*the whole reason I came out here again*, I remind myself.

He takes it from me so delicately. "Is this your mom? She's beautiful."

I smile politely. "No, actually. This is Mr. King's mom."

He reassesses it, this time with that artist's appraisal. "Oh-kay."

"You said you'd paint something for me?"

"You want me to paint Mr. King's mom for you?" Some flutter of curious confusion graces his gorgeous face, replaced suddenly by something that looks a little like jealousy. "Oh. You...know Mr. King well?"

His prying tone makes me smile. "No, I've only met him once. My best friend is...well...I don't know if *dating* him is the right word for what they're doing, but... She asked me to help with his Christmas gift."

"Ah," escapes him like a relieved little bark.

"I was hoping you might be willing to paint his mom...for her," I clarify. "She has no clue what to get a billionaire."

His lips twinge with surprise. "Huh. Mr. King doesn't seem like the sentimental type."

"For her, he is," I say, thinking back on that meeting between Ethan, Cara, and I, how often I caught him smiling at her while she and I spoke. I don't think Cara understands yet just how attached he already is to her. "Smart man, she's amazing."

Kaden turns his intense gaze on me; meeting it head-on is the only defense I have against the sudden urge to look away like a smitten schoolgirl.

He's just some guy, I remind myself...but he doesn't help matters with what he says next.

"Well then, I'll make sure I use all my best colors in this painting."

He motions me deeper into the studio, to a smaller easel set up at the back next to a large window and a big, fluffy armchair that wasn't here last time I visited. I have no idea how he maneuvered it past the junk maze, but he motions me to it as he sets up the photo and reaches for a fresh canvas in the same graceful swing of his arm. Beside the chair, he's set up a little tea table, electric kettle, and two teacups.

It's quaint. It's picturesque. It's...very obviously been set up for me—the little boxes of tea sitting nearby have never even been opened. And no sooner has my ass hit the seat but...

"Do you need an electric blanket? I have one," he offers.

"Please."

He tosses it over my lap not ten seconds later, patting it down around me and showing me the controls before he plugs it in. He murmurs little nothing words while he moves around getting me comfortable—little "there we gos" and "let me justs" and "cozy-cozies" that make me want to tease him about how he's trying to fix things.

He's overcompensating in a sweet way that *does* make me feel a little better.

But we both overstepped. And I won't be modeling for him again no matter how he apologizes. So...

"Hey Kaden?" I ask softly when he's right there, only a few inches away. "Let's just start fresh, okay?"

His body drops into a squat, knees inches from mine, and his eyes widen with some muddled emotion I can't quite interpret. So I reach out my hand to him.

"Thank you so much for letting me come talk to you today, Mr. Malbec," I say, using a slightly warmer tone than I would for strangers. "I just have a few questions, if you don't mind."

The hand hangs between us for several long moments as he studies it, then me, then the hand again. It's long enough I wonder if he thinks it's weird...but...I don't care. I *am* weird. And I'm trying to keep things friendly and professional.

But Kaden seems to want something else. His enormous and blazing hot calloused hand slides into mine as if he's going to shake it, but then he raises my hand to his lips, kissing the back.

"I've heard a lot about you, Ms. Rathbone," he says against my skin before shaking my hand properly. "I hope it's okay if I ask some questions myself."

"You have questions for me?"

"I do."

He's still holding my hand between us, but I forget to pull away from the warmth, too curious for my own good.

"Like what?"

"Well, that depends on you." His thumb sweeps across my skin like a match catching fire.

"How so?"

"I don't want a repeat of last time. I want to make sure I only disappoint you the right way, Ms. Rathbone."

Disappoint you the right way. The words echo through me, calling to mind our last conversation, about the artist he would have made love to if she'd let him. The thought warms me right through. Scares me too.

"You could always just *not* disappoint me," I point out.

"I'm a man, Ms. Rathbone," he teases. "I know what I'm capable of."

That makes me smile. Then I smile wider when his eyes dart to my lips and his hand tightens in mine.

"So what do you suggest?" I ask him.

He sobers then, returning his gaze to mine. "I'm going to answer your questions from Mr. King like I would for any journalist or fan...but if *you* want the unvarnished truth, ask for it."

My brow furrows, but I keep my voice light. "You're going to lie to me?"

"No," he says, wrapping his other hand around mine, sandwiching mine between his. "But I haven't let anyone in in a long time. I don't really remember how to talk to people. So just...ask for more, if you want it, and let me do the same with you. Deal?"

"Deal."

I try to force any expectations of him away as he releases my hand and begins to paint. I let the conversation flow where it needs to, in order to get the information I need for Mr. King.

And Kaden's system for asking for more truth helps a lot, honestly. Any time I can feel him giving a boilerplate answer, I nudge him for 'more' and he gives it. But most of those questions are, well, corporate. *'Have you ever had substance abuse problems'* is not a question I would normally ever ask an artist…nor would I judge him if the answer was yes. And when I ask him the old gimmicky question of *'where do you see your career going,'* we both fall into a giggling fit at the ridiculous nature of the question.

"I think we both know the gods would punish us for making plans, Louise," he jokes.

We keep things light and pleasant for a good long while as he brings Mr. King's mom to life in vivid color.

But…

When I finally leave the chair to roam around the room and the conversation naturally shifts to more esoteric topics like our personal preferences in art and life and why he keeps himself so bundled away up here, the "unvarnished truth" becomes a minefield I wasn't anticipating. Kaden answers every question, then asks a question of me in return, and then glances away with disappointment when I chicken out and give him my own boilerplate answer instead of responding honestly.

I don't *mean* to chicken out. It just happens. I can feel my spine tightening each time we move dangerously close to something like intimacy, to questions I wasn't prepared to answer today.

Until finally, he just turns the conversation on me entirely.

"I looked you up, you know. I've seen your work. You're an artist, Louise."

My spine stiffens, at the compliment that also feels like an accusation.

Then, it tightens more when he asks, "How the hell did you get mixed up with the Russos?"

"What's that supposed to mean?"

His brow arches. "I *know* who they are. Everybody in New York knows who they are."

I squirm a little, even as I toss him a nothing-smile. "So? I was a scholarship kid fresh out of art school trying to make a name for myself. Seemed like a dream come true at the time."

But he shakes his head gently, seeing right through me. "You became a creative advisor for a group of people who couldn't "make art" if you put a gun to their heads."

"What's wrong with being an art advisor?"

"Nothing, if you were one, but you're not."

"I'm actually really good at it, thank you." I try to sound dismissive, to disguise the genuine hurt I feel at his words, but his response surprises me.

"Of course you are," he says, lips curling back a little as if that was never in question. "I just don't know why you gave up your art for it."

Oh.

I glance away. "I don't want to talk about that. It's personal."

"Would you have told me before I messed up?" he asks.

I already know the answer to that one, and I tear my gaze away instead of answering...which I guess is an answer in and of itself.

But a second later, I hear a sound and turn back to find Kaden navigating the maze of junk to reach me. When he does, he's almost haloed by that unfinished canvas sitting square at the center of the room with my form sketched across it, so I can't look at one without looking at the other.

"I just want to keep things professional. Friendly," I say, surprised by the softness of my own voice.

Kaden steps closer, until I'm enveloped in his radiator warmth.

"Well, professionally, I want to tell you that I spent Saturday night calling every person I know until I found the contact information for the guy who purchased your piece *Hourglass* and bought it from him. It'll be here next week."

I recoil a little, studying his face for traces of...a joke? A lie? I don't see any.

And he doesn't back down. He draws even closer to me, and adds,

"And as far as friendship goes, I want you to know that when your painting arrives, I'm going to masturbate to it. And I'm going to record myself doing it, so you finally understand that I don't judge you for modeling for me *or* for sending your friends that picture. I'm only envious that I have no one to send my own pictures to."

Heat flushes through my system in surprise. Heat and amusement. "You want to send it to me, don't you."

His eyes sparkle with mischief. "Yes, I do. But I'd never send a dick pic without permission, Ms. Rathbone."

I smirk. "Will I be disappointed?"

"In all the right ways."

Fuck, that was smooth. And now I'm sopping wet with a guy I've sworn to be strictly platonic with. Fuck.

"Do I? Have your permission, Ms. Rathbone?"

"Sure. But I don't believe you're actually going to do it."

At that, the tiny smile at the corners of his lips returns and I hate myself for how fast my heart starts to beat with anticipation.

"Let's make a deal then," he says. "*When* I send you the video of me masturbating, you agree to come back here and model for the painting again."

My eyes narrow playfully. "When you send it with your face in the frame so I know it's you and not some rando's dick, I will. Deal?"

"Deal."

A few days later…and fifty-three miles away…

CHAPTER 10

NERO

It's Christmas Eve.

It's *Christmas fucking Eve* and I'm standing outside the damned hellhole prison I've been trapped in for five years, freezing my balls off, waiting for my brother to pick me up. Like a fucking chump. Irritation rises in me by the second.

Ethan's such a sore loser.

He's always been the type to take his ball and go home if he doesn't get his way.

It's because he thinks he's special. Lucky. Blessed, maybe. And why wouldn't he think that? Ethan had the world handed to him on a silver fucking platter like some gift...by me, by our mom, by sheer dumb luck. And now that I've claimed the same for myself, he's pissed at me for it.

So what if I bought half his company? He doesn't have to act like such a little baby about it. We're family. *Dyed in the blood family.* The *only* family he has left, by the way. That's not something you flake on after everything we've been through together.

Especially when he knows Otisburg Prison is run by a tight-ass with a god complex who doesn't even have the common decency to let a man charge his cell phone on release day.

Thank fuck calling collect is still a thing.

I give Ethan the benefit of the doubt for another six minutes before the anaconda in my pants turns into a turtle, practically retreating into my body to fight the bitter cold, and I'm forced to make other arrangements.

It takes all of two minutes to shoot off a call to my second in command, Darius. He gives me shit for not calling him first, but I can hear him swipe his car keys off the hook and head for the door in the same breath because *he's* not a dick who's too good for family.

He pulls up in his ridiculous purple Lamborghini half an hour later and I don't even care how loud the color is or how tight the fit is on my six-five frame. Darius is from Atlanta, so he's got the heat on blast like there's a sun in the backseat and I'm indebted to him for it.

"Thank fuck," I tell him, instead of hello. "I lost my balls to frost an hour ago."

"Don't come crying to me," he says, bumping my fist. "*You* told me you were getting out in January."

I don't tell him I was the sappy dumbass hoping I'd get to spend some quality time with my brother before my various enterprises across the city tore my attention away.

Instead, I tell him, "Early early parole. I'm an angel, what can I say?"

"Fallen angel, maybe," he laughs as we drive away.

"If they were smart, there wouldn't be any other kind," I tell him. It's only daddy's special little boys and girls—like fucking Ethan—who act blind to God's favoritism. I learned early on that I was on my own. I carried that burden so he wouldn't have to. Now, I honestly think the constant bullshit I had to put up with growing up was a gift in disguise. I'd be a soft loser if I let it roll off my back like Ethan did.

Darius pulls me from my thoughts. "The real question is…now that you've crash landed on Earth, which do you want to do first—get debriefed on business and start making plays *or* go get your dick wet at Amara's?"

Ooh. Darius knows me all too well. Being away from my business for five years definitely made me antsy to hit the ground running once I got out. But not for the reason he thinks.

We've always made the majority of our money through cyber-intelligence—by getting our hands on information no one should really have *or* by making it nearly impossible for the "wrong people" to get their hands on our clients' secrets (all while *we* keep copies of our clients' information for ourselves, of course). We then use that data to make plays across multiple global chessboards to keep the money pouring in and the power always in our favor.

Those—the money and the power—are the reasons we've never had a recruiting or turnover issue. They afford my entire crew a taste of godliness they could never get anywhere else.

But they're not the reasons I love it. Or why I felt genuine shame when the prosecutor who pinned me with tax evasion charges called me a "twisted fuck."

I love being a ghost in other people's business. I love knowing things I couldn't possibly know. There's just something so...fucking...sensual...about sitting in a darkened room, watching things unfold that I shouldn't know about. That's where the real power is.

Being without a fucking computer for five years, without my favorite live feeds, was *excruciating*.

But...

There's one thing that's better than watching, and as long as I can remember that, I don't think I'm as far gone as that prosecutor thought.

As much as I'm chomping at the bit to get my life back on track, I am fucking *famished* for the sweet taste of pussy. I haven't seen a woman, other than the occasional glimpses of bummed out wives and girlfriends in the prison's visiting room, in *years*. There's just something about the stench of nothing but men that crushed my spirit more than being in prison ever did.

"Man, you got me *drooling*." We both laugh. "Yes to Amara's. Please and thank you. Get the guys to come."

"Great minds," Darius says. "I already told them to meet us there."

"Let's stop by a bank too," I add. "It's Christmas Eve. Let's be generous tonight."

"Hell yes. We were planning a welcome back party for you at Amara's for January. I know the ladies will appreciate it."

I'm genuinely relieved there is no party when we finally roll up in front of Amara's club and enter to deafening cheers from my crew and Amara's women. It's too many familiar faces on both sides. Too much pressure. My nerves spike with unease but I'm a world class bullshitter. I flash the whole room a shit-eating grin and spread my arms wide like I'm some sort of resurrected Messiah.

The thunderous claps of their hands on my back are too much.

Their loud yells of "Congratulations" only remind me of riots in the mess hall back at Otisburg.

But the *women*? The first one I see is a waitress with bright blonde hair and I can't tear my eyes away from her glittered cheeks and ruby-red smile...until I see a regular I've had before who uses the stage name Trixie and I can't tear my eyes away from her either. It's the same with every woman in the room.

There's nothing like a beautiful woman.

Their smell. Their hair. Their nails.

They're a different species, I swear.

But...I realize quickly enough that even *they're* too much for me. Too much for my cock, which should be hard as mahogany, straining against my pants just at the sight of them. Instead, he's fucking shy, the bastard. Limp as a wet noodle. Even when the gorgeous, sensuous queen of the tower Amara arrives.

She arrives at my side draped in gold that accentuates her flawless dark skin, and says, "Welcome back, Nero. It's always great to have you...I see prison has treated you fabulously. Go ahead and flirt a little. Pick one, pick 'em all, and I'll make sure you're set up in your old suite."

"Thank you, Amara."

The normalcy of it is fucking sweet. I missed it. But the noises, the flashing lights, the movement of it all is still too much. I don't know what's wrong with me, but I keep an immaculate poker face in place as I pick a seat amongst my men, order myself a glass of ice cubes to crunch on to take my mind off my sensory issues while I listen to them tell me bits and pieces of the shit they've been doing while I was inside.

I stay calm through it all, I laugh when it's expected, I smile when I don't know what else to do to set them all at ease…but some bitter pang of something nestles deeper inside my chest the longer I listen to them talk.

Until Darius turns down a lap dance and reveals to me that he's about to get engaged to his girl, Pam…and the bitterness tightens its grip on me.

"I'm a taken man now," Darius declares proudly.

"Prick has to be," a guy named Tony jokes, "She's the only one who'd take him."

I missed so much while I was inside.

The sourness deepens as Darius tells me about the proposal he has set up, and how he wants me to be his best man. His plans should make me happy, but I'm envious as sin. Discomfort coils in my stomach like a camouflaged serpent one wrong footstep away from striking.

And it makes me sick, this feeling inside me. Darius is one of my closest friends—it's him and maybe three other guys I'd trust with my life—but I feel the violent need to *ruin* his joy. To say something out of hand about his girl, his character, how marriage is a doomed enterprise in the modern world.

What the fuck is wrong with me?

I keep my fucking traitorous mouth shut and continue crushing ice cubes between my teeth, hoping they quench my need to overshare…which they do, mostly. But the cold can't do shit for the intrusive thoughts that wriggle through my head like worms through rot.

I remind myself I just need to stay quiet until I can get home.

Pfft, as if you have a home, my mind goes out of its way to remind me. *Even your own brother wants nothing to do with you.*

Yeah well, that'll change. Ethan doesn't have a choice. I'll superglue myself to that fucker until he accepts that I'm in his life now whether he likes it or not.

And that thought is the only one that keeps the worse ones at bay. I know I'm not mad at my loyal men who've maintained the business while I was out of commission. Fucking Ethan's the problem; *he's* the bitterness polluting my mind.

But blaming him doesn't help me a few minutes later when Amara approaches again and tells me my usual room is ready. I'm still not up for sex—which scares me way worse than the jealousy I feel toward my guys—but I need something to take the edge off.

Amara can sense it too. She motions me to follow her away from my crew as they cheer me on and shout, "Captain, my Captain's 'bout to drown in pussy!"

She waits until we're alone to say, "You want something hard? Something mellow? Anything you want. Let my ladies take care of you."

My instinct to bristle is lessened by her soothing voice, her hand on my arm. Amara's a class act and she appreciates how much business my guys have always given her, how classy we keep our visits.

"Maybe a massage?" she offers.

"Yeah, that sounds fantastic," I admit, rolling my tight shoulders. "And maybe…"

"Maybe what? We can do anything for you, you know that."

Shit, I don't know why I feel shy asking for what I want. This probably isn't even the hundredth worst ask she's heard this week. Still, I'm a little embarrassed.

"I wanna watch," I whisper. "Do you know if any of your girls can squirt?"

How do I tell someone I need to *see* the pleasure? I need to *know* it's real and that the woman's enjoying it. That she's not just going through the motions. Or at least, I need to know that I can *coax* the real thing out of her even if she tries to hold back on me.

Amara's answering smile is so warm I feel like I could bathe in it. "I have a woman for everyone, honey."

As often as I've come here over the years, none of my past experiences compare to this. How reinvigorating it feels to finally be free again. Two women get me on the massage table and begin to work my stiff body with their soft warm oil-slicked hands. Two others lay on the bed across from me exploring each other's bodies until one erupts with pleasure…and I'm harder than granite in no time.

"You want us all, big boy?" one of the masseuses asks...and I fucking do.

I let my voice go feral as I rise from the table in more ways than one. Commanding, I say, "All four of you on the bed, side by side, two on your backs, two on your bellies."

When they're exactly where I want them, I set my tongue to the first's clit and crook my fingers inside her until she howls. I go along one by one by one, teasing their pleasure out of them one whimper and wail at a time, until I reach the last—my volcano goddess and the spot on the bed that's still wet from where she erupted.

With her, I take my special time.

With her, I edge her to the brink of exhausted ecstasy before summoning a tidal wave. The torturous teasing is how I *know* it's real when the wave finally breaks across my face. That and the fact that she's trembling, unable to get up for several full minutes afterward.

Absolutely exactly what I needed.

But...it's a different story when the four of them try to coax me on the bed so they can take care of me. I don't know what happens. I deflate like a goddamned balloon. *What the fuck is wrong with me?*

And no amount of "It's okay, sugar, we understand," makes me feel any better.

Eventually, my volcano goddess is the one who saves me. She shoos the other women away and locks the door behind them.

With a voice like melted caramel, she slides back onto the bed beside me and says, "Why don't we put on another show for each other? I'd love to watch you take care of yourself while I turn you on."

Fucking angel for a fallen angel. One I'm sure I don't deserve...

Until I notice there's a medical bracelet on her wrist. "What's that for?"

She squirms and covers it suddenly, as if just thinking about it is some terrible reminder.

"It's nothing," she lies.

"Hey-Hey," I assure her quietly. "I'm just curious, I promise."

"I'd rather not say," she begs, and I put my hand on her wrist, to cover it myself as I roll on top of her.

"Okay, that's okay. But I can help you if you need anything. Just let me know, yeah?"

"Okay," she says in a way that tells me she doesn't believe me.

"Seriously, I do it all the time for Amara's girls."

"Really?" she asks, her dark eyes widening.

"Really. Tell me what you need."

"It's big," she tells me.

"I have deep pockets," I tease.

Her perfect pouty lips quiver for a moment as she searches my face. "I need…"

I genuinely meant what I said to her. I *have* helped plenty of the women in Amara's employ pay for rent or a new car or classes if they want to retrain for something else. Hell, before I went to prison, I was practically an angel investor in this place. And I have eighteen graduation photos on my wall at home, sent to me by ladies who made it through school with my "student loans."

But something happens when those words "I need" leave her mouth. Something I've never experienced before.

"I need…" she mewls again. Such a tiny phrase, it escapes her like a whimper. Yet the sound pierces flesh and bone, destabilizing me completely.

Blood *rushes* into my cock so fast it almost makes me lightheaded.

I have to rest my head on her beautiful breasts for a moment to let it pass.

But she notices in a big way. Her eyes dart down between us to the monster tapping her belly button, then back up at me, with a twinkle in her eye.

"I need *you*, Mr. King," she finally says.

There's suddenly *zero* blood left in my big brain, it's all down there. My hands fist in the sheets to either side of the volcano goddess; it's all I can do to keep from impaling her right then and there.

"Fuck don't say that," I beg.

My desperate restraint only brightens her eyes further. Reaching down, she grips the beast in her hand and guides it right to her entrance, tilting up so she can rub my dick against her wetness.

"Didn't you hear me, Mr. King?" she teases, voice breathless. "I said *I need you*. Right now."

And I'm gone. I'm drowning in her hot soaking sweetness. My cock sheaths itself to the hilt before I can even breathe again.

Fuck me, I can't explain it. Not sure I want to. All I know is I spend the best hour of my life in that bed, and when it's done and I leave her to sleep it off, I ask Amara about the bracelet. Turns out her kid's going through a cancer treatment so expensive there's no way for her to ever pay for it with her insurance.

I've never paid for something like that before, but…there's a first time for everything.

She did me a solid in there. She didn't just get me off four times, she gave me some much-needed post-nut clarity. Now I have a clear head to go after what really matters…getting my baby brother to stop acting like a dick and play chess with me whether he wants to or not.

CHAPTER 11

LULU

Whichever time lord rules over those ambiguous few days between Christmas and New Years needs to quit drinking. Those days always seem to blip by in seconds, as if time can't wait to start over fresh on January First. I didn't used to mind, back when the Russos spent their winter holiday in Sicily and I got that week off to party and drink and relax in the apartment I overpay for.

This year is different, unfortunately. I've been up to my eyeballs planning "the Greatest Art Auction this city has ever seen," per a demand the Russos made of me back in June. It's no small feat, considering this is New York City. But I was allowed to hire an actual party planner for the event, and my friend Ivy for the sweets and catering connections, which left me with the job of running around like a chicken with my head cut off trying to coax artists like Koons, Kusama, Walker, and Wiley to put pieces of their work up for sale at the event.

Until Mrs. Russo sprang the *real* reason for the sale on me back in November, and everything went tits up pretty quickly.

"My little prince is finally taking his place among the stars," she'd told me. "We will hang his art with the greats and seed the audience with special guests to talk him up. Then, we will arrange to have private callers on standby to push bids higher for his better pieces. And of course we will have the press cover his success afterward."

Her 'little prince' being Emilio, of course. Emilio the bog beast, whose artwork lives at the nexus of accidental folk, pop art, and porn. Unique in its crassness. Abrasive in its lack of self-awareness. And usually just as gross as he is.

Sorry, I'm being mean again…even if it's true, it's mean and I shouldn't admit it. Especially since the Russos haven't brought up their proposal to me on his behalf since it happened.

I have to remind myself it doesn't matter what *I* think of his art. Emilio *has* had several successful showings in galleries…even if they were only successful because his parents paid for the publicity.

That's how it works a lot of times. Artists that rise to social acclaim are often chosen and helped along rather than emerging self-made from the primordial ooze of creativity.

The problem, of course, is that if we make it too obvious that the sale is rigged in Emilio's favor, we'll lose the goodwill of the artists who graciously agreed to put their pieces up for sale. And if the art world ever catches wind of the grift, it's anyone's guess who will be shunned for it.

Ha! As if anyone would ever talk shit about the Russos. No, no. It'll be me who takes the brunt of the shunning.

I tried explaining the danger to Mrs. Russo many times…and each attempt ended the same way, with her ignoring my warning and telling me to go fetch the work of another great artist—like Curris, like Malbec—to hang alongside her son's.

When she didn't listen, I tried explaining to Matteo, then I went higher to Lorenzo, but neither really understood the ramifications in any way that mattered.

Which meant the added burden of figuring out how to protect myself from the fallout of this auction fell on me.

I spent weeks making special calls to private collectors and museums until I found enthusiastic buyers for every single one of the other artists' pieces. At the very least, no one should end the evening without a bid, and I hope that's enough to protect my name and hide my shame of having to orchestrate this sham in the first place.

Now, with less than an hour left before the event actually begins,

I'm starting to feel anxious again. The wait staff have all arrived, the crates of fancy champagnes and beers are on ice, and Ivy's tiny pistachio petit fours are immaculate as always. The art is all here too, save for one piece of Emilio's he says he'll bring himself.

"You'll love it, I promise," he'd said over the phone.

I didn't bother telling him, I'd only love it if it *actually shows up by the time the party begins so there isn't a massive gap on the wall in the main showroom.*

Which Mrs. Russo will *absolutely* blame me for. Somehow.

That empty spot on the wall is why I hate this job.

But...the artwork on the rest of the walls is why I love it. It's so beautiful in the gallery like this, when there aren't many people and the work looks alive on its own.

Malbec's especially. It's the piece Mr. King sourced for me before I met Kaden. In the painting, shower steam veils a woman standing by the counter, wiping fog off the bathroom mirror. He's captured a beautiful layering effect where the entire painting is veiled by mist but certain parts—like the glass she's wiping clean—are less veiled than others. It's ghostly. It's sensual. It's Malbec.

I sigh a little as I look at it.

He never sent me the video he promised to send. And I...kept waiting for it, like an idiot.

The whole scenario with Kaden was insane to begin with—and I *refuse* to be upset that some guy's dick pic got lost on its way to my phone—but I'll admit he disappointed me in the wrong way. I was even tempted at one point to message him a cheeky reminder, but...no. I have too much self-respect for that.

It is what it is, and the auction tonight is a perfect distraction.

I duck into the backroom out of the way of final preparations with the staff, to hang out with Ivy for a little while.

I catch sight of her luscious wine-red hair the moment I enter. She's a perfectionist with her pastries and she's brooding over the trays of petit fours like a mother hen...as if they aren't already gorgeous works of art in and of themselves. Macarons decorated with tiny hats, bite-sized elderberry tartlets, and even miniature kawakawa tea cakes for our visiting Maori artist, Kura Te Waru Rewiri. I want to eat everything Ivy's made, for their artistry as much as how delicious they probably are.

"Hey, doll," Ivy says when I come up beside her. "Don't worry, they're all good. I tested every single batch—*not that I should have*—and they're going to be a hit. Trust me."

I smile at that. "Oh I *do* trust you, my friend. With my life, with food. I *wish* I had your tongue."

But a tiny, pushed breath leaves her lips as she says, "If you had my tongue, you'd have my hips and *nobody* wants those."

"Ivy, sweetie…" I chide, softly.

"Sorry, the food is perfect and that's what matters," she says with a smile that breaks my heart.

She's always so fierce for everyone else—especially me and Cara—but recently, she's been making these little slips about herself that I don't like. Ever since she revealed she's moving to Paris in the summer, it's like she's discovered a thousand flaws about her looks and can't help picking them apart…which is just *coocoo bananas!* She has curves any woman would *kill* for, like a literal hourglass come to life with tits like a sea ship's figurehead and hips that could smother a man's face at first sit. *And* she can cook. *And* she's kind. I wish I was her all the time!

I want to tell her as much when the door to the back room pushes open suddenly and one of the staff says, "Excuse me, Ms. Rathbone? Emilio's arrived."

"Thank you." I give Ivy a side-hug anyway. "I'll be back, okay?"

"Don't worry about me. This is your night. Break a leg!"

I leave the backroom expecting to find the entire Russo family waiting for me in one of the showrooms…but it's just Emilio. He's wearing a black tux with his thick hair slightly gelled—presentable, all things considered—but as I get closer, I realize he's already been drinking enough that the scent of it tickles my nose from several paces away.

"A little to the left." His voice lilts from the alcohol.

When I arrive, he's micromanaging two moving men as they

position the final painting in its place on the wall. The piece is still wrapped in paper but the canvas is large, larger than any other piece on display tonight. It's so large, it has to be set on the floor rather than on the narrow ledge where it was supposed to go.

"What the hell did I just say? *More left.*" The timbre of his voice goes nasally and one of the men—the younger of the two—rolls his eyes as they make the adjustment.

I've worked for the Russos long enough to know what's coming before Emilio's spine straightens and he suddenly hisses, "Did you just *roll your eyes at me*, you little shit?"

I've also worked for them long enough to know how to ward off trouble.

Before Emilio can step forward, I swing around into his eyeline. "Hey you."

The anger mellows instantly. His gross sloppy arms are around me before I can even pull away from his vodka breath. "Heyyyy. You. Look. Stellar, Lulu."

"Thank you."

"Really classy for once. I mean it."

I keep my face neutral and let the backhanded compliment roll off me. This isn't the first time he's told me he doesn't like how I dress. He makes a point of lavishing approval on me whenever I wear a dress, like I am now...as if he thinks that'll get me to stop wearing pants. Idiot.

"K, shall we unwrap your painting?" I ask to move things along.

"No-No, it stays covered until everyone's here," he says, waving that away. "You'll love it, though. Trust me. You—You'll want to blow my brains out for it."

I ignore what I'm sure is another ham-fisted innuendo rather than a suggestion of violence.

"But you want it to look good, right?" I press, instead of saying what I really want to say, which is that *I want it to look good and not stick out like a sore thumb.*

"It will. Here, stand here and I'll adjust the lighting."

Emilio puts his hands on my waist and nudges me back to stand in front of the wrapped painting before he snaps at a nearby waiter to bring over a ladder.

"You really shouldn't climb that when you've been drinking, sir," I say loudly, just so there are witnesses who can say they heard me if he falls.

But, of course, that's not what he hears. His finger rises to my lips, pressing, as he gets too close and whispers, "It's so sweet that you care, baby, but don't turn into my mother."

I make eye contact with the party planner, embarrassed to see pity on her face. She's tired of having to deal with him too...and she's known him a fraction of the time I have.

At least I feel covered if he falls. I can deal with him practically shoving his finger up my nose for that trade off.

Emilio nearly knocks down a nearby painting as he slides the ladder into position and climbs it, adjusting the lights while I stand there waiting for it to be over. Then I smile blandly as he staggers down, relieved the way a parent of a toddler must feel after avoiding everyday disasters.

"Good job, sir," I say. "What do you say we grab you some coffee, eh?"

"Nah-Nah. Champagne," he says, snapping his fingers again.

I don't argue. Honestly, I'm all for it. Maybe if I pray to the ghost of Gatsby, Emilio will get drunk enough we can store him in the coat closet and have a decent evening after all.

CHAPTER 12

NERO

"Do I have to go?"

I sound like a kid.

I know I sound like a brat.

I'm trying really hard to give a fuck.

"The fuck I look like, your mother?" Darius tells me over the phone. "You said you wanted to start legitimizing your investments and the accountant said art is a sound investment, so I got you an invite to *the* auction of the year."

"But…it's New Year's Eve."

It's my first free New Year's fucking Eve in five years and Darius is trying to pawn me off on some snobby art sale happening in Chelsea. What kinda celebration is that? A bunch of blue bloods mingling with hippies so they can act like they're still "of the people" in any way that matters.

"I know," he sighs. "Maybe it'll be fun. If it's not, make fun of the art or whatever. Make ridiculous bids to drive up prices. Whatever gets you going, man."

I can hear the irritation in Darius's voice at my whining. He's humoring me right now even though he's got places to be and people—like Pam—to celebrate the holiday with. And I'm sitting in my old condo on the Upper East Side, alone, staring across Central Park at the building where I know Ethan has his penthouse. Ugly fucking skyscraper with a mall at the base and a whiny king at the top of the tower.

Prick hasn't spoken to me since I got out. Not one call. Not one text. He even told security in his building not to let me in, as if he forgot I've got deep fucking pockets and nothing more important to spend it on than annoying him daily until he stops being a dickhead.

Ethan doesn't even realize he's making this harder on himself than it has to be; if he would just hear me out, I wouldn't even *have* to go into Star-King. He could keep his little domain all to himself and pay me to stay out of his hair. But now? I'm going to crouch over his desk like a fucking goblin. Dude's *never* going to be able to get rid of me.

I hate that I'm still planning all the ways I'm going to annoy the fucker forty minutes later when I get out of the limo in Chelsea and walk into the last place I want to be tonight.

The art show is exactly what I thought it would be. Bunch of snobby fucks with more money than sense eating canapes, gawking at paintings I wouldn't be able to tell were 'good' or 'bad' if I spent my life staring at them.

As I hand off my coat and ask for a bourbon from the first waiter I see, I take in the landscape and reassess my first impression. I was half right. The rich here are showy rich and the artists are all dolled-up hippies, but there are a bunch of obvious interlopers that stand out from the crowd. Some journalists with their little notepads and glasses on the rims of their noses and photographers on their heels. Some obvious gold diggers and art groupies. And at least one group of modern gothic Italians that are more *familia* than family.

I realize who they are when the crowd parts and I recognize Lorenzo Russo holding court with a group of sycophants. His wife stands apart, talking to her own group but watching her husband like a hawk. Her husband and any young thing that approaches him. The two others I don't know. Their kids, I guess. The female looks bored, drinking and texting on her phone. The male looks like a messy cliché. I can't remember their names, but why would I? Before I served my time, all I knew about Lorenzo Russo was that he only cared about three things— his wife, his business, and his eldest son. Can't remember that kid's name either, but from the way the messy young guy here is hanging on his father's every word, he definitely isn't the eldest.

Either way, that's a trainwreck I want no part of. Leveling up in this city taught me that the more money you have, the more "run-ins" with the mafia you tend to have, and it only took a few to realize I don't want any more. Although, with the dark tattoos peeking out of the collar of my suit and etched across my hands, I'm sure everyone here already thinks I'm one of them.

It'd never occur to most of them that I'm richer than they are...and I wouldn't tell them either. I prefer to let them figure it out for themselves and watch their eyes explode with dismay.

It's one of my favorite little joys.

I catch a blue-haired old biddy trying to read the tattoos on my knuckles and I waggle my fingers at her for fun. The affronted look on her pruney face is priceless. Well worth coming out tonight. The flip side of that, though, is that I want to buck their expectations. Without ever speaking to them, I want to humiliate their presumptions of me.

So, when my bourbon finally arrives, I toast my thanks to the guy who brought it and head in the opposite direction of the Russo familia and everything they represent.

Then I decide I might as well check out the art while I'm here.

Maybe there's something actually worth bidding on. My apartment could use some updating. It's all fancy wainscotting and crown molding, but honestly, it came pre-furnished and I bought it for the bragging rights, to tell people I own on Fifth Avenue with a full apartment view of Central Park just outside.

Of course, Ethan had to buy higher and bigger than me. Little punk.

I make a note to myself to check the high rises to either side of his to see what properties are available. I don't care if I'm scared of heights. With the ten digits in my bank account, I can buy the building and use it to store cardboard cutouts of myself, all facing Ethan's place.

Wandering the gallery, it doesn't take me long to realize I don't understand art. Don't get me wrong, I can *see* that the stuff's pretty...or evocative, I guess is the word. But I only have to look at a few pieces to realize I am in way over my head.

One of the paintings—an abstract rainbow ribbon person, or maybe it's a technicolor lizard with tits—is a prime example. There's a mirror on the floor underneath it that doesn't help matters either. I find myself staring at it for *way* too long. Long enough, I finish my bourbon and order another one, all while tilting my head at the painting, waiting for the shapes to make sense.

It finally does when a melodic soprano voice says, "It's a mind melter."

That doesn't help. I tilt my head more until she giggles, "Look straight at the mirror. And bend down a little, you're too tall. See it?"

"Holy fuck." I *do* "see it" suddenly. The painting is a watery reflection of a person who can only be seen in the mirror. "Please tell me someone told you to look at it that way and my brain's not *that* broken."

"Everybody's brain is a *little* broken," she says, adding quietly, "But yeah, I know the artist. She swears that's how it's supposed to be displayed, but she also had to literally move my head into position to see it, so...you know what that means."

"What?"

She bumps my shoulder playfully. "It must be good."

That puts a smile on my face. I turn to say the first semi-clever thing I can think of...but honestly, I forget everything—the words, the painting—when I see who I'm talking to.

She's...

Tiny. Even in heels. Even with her dark hair done in a subdued beehive wrapped in braids, she barely comes to my biceps. I could pick up six of her and run out of the building if there was a fire...and it feels like there is one, both around and inside me. A pilot light kicks on, at least.

She's...

Lovely. I haven't used that word in a while. Lovely giant round eyes and lovely thick, expressive eyebrows and lips a lovely peachy pink that makes me want to bite them.

As I rise to my full height, the extent of her smallness becomes even more apparent as she tilts her neck back farther and farther to maintain eye contact. I want to take a step away so it's easier for her to look at me...but I can't bring myself to do it. She smells like fruit and her eyes are dark shades of honey, and she's smiling openly, completely unintimidated by me.

"Whoa, you grew a whole extra foot taller," she jokes. "I bet you can't see the painting at all from up there."

I arch a brow at her pointedly. Playfully. "What painting?"

"How about this one?" she teases, inching toward the next piece on display a few feet away.

I follow—of course I follow—letting her guide me to a photograph of feet crushing grapes.

"What do you think of this painting?" she asks, her smirk playful and dangerously adorable.

"That's a trick question," I say. "That's a photo."

"Nope." She crooks her finger at me, calling me down to her height.

I squat a little to get closer, but when I do, she motions to the photo...which I realize really is a painting. A hyper-realistic one.

"Wow," I say lightly.

"Wanna buy it?" she asks.

I want to tell her *not unless you painted it, not unless your fingers were all over it*, but that'd be a weird fucking thing to say, so I go with, "Not quite my style."

"Ah, I see, you're a very discerning gentleman." She motions me to the next. It's a painting of a lady in a foggy bathroom. "Might I interest you in a Malbec, then?"

"Malbec. I've heard that name before."

Her honey eyes light up, nose wrinkling. "I'd be surprised if there was anyone here tonight who hadn't."

"I've been out of the scene for a while," I say. "Is Malbec good?"

"Oh yeah. Well, he's one of my favorites anyway," she says, studying the painting. "You see how he catches the light here, where she's wiped away the moisture from the glass? Isn't it beautiful?"

"It's something," I say, still looking at her.

"Don't worry if this isn't the one," she says. "I made sure we had a variety tonight. There's something for everyone."

"*You* made sure. Is this…your gallery?"

"No," she laughs, waving that away. "But I helped curate the selection of art tonight. *Most* of it, anyway."

"Wow, impressive."

"I think so," she says without a single ounce of ego. She motions my attention away to one end of the gallery, which I can just see through an open doorway, then sweeps her hand slowly around in a clockwise direction. "It's tough to put so many different art styles together and still have them feel cohesive, but that was my challenge, so… I tried to put a natural movement into the progression, as you move around the space. As much as I could anyway. Can you see it?"

I take in the lay of the land again, through her contribution this time…and…it's like one of those optical illusions where you don't see the hidden picture until you take a step back. I don't know shit about art, but I can see the movement she's talking about. Especially when I watch the little crowds of people move from one to the next, like little waves in a swell.

Even though I would have said so anyway, I'm relieved I can answer honestly when I tell her, "I can see it." But I lower my voice and add, "I'm not sure I understand it, but I can see it."

She smiles again and this time, her fingers dart out and land lightly on my hand, when she says, "Thank goodness you can appreciate art without understanding it, *amiright?*"

When she pulls away a second later, her heat lingers on my skin. A shiver of need runs through me as the heat fades. Then panic sets in as someone calls to her and she waves a finger of patience at them like her time with me is coming to an end.

But I don't want it to be over.

My eyes dart across the room looking for something to talk about.

I notice a massive painting wrapped in brown paper that's lit like it's the star of the show.

"What about that covered one?" I ask, motioning to it. "Is it a Banksy or something? You keeping it hidden for a big reveal?"

"*I wish*," she chuffs. "No, it's an Emilio Russo original. One of six tonight."

There's no love in her voice for the Russo family, but there *is* familiarity. Intimacy.

An intimacy I understand a moment later when a male voice suddenly calls out, "Lulu! We need you!" and we both turn to see an older man, dressed like the Russos, waving her to join them.

"I'm so sorry, I have to go," she says. "Please enjoy your night. Be sure to bid on something fun."

And she's gone before I know how to give her a goodbye that leaves the door open for her to come back.

I'm so out of practice with this, it's fucking embarrassing.

But...*Lulu*, he said. Her name is Lulu. No name has ever suited someone so perfectly.

CHAPTER 13

LULU

I wish it was socially acceptable to hand a gorgeous stranger a temporary key to my apartment and tell him to go wait in my bed for me.

Probably a good thing it isn't, or I would have already printed a key for the giant slab of sex on legs behind me.

Men like him are how I know god is a woman. Men like him are why I pray to her like she is one, anyway. Tall, dark, handsome, tattooed, *and* he's nice? I'm friggen *drooling* as I walk away.

Also, I'm a little embarrassed, considering I originally went over to read the tattoos on his knuckles but got so distracted by the rest of him I never found out what they said.

Of course, I had to meet him at a work party where I'm not free to be myself. Where I have to *behave* and tend to other guests. Ugh.

I glance back at him as I walk away. The tattooed man is still watching me, which fills my belly with warmth. I shoot him a longing, apologetic smile that I hope he can understand…because I want him to know I am *not* walking away of my own accord right now. If it were up to me, I'd still be talking to him.

Hell, if it were up to me, I'd already have climbed him like a friggen tree.

Or maybe I'm just a self-saboteur who found the *one person* in the room I didn't know and beelined for him like a snack in the breakroom I wanted to steal and take home with me.

Whatever my problem is, at least he looks interested when I glance back. That's something.

Maybe I'll get a chance to talk to him again later, after I've dealt with whatever new drama has Matteo gesturing at me to hurry up.

"Come on, come on," he says, as if whatever they're about to say will be some time-sensitive last-minute revelation that couldn't wait another second to be relayed to me.

"I'm here, I'm here," I say lightly.

"Beautiful job tonight, by the way," Matteo adds as I step past him, up the couple of steps to the dais where the Russos have been congregating all night. I can tell from the way he whispers it, he knows it might be the only compliment I receive tonight.

"Thanks, Matteo."

"Is everything ready?" Lorenzo asks the second I enter the inner circle. "The microphone? The video screen?"

"Yes *signore*," I say. "The auctioneer will step into position right after midnight."

"Then that is when we will unveil Emilio's piece," Mrs. Russo says.

"No, ma," Emilio counters. "It's the pièce de resistance. We need to reveal it at the end."

"It *will* be the last piece in the auction, my prince," she assures him. "But they must be allowed to *admire* your masterpiece if you want them to bid on it."

That's her way of saying that all the Russo employees planted in the crowd tonight need time to promote and praise the painting before the phony phone bidders buy it. Can't very well have the only thing that isn't sold tonight be the pièce de resistance. And, short of a Banksy, I think anyone with half a brain would realize the auction is rigged if an unknown painting sold for millions of dollars mere seconds after it was revealed.

Emilio grumbles but accepts his mother's declaration for what it is—her bid to help him.

"We will unveil the piece right after the ball drops," Mrs. Russo repeats.

"Yes, *signora*," I confirm.

"Good, and you're sure all the important guests have arrived?" she asks. "We're ready to let Emilio shine?"

That I can answer confidently. "Yes, *signora*, everyone who's anyone in the art world is here tonight."

CHAPTER 14

NERO

I wish I was the type of man who could leave a gorgeous woman's company at an event like this and continue to explore the buffet of painted beauty around me like a civilized human being.

But I'm not.

The second Lulu walks away, the only art that matters leaves with her.

And then she looks back at me as if she really doesn't want to go and I stop thinking about the art at all.

Instead, I move into the next showroom and watch her interaction with the Russos. It's personable but detached. She's not one of them, but she is. She's a part of the organization, and high enough in the hierarchy that none of their security flinches when she joins them. Yet the wife, at least, treats her like a servant. And the son slaps a possessive hand on her shoulder, leaning a little too close in a way I can tell she doesn't like, but humors because she has to.

And the joy that was in her eyes when she was talking to me is gone, replaced by a mask of cordial professionalism I can see all the way from where I'm standing.

Very interesting.

Lulu darts away to do something for them, but when she reappears a little while later, I find her talking to other guests, still in that warm-cool professional headspace. Nothing like she was with me. She never reaches out to touch them. She never beckons them down to her height.

But every few seconds, I feel like her eyes dart to me. O-Or, in my direction, at least. And I meet her gaze head-on—I'm not wasting time pretending I'm not fucking interested in her. That's kid stuff, and the stuff I want to do to her is entirely adult. Each time our eyes connect, I swear I can fucking see them brighten and soften, until some other person pulls her attention away.

I don't…know if I'm reading too much into it, though.

I just know I want to talk to her again.

"Talk," my own mind mocks me. *Is that why half your brain is choreographing an all-night fuck session where her feet never touch the floor?*

I *do* genuinely want to talk to her…before, during, and/or after she's ridden me to victory like a prize stallion at the Kentucky fucking Derby.

Fuck, being in prison does things to a man.

It's the lack of touch—leaving my volcano goddess at Amara's made me realize that. Not even just sex, but the intimacy. My entire fucking body needs it. Going without it for so long fried my brain in ways I'm only just beginning to understand. In everyday life now, I find myself touching things I never did before—curtains, carpet, plants— just admiring how much I missed the sensations of them in my hands. The textures. I even caught myself molesting a coffee mug this morning because it had a chip in it and I couldn't stop rubbing the bare ceramic.

I can still feel her fingertips lightly pressed to my arm. I can imagine the soft graze of her fingernails across my skin. I can almost taste various parts of her on my tongue.

Fuck it's not normal, but it's my normal. My weird normal until I can remember how I'm supposed to act.

It's been years since I've done anything other than bring a woman to screaming orgasm. *That*, I can offer her in spades. But the talking, the timing, the *wooing*—I forgot how to do all that shit.

Until I remember…

I just have to *ask her out on a date*. Like any normal fucking guy would. That's all.

I just need to find my in again. Maybe I can bid on that painting she liked of the foggy bathroom. The Malbec one. Or maybe I can take her to breakfast in the morning after all this pageantry is over?

Minutes to midnight, I'm still thinking about what to say to her when a waiter comes by with tray-fulls of New Year's Eve party favors. Little top hats. Party poppers. Neon feather boas. I grab a gold New Year's horn as the *ting-ting-ting* of metal against crystal quiets the entire party.

Faces turn across the gallery as Lorenzo Russo raises his champagne flute and steps forward to address the room.

His Italian accent adds gravitas and an old-world charm to his words as he says, "Ladies and gentlemen, my family is so honored to have you here to celebrate the start of the New Year with us tonight. There is no better way to spend this holiday than with incredible minds, incredible souls, our incredible community here in the city. Thank you for coming."

Gentle but generous applause fills the room as a large projector screen lowers from the ceiling overhead.

"Before we begin our auction, please join me in counting down to a fabulous new year," he adds, just as the screen pops to life with a video feed of the Times Square Ball and the clock counting down to the drop.

"59! 58! 57! 56!"

I twist my neck, scanning the room until I find the tiny hazel-eyed woman I've been watching all night—I only realize where she is by the sudden gap between upturned heads. She's swallowed by the crowd. She's clearly given up on being able to see anything, I can tell from the way she isn't even trying to look up at the screen.

Making my way over to her isn't hard given my size and look; most people get out of my way when they see me coming. But when I reach her, and she turns her dazzling gaze on me, I'm not sure what to say, or even how to say it.

She's waiting for me to speak.

She's hoping I'll say something clever.

"40! 39! 38! 37!"

At the moment, I have nothing clever to say. My mouth is full of brash, lustful words I know would ruin any chance I have with a woman like her.

So, I change tact instead.

A chair at a nearby table is empty. I reach for it and pull it between us.

"30! 29! 28!"

Then I hold out my hand to her. She eyes it with confusion and curiosity, until her eyes spark with understanding. Her delicate fingers slip into mine and I gently pull her up to stand on the chair, bringing her to my eyeline. I spot a passing waiter and snag a champagne flute for her as well. Handing it to her, I hold my own glass up and she clinks the flute against it.

"10! 9! 8!"

It's one of those moments I think I'll remember for the rest of my life. One of those perfect serendipitous moments that almost makes you believe someone out there actually gives a flying fuck about you.

"6! 5! 4!"

She leans into me and whisper-yells, "Would it be weird if I kissed you at midnight?" with a smile on her face that twists a hook in my stomach and tears a path straight through the center of me.

"Fuck no," I say, with my hand already rising to her cheek, sliding into place against her impossibly soft skin, pulling her into my lips just as the entire room screams "HAPPY NEW YEAR!" and the air fills with gold confetti and the squeal of noisemakers.

It's not a peck of a kiss.

It's not some slathering hungry monster either.

A firework goes off inside my chest as her hand curls around the lapel of my suit, anchoring her, and her smile grows as our lips meet again and again in a conversation of caresses.

I don't want it to end when it does, even though she leans into my ear and wishes me, "Happy New Year!"

I don't want to take my hand away, even when she finally releases my lapel.

I want to luxuriate in this moment that crash landed in my life out of nowhere.

I know it sounds so hokey to say the kiss wrecks me, but fuck…for a moment, I forget I lost five years of my life to a six-by-eight cell. I forget about the bullshit with my brother. I forget I almost spent the night wallowing alone on a holiday meant to be spent with family and friends.

For a moment, I'm just a free man celebrating a free future with a gorgeous woman who likes me, and it feels fucking incredible.

Then, the lights flicker back on overhead and the crowd murmurs loudly between clinks of champagne glasses, and Lulu holds out her hand to me to help her down, which I do. All while some part of me is mourning that the moment is over.

"Would you…" escapes me before she can take her hand away, not that she could while I'm clutching it like a lifeline. "…like to go out to dinner with me sometime?"

"What?!" she asks.

Shit, she didn't hear me.

I bow down and press my lips to her ear so fast I feel second-hand embarrassment for myself.

Who cares?

"Want to get dinner sometime?" I ask again.

I hear a giggle and turn to find a wily smile on her face. She kisses my cheek and slides back to whisper in my ear, laughing, "I heard you the first time, Big Guy. I'd love to."

Ohhh man, I am so fucked.

Especially when she turns my hand in hers and reaches for the other one. She runs her thumbs across my knuckles, across the bright black tattoos there.

"'*Need*' and '*want*,'" she says, reading the letters. "Are you right-handed or left-handed?"

"Right," I say.

She runs her thumb across my '*need*' tattoo a second time.

"Hmm," she says. "And what do you need?"

"What a question." I definitely can't tell her the first thing that pops to mind—*I need to hear what my name sounds like when you scream it in pleasure*. Instead, I say, "How 'bout we start with your number."

Her eyes light up again and she holds out her hand for my phone. I fish it out of my pocket and watch as she quickly types the number in. When she hands the phone back, I stare at her contact info like the temptation it is. She has no idea how fast I'm going to feed her name into my proprietary search engines and learn everything there is to know about her before we meet again.

"Lulu Rathbone," I read aloud.

"That's me."

"I'm Ne—"

Pah-Pah-Pah. Someone taps a microphone with their fingers, cutting me off. We turn to find an elegant smiling woman with a high ponytail and her bangs tied into a braided bow at the side of her head standing behind a podium where the Russos were a few moments ago.

"Hello everyone, I am Eustice Lau, your auctioneer for the evening," she says, her voice unharried, inviting, and commanding. "Happy New Year and welcome. Thank you to the Russo family for inviting me. We are thrilled to have you here."

Lulu releases my hand and her full rapt attention goes to the auctioneer. The look on her face tells me she might not like the Russos, but she adores this part of her job.

"Given the geography of this gallery," Eustice announces, "we would ask that any serious bidders step into this main room, please."

Lulu nods as if the woman was speaking directly to her, before her eyes dart back to me. "That's my cue, unfortunately, I have to go stand with my boss for the bidding. Are you going to join in?"

"Eh, I wouldn't trust myself without you there to tell me what to bid on," I say, half-joking.

"Oh, I couldn't do that," she says, taking a step back.

"Why not?"

I don't know why, but I expect her to say something unintentionally backhanded about whatever she presumes my budget is, or how clueless I am about art. She doesn't.

She smiles that wily smile again. "That's the sort of thing I discuss on a third date."

Clever girl. "I'll remember that."

Off a smile that makes me want to literally hoist her off the ground and kiss her again, she waves goodbye and disappears between guests. The movement of the room is swift and prim as entire sections of the crowd switch places with one another…and I stand like an immovable stone in the middle of it all, just taking it all in. It's wild how polite the shuffle is. How civilized. It's such a far cry from everything I've known for the last few years it feels uncanny and unnatural. A glimpse of a strange new world.

Then I remember…humans are wild creatures who learned how to hide their animality. It's still there, right below the surface, lurking under the elegance and airs they wear like fur coats, waiting to be provoked. These blue bloods may behave in public, but in private their animal nature is on full display.

The crowds are still shifting when the auctioneer calls out again, "Before we get started, we have one more piece to unveil. Lot 47—*Eager to Please*—is a last-minute addition and new acrylic by Emilio Russo. It will be available for bidding later in the auction."

She draws the room's attention to the far wall, where the hidden painting sticks out like a sore thumb. The Russos loiter beside it, impatient and distracted…

Until Lulu reaches them. The moment she appears, the son—Emilio—stomps toward her like a knuckle-dragging neanderthal and grabs her upper arm. He hustles her over to the side of the painting quickly, whispering something directly into her ear.

There's no look of pain on her face—or even surprise—but her brow furrows, her eyes dart in my direction, and she shrinks away from him enough that my hackles rise all the same. Then she tries to slip delicately out of his grasp and he yanks her closer instead of letting go…and I take several large strides in their direction.

My hands fist.

My muscles tighten in anticipation of the punch my body already wants to throw.

I know starting a fight with the Russos over a woman I just met would fuck up my life in ways I can't even imagine, but I can't just watch him leave bruises on her arm like that either.

I won't.

I'm halfway across the gallery when the crowd finally simmers down and Emilio releases her—when he knows he has an audience. I stop in my tracks to watch. Even with everyone's attention on him, I can tell from the mean mug face he flashes Lulu when she's not looking that something's wrong. His body language is defensive, like a dog that did something naughty while his owners were out of the house; he's acting like he knows she's going to be angry at him soon. He's tense and stiff and ready to bite.

As if I'm any different.

But looking at her, I can tell she has no idea why he's acting this way. She's wearing a pacifying expression on her face I know all too well. One I saw on my mother all the time growing up, whenever my dad would come home with a chip on his shoulder that he wanted to offload onto her, or me.

I spent my entire childhood learning how to read body language to avoid exactly how Emilio is looking at Lulu now.

And then, Emilio turns and lifts the canvas away from the wall, so he can release whatever's holding the cover in place. Then he tears the brown paper away from...

Fuck.

My blood runs cold as the painting is revealed for all to see.

Oh fuck.

Camera flashes go off and the crowd gasps and murmurs so loudly it might as well be a roar of second-hand embarrassment in my ear.

My eyes dart to Lulu, to her mortified face as her mouth drops open in horror. She wears shades of humiliation that tell me what's on that canvas is as much a shock to her as it is to everyone else in this room.

Her wounded gaze shoots from the painting to Emilio to the Russos, back and forth in a terrible dance, her chest heaving, while the rest of her seems frozen, unsure of what to do.

And the Russos, well…their expressions run the gamut.

I feel the barest flicker of relief when I see incredulous anger on the older man who pulled her from our conversation earlier, and confused embarrassment from Lorenzo and the daughter.

But the wife, Mrs. Russo. The surprise on her face settles into a cruel and indifferent mask that makes my blood boil.

And Emilio—that disgusting little shit—gives Lulu a passing glance before he swipes a microphone off a nearby stand and flicks it on, ignoring her entirely as he says, "*Eager to Please* is an exploration of exhibition, shamelessness, and modern society's attempt to sexualize women."

It's obvious from the first syllable that someone else wrote that for him…and the only shameless person in this room is the painter of the garbage he just put on display.

Or, he *was* the only shameless person in the room until this moment. I didn't leave my house tonight thinking I'd kill a man, but life's unpredictable like that.

I'm tempted to snap his neck right here in front of everybody.

I'm tempted to shatter his teeth with that microphone and shove it so far down his throat, they have to break his jaw to remove it for the funeral.

I'm tempted to rip the painting apart and stake him with the wooden frame, then call it "an exploration of exhibition, shamelessness, and modern society's attempt to butcher men."

No…

I'm tempted to ask Lulu how she wants him to die and then do exactly what she says.

CHAPTER 15

LULU

I'm frozen-frozen-frozen.

I need to move and I can't. I can't because the shame is lead in my legs and glue in my heart and I know if I dart away from this spot right now while everyone is watching, the Russos will punish me more than they already have.

I don't know how to process the image on Emilio's canvas. Not all at once. Not in pieces either.

It's awful.

It's the worst thing I've ever seen.

The painting is...*god I feel like I'm going to vomit*...It's a painting of me...but it's not me.

It's my face—he's spent an inordinate amount of time and detail rendering *my face* at the head of the canvas—but the rest of it is...*I'm going to be sick*.

A contorted female figure with bruised, misshapen breasts wearing a dog collar around her neck lays partially reclined with her legs bent and spread. She stares the viewer down while exposing her sex, using her fingers to hold her entrance open for inspection. The vagina is enormous and warped and intentionally ugly, discolored, with exaggerated asymmetrical lips crowded with coarse hair, and the fingers pry it open to display a vaginal canal dripping with secretions and bruised from intercourse.

He could have stabbed me and hurt me less.

He could have burned me alive and at least I would've died with my dignity intact.

It's not my body, but what does that matter when it's so obviously, intentionally, unignorably *my face* above the rest of it.

Worse still, I can't tell which of the Russos knew. They all seem surprised, but...no one says anything. Then Emilio begins to address the room and any hope I have that they'll stop this disappears.

I tear my gaze away and focus on the floor, squeezing my hands together to the point of pain, savoring the piercing bite of my nails as they cut into my skin, to take my thoughts off the desperate scream in my head to *run*.

Emilio is still speaking, but I just focus on the floor. I focus on the floor until I hear Eustice's voice crack as she scrambles for something to say, "Well, th-thank you to the Russos for contributing...such a special piece. Remember, that's Lot 47. We'll come back to it later tonight. For now, please give your attention to our first piece up for bid tonight, *Limerence* by Nancy Ruida..."

I peek my eyes up from the floor, hoping everyone is turned away so I can escape before—

"Lulu, are you all right, sweetheart?"

The voice catches me off-guard. It's Matteo. Matteo's suddenly in front of me, partially blocking out the Russos behind him, who I notice have swarmed Emilio in a strange little huddle of tension.

But I can't look that way for long. The painting is right there, larger than life between me and the only employers I've had my entire adult life.

"Are they firing me?" I ask. "Is this how they fire people, Matteo?"

The thought breaks my heart as badly as the painting does. Is this insult to injury? Did I do something wrong to deserve this? What do I do now that everyone who's anyone has seen that painting? The *entire art world* is here. We invited the art editors from *The New Yorker* and *The New York Times* tonight, for God's sake.

"No-No-No," Matteo says, but I'm not sure I believe him. "I don't know what this is, but don't worry. We'll—I'll talk to them, all right."

"I don't feel good." I hate the quiet sound of my own voice. "I need to go. Will they fire me if I go, Matteo?"

My mind feels like a tornado that whipped through a knife factory, full of blades that slice and cut with each new thought that pops up in my mind.

I'm ruined. If they're firing me, I'll never work in this city again.

But I'm also a laughing stock. By the end of day tomorrow, that image will be in the private art grids of hundreds of art advisors, magazines and websites. I'll never live it down. I'll never know when I walk into a room whether the person I'm speaking with has seen it.

And then I see him.

My tattooed stranger. He's so tall that even from here, I can see his beautiful green eyes are fixated on that painting as if it's changing every thought he ever had about me.

Fuck, and we shared such a lovely moment too.

I can't imagine what he must think of me now. Seeing that 'version' of me after we kissed? And I don't even know his name? I'm mortified.

I can't take any more of this.

I manage to squeak out one more, "Please tell them I'm sorry, Matteo, I'm just not feeling well," and then I'm moving.

"Lulu, wait. Wait!"

I don't know whose voice that is, but it doesn't matter. I reach the backroom door and dart behind it before I even look up again.

The 'backroom' is just a name for the staging area of the gallery, but it's several hallways and rooms serving various purposes, all crowded with staff. As I dart between them, I can tell word about Emilio's painting has already spread back here. Some of them seem to pity me, others are laughing.

"Ivy? Ivy Montclair!" I need my friend. I need... "Anyone know where Ivy is?"

"Lulu?"

Ivy barely has time to peek out of the room she's in before I burst into tears and fling myself at her. Her arms catch me like they always do, spreading warmth through me.

"Oh, sweetie, what happened?!" she asks, only making me cry harder.

How do I explain? How do I describe my own humiliation to her?

Like a tiny gift from the universe for my troubles—someone else steps up to explain for me. A waitress leans into Ivy's ear; I don't have to hear what she says to know she's telling Ivy everything. Ivy's body language bristles and stiffens. Her eyes widen, her jaw tightens. Everything I wish my own body would do, hers does.

"*Those fuckers!*" She wraps her arms around me again tighter and her hand pets my head so gently. "You're okay, Lulu. You're okay, I promise."

"But I'm not!" I almost wail.

"I know, but you will be," she says, and I almost believe her.

"What did I do to deserve this?"

She pulls back at that, and the fire in her gray eyes surprises me. "*Nothing!* Do you hear me? This is their twisted fucking problem. *Fuck* that family."

I would laugh if the sadness wasn't close to drowning me already. "Maybe he wouldn't have done this if I had."

"Huh?"

I don't have the heart to tell her about the proposal I turned down, or the fact that I'm wondering whether he still would have done this to me if I had said yes.

Ivy's next words tear me from my thoughts. "I'm calling Cara."

"Don't interrupt her night," I say limply, even though the thought of her here makes my heart a little lighter. "She's probably with Mr. King."

Already on her phone, Ivy nods with a twinkle in her eye. "Oh, I'm counting on it."

CHAPTER 16

NERO

"Just. Let. Me. Back. There."

I don't want to be a prick, but the security guy by the door Lulu darted through won't give me access to speak with her. I tried her number, but she's not picking up. I tried bribing him, but he's a bootlicking self-righteous shit.

"Sir. I have already told you, the backroom is for staff only."

"At least tell her I want to talk to her. Lulu Rathbone, she—"

"You can tell her later when she comes back out. Right now I need you to stop making a scene. Just back off before I'm forced to have you removed from the building."

Fucker.

I do step back, but I'm fuming. Especially when my gaze lands on that disgusting fucking piece of "art" again. The second Lulu disappeared, Emilio tried to follow and the Russos' security closed rank around him and his garbage, holding him back and protecting him in the same motion.

They've sort of locked him in place alongside his painting, which is garnering the most attention of any of the art on display. One photographer *has not stopped* taking photos of that ugly fucking thing since Emilio unveiled it.

Each click of the camera shutter rings out like some sort of ill omen about what tomorrow will bring for her and I'm half tempted to rip the camera out of his hands and smash it on the ground, until I remember

I don't have to. Money is a cure-all.

I don't waste my time begging apologies. I navigate the crowd on a single-minded mission until I reach the photog and land a sobering hand on his shoulder.

"How much." I don't ask it as a question, because it isn't one. He either lets me pay for it, or I'm taking it.

"What?"

The man's thick skull turns in my direction and I have half a mind to knock on it.

"The film in that camera. It's mine. How much."

"Listen, buddy—"

I keep a soft discreet smile on my face and barely move at all, just my hand as I clamp down between his neck and shoulder in a sort of Vulcan nerve pinch. His mouth falls open like a broken mailbox.

"How much."

"Uh-uh…ten—FIVE! Five thousand!"

Pocket change.

Still holding him in place, I ask for his payment information and wire it directly, then I hold out my hand for the film, which I realize is a digital film card. He removes the chip from his camera with a dramatic flair. As if I demanded the head of his first born.

But we're not done just yet. Still holding him, I lean in close. "Not another fucking picture of that painting, do you understand? If I see a single image of that painting anywhere tomorrow, or the next day, or the next, well…let's just say I'll be paying you a special visit, all right pumpkin?"

"Dude, this is just my job."

"Exactly. It's not worth your life, is it?"

I hold his gaze and wait until he shakes his head before I release him. Then I watch him scurry off to another part of the gallery like a rat escaping a sinking ship, as if I can't find him if I can't see him. He doesn't seem to understand I already have him; he gave me his payment information. He might as well have handed me keys to his entire fucking life—one I can very easily destroy if he goes back on his promise to me.

I don't think he will.

But…I'd be better off assuming every person in this fucking building has a camera tonight than leaving something like this up to chance. The internet is forever and that painting could haunt Lulu for the rest of her life.

I snap the film card in half and stuff it in my pocket, then I pull out my phone. I take a photo of that horrendous fucking painting and rattle off a quick email to my team explaining the situation.

They'll take the guest list for tonight and invade the private online accounts of every single one of these fuckers until no image of that insult against Lulu exists anymore.

While they're doing that, I'll be destroying the insult itself.

"And that's it, ladies and gentlemen. At twenty-three million for the Koons, selling here at twenty-three million."

The auctioneer taps her gavel, and applause erupts at the sale as I step into the bidders' huddle, enjoying the thrum of energy, the collective excitement. I have no idea what I'm doing, but… how hard can bidding on a painting be? It's spending money. I know how to do that.

"Finally, we come to Lot 47," the auctioneer says as two men carry that ugly fucking insult onto the dais. "*Eager to Please.* The newest piece by the artist Emilio Russo who's already sold five seven-figure paintings here tonight. We'll start the bidding for this final piece at nine-hundred thousand. Do I have nine-hundred thousand?"

My hand rises into the air with all the humor of a guillotine blade, and the crowd murmurs around me.

"Thank you, sir. Nine-hundred thousand. Do we have a million?"

There's barely a pause at all before she points off toward the far windows, "Thank you, one million, coming in over the phone."

Phones. I forgot there were others bidding on the monstrosity they're not even here to see. Whoever they are, they're going to be fucking disappointed.

"Do we have one-point-one million?"

My hand rises again.

"Thank you, sir."

But just as quickly, the same phone bidder bids again, and the auctioneer swings wide to ask me for a higher bid. No sooner have I bid, but the phone bidder does the same.

It moves so fast, it's like a game of tennis. No one else is playing. It's me-them-me-them.

Back and forth until, "We have three million. What do you say we make things interesting. Will you go to three-point-five?"

I nod before she's even finished asking.

Four million.

Five million.

Eight.

Fuck, I don't care about the money, but damn it all if I don't wish I could look the prick who's bidding in the face. No one should want that painting. Not bad enough to pay—

"Ten million, on the phone now."

The crowd titters with obnoxious drama. And my hand is already rising in the air to bid again when someone reaches for my hand, yanking it back down.

"*What are you doing?!*"

I turn to find Lulu standing beside me, her face painted in shame and heartache and anger...at me, I realize. She's mad at me.

"I'm bidding for that piece," I tell her.

"Please don't," she begs through gritted teeth.

"I don't want anyone else to have it. I want—"

But she interrupts me before I can explain, "I thought you liked me."

My back bristles. "I do."

"Then stop it. Please don't take that home. I'm humiliated enough, please."

"Lulu, I wasn't—"

"Sir in the black suit. Do I have eleven million? Sir? We're going to have to close the bidding at ten million unless there's another offer?"

"Please," Lulu says again, still clutching my hand. Her hazel eyes are so big and lined with silver tears, it's like catching sight of gold flecks in a riverbed.

"I was trying to help you," I tell her quickly. "I just wanted to help you."

"Please," is all she says with a desperate shake of her head.

Fuck.

So reluctantly, I look up at the auctioneer and shake my head. And just like that the tension in the room pops as she finishes the sale, taps her gavel, and the audience erupts into applause again...for some prick who isn't even here.

The second the moment ends, Lulu lets go of me and darts away and it's like someone set me adrift in the sea with no paddle to get back to shore. I can't even keep my eyes on her as she slips between people.

And then...a sudden brutal lick of winter wind tears my gaze to the far gallery door as it wrenches open and the last person I'd ever expect steps in out of the cold.

It's Ethan with some pretty brunette.

My fucking kid brother walks in with a scowl on his face, murder in his eyes, and his cell phone pressed to his ear. He doesn't even glance my way. He doesn't look at anyone or anything, except that painting. And he doesn't hesitate. Like a fighter stepping into the ring, Ethan marches through the crowd, walks right onto the dais, right to that abomination of a painting, and yanks it off the stand.

The auctioneer blinks and stammers, "Oh! Ladies and gentlemen, it seems our phone bidder has come to collect his prize himself. Congratulations, Mr. Ethan King."

Another round of confused applause fills the air, but Ethan pays it no attention. He leaves the dais with the painting tucked under his arm and swerves around the older man with the Russos who tries to speak with him. Ignoring the Russos entirely, Ethan walks right over to...Lulu, who's sandwiched in a fierce hug between two women. One has dark red hair. The other is the brunette Ethan walked in with. I've never seen her before, but Ethan's hand slides into hers without hesitation and his entire expression changes when she glances at him.

Words are exchanged and like a knight in shining fucking armor, he leads all four of them right out the gallery door without looking back.

The second they walk out, the silence in the room gives way to chatter. Loud, obnoxious gossip deafens everything else around me, save for the sudden blaring thought in my head to go after them.

So many questions swirl around in my head, I don't feel the cold at first as I arrive on the sidewalk outside. I don't know what to say either when I find my brother holding open the back door to an SUV while the women climb in.

The only thing to say is, "Ethan?"

His head snaps in my direction. "Nero? What the fuck are you doing here?"

I almost want to make a joke, but it's not the time for it, so I just say, "How do you know Lulu?"

"How do *you* know Lulu?"

"I was trying to help her in there."

"Pfft, yeah, I'll bet. Sounds like I got here just in time, then."

The words escape him on a puff of air, like an exclamation he couldn't keep to himself. My spine stiffens instantly. I don't think I'll ever forget what he said to me in prison the last time we saw each other. Outta the blue, he accused me of poisoning his girlfriend, Sam. No, excuse me. He accused me of helping that flunky Troy Singer poison *two* women, Sam and someone else—

"Ethan? Baby?" The brunette pops her head out of the car, calling for him, and I take a moment to absorb her presence a little more fully this time. *Baby?* Who the fuck is this? Whoever she is, she's not Sam.

"I'm coming," Ethan says, turning his back on me.

"E, let me explain. Let me come with you—"

"Goodnight, Nero."

With that, he slams the car door shut behind him and the SUV speeds away into the night.

CHAPTER 17

LULU

I have the painting, that's all that matters.

The thought repeats on a loop in my mind. I don't know anything else—what my life will look like tomorrow, what my job will look like—but at least that painting won't go to a museum or end up on some rich jerk's wall for others to gawk at.

Gratitude wells in me like oil burbling out of the ground. This is one of those SUVs where the back seats face each other. Ivy and I sit across from Cara and Mr. King, who has that horrible painting shoved to the side, facing away, as if it's contagious and he's trying to keep it from contaminating us.

"Thank you, Ethan," I say limply, as we drive through Manhattan. "I don't think I can ever repay you, but—"

"No, forget about that," he says with more sympathy than I know what to do with. "People like the Russos forget their humanity sometimes. I don't mind reminding them. And giving you back your peace of mind is a no-brainer, I mean that, Lulu."

It's such a simple statement, but he delivers it with a casual sincerity that makes me think he genuinely means it. Like this is something he'd do for any friend in need. But as I watch, he slides his hand into Cara's almost soothingly, rubbing his gloved thumb across the back of her hand. It makes sense that he's doing this for me, for her, and honestly, I don't care at all. More gratitude wells up into my eyes; I wipe away the tears before more can spill.

"Thank you again."

Ethan nods, then turns slightly to address his driver. "Chuck, the old dump."

"Yes sir."

"What dump?" I ask.

I like the sound of it. A 'dump' is exactly where that painting belongs.

"In Jersey just over the bridge," Ethan says, wiggling the frame of that horrible painting. "They have a massive shredder there. A disintegration tank too. Pretty much any tool you want to destroy this thing."

"Destroy?" I couldn't have heard him correctly. "You're going to let me destroy it? A ten-million-dollar painting? Just like that?"

I'm surprised by the look I find on his face. It's a mixture of indignation and confusion.

"Unless...you want to keep it?" he asks.

Cara and Ivy glance at me, as if the decision is entirely mine to make...ha! I didn't even know it was an option!

"N-No," I stammer. "I want it gone."

"Damn right you do," Ivy says. "We're going to help you find a new job, too, sweetie."

Cara nods adamantly at that. "If Ethan says it's okay, I could maybe make some calls to our clients, see if anyone has a foundation or something in need of an art advisor?"

"And the Director at MoMA owes me a favor," Ethan adds so casually, as if that's not the most insane name drop humble brag I've ever heard.

Then he drops a bomb.

"You could—technically—try to sue Emilio Russo for slander and right of publicity, if you want to. I don't know that you would win, given how nebulous those laws are in New York, but it's an option."

But my head's already shaking before I point out the obvious. "*Sue the Russos?!* Are you *nuts?* I can't even leave the Russos, much less sue them."

"Sweetie, of course you can," Ivy says, her voice high and sharp. "You can't stay after what that gross little pervert did back there. The way he painted you and put it up for display in front of *all of your peers?*"

"I wouldn't let that slide," Ethan echoes. "People will treat you how you let them treat you."

Cara doesn't add her two cents…and I know why. After fifteen years with a guy who treated her like garbage, she knows it's not always that easy to leave.

Usually, I'd just shake my head again and let it lie, especially around a group of people who just went to bat for me like they did, but they deserve more than that.

"It's not that I don't *want* to quit," I admit. "You know how powerful the Russos are. They're already acting like I sullied their entire family's reputation by leaving."

With that, I hold up my phone so they can all see the *glut* of text messages that have come pouring into my phone in the last fifteen minutes. There must be forty or fifty of them now. The phone hasn't stopped vibrating in my hand since we left.

I'm not brave enough to read the messages just yet, but I saw one of the first. Mrs. Russo threatened to have me blacklisted for "overreacting."

No, the Russos have trapped me in a corner with only one way out I can see.

"I have to let them fire me," I tell them, even though the thought makes me want to burst into tears. "If I leave, they can say terrible things about me."

"They can say terrible things about you if they fire you," Ivy counters.

"But it'll soften the blow," I say, trying to convince myself. "If they feel like they already hurt me, they'll be less likely to retaliate, right? They'll…think they won and let me go."

Does that make sense? I'm not sure. I just…

I know it sounds like a weak excuse, but *they know everyone*. I didn't know the full extent of who the Russos were when I originally went to work for them. As far as I knew, they were just some rich family that liked art, Lorenzo seemed like a dream boss who trusted me *and* didn't micromanage me, and Matteo and Carlo were kind enough otherwise to make the day-to-day fun. I turned a blind eye to the rest of it because it had nothing to do with me. For the most part, I didn't even know what they did beyond the couple hours a week when I would meet or talk with them over the phone. So long as I kept the investment pieces high quality and the collections well maintained, they let me be. It was a great job.

A great job aside from Emilio, but...I could put up with a gropey guy if it meant I got to spend all my time worshipping the art and artists. Plus I got to build a massive private collection I was *and still am* damned proud of!

It wasn't until Carlo left the family that things got bad.

I'm sure if I go back to the Russos now, they'll make excuses for what Emilio did. They'll make it up to me.

Right?

They seemed just as surprised by the painting as I was.

And regardless of whether they knew, I just want to slink away without losing everything I've built over the last ten years.

"I hope it's that easy," Ethan says gently when the silence settles around us like a wet blanket. "But either way, by the time you're done with them, we'll have you set up somewhere else."

I hope that's true. On the drive to Jersey, I push the prayer that everything will be okay out into the universe in little mental bursts. I hope and hope and hope until the SUV comes to a soft stop inside a junkyard right on the water, and the driver opens the door for me.

But when the dump's owner shows up and Ethan asks me again how I would like to destroy the painting, my mind makes a connection I wasn't expecting. I've never been religious, but I know a lot of religious people light candles when they say their prayers, to give them more power, more focus.

I may not have a candle, but a flammable canvas should do.

Cara, Ivy, and I huddle together for warmth while Ethan, Chuck, and the dump's owner build a bonfire with flames that are almost as tall as I am. Then, with all the reverence of a witch burning, I toss the painting in. It catches just right, slightly tilted toward us so it's almost on display when the flames begin their feast.

As the offending image disappears in a blackening landscape of boils and ash, the flames purge the worst of the worries from my mind, and relief splashes across the wounded parts of my self, reassuring them.

At least the image doesn't exist anymore.

With time, it'll fade from the minds of everyone who saw it too.

And by then, maybe my prayer will have been answered.

It has to be. I just...wouldn't survive being shunned from the art world I love so dearly.

CHAPTER 18

NERO

Hey Lulu. I'm the guy you kissed at midnight. I know it's late to text, but I need you to know I wasn't trying to buy the painting so I could keep it. I wanted to get rid of it for you. I saw how much it hurt you.

...

You won't have to worry about anybody seeing that painting again, I promise.

...

And I still want to take you out to dinner when you're free.

...

My name is Nero, by the way. Nero King.

...

Whatever Ethan said about me, please let me explain.

***

It's nearly ten a.m. the next day when I step into an office I haven't seen in over five years...and I hardly recognize it when I do. This building in the Flatiron District used to house the NY branches of eight tech companies based out of Palo Alto, but it seems a bunch of tiny startups have infested the building—startups, and things that sound like money laundering tech pipe dreams. Maybe we pushed the other guys out. My company, Omnisight Analytics, used to be on the third and fourth floors, but in my absence has grown to incorporate the fifth and sixth too.

The expansion should make me proud, especially since data mining is practically gold farming, but I can't help feeling a little unnecessary. After all, it happened while I wasn't here. With my money, with my initial investments, with my blood, sweat, and strategy, and following my plan—but still without me.

I hate that it bothers me.

I hate that my brain is trying to eat away at my own achievements.

I came from nothing. Everything I have, I worked for. I built this business off the back of a $500,000 loan I took out myself and repaid within two years. With this place and my acquisition of half of Ethan's company, I'm worth over a billion dollars now.

I'm a fucking money alchemist.

But none of it feels real.

Back when Ethan and I were kids, we'd find those old cicada shells stuck to the trunks of trees sometimes. I feel like one of them, dry and hollow and like something that outstayed its fucking welcome.

There came a point while I was locked away when I realized that even though watching people's private lives *does something for me* on a primal level I can't explain, a digital life isn't…enough. That watching other people live their lives is a fake approximation of living one of your own.

In the early days, this business gave my hunger and anger an outlet as well as a sense of purpose and direction. Then I had to give it up and all I had was endless time in a cell to fixate on what I didn't have. I missed women. I missed good food. I missed my freedom. I missed being a fucking voyeur. But I never missed work.

I keep trying not to think about what that might mean, but that's hard to do when the elevators open and my small, but mighty crew greets Darius and me with a pounding, stomping roar of applause. I ring the old bell hanging from one of the office walls, the one we rang to signal another million made, another client landed, another juicy piece of intel acquired. I smile and fist bump a couple guys and wish them Happy New Year in passing.

But I feel almost bad for them when they quiet down, expecting me to have some sort of grand speech prepared or something. I don't know what to say.

The words tumble out of my mouth, half formed and mumbling. "It means the world to me that you guys stuck it out here and grew this place while I was gone. I'm impressed. Proud. Blown away, honestly." Someone claps me on the back, and I wish I had more to give them. "Gimme a chance to get back on my feet, then the sky's the limit, I promise."

The words taste like bullshit, but the only one who seems to pick up on it is Darius, who gets them clapping again before he says, "Hell yeah. You heard the man. Now that Nero's back, I think it's time we took over the fucking world, what do you say, gentlemen?"

My team cheers louder at that and I fake a reaction, as if Darius read my mind. Then I let him pull me into a quick round-robin reconnect with all our people. It's not really necessary, considering Darius visited me at Otisburg every week and kept me apprised of all the big moves our clients and targets have made, but it gives my people the chance to show off a little. To brag about their recent big catches.

One team shows me proof of a world leader's infidelity caught in 4K and high definition—the sort of thing that should guarantee his rival's win in an upcoming election…and act as a nifty bit of collateral should we ever need something from him.

Another team just found the corporate mole terrorizing a PharmaTech firm in Canada…and helped him slip away to another company, where he could facilitate *our* interests moving forward.

Another just spent three months poking and prodding at the weak spots in a new data collection system used by a third of the world's banks. In another few months, we'll be able to reduce the vulnerabilities in that system down to one—us.

Of course, we're not going to pull the triggers on these loaded guns any time soon… The point is just that we can. It's the type of power that makes miracles happen.

Miracles such as erasing the Lulu-Russo situation from digital existence.

The very last desk we visit belongs to Kenzo, a kid who might as well be a godfather for the internet despite being all of twenty-five years old. I recruited him fresh out of juvenile hall when he was seventeen after he was arrested for "accidentally" hacking into a government agency's website. He's the first person I texted last night while I was at the gallery.

"Looking good, Kenzo."

"Thanks. It's good to see you, too, boss," he says with a wide, dopey smile I genuinely missed while I was away.

"Last night's assignment give you any trouble?"

"Hardly." He laughs, swiveling his giant black leather chair to face his monitors. "Pretty easy to worm my way into the hearts, minds, and cloud accounts of a bunch of artists and blue bloods. Half a dozen guests took pictures of the painting on their phone—I deleted those. The couple of journalists who've written about the auction so far have mentioned the painting, but I broke the picture link on the articles pretty immediately after they were published. The journalist for *The New Yorker* refused to print a picture of the painting because it was crass and said the only memorable thing about it was that your brother purchased it. I'm monitoring the others. I had all the videos people posted taken down for copyright infringement, and as far as I can tell, Emilio Russo didn't tell anybody about the painting before he debuted it, but I'm monitoring his emails and messages. So far, he hasn't sent any pictures of it to anyone, but his family is nuking his phone with messages scolding him for it. I do not envy him right now."

"Good, the fucker. Keep an eye on this; prioritize it. Not a single photo of that painting anywhere, all right? Kill it in the cradle. Break into that prick Emilio's cloud account and delete any copies of it. Watch his email too—any mention of it from anyone, block him from seeing it. And if he talks about it in any interview or article, I want the comment sections overrun with people calling him a little bitch."

Kenzo chuckles. "What'd that guy do to piss you off, boss?"

Darius leans it at the question, curious as well. But I don't want to explain any of it—at least not while Lulu isn't answering my texts—so

I do the easy thing of lying through my friggen teeth. "Fucker cockblocked me. Ruined my chance of getting laid last night and I'm going to fucking punish him for it."

Both men smirk at that.

"Is it the chick in the painting?" Kenzo asks. "Seems a little ran through."

That's an expression I haven't heard before, but I hate it the second he says it. It proves how vicious that painting was on even the most superficial level. Emilio Russo didn't just hurt Lulu, he tried to ruin her professionally and personally. He tried to reduce her.

Makes me want to get him alone and pry open his undercarriage with a pair of steak knives.

"The face is hers, the body's a figment of his fucked up Freudian nightmares," I tell Kenzo. "But while you're at it, make Lulu Rathbone a priority as well. Send me whatever you find out about her."

"Who is she?"

Honestly, I'm not sure I even know; I spent all of twenty minutes with her. An incredible twenty minutes, but still. But after what happened—after *Ethan* of all people swooped in like Batman and bought her painting—I feel like I need to know more.

"I know she works for the Russo family," I say. "Seems close to them, despite everything. She curated the event last night."

News of her connection to that family almost has Kenzo's tail wagging. "Ooh, interesting. I'll find out what I can."

Darius eyes me too. "What are you thinking? We going to war with the Russos, Nero?"

There's no judgment in his voice, only curiosity.

"I don't know yet," I admit. "Maybe."

That's up to Lulu, isn't it.

If she'd just text me back, I'd have my answer...and I might actually enjoy taking the Russo empire down a peg or two. Or razing it to the ground entirely. It'd give me something to do, at least. Hell, it might even reignite the spark for my work again.

"Be prepared for anything," I add.

"Always am," Darius smiles.

He motions me to follow, and I do, to my old office—a room I've always love-hated. I love it because it's a cozy windowless burrow with little more than a fancy computer on a desk and it's where I used to go to watch live feeds of some of our most active clients and targets. I feel comfortable here. Powerful. In control. But I hate it because I realized after a while that nobody cared I was here, watching their every move, judging their every decision. Nobody cared that I was off by myself.

Eventually, I started working in the bullpen with the rest of my crew.

They thought I did it so I could watch them more closely.

I never told them the real reason—that it was fucking lonely in the control room, listening to them laugh and talk through a door.

"I got you set up with all the latest feeds," Darius says as he flicks on the light, revealing the same setup as five years ago, except with a brand-new computer. "Since I thought you were getting out in a few weeks, I scheduled client meetings for then. That gives you a good chunk of time to get caught up...unless you want me to schedule them sooner."

"No, that's great, thanks D," I say, dropping into the swivel chair that still has my ass impression in the seat. I hate that I both fit and don't fit anymore.

"I'll be out here if you need me," he says, hand on the doorknob.

"Thanks again."

I hate this room, this chair, even more when he shuts the door behind himself. This isn't a small room by any stretch of the imagination, but the second I'm alone it feels like a punishment to be in here, not a return to form.

I turn on the computer anyway, hoping that by the time it boots up, some old part of me will boot up too.

But while I'm waiting, thoughts of last night—of Ethan—return and catch like a song stuck in my head. How the fuck does he know Lulu? How does he know her well enough to drop ten mill the second he finds out she's in trouble? I don't think they're together—they better not fucking be—but he was there the second she needed him. Him and that brunette I don't know.

It's too much mystery for me. I hate mysteries. Especially where my little brother is concerned. And after last night, I think it's high time I paid him a visit where he can't avoid me.

CHAPTER 19

LULU

"Friendly and professional. That's what I am. Unbothered. Friendly. Professional."

I repeat the words to myself like a little mantra, for courage, as the car the Russos sent for me pulls up in front of their Long Island home. It's a house I've visited hundreds of times before. A beautiful, 25,000 square foot mansion designed and built by an American senator back in the early 1900s. In the springtime, flowers fill nearly seven acres around it, turning the whole thing into a mini botanical garden, an idyllic retreat forty minutes outside the city.

But now, in the dead of winter, everything is cold and lifeless and that's how I feel when the front door swings open and the butler, James, greets me with a polite, "How are you, Ms. Rathbone?"

I had hoped that I would be able to tell if he knows I'm getting fired from his tone, but I can't.

"I'm fine, thank you, James," I say, letting him take my coat. "How are you?"

"Busy," he says.

I know he doesn't mean it as one, but the single word response feels like an accusation as I follow him deeper into the house. No one's in the kitchen, even though that's where the family often likes to meet. No one's in the downstairs office either, which means Lorenzo isn't here.

No, James guides me to one specific staircase in a house full of them and I realize that we're headed for *the den*, the part of the property

Emilio prefers most when he's here...and my stomach flops over itself with dread. The den is...basically a playground for adults, a huge portion of the lower level is outfitted with a restaurant-sized bar beside two bowling lanes, a wine cellar larger than my apartment in Brooklyn, and doors leading to the cinema room, indoor basketball court, and the indoor pool.

It's a fun entertaining space...when it's used for that.

But as we reach the bottom of the stone stairs, I know entertainment is the last thing on anybody's mind today. I see only two people waiting for me, and they're the worst combination of Russos there can be.

Emilio stands by one of the bowling lanes with a massive black bowling ball in his hands...and I steer clear to Mrs. Russo, who sits at the bar sipping coffee as if it's any other Tuesday morning. As if they didn't humiliate me only a few days ago at that party. I haven't spoken to anyone in the family since that day. I knew they'd send a car for me when they were ready. But I'm surprised by the look on their faces when they see me, the slight shift of their bodies as I approach. I'd expected defensiveness, hostility maybe, but there isn't any. Emilio glances my way, then sends the ball careening down the lane where it hits the pins with a loud clatter while Mrs. Russo dabs at her face with a napkin.

It...makes me more nervous. And less.

Maybe I blew things out of proportion? Maybe they won't bring it up at all. Maybe they just want to move on and pretend like it never happened. I'd take that. I'd be *happy* to pretend that painting never existed. After all, they got ten million dollars for that friggen thing.

"Good morning, Mrs. Russo, Emilio," I try, forcing a polite soft smile onto my face.

"You're looking well, Ms. Rathbone," Mrs. Russo says. "Considering how you left things last week."

How *I* left things? Nope, I'm not going to rise to that.

"So do you both," I say quietly, keeping my voice polite and friendly.

Afterward, I let silence fill the space around us for a long beat—something I know they don't know how to deal with. I do. After years of working for them, falling into the background with the rest of the staff while they move around me like I'm a piece of window dressing, I'm entirely comfortable not speaking unless spoken to. And it feels like the right thing to do. I want them to understand I'm not going to make a big deal out of it. We can just move past this.

"We've been waiting for an update on the auction," Mrs. Russo says after a moment.

"Of course! Yes!" I already have my consolidated notes cued on my laptop, which I brought with me in my saddlebag just in case. I pull it out almost thrumming with relief and set it on the bar opposite her. "It was *incredibly* successful, Mrs. Russo. Collectively, the art sold for a little over one hundred and sixty-four million, and three sales were the highest ever for their artists. Congratulations, really."

"Aren't you going to congratulate my son? He was one of those three."

I pause for only a moment. "Of-Of course. Congratulations, Emilio. I read *The New York Times*' article. They dedicated an entire paragraph to your work. If you want, I can have the article framed for you."

"That's generous," he murmurs, sending another ball down the lane, even harder this time. I feel the force of the hit in my bones as it strikes the pins.

"You know, it's weird," he says. "I see you kissing this stranger at our party and then suddenly he's bidding on my painting. Him *and* Ethan King."

I don't know where he's going with this.

"You kiss one brother, but you leave with the other. What happened there? You fuckin' both of them, or what?"

I blink at that. I never got the tattooed stranger's name before I left. I thought I heard him talking to Ethan right before we drove away, but my mind was on other things and Ethan never mentioned it. Even if he *is* Ethan's brother, I don't know what that has to do with anything.

So I say, "Mr. King is dating my best friend. He's also how I got in contact with Kaden Malbec to source the piece for the show for you."

"*Really*," Mrs. Russo croons, as if she doesn't believe me.

"Yes, *signora*. Mr. King represents Mr. Malbec."

There's a twinkle in her eye I don't like, then a cruel little smile. "I didn't take him for much of an art enthusiast. Strange that he would pay such a high price for my prince's piece *and* come to collect it himself...considering he wasn't invited."

Discomfort crawls up my spine. I can't tell if she's trying to trap me or pick a fight so she can finally fire me. I almost wish I could just ask her if that's where this is going. I wish I was brave enough to cut to the quick and save us all some time.

But I'm not. Every time the thought of termination enters my brain, thoughts of everything else I'll lose crowd around it, almost like burs caught in cotton.

"Would...you...like to send him a thank you card?" I try.

Emilio sneers and releases another ball as a laugh barrels out of Mrs. Russo's throat, deep and mean. "Do you take us for fools, Ms. Rathbone?"

"...No?"

"Mr. King embarrassed us when he took that painting. For you. Because you called him. Why you didn't just let your little boyfriend bid on it, I have no idea, but instead you brought one of the most recognizable faces in New York City to our event to cause a scene. And then he doesn't talk to us, he just takes it, and you walk out with him like you want to insult us. Is that what you were trying to do?"

"No!" The word leaves my mouth high and panicked. "Of course not!"

"We have been trying to contact Ethan King since that night. He has ignored every single call and email we've sent. What am I left to assume but that you badmouthed us to him."

I don't mean to. I genuinely don't mean to, but I get my back up and I speak before I can think, "*I* badmouthed *you*?"

Damnit. I hate myself. I already know what she's going to say before she leaps at my words like a jungle cat after a piece of meat.

"Are you saying *we* did something?" The volume of her voice swells. "Is that what you're saying? Ungrateful. Selfish. We don't employ anyone like that, and yet here you are!"

Tears rush for my eyes as my shoulders tense.

"*Che porca troia!* Your little stunt damaged my prince's reputation. We expected articles, profile pieces, invitations for Emilio this week, and there's barely anything. No pictures of the art anywhere. No requests for interviews."

I balk. "*Signora,* I don't have any control over that?"

"This was supposed to be Emilio's breakthrough moment, you stupid girl. Not only did you ruin it, you humiliated him in front of the most successful talent mogul in New York City."

Guilt rushes into me at the thought. She's right…the whole point of the auction was to launch Emilio's painting career into the stratosphere. I forgot about that when he revealed that painting, but…she's right. I stole focus. If Emilio's star fails to rise because of what I did, then they have every right to be angry at me.

I should have just let my pride go. I should have just left that painting alone and bore the humiliation until it eventually died down. I forgot I'm nothing without them. I forgot I don't have "fuck you resources."

"Already I've had people asking what happened," Mrs. Russo says.

She presses something on her phone and a text message chain pops up between her and Sarah Stout—one of the top editors at one of the most prestigious art publications in the world, *ArtForum*.

Sarah writes, *I was so shocked by Louise's behavior at the auction. How are you and your family coping?*

Mrs. Russo replies, *We're heartbroken. It was so unprofessional, but we want to believe she has her reasons.*

Sarah's reply to that chills my blood: *Let me know if you're cutting ties with Ms. Rathbone. I'm prepared to do the same.*

"I have half a mind to call up *everybody we know* and tell them *this* is what they can expect if they ever rely on you," Mrs. Russo says as she takes away the phone. "Nothing but failure and embarrassment after everything we've done for you."

"I'm sorry!" I blurt.

"Don't say sorry to me! Say sorry to my son!"

I recoil, my gaze darting to Emilio. I don't know what I expected from him. I've never expected much, but…the look on his face is vicious in its entitled indifference.

And as much as I wish I could say those two little words to him, I can't.

The thought of apologizing to *him* after what *he* painted? It's one step too far. The words stick in my teeth like toffee, practically fusing my jaw together. I tear my gaze away from him and focus on her instead. Her shrillness is tolerable compared to that.

But she pushes. "Mr. King might have represented him if you hadn't humiliated him!"

I try to assure her as gently as I can, "No, he wouldn't have, but we can find someone else—"

"*Excuse me?*"

"He wouldn't have, *signora*. Mr. King rarely reps anybody. The only painter on his roster is Kaden Malbec and only because—"

"Are you trying to say my prince isn't as good as him?"

"I didn't say that."

"Well if I'm not good enough to represent, then why'd he buy my painting?" Emilio doesn't say it as a real question. He stalks forward toward the bar and it takes everything in me to stay rooted to the spot so he won't think I'm backing away from him. If he does, it'll only make this worse. "You know what? Fuck that and fuck him. If he's too good for me, then I want my painting back."

I keep my mouth shut again, and not just because the painting literally doesn't exist anymore. I keep it shut because I'm hoping Mrs. Russo will talk some sense into him.

"Don't overwork yourself, *amore mio*," she says.

"No. I want it back, Ma. I spent a lot of time on that piece. It should go to somebody who'll appreciate it. It should be on fucking display for everybody to see."

It's surreal as they suddenly transition into Italian and Emilio begins whining about how much heart and soul he poured into that humiliating painting of me. A painting he did *without ever consulting me*. It makes me sick to my stomach how Mrs. Russo reaches for him. How she pets his hair consolingly. How she talks about the piece like I'm not here at all. I feel like I'm in a nightmare.

Then worse still when she says, "All right, *amore mio*. We will get the painting back." Her dark eyes flitter back to me full of expectation as she adds, "This week, Lulu. Then you'll find a new buyer for it."

"A museum," Emilio mumbles. "Or a socialite."

"*Si, amore*. A better buyer."

Oh fuck.

"But..." I say.

"But what?" Mrs. Russo snaps.

I scramble for anything. "Mr. King already paid for the painting. In full."

"So?" Emilio asks.

"You...want to refund him ten million dollars? It's your most successful sale to date. You've never hit eight-figures before. It's better to have that as part of your lore moving forward, right? The next piece will sell even higher thanks to him."

His lip curls petulantly. "Who fucking cares? I don't need the money. I want my painting. It wasn't even finished anyway. If I get it back, I can do final touches and sell it for even more next time."

"Of course you can, my prince," Mrs. Russo says before turning her icy gaze on me. "Go fetch, Lulu."

I'm frozen to the spot for a long, painful second as *I'm ruined-I'm ruined-I'm ruined* streams through my mind like ticker tape until Emilio sends another bowling ball down the lane. The crash of it against the pins sounds like a mourning roar in my ears—the death knell of my entire career being shattered to pieces.

CHAPTER 20

LULU

It's gone. It's over.

I feel like I've spent my life running across a slowly collapsing bridge. I take a step thinking I've finally reached solid ground only to feel it give way beneath me the moment things start to feel okay.

My dad.

Then my mom.

Then the man I *thought* saved me from my mom, who turned around and hurt me a thousand times worse than my shitty parents ever did.

Even the Russos—the only reason I went to work for them in the first place was to escape my supposed "savior." And I stayed because it felt like I'd finally found the bedrock I could build a life on. A blind eye and a thousand mundane cruelties were the price I would happily pay to protect that.

But the bridge is giving way again and it's my fault, isn't it.

And this time, I don't think I'm going to make the leap to safety, not even by the skin of my teeth.

I mean, the painting the Russos want doesn't exist anymore. And when they find out I burned it…who would ever work with an art advisor who burns paintings? What artist would ever trust me with their work? I didn't even take a picture of the offending painting to help me explain, if anyone ever asked. I just wanted to forget it ever existed.

I don't know what I'm supposed to do with myself now, but I need comfort. A hug. A cry. A friend who can make the pretty lie that 'everything will be okay' sound like the truth. Ivy flew to Paris yesterday, so that leaves Cara.

I walk into the Star-King lobby like a zombie. I know I shouldn't be here. I know she's working now and has her own problems, considering everything we found out about what her ex did to her last month, but...she's all I have and—

"Hello again, Ms. Rathbone. Can I help you?"

My head swivels groggily in the receptionist's direction. She remembers me from my last visit, which should make this easier, but my throat is tight with tears or vomit and I'm not sure which will come out if I speak.

"Cara, please," I whisper. "Miramontes."

Her eyes tighten with concern, but she picks up her phone and whispers into it. Then she sets it down. "Do you need a water—ooh! Careful!"

I don't even realize my knees are giving a little until I catch myself on her desk.

"I'm sorry," I say, because I am.

"Sit down, honey, before you fall." She leaps out of her chair and comes around to me, but I feel like my head is swimming and the seats seem so far away.

"I'm sorry."

"Lulu?"

Cara's voice carries. I turn to find her wearing more of those beautiful clothes that fit her so well. She looks so polished and bright. Her cheeks are flushed, her eyes are happy...until she sees the state of me.

"Oh, baby, what happened?" she asks, darting forward.

"I'm finished. Ruined."

"No. That's not true," she lies to me.

"Should I call somebody?" the receptionist asks, but Cara waves that away.

"No, I'm going to sit her down somewhere quiet. Could you please let Mr. King know I won't make the next meeting?"

"Sure."

Cara's hand goes to my waist, the other to my hand, and she helps me down the hall to an office that's half empty and full of boxes otherwise. The only thing unwrapped is a swivel chair that looks sort of...hobbled...but she sets me down in it anyway. And before I can protest, she drops to her knees beside me to hold my hand.

"I'm sorry," I say again.

"There's nothing to be sorry for, I'm here for you. Tell me what happened."

So I do. It doesn't take long. In fact, the explanation of my meeting with the Russos is so short I'm almost embarrassed by the way my chest hitches when I explain it.

Then I'm embarrassed again when a massive figure catches my attention out of the corner of my eye and I look up to see Mr. King entering the room. He steps in and shuts the door, his face set with concern...and something I've seen a couple of times now—resolve.

"What's happening? What's wrong?" he asks, coming to stand just behind Cara. His hand goes to her hair almost instinctively and the way she looks at him—it's almost enough to distract me from the mire of my own thoughts. I know I'm in no place for love, but I can't help thinking everything would be easier, lovelier, if I had someone to help lift my spirits; verdant green envy trellises up my spine and I watch it climb higher as he helps her to her feet.

"The Russos want the painting back," Cara says. "Lulu thinks they'll get her blacklisted if anyone finds out we burned it."

"I'm sorry, Lulu," he says.

I shrug. "It's my fault."

"No. It's not," he almost chastises.

"I embarrassed Emilio," I point out. "I ruined his big show."

"Oh, fuck him," Ethan sneers. "They knew what he painted. They saw it. They're not blind. Fuck, the second I walked in that gallery, *I* saw it and wanted to knock his lights out. Did they ask you if you consented to him painting you?"

"No, but—"

His head shakes. "Then they're just trying to cover their asses. Or they're fucking narcissists. Either way, it's not your fault."

"Well...thank you." Genuinely, it's nice to hear the words, even if they don't matter. "I'm just..." Emotion wells in my throat, tight and painful. My eyes dart to Cara. "I'm scared."

"Oh, sweetheart," she says, reaching down to hug me. It's a good hug, a *great* hug. I need every second of it she'll give me. "I'll help you."

"We'll help you," Ethan echoes. "No one knows the painting is gone, all right? No one has to know either."

I blink. I hadn't thought about that.

"What are you thinking?" Cara asks Ethan, taking the words right out of my mouth.

"Well, I don't want to push you to anything," he tells me. "This is just my two cents, but...use this time while they're waiting to figure out what you want, all right? They're not expecting the painting today. Take the next week and do whatever you need to set yourself up in a better place, then tell them I want to speak with them. Have them reach out."

"What are you going to say?" I ask.

"Cara and I will think of something, okay? Don't worry about that. We'll buy you some time," he says.

Buy me some time.

Such a lovely idea...except when I wonder what we're buying time for. Are we buying time so I can finally find some solid ground to stand on or just so I can jump to the next board on the collapsing bridge?

CHAPTER 21

NERO

Her name isn't Lulu Rathbone.

It isn't even Louise Rathbone, like it says on all her financial documents and the contracts she's signed over the years while working for the Russos.

Her birth name is…'*Unknown*,' which seems impossible in this day and age. My crew has had almost twenty years to perfect our invasion of the digital privacy of literally every person we've ever met. We've gotten so good that even if we *didn't* have a password breaking program, we could probably guess correctly nine times out of ten.

And yet…

Kenzo wormed his way into every facet of Lulu's life and came back with half a story. There weren't even *holes* in her story, just a massive gap before the age of nineteen. One random morning, she showed up at RISD as a scholarship student and less than four years later, she was in deep with the Russos. That's an insane trajectory.

Kenzo's digging deeper…but so am I. I step out of the elevator into the Star-King lobby with exactly two goals for the day—take part in my first board meeting at Ethan's company—*our* company—and somehow annoy my childish brother into confessing everything he knows about the tiny woman who *still* refuses to call me back.

"Hello, sir," the receptionist says. "How can I help you today?"

"Could you call Ethan King out, please?"

She blinks at me, eyes raking over my tattoos, before her lips curl into a tight smile. "Is Mr. King *expecting* you?"

Her tone is laughable. Just the right amount of arrogant disdain and disbelief. I love it.

"He should be," I say.

So reluctantly, she reaches for the phone on her desk, as if she's going to pretend to call him, then lie to me that he's not available. I know he is. I saw him through the security cameras this morning.

"May I have your name, please, sir?"

I already have my ID card in hand. "Yeah, Nero King."

She freezes with the phone to her ear. The look of surprise is tasty enough to eat, but I love pushing people who are already uncomfortable that extra inch further.

"You know what? Don't worry about it. Why don't you show me to my office, please, Ms...?"

"Rita Carmine, sir," she almost whispers, rising to her feet.

"My office, Ms. Carmine?"

"Uh, it's being used at the moment."

"By whom?"

"Mr. King, sir."

I smile at that. "Well isn't that lucky. We don't even have to go looking for him. After you."

It's barely fifteen feet to the closed door, and I can hear people talking inside before Rita knocks. The voices shift, one draws nearer, and I put on my favorite shit-eating grin in anticipation of the delicious surprise on Ethan's sour little face.

And it. is. *glorious*. The distraction in his eyes shifts darker when he sees me. I eat it up.

"Hey bro," I almost sing. I don't wait for him to stop me. I reach beside him to push open the door. "You in my office planning a welcome party or something?"

But I fall silent the second I see who's in here with him. Thanks to Kenzo, I now know the pretty brunette is named Cara Miramontes—Troy Singer's ex. Here I'd thought I'd messed with Ethan by having Troy steal Sam away. Turns out, I'd only opened up a vacancy, one he filled immediately. Kenzo showed me a video of Ethan telling journalists at his Christmas party that Cara was the love of his life. She seems to have infiltrated his existence as thoroughly as I plan to, and in record time. I'd be impressed if I thought it would last.

She's tomorrow's problem, though. Today's is...

"Lulu." I don't mean to murmur her name like some sort of prayer, but I do. I'm surprised to see her. Excited. A weird flush of relief goes through me. "Are you...here to see me?"

I realize she's not when she jerks her tear-filled gaze away from me. "I should go."

"No, wait—"

The words are barely out of my mouth when Ethan's hand lands at the dead center of my chest, as if he's prepared to hold me back. I want to shove it off—really, I want to put him in a headlock for it—but whatever's going on with her matters more right now.

"Lulu, just talk to me. I need you to know I *never* wanted that painting, all right? I wanted to destroy it for you. I *would have destroyed it*, I swear."

Her eyes meet mine again, studying me, and it feels like a win, until she turns away.

"I'll call you later, Cara," she says, before giving her a hug. "Thanks, Ethan. I'll take the week, okay?"

"Yeah, no sweat," he says, as if I'm not even there.

But Lulu turns to me next. She steps toward me, her neck craning higher and higher the closer she gets. "You're Nero?"

She knows my name—my heart goes giddy for a second and I shut that shit down *immediately*. I'm not some lovestruck little schoolboy; that shit's embarrassing. I only nod instead.

"I'm sorry I was rude to you that night," she says. "I'm sorry I never called."

"That's okay, I get it." Of course, I get it.

"I was really ashamed of...everything." Her voice is so small, so heavy with tears she's holding back, I reach for her automatically. My hand cups her cheek, slides across her soft skin—

Ethan's hand knocks my arm back. "Hey. Let her be."

Anger spikes in me instantly—at the interruption, at the insinuation that I would hurt her. I'm halfway to saying, "*Don't fucking touch me,*" when Lulu beats me to it, "No, no. It's okay. He's not a bad guy."

Her hand slides into mine, her thumb traces the '*need*' tattoo on my knuckles.

"Nero, things have gotten worse for me since the new year, and it's not the time for...anything. Maybe someday things will be better. But right now, I have to fix my life before it's over. And if it *is* over, then I won't be worth anything to anyone anyway."

"Lulu, that's not true!" Cara almost mewls.

"It's okay, I-I'm gonna fix it." Her voice breaks and she lets go of my hand. "Thank you, Nero. I always wanted a New Year's kiss like that. It made my night, really."

I...hadn't expected her to say that. It takes me aback for a moment.

But it also feels like a goodbye, one I wasn't prepared for.

By the time I have a reply ready, she disappears down the hall. My feet go to follow, but it seems Ethan can sense the shift in me before I lift my foot; his hand latches onto my bicep as if he thinks that'll stop me from going after her.

"What kiss is she talking about?" he asks.

"Like you give a fuck," I say. "What does she mean she has to fix her life?" When he doesn't say anything, I turn to... "Cara?"

"You know who the Russos are, right?"

I doubt there's anyone in the city who doesn't know who they are. "Yeah."

"We burned the painting, the Russos want it back."

Shit.

"They're not going to kill her for it," I say in reassurance. In promise.

I wouldn't put it past them to retaliate, but...

They'll never get the chance to.

I won't let them.

"No, but she *is* the art," Cara says, glancing between us like her meaning is obvious. "She...has no idea who she is without it."

CHAPTER 22

LULU

My feet pound concrete as I step outside the Star-King building. I feel lighter than when I went in, and more focused than before too. Cara's office isn't on the way home; I had to go out of my way to come here. But I'm so glad I did, and not just because she and Ethan gave me the guidance, kindness, and consolation I desperately needed.

Nero was there. I-I hadn't expected it, but I was glad to see him. Glad to clear the air between us so he doesn't have to keep texting or trying to call. He seems like a good guy—too good for me, really—and I don't want to lead him on. Some embarrassments are just too big to overcome, and knowing that he saw that painting, that he knows how awful it made me look, I couldn't go out with him even though I'd like to.

And I wasn't lying when I said I'm too busy anyway...or that that visit was worth it. I never expected Cara and Ethan to give me an idea for how to fix this, but they did. *They did.* Now I feel like I'm leaving with a purpose. A mission.

Mr. King offered to buy me time, and time is all I need to replace that ugly painting.

Time is all I need to get Malbec to repaint it.

He's the only artist I'm pretty sure has no connection to the Russo family whatsoever.

And he's the only one I know who might understand why I burned that painting.

I know it seems like a crazy idea, nothing but a Hail Mary pass. But it's better than nothing, right? It's better than just sitting there and waiting for the end of everything I love. Malbec and I may have left things in a weird place, but weird is fine. I know weird—I can work with weird.

I just have to convince him to help me, that's all.

If I can replace that painting, then the Russos won't destroy me.

They might even forgive me.

With that thought keeping my head above the murky waters of my fear, I set out for home to get my car...so I can pay my favorite reclusive artist a very unexpected and very important visit.

CHAPTER 23

KADEN

I have been in a terrible headspace and it's ruining everything.

I hate myself, and I'm embarrassed when I get like this, but of the two emotions, the self-loathing is more manageable. It's quiet. By contrast, the embarrassment is laughter ringing in my head whenever I think about what I let get to me this time.

I haven't painted in twenty days—fuck, I'm actually counting them now. Pathetic.

Not since Louise left. Not since I made her that promise I didn't keep.

Yes, that's it. I haven't painted in twenty days because I didn't follow through on a promise I made to a woman to send her a video of me masturbating. So fucking pathetic!

It's such a small thing. Such an easy thing to fix either way—by apologizing or just *getting it up for her*. But day after day passes where I don't and then I can't paint because I feel like I shouldn't and it's this doom spiral that's ruining the solitude and inspiration I hoped I'd find if I holed myself away up here for a few years. To get away from the expectations and influence of other people. It only followed me here.

It feels like my brain is screaming at me to *just fucking do something about it already!*

But therein lies the rub. Worse than the embarrassment, the self-pity, etc…is the self-awareness. I don't think anyone understands how *crippling* it is to actually be *aware* of what's wrong with you and still feel stuck in quicksand when it comes to fixing it.

It's my own damned fault I'm like this. I could call a therapist. I could call *Louise* and sort this all out in a second. I could go to a museum or do anything that gets me out of my own head for a little while...but I know I won't because I'm a fucking chicken shit.

Why didn't I masturbate for her, you ask?

Why couldn't I sacrifice a little of my dignity to show her that I respect her?

Great question.

Maybe it had something to do with the art piece that arrived in the mail a few days after she left the last time. Her painting, *Hourglass*, is sitting in my bedroom, leaning against the wall across from my bed, catching the mid-day light. Taunting me.

Anyone can call a painting beautiful, just like anyone could call Louise beautiful. But beauty isn't all I see when I look at it.

It's a deceptively simple piece. A nude woman in a sandstorm. From tip to toe, she's the same color as the sand that whips and billows around her. Even the 'whites' of her eyes are dune-colored. And yet she stands out like a lighthouse in the darkest night. Her hand is extended slightly above and ahead of her, as if it's trying to keep the sand from blowing in her eyes, but...the hand is *pressed* to curved glass we can't see. It's the only part of her that's slightly lighter, with a faint pink from the pressure and the dark lines on her palm on full display. She's literally trapped in an hourglass, but the only way to tell is in the hand and the slight curvature of the wind-swept sand above her head.

More than what it *is*, it's what it makes me feel. She's staring right at me with an expression painted on her face that I've explored plenty of times in my own work—she's condemning me. Calling me out. Imploring me to break the glass I can't see and help her escape.

The painting is alive. That's what it is.

Far more alive than half the paintings I've done in the last three years.

It's as alive as Louise is. *Was*, when she posed for me.

And it might as well be calling me out for how dead I feel inside.

That's what art is meant to do—it's meant to make you feel something, to hold up a mirror—but when it arrived, all I felt was impotent. Like I shouldn't paint anymore. Not unless I can bring myself back from the dead.

But the voice in my head keeps saying *then do it already!*

And I keep mentally yelling back *how?!*

And nothing's getting done. Twenty days of nothing.

Well, not *nothing*. In that period of time, I've been forced to face an uncomfortable realization about myself—my impotence is pure self-sabotage.

And I know that because I haven't stopped masturbating since Louise left.

Every single time I've thought of her, my cock has surged to life like a lightsaber made of steel, commanding me to give her *exactly* what I promised her. I think I've come more often in the last three weeks than I have in the last three years. At this point, I could have painted an entire canvas with myself. Which only makes the fact that I *haven't* sent her the damned video that much more pathetic.

But then my self-awareness rears its ugly head. If I send her that video then she'll actually come back here.

I'm fresh from a shower when a strange noise tears me from my obsessive sad-sack thoughts. It sounds like a door opening. I almost dismiss it until I hear—

Boots on hardwood—

—A sound like someone moving around trying to get warm.

Then... "Mr. Malbec?"

"Louise?" It can't be.

"S-S-Sorry to just barge in but it's s-snowing really hard outside and your door was open."

I can hear her teeth chattering, all the way from upstairs. And I'm moving before I've even buttoned my jeans. We're getting a blizzard today. Through the window, there's like two feet of visibility out there before it's a whiteout; there is *zero* reason to drive in this weather.

I hit the stairs at a trot, but I stagger a step when I see her there. She's just taking off her coat and hanging it on the hook, but she naturally does this thing where she tips her ankle forward so she can rest on the ball of her foot, bending her knee a little, and I feel that flicker she inspired the last time she posed for me spark to life. The lines of her body are beautiful.

She's beautiful, as she turns to me, her round eyes wide and staring.

I half expect my cock to rev to life, but the lust is only half of what I feel. The rest is pure inspiration. There's a twitch in my fingertips to find a pencil and draw her before I lose this moment. It's the first such twitch I've felt in weeks.

The heady cocktail of inspiration and lust almost knocks me back, but then the yuzu and pineapple smell of her hits me and I move toward her quicker than before.

"You're freezing," is the only excuse I can give as my hands go to her arms and begin rubbing long, slow arcs down the length of them. "Come on, let's get you a coffee or something."

"Thank you."

I don't take my hands off her. I only slide them around to her back to guide her into a room she hasn't visited before. There's not much in the kitchen—I barely use it—but I've got an entire cabinet of coffee. I release her to get settled as I move around making a fresh batch.

"I'm sorry for interrupting your day."

I rush. "You didn't."

She blinks those beautiful amber eyes at me. "How have you been?"

A wreck, I want to say. Instead, I tell her, "Fine. You?"

"I'm...awful, actually."

Well, at least that makes two of us. I leave the coffee to brew and turn to face her fully, intending to stay on this side of the island, but...she tucks her hands inside the sleeves of her black sweater and presses her mouth to her hand as she stares at me and it's another fucking perfect accidental pose I want to sketch.

"Do you want to talk about it?" I ask.

"No, I've talked enough with my friends." She flicks away a tear at the corner of her eye and adds, "But...I think I need your help. I know we don't know each other well enough for that, but honestly I'd do anything right now. *Anything* if you say yes."

Her voice rises as she speaks until it's almost squeaky with tears. My legs propel me forward on a collision course with her without any input from me whatsoever. She swivels in my direction as I approach, staring up at me with eyes so bright with need and hope and fear and *life*, I feel hypnotized.

"Hey, it's okay."

I want to touch her again—the arms seem safe. Warm under my fingers. The tension in them eases with each passing second of connection.

"I mean it, Kaden. I have a really big favor to ask, but *please* don't immediately say no. I-I'll do anything you want—"

I can't hear her say that again. It inspires too many inappropriate possibilities. So I whisper, "Shh, calm down. It can't be that big."

But silver tears flood her eyes, and I know it *is* that big, and my hand slides over her shoulder and plants itself against her cheek, under her ear. She leans her head against my palm and my grip tightens just a little.

"I need you to paint something else for me. Something…you won't want to paint, but I'm not exaggerating when I say you'd be saving my life."

I want to smile at that, because that *does* sound like an exaggeration. Art can save lives figuratively—it can definitely save our souls—but I don't know that it's ever literally saved anybody. The importance of this painting to her, though, is undeniable and I can understand that better than anyone. I'm not sure why she needs *me* to paint it, when she's an exceptional talent herself, but…

Maybe…this is how I get my spark back.

I don't know what it is about her that makes me *crave* my brushes, my easel, but I do. My twenty days of nothing feel like a fugue state. Like a weird dream that popped out of my thoughts the second she stepped in out of the snow.

"Just…tell me what you need," I offer. "Let me see if I can do it."

"Really?"

"Sure, I owe you one anyway," I joke.

She glances around until she spots a little notepad I keep by the house phone that rarely rings anymore. She grabs it, and the pencil beside it, and brings it back to me, wafting more of her fruit-kissed scent in my direction. Then, she begins to sketch.

It doesn't take her long, and neither of us speak while she does. I just stand beside her, watching her fingers move across the paper for a few minutes.

Until she finally turns the page toward me. "It's like that. In neon colors—I can pick out the shades, tell you where they go. It's done in a hybrid pop-folk art style, sort of Andy Warhol meets Maud Lewis. Does that make sense?"

I don't answer right away because I can't. I have a hard time comprehending the sketch at first glance. She's drawn a headless woman with bruises on her chest and her legs bent and splayed, exposing her vagina to the world while prying it open with her fingers.

Don't get me wrong, the sketch is good. Crystal clear as far as headless women and genitalia go…but I'm not sure why she wants this.

Until she points to the bare space she left at the very top of the sketch.

"Once the rest of it is done…I need you to paint me wearing a dog collar."

"What…are you talking about?" I eye her, then the sketch, then her again hoping she's joking, but there's no levity in her eyes. "Why?"

She doesn't answer. She just asks, "Can you do it?"

"Yeah, but I won't."

"Why not?"

"*Why not?* Louise…why would you want your face above that? Why would you want me to paint that at all?"

She looks away from me, almost ashamed, but her fingers go to the edge of the counter and grip it, like she thinks I'll kick her out and she's welding herself to the spot just in case.

I can't tell if she wants this painting because she hates herself and her body and is trying to punish herself. Or worse, if that first mistake of mine—accidentally shaming her for modeling for me—made her feel *that* self-conscious.

I reach for her chin, tugging, so she'll turn to face me again. The second those hurt hazel eyes meet mine, though, I feel the need to pull her in more—so she has zero doubt that I mean what I'm saying. I tug her closer, until she's almost looking straight up at me.

My voice emerges deep and firm, but warm. "Louise, if you...*want*...a nude of yourself, I'll paint you one. Gladly. But only as you actually are. That is not your body. Believe me. Every time you walk into this house, all I want to do is paint you. All I want to do is..."

I force my mouth shut. God, am I *incapable* of keeping the barest semblance of professional boundaries intact between us?

I don't know, but I try.

"What made you come up with that concept? Maybe I can give you the same thing but—and don't take this as an insult—with far less hate."

She tears her gaze away then and steps out of my grasp; I feel the absence of her like a sting on my skin.

"I need that exact painting," she says.

"No, you don't," I counter. "Nobody needs that."

"Yes, I do."

The quiet conviction in her voice spikes fury through me. I don't mean to hiss, but I do. "Why?"

"Kaden, please..."

I can't stand the thought of someone like her filled with that sort of hatred toward herself. She's not like me. I don't want her to be anything like me. Hell, *I* don't want to be like me either.

Burning hot anxiety roils inside me, pushing me forward, desperate to close the space she's just put between us. She sees me coming and backs away a little, but she hits the wall behind her and I don't slow until I'm almost pressed against her. Until I can feel her panted breaths each time her chest heaves and grazes my abdomen.

"Kaden," she whimpers, staring up at me.

For a moment, my mind whites with panic that she's scared of me, that I've overstepped again.

But then I realize it's not fear in her giant round eyes. It's thirst. Hunger. Heat. Hope.

Fuck if I don't feel all of that too. My cock swells so fast against my pant leg I hear the actual fabric stretch. Suppose it doesn't help that she's the only fantasy I've been able to get off to since she left in December.

Maybe I can find a tactful way to let her know. Hell, maybe I should just say it outright. No, that's not enough. If that sketch is how she sees herself, then I need to dissuade her of that delusion immediately. I need to show, not tell, her how fucking *flawless* she is. How badly I want to—

Fuck it. If she says no, she says no. I'm going to ask anyway.

"May I touch you, Ms. Rathbone?" My voice rasps across the inches between us like a stone across a frozen lake.

A tiny groan of need escapes her and she pants harder, but I wait. I wait and draw closer, lowering my head until I can almost run the tip of my nose along her cheekbone. Until I know she can feel the puffs of my breath against her skin, and I can feel hers.

Staring into her eyes, I tell her the raw, unvarnished truth. "I need to worship you, Louise. I need to touch and kiss and nibble and lick you until you understand."

Her eyes blow wide with unmistakable desire and I put my hands to the wall to either side of her, just to keep them from getting ahead of me.

"Understand what?" she asks…and I'm so glad she did.

"You're a goddamned work of art."

Her eyes flutter shut for a moment, in ecstasy, in need. But still, she resists what she so clearly wants too.

So I lean in a little closer until her gaze begins a relentless back and forth between my eyes and my lips, my eyes and my lips, and I ask again, "May I touch you, Ms. Rathbone."

CHAPTER 24

LULU

"Yes. God Yes."

The words blow out of me in a moan that melds with his sigh of relief as he captures my lips with his. It's not a soft kiss. It's urgent, needy. My head taps the wall behind me, pressing, as he claims my bottom lip with his teeth and plunders my mouth with his tongue.

Fire explodes in my belly, and lower; the sudden squeeze of my pelvic muscles almost knocks me off my feet. But it's nothing compared to the way my mind *sheds* thoughts of embarrassment, shame, uncertainty, disbelief—everything from the outside world influencing my behavior.

What I need is comfort, a type of comfort no one *out there* can give me right now. My friends, and Nero, saw that painting, saw me the way Emilio sees me, and they pitied me for it.

But Kaden doesn't know it's real. He thinks that cruelty came from my own mind, not someone else's—and he's mad at me for it.

He's defending my honor against me.

I can taste his anger and desperation on my tongue.

And it comforts me in a way I can't qualify. It's one thing to see Emilio's painting and rush to reassure me that my face doesn't belong there; it's another thing to refuse its existence entirely.

The kiss begs me to see myself another way. The way he sees me.

And for a long moment as I listen to his hungry little groans and taste his impatience, I do.

I can bring the painting up again after. For now, I want to live in a world where that painting never existed. I want one more lovely night with a work of art who doesn't know about my shame.

My hands dart forward to wrap around his neck, but he doesn't let me pull him closer.

A sizzling burst of need spirals through my pussy as he grabs my wrists and presses them back to the wall to either side of me. He tears his lips away and stares at me as if he can't believe I dared to touch him.

"Let me worship you," he chastises, clicking his tongue. The sound travels over my body in a shockwave that has my pussy trembling.

So does the insane intensity of his eyes. Barely blinking. Never wavering. They're like desert oases on a windless night; I can almost see my heaving reflection in them.

Sliding, he raises my hands until they meet above my head and he captures both of my wrists. Then the very tips of the fingers on his free hand tease a feather-soft trail down-down-down my arm and curve around my underarm.

Right when his fingers reach the swell of my breast, he drags a little harder, just enough to pique my nipple in passing. But then his fingers swerve back around, teasing circles around the tip of my breast until his thumb brushes my nipple again, riling it more. It's suddenly hard as diamond, begging to be tweaked and touched through the fabric of my sweater.

He leaves it and does the same on the other side, dragging his fingers, then his nails across the soft expanse of parts of my body most lovers have all but ignored—my wrists, the undersides of my arm, the sides of my breasts. Only then does he tease the other nipple until it matches the first. And when it does, he leaves it begging for a mouth to warm it in the slight chill of the kitchen.

Tantalizing sensation spirals away from his every caress.

Never lingering long.

I love the denial of it. The promise that he'll come back to let me feel those touches again, but only when he's ready. Only when he decides *I'm* ready.

Hate to tell him—or maybe I'd love it—but I'm already wet for him. And my pussy's already complaining that his fingers are devoting too much attention elsewhere.

But it all feels so...*good*. Too good to stop.

The fact that he isn't in a rush. That he isn't racing to his own satisfaction.

It makes me realize how long it's been since someone took their time with me.

As if he can hear that thought, he leans in until his lips are a hairsbreadth away from mine and asks, "When's the last time someone lost themselves in you?"

"I can't remember," I admit.

He nods so seriously, as if it's all the confirmation he needs that he's doing vital work here.

Kaden lowers himself just enough to run his fingernails along the side of my leg, from my knee, up-up-up to the crest of my hip, disregarding my skirt entirely. It's simply in the way. Then he does the same on the other side before grazing his touch across the inside of my knee.

The tights on my thighs, he seems to love....because I think he can tell from the way my body is responding that the tights are muting his caresses and I want more—*need* more—sensation.

"Please touch more of me," I beg when my pussy begins to cry.

Like a first brushstroke, a smile streaks up his angular cheek pretty enough to paint...but since I can't do that, I'm left to marvel as he growls, "With pleasure, Ms. Rathbone."

I expect him to rip my clothes off—and honestly, I think I would've loved it if he had.

But what he does instead...

He releases his hold on my hands and lands on one knee. His fingers find the little hook holding my skirt in place and undo it. The zipper goes too a second later and he lets it fall to the floor at my feet until I'm standing in my sweater and tights and nothing else.

Then he freezes, seemingly awestruck, staring relentlessly at my lower half.

"What is it?" I ask after a moment. "Is something wrong?"

He doesn't answer. Not with words. Taking hold of my hips, he leans in and kisses the mound of my sex so tenderly, before his mesmerizing blue eyes shift to my face. Rising to his feet, he whispers "Wait here, Ms. Rathbone," before he turns and walks away.

I want to do what he's asked of me, but...I also want to know why he stopped.

My eye catches on a large mirror on the wall between the kitchen and the living room and my curiosity gets the better of me. I'm so glad it did. I realize the second I step in front of the mirror why he kneeled there in awe.

My black tights are sheer. Sheerer than I ever gave any thought to before.

Through them, the outline of my mauve lace panties isn't just visible, it's almost highlighted. The narrow triangle of underwear covering the back shines through the translucent material of my tights, dark against my creamy skin.

It's a veil.

I accidentally wore a veil for him—one I desperately want him to pull back.

"God, I want to paint you."

I turn at the sound of his pebbled voice to find him on slow approach, almost prowling toward me like a panther, carrying a tube of paint in his hands.

He rakes his hungry gaze down my body and for the first time in my entire life, being painted isn't the thing I want most in the world.

Until he asks, "Are you attached to that outfit?"

"No." It's a black sweater, black tights. My underwear doesn't even match my bra today.

That smile reappears on his face as his nose crinkles. "You will be after this."

I realize what he means as he unsnaps the cap on the paint tube and pours a large dollop of red-orange paint right into the center of his palm.

"I keep an extensive assortment of rare pigments in my paint collection, Ms. Rathbone."

Setting the tube aside, he steps behind me and drops his chin onto the top of my head, turning us so we're both facing the mirror. Showing me the paint in his hand, he meets my gaze in our reflection.

"What color is this?"

I stutter a moment. I know exactly what color that is. Modern variations are safe, but the original color is deadly. Toxic. I hope he's not suggesting that that's what he's holding in his bare hand. My heart revs at the thought.

"Vermilion," I whisper.

He smirks at me approvingly, and my pussy thrums to life with an obscenely dark desire to beg him to touch me with it, to slather me in toxic paint...all while some rational part of my mind reassures me he wouldn't.

Or would he?

Holding my gaze, he brings his hands in front of me and presses the paint between them, until both palms are coated with it.

"The first day you came here, when you posed for me? All I wanted to do was touch you...here."

A single paint-covered finger begins a circular route along my breast, spiraling until it lands on my nipple...and pinches lightly, leaving a tiny starburst of orange.

My body recoils a little from the surprise of it; Kaden only presses to the back of me harder, to keep me in place, to reassure me he's not done yet.

"And here," he growls, cupping my other breast with the entire palm of his hand, leaving a giant print.

For good measure, he scrapes his nails along the peak as he pulls away, scattering sensation through me.

"But this?" he says, trailing a single line of vermilion from the center of my chest to the mound of my sex. "*This* has haunted my thoughts since you left."

It happens so suddenly, I yelp with desire. His hand curves around the apex of my thighs and "takes hold," clutching the spot between my legs, almost lifting me off my feet. My heart tumbles over itself when he pulls away and I see his claiming handprint there.

His mouth darts forward and captures the helix of my ear between his teeth.

"Do you see?" he rasps, almost angry at me. "Do you see how fucking flawless you are? I could paint you a thousand times and find something new to exalt every time."

As if he can barely contain himself, his hands rub a slow, slanted red-orange arc between the place he just marked and my hips, back and forth, back and forth.

"Jesus, Louise. You have no idea how many times I've thought about taking a paintbrush of vermilion and fucking you with it."

Fuck.

I almost swoon. I almost *swoon* right off my feet at the thought of it. Of a thick wooden brush slamming inside my soaking wet pussy, coating my insides with his toxic color.

He catches me the moment I begin to sway away from him. He grips my hips to bruising, leaving handprints there, and pulls me flush against him so I can tell just how excited the thought truly makes him. He's not just rock hard. He's almost wagging with anticipation.

But when I meet his eyes in the mirror, the expression I find on his face surprises me. He looks like he hates himself.

"What? What's wrong?"

"I shouldn't have said that," he says.

"It's okay," I insist.

"It's not. I'm supposed to be worshiping you."

The words trip me up. Doesn't he understand that he already is? This is *exactly* how I would demand worship in my temple. Well, almost...

"Worship me with your cock," I offer. Reaching behind, I pop the button on his jeans and take hold of the behemoth within. Its warmth falls into my hand and I run my fingers softly across its surface, coaxing it out of his pants.

He's just the right height...

I tuck his beautiful length into the soft elastic band of my tights and begin to sway, running the soft fabric across the length of him. In bated silence, we watch together as his cock moves within the sheer material, against it, visible and pressing, teasing.

The growl that escapes him at the sight of it—it's a feral sound that soothes away every terrible thing that's happened to me in the last few days. So does the sudden vital grip of his hands on my hips as he takes control of the movement, coaxing me back and forth so his cock dips farther into my tights, then rises to the very edge, threatening to pop out.

The feel of his soft skin against mine—my body feels so poised to come, I genuinely have to stop myself, squeezing against the flutter in my pussy, the urge to let myself go too early.

I want to come when he can feel it.

But he's making it so. fucking. difficult to wait!

Still sliding himself against the sheer material along my hip, he suddenly slips his hand around my throat, cups my jaw, and pulls my head back into the crook of his neck, holding it there. The only view I have is his gorgeous stubbled jaw, his high-hollow cheekbone, those full lips.

It's almost hotter that he *isn't* looking at me. His face is so expressive—contorted with raw lust and hunger. He's so fixated on the movement of his cock beneath the pantyhose, against the soft expanse of my hip, his eyes are blown wide with a need echoed in every guttural gasp he makes.

His claiming grip, his beautiful face. I'm so turned on, a finger—hell, a butterfly wing—against my clit right now would summon a tsunami.

And that's exactly what he gives me. As if he heard the thought loud and clear, his free hand reaches around to cup my sex again, then nuzzles deeper until his finger lands on my clit through the tights.

A few soft strokes.

A needy press and grip.

He whispers, "God I want to fuck you on a canvas."

And my body seizes like it's being electrocuted with pleasure while he holds me. Devours the sight of my ecstasy. Spills himself onto my hip, spreading warmth down my thigh.

Shaking. We're both shaking, frozen where we stand, staring into each other's eyes as we try to get ahold of ourselves again.

After a few moments, he groans, "Let me paint *this*. *This* is your glory. *This* is your perfection. You're *nothing* like that drawing of yourself."

I smile at that; it's all I can do until the twang of pleasure inside me subsides anyway.

"Both," I finally say.

He shakes his head. "No, Louise."

What?

"But I *need* that painting," I try.

He only shakes his head again…and releases his tight hold on my body, robbing me of the surety and comfort of it. He steps away and my tights snap back against my body, trapping his fluids against my skin, making me miss his possessive hold even more.

"You can't hate yourself that much," he says.

"I don't."

"Then who is that fucking painting for?"

I open my mouth to speak, but I don't know what to say. I should have known that question was coming. I guess I did, really, I just couldn't come up with a good answer for it before I got here. I don't know how to answer that one question without opening the floodgates to a thousand others.

"Who is it for, Louise?"

I feel so small. I can't even look at him when I say, "It's to replace one I burned."

"Whose?"

"…Emilio Russo."

I expect him to ask more questions, to demand more answers, to make me replay the whole nightmare again, but instead I hear movement. I look up as he stalks toward me, his eyes a ruinous blue.

"Emilio Russo painted you like that?" he demands.

I nod, biting my lip to hold back tears.

"I'll kill him."

What?

I blink, watching as Kaden turns on his heel and marches off deeper into the house. I pursue. There's not much else to do. He can't be serious, but he's angry enough I wouldn't put it past him…

"Where are you going?"

"To paint him something he'll regret accepting."

I almost laugh, because he says it so casually, but he means it. Oh boy does he mean it.

We soon reach a room on the main floor I haven't seen before. He wrenches the door open and flicks on the light, revealing a storage room.

No, it's not storage. It's a micro-museum. A very volatile museum full of ancient-looking bottles of paints and pigments in glass cupboards.

Lead white.

Radium orange.

Scheele's green.

These paints aren't just toxic. They're coffin colors.

Glancing down at the paint patterned across my clothes, I ask the obvious, "You didn't really touch me with vermilion, did you?"

It's kind of a joke, so his response is kind of funny. "I told you; I'd only ever use my best colors with you."

Then I hear the click of a lock opening, the *tink* of glass against glass.

"Okay, stop, this isn't funny, really."

"I'm not laughing, Louise. Art is many things—a mirror, an apple box, a source of willful liminality—but it is not a tool for punching down. That's when it becomes something else."

He emerges from the cupboard holding the ancient, crusty, cracked jars with his *bare fucking hands* and I grimace with my entire body. "Put that down! No gloves, are you *insane*?! Look, I'm not going to poison my employer's son, as if that was ever an actual option."

He raises an accusatory eyebrow. "Then what *are* you going to do about it?"

"I'm going to give him the painting back before he destroys everything."

"And then…?"

"I don't…" I don't know.

"You're going to quit, right? You're going to burn their fucking house down, *right*?" He doesn't say them as questions. He's scolding me. "What if he shows that thing to anybody?"

I don't have the poker face to survive that question. The second it leaves his mouth, my entire body flinches at the memory of that auction. For a long moment, I have the *very visceral compulsion to SCREAM just to purge the negativity that's rushed back in* since he stopped touching me.

He sees my reaction and his tone spikes. "Fuck, who's seen it?"

"It doesn't matter, all right?" I snap. "The Russos will destroy me if I can't put that painting back. I need your help, Kaden. Please. Anything you want, I'm begging you."

I hear the clink of glass and when he rounds the cupboards again, his hands are empty. With a scowl on his face I can feel in my soul, he walks over to a small sink in the corner and scrubs his hands before approaching me.

But when he draws closer, his scowl softens to that horrible pity I didn't want to see on his face. I push the shame from my body, to focus.

"I would need a picture of it to copy it," he says.

"I remember—"

"No." He shakes his head firmly. "You're asking me to copy another artist's work. If I'm going to do that, I'm going to do it right."

My chest swells with hope. "You'll do it?"

"Just…let me see if it's even possible first."

"Okay! Let me grab my phone."

I practically sprint down the hallway to the kitchen. Thankfully the phone isn't busted when I fish it out of my fallen skirt. A few seconds of finagling and I log into the Russo Trust's cloud account—where Emilio has always uploaded images of his work for publicity and archival reasons.

But…it's not there.

I refresh my phone screen about twenty times. Look in *every* folder. Then I go to my email account and check for any attachment he might have sent me in the last three months—there's nothing.

Which is impossible.

Everyone's been talking about the auction. Since New Year's Day, every artist that displayed that night, save Malbec, has sent me an update about the requests they've received for interviews and profiles, plus additional career-defining sales they've made. They couldn't wait to brag about their successes, and I was thrilled to hear about them all.

Next, I try *The New Yorker* and *The Times*. I know both pieces mentioned Emilio.

But neither has a photo of that painting. What the fuck?!

I mean, I'm not complaining—honestly, the fact that *nobody* seems to have covered it feels like a gift I never expected—but that doesn't fix the current problem.

I go to literally every single art forum and website I can think of off the top of my head. Emilio's painting is gone. It's just gone. Even on the sites where the painting is mentioned in the caption of a photo, the photo link is broken.

Impossible.

I hear Kaden come in behind me, but I have to focus. I dial a number on my phone and wait for an answer.

"Hey Lulu." It's Taylor, the event coordinator from that night.

"Hey. I'm so sorry to call, but…do you have a list of the photographers we used for the Russo auction?"

"Sure, is it urgent?"

"You have no idea. Please."

"No worries. One sec." I wait an absolute eternity until my phone vibrates in my hand. "There, just sent it to you."

"Thank you! You're a lifesaver."

I end the call, pull up the sheet, and dial the first number.

"You okay?" Kaden asks.

"No. It's gone."

"What's gone?"

"Photos of that piece."

His broad warm hand lands on my shoulder. "Maybe that's for the best—"

"No!" I grumble, pulling away.

The phone rings for what feels like forever, and then I ask the person who answers if they have photos.

"Fuck..." the photographer says. "I don't know what's going on. I-I uploaded the photos *that night* when I got home. Let me look and I'll get back to you, Ms. Rathbone."

The next photographer tells me the same. "This is so strange. The rest of my photos are here, I swear."

It's the same for all six of them...save the last. The last guy is a piece of work, but he's so pissed, I believe every word he tells me.

"No, I don't fucking have any photos," he snaps.

"Why not?"

"Because *some guy* took them from me. Grabbed my neck and forced me to sell my film card to him for five grand."

"What guy? What did he look like?"

"I dunno. Tall. Dark. Asshole. Covered in tattoos. All black suit."

Nero.

I grab my skirt and force it back up over my paint-stained tights. Then I'm moving toward the front door, for my coat, for my shoes.

"Louise? What's happening?"

"I have to go."

He laughs like he doesn't believe me. "There's a blizzard out there...?"

"I'll be fine."

"Wait-Wait."

His hand slides into mine and tugs me to stop and face him. The soft expression I find on his features gives me pause. He actually seems sorry to see me go.

"Just stay, huh?" he asks. "Let me take your mind off this. You can use this place to help you think about what comes next."

"What do you mean, 'what comes next?'"

"After you leave the Russos."

That full-body flinch happens again, lancing discomfort into my shoulders. "I can't do that. They'll take everything from me. Why do you think I'm going to all this trouble? The only thing I love is the art. The only thing I have is the art. There's no 'next' without it, Kaden. I thought you of all people would understand that."

"Your passion, I understand. But no one can take art away from you—you're an artist in your own right. You don't need those people. You don't need anyone."

An acidic disgust rises in me at that. "Fuck off with that nonsense."

"Excuse me?"

"You heard me. You live up here alone, wallowing in your own loneliness, wondering why you can't paint anything even though *most of your art is people*." I twist my tone into a soft mocking one. "'I wonder why I'm not inspired,' says the man who hasn't spoken to a person voluntarily in years. I like people. I like the artists as much as the art, you...ding dong."

Okay, maybe that last insult hit like a kitten paw, but I stand by it.

"I'm so grateful for any help you're willing to give me with this. I genuinely am. Because if this piece is the price of continued admission to the world I love, then all I can do is make myself the ugly whore for the gatekeepers and hope they'll get bored with me. But I can't take life advice from someone who's so scared of connection he detaches himself from everyone and everything and then acts shocked that he's lonely."

He looks like I've punched him. Like I knocked the wind out of his sails. I feel bad, I really do, but the guilt is too mixed up with the frustration and fear I feel to go back now.

"I'm sorry, Louise," he says. "I'm not judging you for trying to...survive."

My shoulders untense a little, surprised by his words...until he ruins it.

"But doormats end up getting trampled until they break down and get thrown away. Maybe you need to grow a spine and stop avoiding conflict if you want things to actually get better for you."

There's only one thing I can say to that. "You first."

I tear the doorknob open and walk away, never looking back. By the time my car's warmed up enough to drive, I'm making one more phone call, perhaps long overdue.

Cara picks up on the first ring. "Hey Lu, you okay?"

"I need you to tell me everything you know about Nero King."

CHAPTER 25

NERO

Right around the time I'm lockpicking Lulu's apartment door, I get a notification from the tracker I have on Lulu's GPS; she's on the move again. She's left the Catskills and is headed back to the city, if she stays on the current road she's on.

It leaves me plenty of time for what I've come to do.

As the lock clicks open and my employee Tony and I step into her flat, I make a mental note to convince her to get a deadbolt since it took less than a minute to get through the two locks she already has on the door. But she's also got a patio door with nothing but the lock it came with and a wooden dowel in the lower track, and I want to call her and offer my legitimate services just so I can educate her on the dangers of leaving herself unprotected like this.

A single woman living alone in New York City should have more than a piece of scrap lumber wedged into her patio door for security. Hell, she should already have cameras in every room.

And a gun.

Considering she works for the Russos, it's even worse that she doesn't have one.

"Want me to start in the bedroom, boss?" Tony asks.

"No. Kitchen and living. I'll do the bed."

Smirking, he yips, "You got it, boss," before he slides his toolbox onto her kitchen counter and gets to work. Well, 'toolbox,' is relative, I guess. It's a briefcase full of audio bugs and hidden camera options—

pens, USB chargers, the works—and the tools we need to install them.

Standard-issue in all the kits my guys carry are dual smoke detector cameras that we can wire right into the building's electrical so it never needs to be charged. That's where I start when I step into Lulu's room. The smoke detector's located right above the bed...and I ignore that yappy little voice at the back of my mind telling me this is an invasion of her privacy. I'm not some pervo creep who's going to watch her undress every day. This is security, pure and simple.

Liar, my mind scolds.

Only half of one, I respond.

Before we came here, Kenzo did a preliminary, barebones assessment of her connection to the Russos. Within *ten minutes*, he had proof that Emilio didn't come up with the idea to paint Lulu randomly one day out of the blue. His cell phone's GPS has pinged outside Lulu's building so many times, you'd think he lives here.

He only comes when he knows she's here, which...begs other questions. But we checked her wifi and there were no "unknown devices" connected. We also carry CIA-grade detectors in our pockets, and they're not going off as I move around her room, so it's unlikely he installed hidden cameras here.

But he doesn't even need to. There's a new technology developed by a professor at Northeastern that allows anyone with an antenna, a few pieces of equipment, and engineering training to capture video feeds *through the walls of people's houses*.

Emilio's not savvy enough for that, but with his money he could hire someone.

The easier possibility is that he's renting an apartment across from hers with cameras or people watching for signs of movement. I move to the window and peek through the curtain, scanning the opposite building for possible voyeurs. I don't see any right now, but...that doesn't mean they're not there. So, I remove two mini wireless surveillance cameras from my toolbox and slide her window open, careful to attach one so it faces the far building, and the other so it faces the street.

Her place is in a good part of Brooklyn, and about as swanky as this borough gets, but it took all of half a string of computer code to bypass the front buzzer system and the building's security cameras are self-monitored. Or they were, until we absorbed their feeds into ours.

What Tony and I are doing isn't enough, in my humble opinion, but it'll do until other arrangements can be made.

As a collective, the Russos are clever, ruthless, structured, which makes up for their eccentric individual shortcomings. That's not a surprise; the entire point of family is collective survival. The weaknesses of one member are bolstered by the strengths of another, and a rising tide raises all ships, no matter how holey. The Russos just take that to the extreme. They've weathered storms together that would break most normal people. And as a pack, they've decimated enemies.

They did, at least, until last year. Kenzo did a little digging and apparently, the Russos' eldest, Carlo, betrayed the family. He returned to Italy to marry the daughter of a rival Sicilian family and gave up the Russo name.

Seems to have knocked one of the foundational pillars out from under the rest of the Russos.

Not that that's Lulu's problem.

I mean, she was there when that all went down. Being in the midst of that was probably like surviving a nuclear bomb, but if anything, Lulu staying by their side should have made her *more* like family, not less. They should have valued her loyalty to them. Instead, they let their dipshit youngest son humiliate her in front of her peers.

I wish I could just crush Emilio like a bug and then scrape him off the chessboard without starting some sort of war with the largest crime family in the city.

I can erase him.

I can haunt his digital life forever.

But it doesn't feel like enough. He needs to be humiliated publicly. Ideally in a way that makes Lulu feel like her reputation has been salvaged.

In the meantime, I wouldn't put it past them to do worse to her, which is why I'm bothering with the dozen cameras we hide in her apartment. That painting Emilio did was personal. A product of infatuation—one that became more obvious once Kenzo checked his private messages and emails. From the small selection Kenzo sent to me, all I can say is *yikes*.

I don't think Lulu knows how closely Emilio keeps tabs on her when she's in the city.

"You done?" I ask Tony as I come out into the living room.

Tony nods, halfway through screwing a light outlet back in. He glances around at her place with a nervous sneer on his face, taking in the plentiful curtains, the walls so covered in artwork it's almost impossible to see the drywall in between. And yet it still all goes together—the plants, the cushions, the mismatched rugs. It's not just bright and inviting, but fucking cozy as hell in here. A *far* cry from my stuffy outdated apartment that feels like a hotel from half a century ago.

"Kinda nice," he says, even though the look on his face would suggest otherwise.

"Maximalism, I think it's called."

His sharp gaze turns on me, still smirking. "Five syllables, boss? You got it bad for this chick, or what?"

"Man, shut up," I grumble, even though I can't kill the smile on my face.

Tony's more than a regular at Amara's. If they had a loyalty punch card, it would be one punch away from a free lap dance every other day. So I figure genuinely liking *any* woman probably seems like foreign territory to him. Then he surprises me with…

"You're allowed, you know."

"Gee, thanks."

"No, I just mean…it's better than listening to you yammer on about your brother all the time."

Anger flares bright in me at the accusation, but I keep my voice calm. "What the hell's that supposed to mean?"

Tony raises his hands so innocently. "Nothing. I just like the idea of you putting all your energy into somebody who actually wants it for a change."

My hands fist reflexively, surprising me. I'm only lucky they're tucked in my coat where he can't see.

"Although, I'm not sure you should bug her apartment, if you wanna keep her, boss," he says after a moment.

"I'm not worried about that."

Because I'm not. These cameras are just insurance while Lulu's trying to figure her shit out.

Eventually, I'll replace the need for them...with me. She'll have nothing to fear with me sleeping next to her every night.

And that's all I want to do.

The second she said that New Year's kiss was a dream I fulfilled for her, the second she told Ethan I was a good guy, something long dormant inside me woke the fuck up. She didn't look at me like a broken waste of space. She didn't even look at me like some wild oat to sow that would make a fun story to tell her friends, although I'll happily give her plenty of stories once we get there.

She just liked me.

I don't want to ponder all the fucked-up reasons why that feels unique to me.

But the fact that she didn't make some snap judgment about me that first night. The fact that she was just open and nice and interested in *me* as a whole fucking human being?

Fuck I'm hard just thinking about it.

Heart hard too.

Honestly, I don't want to leave her apartment when it's time to go. I want to sit on her soft green couch and wait for her to walk in so we can talk for hours before I fucking *obliterate* the memory of her last good lay. I want to fuck her so well, I have to bathe her and feed her and carry her to work tomorrow because she can't fucking walk.

I want her so breathless screaming my name, she can't even fucking *talk*.

In preparation of that fantasy I *will* make a reality, I take one last long look at Lulu's apartment before we leave and make note of the flowers she likes—orchids—and the colors—pinks, greens, and zebra stripes. There's also a giant, unignorable grid of photographs on one wall in her living room, all featuring her with people who are clearly important to her, celebrating birthdays, gallery openings, moving into this apartment. I see Cara in a few of them, along with the red-haired woman I saw with Lulu at the gallery—someone Kenzo told me was named Ivy, a pastry chef who provided the ridiculously delicious desserts that night.

But there's one photo that catches my special attention.

How could it not? It's the only one on the wall with shattered glass in its frame. The impact suggests someone slammed their fist into the exact part of the photo where Lulu is. I have to get within a foot to catch a glimpse of Lulu's smiling face through the spiderweb cracking.

I wonder why she kept it this way. She can obviously afford to buy a new picture frame, so I wager something about this act of violence is important to her. Unless her self esteem really *is* that low. Fuck I hope not.

The photo…sets off alarm bells for me in more ways than one. In it, a teenage Lulu lays reclined on a couch wearing a lacey dress that barely covers her. Behind her, a man looms over her, leaning with his hands on the spine of the couch. He's good-looking, with dark eyes and brown hair just beginning to grey, but clearly much older. Maybe in his early forties back then. It's his expression that I don't like. Cocky and controlling. He's staring at her, but not her face. He's leering at her body like he owns it, or wants to.

He's a fucking predator admiring his prey.

Makes me want to reach through the photo and bust his fucking teeth in.

Instead, I pull my phone out and take a picture of him. Whoever he is, I'll know soon enough, from Kenzo's research or because Lulu offers me that story herself. I prefer the latter, but I'll take the former.

And if this guy's problem is anything like Emilio's, well, it's just as easy to dig two graves as it is one.

CHAPTER 26

LULU

I wake up completely exhausted and getting out of bed feels like an Olympic triumph. It's partially my fault; I tossed and turned for hours before I self-medicated by using my vibrator until the battery gave out. I needed the dopamine hit.

It's been seven days since Mrs. Russo told me to get the painting back.

Today is the day Mrs. Russo and Emilio speak with Mr. King.

Today we'll know if the excuse he's come up with will buy me more time. The only problem is, I can't help wondering *what exactly I'm buying time for*.

Replacing the painting is the only way I can keep my job. I can't do that unless I get the photograph of it from Nero, and I can't do that unless I actually call the guy. I should have called right after leaving Kaden's house, but Kaden's parting words stopped me. So did my call with Cara. Together, they became a perfect recipe for procrastination.

I knew Nero went to jail for tax evasion. I didn't know Nero owned a 'cyberintelligence firm,' whatever *that* is. I mentioned to Cara that photos of the painting went missing online and Ethan cut into the call to say that was something Nero could do.

"Why? He barely knows me."

"I don't know, babe," Cara said. "You'd probably have to ask Nero."

"I wouldn't," Ethan countered. "This is just his twisted way of getting something out of you."

The problem with that, of course, is that I'd do pretty much anything to fix my problem, so Nero wanting something out of me is fine. Great. You blow my back out, I'll blow out yours. A little negotiation on safe words, and we're good to go.

That's where Kaden's parting words about needing to be braver tripped me up, though.

"Maybe you need to grow a spine and stop avoiding conflict if you want things to actually get better for you."

He implied I was a coward for not telling the Russos to go fuck themselves and prancing off into an uncertain future of my own making.

Kaden said that with zero self-awareness of the fact that he's a financially independent man with no one to answer to except the audience of his paintings. I'm sure Nero would say something similar, forgetting all the while that he's also a financially independent man with no one to answer to, period.

Whereas I am one tiny part of a much larger organism. Powerless, really. The Russos pay me well, but not so well that blacklisting me from further employment wouldn't permanently cripple my life. And there's the added complication that they're the only reason I have my life at all.

Considering what they helped me escape, it feels like I owe it to them to undo my snap-mistake. I should have already called Nero and done what was necessary.

But I'm still embarrassed about being "laid bare" in that gallery. I haven't had a single meeting with any of my normal contacts since that day. Phone calls, yes. Emails, sure. But I don't want to talk to a benefactor or museum director and see that look of pity in their eyes.

Just like I don't want to see it in Nero's lovely green ones.

But I'm more scared that I may not need to contact him at all. If the call goes wrong today, well…

I try not to think about it a few hours later as I walk into the Russos' Manhattan skyrise and take the elevator to their city apartment on the 76th floor. It's a corporate flat that's technically one floor sandwiched between three empty floors to either side for...sound proofing. The apartment itself is a concrete and glass box with an incredible view and a palpable aura of intimidation. The many windows are there to mock those the Russos bring here to punish; to add a touch of insult to injury in the fact that you can see the entire financial district but no one can see you. Or hear you scream.

Matteo asked me to join the family here for the call with Mr. King.

They could have saved themselves the commute; I already know this is where they intimidate people, and I'm already intimidated.

The elevator door opens and Matteo is there waiting for me.

"Hey Lu," he says, wrapping an arm around my shoulders to hustle me along the second I step into the foyer. "You okay?"

"I don't know," I answer honestly. "Am I?"

His gaze flitters away for a moment, riling my anxiety. "They're a little squidgy about this whole thing with the painting. I don't know why Emilio's making such a big deal out of it, but with his mother involved, Lorenzo's trying to keep the peace."

That's not surprising. Lorenzo has always been obsessed with his wife. She's the one woman he continues to chase, even after 45 years of marriage, which sounds sweet except it means he never stands up to her. He'll take her side no matter what she wants. That loyalty, in turn, has a weird trickle down effect with the rest of the family. With Carlo gone, Emilio's both Giulietta's favorite *and* Lorenzo's heir...because Lorenzo is a tragic patriarchal old fart who can love, chase, and defend a woman for decades, but can't give power to the only one in this family—his daughter Bianca—who's genuinely trying to follow in his footsteps.

I've never understood their family dynamic or the decisions they make in the name of "keeping the peace." That wasn't an option in my family, although I wouldn't call what I had a family in the first place.

But their loyalty to each other is part of why I was drawn to the Russos, when they saved me. It's why I took the job they offered. I remember thinking to myself, *"I'd rather be a pet in their family than a daughter in mine."*

I never regretted that decision either, until Emilio whipped the cover away from that painting.

"Good, she's finally here."

We reach Lorenzo's preferred office on the far south side of the apartment where the family is already seated like some sort of Victorian painting, with Lorenzo at his desk, Giulietta smoking by the window, and Emilio and Bianca almost framing her where they sit on the couch.

It makes me wish I had my sketchbook, not that this is a moment to remember.

"Good afternoon, Mr. and Mrs. Russo," I say as Matteo finally steps away from me. "Bianca, Emilio."

"Did you speak with Enzo this morning?" Mrs. Russo asks right away.

"Yes, *signora*," I say. "He's acquired the Batari Wenda abstract and is taking it to the gallery in Berlin. The paperwork is signed. The trust just needs to wire the final payment."

"Very good, *passerotta*," Lorenzo beams. "She is an exceptional find."

My smile in response is genuine. I *was* really proud to find Wenda at a Southeast Asian juried exhibition back in October. She only had three pieces on display but I had an inkling about her, so I asked to visit her studio and lo and behold…she was a little master in hiding.

Too many artists forget that politics and personality can make or break them.

And even more are shy little things with debilitating imposter syndrome—I used to be one of them until I realized I wasn't good enough to be an imposter in the first place.

Which is why I like to visit artist dens, make them comfortable. Wenda. Malbec. There are gems hidden in plain sight all around us. They just need someone to find them and offer them the chance to shine.

"We would like you to acquire another of her pieces for an exhibition we want to host in April," Lorenzo continues.

My spirit trills a little at the request. Not just for Wenda's sake, but for myself. I'm the only person in the last ten years they've entrusted to run an event of this kind. If they're asking me to again, then maybe my job is secure no matter how the call with Ethan goes.

"Of course, *signore*, an exhibition is a lovely idea. I'll begin preparing right away."

"This time, you will do things right," Mrs. Russo cuts in. "Emilio and his work will receive the respect they deserve, without any tantrums."

I school my face carefully. "Yes, *signora*."

"And the painting we reacquire from Mr. King today will be a centerpiece."

I can feel another full-body flinch coming. At the last second, I tuck my hands behind my back and squeeze my fists to keep from giving anything away.

"Oh-kay."

I'm doomed.

"I've decided to make it part of a triptych," Emilio adds, surprising me. That's the highest-score Scrabble word I've ever heard him use.

But the snark in me dies pretty immediately. A triptych is a *three-panel artwork* that usually tells a story through progression from one panel to the next. He can't mean that he's painted me *more than once* and in *progressive poses* compared to the one I already saw.

I feel sick.

I want to vomit.

Literally, my mouth begins to water with dread. My eyes dart to Mrs. Russo, Mr. Russo, and Matteo in that order, looking for any sympathetic faces. The only kindness I find is on Matteo's face.

And then Matteo speaks and I realize he's doing it for my benefit. "You...exploring something in particular, Em?"

"I'm really challenging myself this time, doing a hard dive into 'the many faces of womanhood,'" Emilio says without *any* self-awareness whatsoever about how insane that sounds! What the *fuck* would he know about womanhood?!

"That will be the theme of the exhibition," Mrs. Russo clarifies, observing me through her cloud of smoke. "Of course, I will need to assess every piece in advance to ensure it meets our high standards, Ms.

Rathbone."

"...Yes, *signora*."

"I have no doubt it will be a triumph, *mi amore*," Lorenzo croons to his wife as he picks up the phone. "Now let us call Mr. King and be done with this. I have a meeting in Hell's Kitchen in an hour."

The ring of the phone fills the air as he puts the call on speaker, and for a long moment I almost wish I could call Ethan off. I wish I could bring myself to quit right now and refuse to be part of whatever future humiliation Emilio has in store. I wish I could threaten them with legal action if he paints me without my permission again.

But...I realize something tragic as we all wait in silence and my voice never erupts out of me to protect my dignity, my self-respect, my self-esteem. Kaden might be right about me. I might be a coward after all.

CHAPTER 27

NERO

I heard through the tap I put on Ethan's office phone that he's having a call with the Russos today, about the whole thing with Lulu's painting. And this morning, I watched Lulu have a mini meltdown in her apartment before her GPS disappeared into the subway.

I also...failed in my promise not to be a creep.

Completely out of my control, I swear.

But at two this morning, I got a motion alert on the smoke detector camera and opened the feed to find Lulu pulling a little battery-powered friend out of her bedside drawer.

I went to exit out of the feed.

My mouse cursor was literally poised over the X as her toy disappeared under her covers.

But then...she moaned.

Fuck-Fuck-Fuck.

I could only see shapes, suggestions of movements under the sheets, but her face.

The way her head tilted back.

The way her eyes fluttered shut.

She bit her lip as her pleasure deepened and I couldn't tear my eyes away.

She gave into her swelling bliss. Surrendered to it. Whimpered and then finally roared as her body erupted with joy, leaving me fucking transfixed.

And then…she did it again.

She waited all of two minutes and I heard the buzz hum back to life, heard the siren's call of her soft, breathy whimper.

I didn't touch myself. I showed at least that little bit of self-control. But I watched her go at it for *hours* until she *and* the vibrator conked out at the same time.

Fuck if I didn't want to offer myself as a replacement.

But when I heard Ethan talking about his call with the Russos, I realized she was fucking stressed as shit and there might be another way I could help her.

The fact that Ethan thinks his call with the Russos will happen without me there is laughable. Or it would be, if it wasn't another feeble attempt to lock me out of his life. For that alone—just to rile him into a fight we should have had the first day of my release—he couldn't keep me out if he tried.

But as I step into the Star-King offices, an anxious desire to leave again competes with my need to fuck with him. I've come in a couple times since I last saw Lulu in person, but each time has felt more pointless than the last. Ethan refuses to speak with me. He stays in his office whenever he doesn't have a meeting, and the windows are always frosted. Even his phone seems programmed to send me straight to voicemail. I think the only reason he hasn't outright blocked me is because he thinks I'll leave some incriminating message he can use against me to wrestle my share of his precious company away.

The irony is that if he just talked to me, I'd give it to him. If he'd just *have a fucking civil adult conversation with me*, and maybe let me put him in a headlock for half of it, he could have Star-King. I'm not going to tell him that; he's gotta come to me.

I've had better luck with Cara, who moves around the office a lot more, but I feel pathetic trying to go through my brother's girlfriend to get to him. And Cara's smarter than I gave her credit for initially.

Every time I ask her about him, her face softens with…knowing. The expression is so bald and piercing and unjudgmental, I feel embarrassed that she can read me so easily.

And then she puts her hand on my shoulder and imparts some tidbit about how he's doing, like she knows I need it. Like she wants us to be friends without betraying her intimacy with him.

She's already hinted at us getting dinner—the three of us—as soon as Ethan's removed the stick he shoved up his own ass. And she seems to know he's the only one who can remove it.

I've only seen them together a couple of times during my visits, but he's a whole different person with her. So...*aware* of her. Thoughtful, I guess the word is. And she's like a hug in human form.

Fuck, I hate that I like her for him. I hate it even more that I'm jealous of her...and what they have.

Despite never actually meeting Sam in person, I knew she never loved him, so it was no skin off my nose to remove her from his life. I thought if I got rid of Sam that he'd...that we'd...

Cara's different.

She asks me real questions each time we talk—questions about what I want that I'm never in the right headspace to answer.

I don't even know how to describe what I want. Except for him to stop treating me like he did when we were teenagers moving out of our dad's house. He didn't want to leave so I had to pin his arms down with mine and literally carry him down the porch stairs kicking and screaming to get him to go. Then he iced me out for three months. Didn't say a word to me, or Mom.

It's because he's 'the good guy.' He thinks he has the moral high ground to cast me out because of my supposed offenses against him. He thinks his life is so great because he's some paragon of virtue, does everything right, and the universe rewards him for it.

Which is, of course, absolute horseshit.

I learned a long time ago that life doesn't care how you want to live it. It'll blow you around like a piece of trash in the wind forever...unless you latch onto something that gives you purpose and begin charting your own course.

Which is what I did. What I helped Ethan to do, whether he'd admit it or not. *I* never got to go to college, did I, but I made sure he did. The extra-collegiate connections I helped him forge were integral to him being able to build Star-King in the first place, but god forbid I point that out.

That's why I've come today. If he only sees me as the 'black hat' to his white, then maybe if I show him that I actually *want* to help Lulu—that I'm capable of caring about someone other than myself—he'll stop icing me out.

A guy can dream.

I spot Cara and Ethan walking into the main conference room a second before they frost the glass. I cut through the bullpen and snag the lip of the soft-close door before it finally shuts.

"Good morning, Ms. Miramontes, Mr. King," I say, ignoring the look of frustration on Ethan's face that threatens to summon a petty smile to mine.

I drop into a seat as quickly as I can without looking desperate, so they know I'm not leaving. When the silence sours, I add, "Are we waiting on the Russos?"

"Yeah," Cara offers when Ethan doesn't. "They should be calling any minute."

"Where's Lulu?" I thought she'd be here.

"She's with them," Cara says, as Ethan leans forward and wraps his hand around hers on the table, as if in silent warning not to divulge too much.

But *I'm* the one who needs a warning squeeze. The thought of Lulu with the Russos right now makes my spine itch with dread.

"That seems dangerous," I say. "What if they retaliate when you tell them you don't have the painting?"

Cara's eyes widen with concern and dart in Ethan's direction and I can't tell how much she knows about Lulu's history with the Russos. Obviously, she knows Lulu works for them, but anyone with any insight at all into their various enterprises would already have been worried about her proximity to them.

"She'll be fine," Ethan says, more to Cara than to me. "Legally, they have no way to demand the painting back since I already paid. If they don't buy our excuse for why we can't give it back, then I'll act like a brat and refuse to give it up. They can turn their ire on me, okay?"

That soothes Cara's nerves, but not mine. "That's all nice and well, but they can still come for you *after* hurting her."

"Why would they hurt her?" Cara's tiny voice yips in pain.

"Nero!" Ethan snaps. "Why the fuck are you here? To make things worse?"

It's amazing how quickly I mute his twerpy little voice. I pull out my phone instead and look at Lulu's GPS tracker. The last ping shows her entering a building in the financial district before her cell signal disappeared. Discomfort rakes its claws down my back.

Then, like the dark messenger he's always been, the last person I expected to see today walks into the room. Valerian Fox—one of my oldest friends in the world and the guy who used to be one of my best employees before I went to prison and he bowed out of everything having to do with Omnisight.

Never has a name fitted anyone more. He moves with the slinky grace of his animal namesake, removing his coat and sliding it onto the chair beside me. Then he claps a hand on my shoulder as if there hasn't been an awkward silence between us since I got paroled. As if he isn't surprised to see me at all.

"Good day, family," he says in that accent that makes him sound like a British action star. "I see spirits are high this afternoon. We waiting on the call?"

"Yeah, any minute," Ethan says.

But I'm not waiting on jack shit. If Val is here, that means Ethan has likely been keeping tabs on Lulu too. Or at the very least, investigating the Russos to help her. So, I lay my phone on the table open to the GPS tracker.

"Lulu's there right now," I say to Val, shoving the phone his way. "Do you know anything about that building?"

"Are you…tracking her location?" Ethan's self-righteous tone grates on me.

"Like you're not?" I snap back.

"We have her permission, asshole," he says. "Do you?"

I can't focus on him when usually-stone-faced Val suddenly blanches. He's already pale enough without actually losing color to fear, but he pales anyway.

"Fuck," escapes him in a whisper.

"What? What's wrong?" Cara asks.

"It's…a processing building for them. They have several apartments there, but let's just say only one of them has a two-way door."

I'm on my feet before I can really think about it. Coat's on faster than that.

"Where are you going?" Ethan asks.

"Where the fuck do you think?"

"Relax. Let's just see what they say," Val says, always the mediator. "She's basically family to them. There's no need to escalate prematurely."

"Cara, I'm calling you right now," I say, ignoring him. Her phone rings a second later. "I'll mute myself so I can listen to the call on the way, okay?"

"Okay."

Ethan's face twists with confusion. "Nero—"

"I'll just go as insurance," I tell him. "Just in case."

I'm out the door before he can respond, but as I reach the elevator and press my phone to my ear, I'm surprised to hear Ethan say, "He'll be okay, right?"

"As long as he doesn't play savior," Val replies.

For a moment, warmth diffuses through me…until Ethan ruins it.

"He's fine then."

Self-righteous fucker.

"Shh, he might hear you," Cara whispers faintly.

"Oh, the dick hears everything I say…he just never listens."

CHAPTER 28

LULU

Ethan picks up the call on the fourth ring. There's a click, a throat cleared, and then he says, "Hello, Signore Russo?"

"Yes hello, Mr. King. It is good to talk with you finally."

"You as well."

"I know there was quite a...rush...the last time we saw you," Lorenzo says magnanimously. "We would have loved to speak with you about Emilio's painting before you left."

"Yes, I had an entire special night planned for my girlfriend, but once she saw that painting, I knew I had to get it for her before the evening could continue. I hope your family took no offense."

My eyes dart to Mrs. Russo and Emilio. Their expressions almost match as they sneer. They're not used to having to hold their tongues. Ethan's tone is quite convincing; they don't know whether to believe him or not.

Lorenzo seems the most surprised by what Ethan says. As if his wife whispered poisoned words into his ear before this meeting and Ethan has robbed him of ammunition.

"Oh no, no offense, of course," Lorenzo says. "But we do have a concern we wanted to discuss with you."

"By all means," Ethan says.

"My son is very proud of his work, and...well...he had hoped the painting would be displayed publicly in the future. Do you have any plans to do so?"

"Huh," Ethan says, as if the thought never occurred to him. "Signore Russo, I have to be honest with you, I own properties all over the world and I regularly acquire artwork for them. I've already sent the painting to my pied-à-terre in Paris."

Like a log popping in a fire, Emilio sits forward and grumbles, "That's bullshit, Pops."

Lorenzo's hand rises, demanding silence.

"You buy this painting for your girlfriend but then send it to France?" the Russo patriarch pushes politely.

"Yes," Ethan replies so casually. "Don't tell my girlfriend, but I plan to propose there later this year. I want to fill it with keepsakes from our time together to surprise her."

Emilio shoves off the couch like it's the only way to keep whatever he's feeling pent up. He rounds the couch and grips the spine as his dark gaze lands on me—

I tear my gaze away. The way he's standing… A memory I've long pushed to the darkest corners of my mind threatens to surface. I shove it back into the dark.

"It will be on display for my friends and guests," Ethan continues. "I hope that gives him some solace."

Lorenzo's gaze darts to his son, in question…Emilio shakes his head slowly, like a bog beast shaking moss off its neck.

"This is no good," Lorenzo laments.

"Oh?" Ethan asks.

"I'm afraid my son will be very disappointed. He spent many hours painting it, you understand. Too many for it to remain hidden away."

"I see."

"I am just a father, you understand," Lorenzo laughs lightly. "I try to keep my children happy. I am not always successful, but I try. In this case, I would request that you give us the painting back. We will, of course, refund you, Mr. King. And we can invite you to our next exhibition so you can invest in another piece."

Ethan is quiet for a long moment. A *long* moment.

"Hmm," he says finally. "I might end up in the doghouse for this.

Could you give me a bit of time to speak with my woman?"

"Yes, of course," Lorenzo says, raising his hand preemptively to stop Emilio from saying anything.

Thwarted, Emilio shoves off the couch and begins a strange circuit around the room…one I realize is leading him straight to me. It's like watching a slow-motion car wreck, one I can't avoid because if I move away, they'll take it as an insult. *He'll* take it as a challenge. My stomach plummets with fear, splashing acid into my throat.

But I stay put.

"Thank you," Ethan says. "I'll be in touch soon."

"Very good, thank you," Lorenzo finishes, ending the call. His eyes track his son, who I know has almost reached my side, even though I don't look that way. "You see that, *amore*? We will have this fixed long before the exhibition."

"We better," Emilio says, practically in my ear. He doesn't touch me, but he swerves around me so close, I can feel his cloying warmth in passing.

"Your father has handled it," Mrs. Russo echoes. "And if he hasn't, you and your model can simply work together again to recreate it."

It takes a moment for her words to penetrate and when they do, the full-body flinch hits me. Like needles across my skin. My eyes zip between Mr. and Mrs. Russo, unsure of what to say or do.

"Yes," Lorenzo says. "*Passerotta*, you would not mind, would you? Since you've modeled for my son before?"

My mouth pops open involuntarily. I can tell from Lorenzo's composed expression, he actually thinks that's what happened. They told him I modeled for *that disgusting painting*.

"Of course she doesn't mind," Mrs. Russo says. "Lulu's always been so grateful for the help we've given her. She's told me many times that she wants to pay us back."

"*Passerotta*," he says, almost moved. "That is not necessary, your wonderful heart is gift enough for me. You have always been like a daughter to us, and this will make Emilio very happy."

I feel sick. The vomit is rising. The pain in my clenched hands is almost numbing. But all I can do is nod.

Nod and say, "Let's just wait for Mr. King. I'm sure he'll get the painting back soon. I'd hate to waste Emilio's time."

"Yes," Emilio says, brushing his arm against me. "We'll be busy with my other paintings anyway."

"Good, that's settled," Lorenzo says, turning to his wife. "*Mi amore*, do you need more of me?"

"No, but Lulu and I will stay to discuss the exhibition."

"*Va bene*," he says, dismissing us all to our various fates.

But I can't stay here one more second, certainly not alone with Emilio and his mother, who in ten minutes have managed to stir a vile hatred in me, the likes of which I haven't felt for *anyone* in over a decade. All I want to do is break my fingers against Emilio's cheekbone. But I know I can't do it. I can't do it! So the only way out of this is *out*, to literally leave.

My chest tightens so painfully for a moment, I fully expect my chest bone to just crack in half under the pressure.

And then...

"Excuse me, sir," Matteo says. I turn to find him with his phone pressed to his ear. "Your boyfriend is downstairs, Lulu. He's causing a bit of a fuss."

As if someone reached into my chest and popped the balloon of tension, my breath whistles out of me with relief.

"Yes! My b-boyfriend. I told him to meet me outside, my apologies, *signore* Russo."

I feel Emilio flinch beside me, but I don't give him time to respond or ask questions. I don't even care who's out there claiming to be my beau. I'd take Pennywise at this point.

So I push. "This *is* my day off technically; I would hate to keep him waiting."

"Ah, yes, of course," Lorenzo says, as if it's the most understandable thing in the world. "We will see you tomorrow."

God bless that European respect for rest.

"Come, we'll walk you out." Matteo opens the office door for me, and I don't look back. I keep my face friendly and professional as I follow Lorenzo and Matteo down the hall to the elevator, and take my first breath since entering this building when the doors seal us in.

But I rethink my gratitude the moment we reach the ground floor and I see who's there.

Nero turns and stalks across the lobby like he owns it.

"Hey gorgeous," he says, leaning down and planting a tender kiss on my forehead before turning to greet Matteo and Mr. Russo. "Good afternoon, gentlemen."

"It is the man from the gallery," Lorenzo says, offering Nero a firm shake. "You are quite a surprise, so big!"

Lorenzo's voice is all Italian grandpa, the tone he uses to disarm people while still assessing them. Nero matches the same jovial tone as he shakes my boss's hand.

"Thank you. Lulu seems to like it."

"Treat her well," Lorenzo half-teases, half-threatens.

"Always, sir," Nero says with a smile that tickles deep parts of me.

He keeps that smile on his face as Lorenzo and Matteo walk out into the city, and I try to match it, hoping it disguises the wariness I feel.

After all, Nero shouldn't have known I was here.

And given how Ethan talks about his brother, I *know* he didn't tell Nero where to find me.

Which leaves only one possibility—Nero is keeping tabs on me, and not just digitally.

But I need to talk to him anyway, and if I don't focus on something else right now, I'm going to spontaneously combust.

So when he smiles at me and offers, "Dinner?" I slide my hand into his giant warm one and say, "Please."

"Sushi?" he asks, guiding us to the door.

I shake my head. "Let's get whatever you craved most while you were locked away."

His beautiful smile deepens. "With pleasure, Ms. Rathbone."

CHAPTER 29

NERO

She took my hand. It shouldn't matter, it might just be a gesture, but...now that it's enveloped in mine, it's all the excuse I need to deepen our connection. I intertwine our fingers as we reach the corner and pause for the crosswalk light.

My heart beats like a jazz drum when she doesn't pull away. I catch a smile on her face, but it's so soft I don't know if it's poking fun at me or sincere...and I want to know more than I've ever wanted to know anything in my life.

Until she frowns, peering up and down the street.

"Where are you taking me?" she asks.

"Do you want me to spoil it?"

"No, just...is it far?"

"A little. It's in Harlem."

"A *little*?!" she squeaks. Her other hand rises in plea, and I think she's going to say she no longer wants to go. She surprises me instead. "Gimme a second."

She has a handbag over her shoulder, which she drops down until it's balanced on our intertwined hands—the thing's *heavy*. She rummages for a second before pulling out a pair of black sneakers. They land by her feet as she reaches for one of her high heels, all while still holding my hand.

In fact, her hold on me only tightens as she uses me for balance.

"Sorry," she says.

"It's fine," I say, trying to hide the sudden tightness at the back of my throat.

"I hope you don't mind if I choose to be comfy as we walk."

I resist the dark, thirsty urge to tell her *I* can make her comfortable too.

So comfortable.

My tongue, my fingers, other parts of me too—she can take her pick.

Then I resist the urge to help her when she hops a little to get the sneaker heel in place. But, I give in half a second later, reaching down to scoop up her heels so she doesn't have to.

"Sorry," I say.

But the smile she rewards me with is so bright, I'm not sorry at all.

"Thanks, Big Guy."

She holds out the handbag for me to drop them in and I get a glimpse of a wallet and something that looks like a sketchbook before she shuts it again. Then the crosswalk light changes and she takes a step down from the curb before she suddenly stops and turns back to me.

"Is it okay that I call you that?" she asks. "Or does it bother you?"

"It's more than okay, Ms. Rathbone. The name suits me in ways you can't imagine."

I don't say the line as an innuendo. Not intentionally. *Big Guy* is what she called me on New Year's right after we kissed when I felt like a champion. *Big Guy* is how I felt when she craned her neck up at an angle to continue meeting my eye. *Big Guy* is how I felt when she ran her thumb over the '*need*' tattoo on my hand and something shifted inside me. I wanted nothing more than to be *her Big Guy*.

But pink spreads across Lulu's face, and I'm tempted to tell her the accidental innuendo also suits me.

We spend the next hour as we catch the subway to Harlem "clearing the air" between us.

"*That's* why you didn't call me?" I finally say when she reveals why. "You were embarrassed because I saw that painting?"

"Still am," she admits.

I'm struck with two wildly different, competing desires. Half of me just wants to haul her off her feet and, like, cloak her in my coat, against my chest, until that nonsense thought is long gone.

The other half wants to find a soft perch on which to splay her wide and lick her until she *knows* there's nothing to be embarrassed about.

But before I can respond, she adds, "I just didn't want you to pity me."

My brow arches at that. "Lulu, I don't pity you. I just want to know you."

Her hazel eyes stare at me for a moment before she turns away to hide a bashful smile, but she leans in and hugs my arm a little at the same time, and it's all the answer I need to know that dipshit Emilio didn't ruin the chance between us.

I make myself a silent promise not to ruin it either.

Especially when we reach our stop, and Lulu's eyes *light up* when she realizes which restaurant I'm taking her to. "No!"

"Yes."

"Amy Ruth's?!" she squeals with excitement, pulling me along. "You're a chicken and waffles guy?"

I groan loudly at the mere thought of the mouthwatering food I'm about to devour. "I had actual dreams about this place. Even cried once thinking about how long I'd have to wait for it. Thank God for early parole."

When our food finally lands in front of us—perfectly golden fried chicken with perfectly golden waffles, whipped cream and syrup—Lulu literally claps; her hands beat a tiny, excited rhythm at her chest as she thanks the waiter.

And I watch her dance a little as she tucks a napkin into the top of her blouse and reaches for a drumstick with her hands. The second I hear that crunch between her teeth and see the tip of her tongue flick out of her mouth to lick her lips, my body revs to life in some sort of perverted Pavlovian response.

The woman I want eating the food I want?

My cock hardens so fast, I flinch in my seat. Knock down the Brooklyn Bridge tomorrow, and you could replace it with the steel in my lap.

Dropping a napkin over it does nothing; if anything, it highlights it. My only saving grace is that Lulu can't see it from where she sits across from me. But she notices the shift in my body language.

Her round eyes widen with concern. "Is something wrong?"

"Ahem, no," I say, scooching my chair in. "Just being here. It's a lot."

"What do you like about this place?"

"It's where my brother and I used to come when we needed to escape our dad's house. We lived in the Bronx back then. Didn't have much, so we'd race each other here instead of taking the subway and split a plate."

She nods, and I catch a micro-expression on her face I don't think she even knows she's making. It's a tiny tell that says she's experienced that level of poverty before. Knows it well.

And a whistle of relief blows through me outta nowhere. I can't explain how comfortable I suddenly feel knowing we have that in common.

But I can't ask about that outright, so I go with, "Are you from New York originally?"

The corners of her eyes crinkle with sorrow. "No. Philadelphia."

"Do your parents still—"

"I don't like talking about that time in my life." Her voice brims with a politeness that's almost manic. Like it's an armor she throws on when things get too real.

"Sorry," I offer.

"It's okay," she says, regaining that happy-go-lucky quality I think might be camouflage. "T-Tell me about yours."

I bark out a laugh, catching her off-guard. Her eyes light up, though, as if she'd love to be in on the joke.

"If I told you about them, *you* would pity *me*, Ms. Rathbone."

"Oh no!" she croons. Her hand lands on mine so playfully. "Did we both win the shitty parent lottery?"

"Worst lottery in the world," I grumble, smiling with her. "Is it too late to return my ticket?"

"Yes," she says. "If you did that, you'd never have met me, so…"

That makes me smile until my cheeks hurt.

"Quite selfish of you," I tease.

"Didn't you know? Existential selfishness came in the lottery prize package."

"Damn, I…"

She called herself selfish so casually, as if she made peace with it a long time ago, and I've never heard someone admit that before. Existential selfishness. The concept sort of smacks me in the face; I couldn't name the ways in which I'm self-serving, but the moment she mentions it, my mind floods with examples that leech shame into me.

"What?" she asks.

"I just…never thought about that. Kinda threw me."

I feel small all of a sudden.

"Oh no," Lulu says. Her chicken drops onto her plate and she wipes her hands quickly. "I'm a hugger. Can I give you one?"

"Oh, sure."

The words have barely left my mouth when her chair screeches back and she darts around the table. She hugs me from the side and her arms only just reach my opposite shoulder. Still, she squeezes, with her cheek resting on me, and I could swear my heart jolts in my chest.

"I didn't mean to make you feel some kind of way. I can be a lot," she murmurs. "I know this is probably too early for this, but *please* feel free to be a lot around me. I like full-on people."

She releases me as if she didn't just drop some profound shit that's left me reeling. A second later, she's back in her seat, forking fluffy waffle into her mouth.

And I'm trying to make sense of her in the context of everything else I know.

She's nice. Kind. Might even be genuinely good. She's smart. Capable.

How does someone like her end up working for the Russos? How does someone like her *continue* working for them after what they did to her? I know Cara said Lulu does it for the art, but there has to be more to it than that. In my mind, there are only two possibilities—either she owes them for something, or they give her something she can't get elsewhere.

I didn't notice any drug paraphernalia in her apartment.

She doesn't have any debt.

Maybe she needs a different sort of help—

"I have something to confess, Nero," she says, pulling me from my thoughts. "I'm being a little existentially selfish with you right now and I hate that I have to be, but I do. I want to get that out of the way, so I can go on a proper date with you."

"Chicken and waffles not fancy enough for you, Ms. Rathbone?" I tease.

"Fancy, rustic, it's the story that matters to me."

"Really?" I croon playfully.

Her lips twist and she leans forward, "Would it surprise you if I told you I used to eat out of dumpsters, Mr. King?"

I eye her for signs of fibbing, but I know almost immediately that she isn't. It's just another...*fact*...she's accepted about herself.

"Why?"

"Not important, my good sir," she says, reaching for my hand. Her fingers curl around mine as she adds, "What *is* important is that I need your help."

It happens too fast to stop; my hand tightens around hers with something I only realize is longing after she's already felt it through our touch.

I expect her to pull away from the neediness of it, but she doesn't. She deepens her hold on me—the move eviscerates my self-control. I feel hypnotized, beholden to her somehow. Is beholden a word?

"I'm sorry to ask, but please hear me out," she offers. "I-I know you bought a film card from a photographer at the auction."

"I did," I say. "He just kept snapping shots of that fucking insult to you."

Seventy-two photos of that painting, in fact. I watched him snap that button seventy-two times before I stopped him. Fucking prick.

"Thank you. I think you might be the only reason I'm not a city-wide embarrassment. Maybe even farther than that. I noticed there aren't any photos of that painting online anywhere. Ethan mentioned that might be something you could make happen."

"I did," I admit. I could lie, but what would be the point? "It's not a big deal."

"It is to me. Thank you again."

I squeeze her hand on purpose this time, hoping she believes me when I say, "Hey. It was my pleasure, Lulu. That prick Emilio should *never* have had the chance to display it in the first place. He'll *never* get the chance to again, now that you've burned it."

She grimaces. "You know about that?"

I nod. "Frankly, you should've burned that painting and then burned their entire life down. Emilio's infatuation with you is dangerous. He's a spoiled brat who's never had to face any consequences. He sits outside your apartment building at least three times a week, for Christ's sake. It's a miracle he hasn't escalated things already. And it wouldn't even be hard considering you don't have any security measures in place."

I don't realize I overspoke until I notice how high her shoulders are against her ears. "How do you know…?" She flinches and waves that away. "It's not important right now. I just need the film card, Nero."

"Why?"

"It's complicated. I need a photo of that painting."

"For what?" The memory of what Cara said—that the Russos want the painting back—returns to me. "To give to the Russos?"

"Can you just trust me that it's important? I don't have much to offer you, but I can give you the five grand you spent on the film card."

"No, I don't need your money," escapes me like a knee-jerk reaction. "Do *you* need money? Do they have something on you? Are you in trouble with the Russos?"

"N-No," she says, and I can't quite tell if it's the truth.

So I push. "Are you sure? Cuz I'll give you twenty million dollars today if it means you stop working for that family." She tries to pull her hand away, almost in offense, but I hold tight. "I'm absolutely serious, Lulu. We can call my accountant right now, have it wired and cleared in your account by tomorrow, and then your life is *yours*, no matter how they own you."

At that, she snaps her hand out of mine. "They don't own me. Nobody owns me."

"No? Then how did they react when you told them how bad he hurt you?" I ask, knowing she likely didn't bring it up at all.

"It's just a point of pride for them."

Anger-flavored disappointment coats my tongue. "What about *your* pride? Why does yours matter less than theirs? I've seen this over and over again with abusive pricks like them. They come for your pride so they can call you ungrateful when you attempt to defend yourself. Then they act like you sinned against them in some other way so they get you chasing their approval. Until eventually, they've convinced you that taking care of yourself is selfish, and you're tying yourself in knots to "meet their needs" while they ignore yours."

"Whoa!" she almost yelps. "Projecting much? You don't know anything about my relationship with the Russos."

"You're right. Enlighten me."

She almost laughs at that. "What...you want everything? I've worked for them for over a decade. They've treated me well i-in the past. This was just o-one incident."

"Could you walk away from them tomorrow, Lulu?"

I can see the burst of panic as it shoots through her body. I push before she can say anything.

"Are you confident that they'll never let Emilio do that to you again? Or worse?"

She jerks her gaze from mine. "*Please* give me the film card."

"It's broken."

"What?"

Guilt streaks through me at her tone, she sounds devastated. But I don't back down.

"I broke it the second I made that guy hand it over."

"But…you have someone who took the photos down online, right? They could…undo that?"

"They could," I say. "If you tell me what they have on you."

"Goddamn it, Nero!" she almost pleads. "Giving them that painting back is *my* decision. It has to be *my* decision."

"But is it? Are you giving it back to them because you want to?"

"Yes!" she snaps.

Heads turn in our direction from across the dining room. I don't care. I want to keep our momentum going.

"Why?" I push.

"Because I owe it to them—"

She seems to realize she let something important slip and her whole body crumples before she finishes her sentence. All I want to do is reach for her—she needs that, she needs me, even if she'd never admit it—but I resist. This is more important.

"You're too smart to be this naïve," I tell her as gently as I can.

"Excuse me?"

"You should be spending your time extracting yourself from their hold on you, not trying to get in deeper with them. Unless I've totally misread you and you're some sort of mafia groupie."

"Fuck you," she says, although it hits with all the softness of a bean bag to the face.

"With pleasure, Ms. Rathbone," I offer—because this argument has my cock as hard as diamond. I'm about two seconds from apologizing on my knees right here in the restaurant just to convince her to take me home so we can have a…deeper conversation about all of this. Preferably while I'm pounding dopamine and oxytocin into her shuddering body.

Fuck, I want to make her feel so good.

But…I also want to make sure she's okay.

I push on. "I'd love nothing more than to hear you scream my name all night long. But I need to know you understand what giving them that painting back will mean."

"It'll mean my life doesn't implode," she says…but she's lying to herself. I can see it on her face, hear it in her voice.

I don't feel pity for her—that's not it exactly. It's still disappointment. She knows better.

"Lulu, the internet is forever," I say. "They'll put that painting on display for everyone to see. They'll talk it up. They'll show it off. Anytime someone googles your name, that painting will be connected to you. It's cruel, what they did. Just plain old cruelty."

Then I think twice about that. "Actually, it's worse. It's cruelty with a goal."

She doesn't want to ask, but I see the moment her resistance breaks as she says, "What goal?"

"Emilio wants his thumb on you. My guess is he's made passes at you before and you turned him down, right?"

She doesn't speak but her wayward eyes tell me I'm right.

"If you give him back that painting, he *will* own some part of you. It'll be like working with a knife to your heart for the rest of your life. With that painting, he can manipulate how every person you ever meet will think of you. It's not fair. It's not just. But it's true."

Once I've said that, I realize I can't give her what she wants. I won't. For her own good.

"And if you won't protect yourself, then you leave me no choice but to do it for you."

I expect another 'fuck you,' but what she says is infinitely worse and hits like a wrecking ball.

She sneers softly and rises from her seat, grabbing her bag in the same movement.

"Who's trying to control whom exactly, Mr. King?"

Then she walks right out the door.

CHAPTER 30

KADEN

It's some time between three in the morning on a Wednesday and seven at night on a Saturday when I decide I can't live like this anymore. I can't allow whatever creative block is fucking with my mojo to stay in place for a single minute longer.

I've wasted half a dozen canvases trying to paint...literally anything. A smear of blue. A splatter of green. A deer perfectly positioned outside, obscured by great big snowflake-shaped frost crystals on my window. All turned to shit on my canvases.

Louise is holding me hostage again. And it's my own damned fault. I called her a doormat—what the fuck did I think that would accomplish? I have no idea. She called me out for it and every inkling of inspiration I felt in her presence winked out.

"You first," was all she said in response to my insult, but she might as well have set the studio ablaze for how *torched* I felt after she left. How creatively blocked.

And, of course, I haven't been able to stop masturbating since.

Which wouldn't be a bad thing if I wasn't picturing the extended DVD director's cut version of our encounter in the kitchen. How my cock looked through her tights. How it felt against her silky skin. How her big round eyes stared at me when I touched her and how I watched pleasure swell in them until she finally burst.

In the extended cut, though, it doesn't end there. I take her into the studio and we paint each other's bodies and make art and love on the canvas. Then we wait for it to dry and hang it above the bed. Our bed.

I don't know if that'll ever happen now, but fuck if the thought of that scenario isn't motivating. Louise waltzed right in here and laid down the gauntlet for me to pick up; I just have to actually do it.

I'm standing naked in my bedroom with my phone set up to record video and Louise's *Hourglass* painting leaning just beside me in frame. My dick's standing at attention, my balls are tight and ready.

And yet, something's stopping me from just hitting record and giving part of myself to her.

It isn't even a failure to launch at this point; someone fell asleep at the controls so the machinery's in full gear, but nothing's actually happening.

Stupid.

Useless.

I'm giving myself blue balls while my cock just waves at me for attention…even though it's chafed from the eight times today I've already given myself a release.

And honestly, I don't know if she even wants this anymore. Maybe I missed my window. Maybe she'll think this is tone-deaf, considering what Emilio Russo did.

Disgusting sack of shit.

Just thinking his name has me wanting to pull out my toxic paints again. I think a poisoned painting would be very apropos. To abuse the art the way he did, to abuse *her* that way. He deserves to die by a thousand cuts.

I can't find out anything about the painting online, except a few statements regarding how vulgar it was. But the mentions I do find also say that the who's-who of the New York City art scene were in attendance, so he didn't just attack her, he set her body on fire and put it on display for the world to see.

I've never hated anyone like that.

And coupled with that thought is the still-unsatisfied desire to worship Louise like she deserves. She doesn't 'light up a room,' she robs it of oxygen when she leaves.

Then, it hits me.

I don't want to pleasure myself to the piece she painted. I want to "worship her with my cock," like she asked me to.

Moving a second later, I grab my phone and the ring light I set up like a dork to give my video some production value, and head for my studio. I shove junk out of my way until I reach the unfinished painting on my largest easel—Louise's painting. *Blue Ruin*.

I don't even care that I'm naked, the paint will go where it wills.

I only know that my fingers are twitching to pick up a brush for the first time in weeks.

I pop the lid on the half-full blue paint can and literally sigh with relief when I reach for one of my brushes and it fits into the well-worn grooves between my fingers.

I don't want to lie and say I paint faster and better than I ever have before. It's like riding a rusty bicycle for the first hour, but then I lose myself in the process, the smell of it, the quiet stillness of night when no one else is awake.

I spend hours getting her face right. That more than anything. I want exactly the right expressions there. Exactly her eyes. Exactly her lips.

Eventually, dawn creeps in around mc, a paler shade of blue ruin, and I'm forced to take a break so I can put more logs in the woodstove and tamp down the goosebump chill all over my body.

When I return, I take in what I've done. *Blue Ruin* still isn't finished—I only completed the three-fourths of the canvas Louise was actually here to pose for, leaving the last quarter blank for her second sitting—but it might be my favorite piece in years.

It's totally different from the rest of my work.

Maybe that's why.

I used blue ruin as the unifying color, mixing it into every other shade of blue, white, and black I used, and paired it with post-impressionism techniques, leaving the brush strokes noticeable, almost "chunky." I used these to give the painting a slightly three-dimensional quality, so each of the iterations of Louise look like they could step right off the canvas.

It doesn't have a veil, and I'm not going to give it one.

I don't want one there between us.

If anything, I want her raw and here and pressed like paint to my skin.

And that's how I know it's time to get this show on the road. That, and the fact that my dick is standing at attention again, just thinking about the paintings she and I might make together once I apologize.

Fuck, it's insane how hard that fantasy has me as I hit the record button on my phone and step back so both I and the painting are in frame.

I don't have any lube handy, and I almost spit into my hand…

But then I think, this is a special occasion. She deserves special treatment. The paint I used on her clothing was body-safe. I dart out of frame momentarily to grab the blue tube of body-safe paint I have; it's not the exact shade of blue ruin, but…I'm trying here.

Pouring a dollop into my hand, I get myself back into position, and imagine Louise sitting where the camera is, reclining on a chaise lounge or something, watching with a cheeky smile and curiosity and bratty neediness on her beautiful face.

"Go on," the phantom version of Louise teases. *"Show me what I'm missing."*

"With pleasure, Ms. Rathbone."

With that, I wrap my hand around my cock and begin to stroke.

CHAPTER 31

LULU

These past couple of days have been…brutal. It's like I slipped into a nightmare mirror version of my life where everything is topsy turvy and nothing quite feels real, but it's all painful and I don't know how to get myself back to my own dimension again.

After leaving Nero at the restaurant, I cried for about three hours straight, slept all night, then burst into tears the next morning just thinking about what'll happen when the Russos realize the painting is truly and permanently gone.

That, and the fact that every single person I care about seems to think I'm a coward for trying to hold my life together instead of letting it fall apart. It's not their fault that they don't know the real reason I'm scared to start again, but…damn. Everything Nero said to me made me feel like my life is over anyway.

I'm damned if I replace the painting, damned if I don't.

And until the Russos fire me, I still have to work for them and pretend everything's okay.

I got the waterworks under control by the time Mrs. Russo called to send me on a wild goose chase around the city looking for the perfect place to hold their "*Faces of Womanhood* Exhibition."

Bleck.

She chose a recently gentrified old meat-packing plant. *A meat-packing plant!*

What. the. fuck doesn't even come close to how I felt showing up to that place. Dread—just so much dread filled my stomach.

Phone in hand, video chatting with her as the guy gave us a tour, I already knew she'd pick it before she finally said so. And when she did, I had to swallow my bile and smile while she could see me on camera and accept that this was my reality for the foreseeable future...

Until they fire me because the painting is gone.

I can't stop worrying about when it'll happen because it's coming; I've already ignored three texts from Emilio about scheduling a modeling session for his other paintings of me. There's only so long I can pretend to not see his messages before he'll sic his mommy on me.

I have no idea what to say to her when she asks. Suppose I could use the proper Italian word—*vaffanculo!*—to tell her to go fuck herself. Why not? She would take "No, I won't do it," as an insult too.

It's just all awful, you know?

But I can't wait for the Russos to torpedo my life. After seeing that text exchange between Mrs. Russo and the *ArtForum* editor, I have to make some big moves now before they call up the other bajillion people they know and burn every bridge I built for myself.

Which is why I've invited Cara and Ivy over to my apartment for an emergency strategy session. They're the only people I trust implicitly with my life, my soul, my heart. They're also just really clever women. Like resource-poor MacGyvers.

"Hello, sweetie," Ivy says when I open the door and find them both holding takeout bags and bottles of wine.

"Hey Lu," Cara adds, giving me a hug I desperately need.

"Thank you for coming." I groan as the succulent scent of barbecue—burnt ends and brisket and macaroni and cheese—hits my nose. "Oh my God, is that *Hometown*?"

"You know it, baby," Ivy says, heading into my kitchen to grab plates. "We are going to scheme in style."

It takes less than ten minutes for us to plate up, pour wine, and collapse back onto my sofas with audible groans of comfort and relaxation—nothing beats people you can just be yourself around. And I finally unwind listening to them talk about Ivy's latest trip to Paris.

"I signed all the paperwork while I was there, so…I officially own a pastry shop in the seventh arrondissement, right off the Rue du Bac."

"Ivy! That's so great! Congratulations!" Cara says, almost bouncing. "We'll have to come visit you as soon as you're settled, right Lulu?"

"You couldn't keep us away," I tease, even though it isn't a joke.

"You two are always welcome, you know that," Ivy murmurs, her voice shyer than normal.

"You okay, babe?" Cara asks.

"Oh yeah, just…" Ivy says, "I had my first…I don't even *know* what it was. Like a turf battle? Anyway, Hugo and I were taking measurements when this guy walked right in and started picking apart *everything* in the shop."

"The *empty* shop?" I ask.

"Yeah. He didn't like the crown molding—which has been there since 1867—he didn't like the display cases Hugo chose. He just had something to say about everything, had no regard for personal space. I had to ask him to back up twice. I think I was lucky Hugo was there."

Hugo. The mysterious businessman who walked into Ivy's award-winning patisserie in Brooklyn one Tuesday morning and changed her life forever; the man who *brazenly* and *lavishly* tempted Ivy to uproot her entire life and open a shop in Paris.

The man neither Cara nor I have ever met.

"I want to hear more about *Hugo*," I almost sing. "Sounds so dreamy."

"No," Ivy chides as a blush pretties her cheeks.

"Or how about Ethan?" I tease again, glancing at Cara. "And his promise to propose to a certain friend of ours this summer."

"Hush," Cara dismisses that.

"What?!" Ivy squeals.

"Yep," I say. "He told Mr. Russo."

"Cara! Do you think you'll say yes?" Ivy asks.

"It was just part of the excuse we used to buy Lulu time," Cara says. "It wasn't real."

"What if it was?"

"It's not," Cara says, but her gaze darts away and I can't tell whether she's worried what Ethan said might be true or that it isn't. "I'm still legally married to Troy anyway. Either way, what matters *right now* is helping *you*. So, let's get back to that, thank you."

I groan, forcing myself to sit up a little straighter. Ivy and Cara have listened to me talk more about the Russos these past couple of years than anyone or anything else in my life. Pfft—*what life?* That family has *become* my life!

"It's so stupid," I admit. "I feel embarrassed, but I need help, and I honestly don't know what to do. If I did, I wouldn't trouble you guys with more Russo stuff. I know I'm like a broken record at this point."

"Maybe just a little bit," Ivy teases.

"Thank goodness we like your music, babe," Cara adds, smiling at me.

It doesn't take as long as I thought it would to tell them that I went to both Nero and Kaden for help, and that I don't think there's any way to replace the painting now. It also doesn't take long to tell them that the Russos expect me to *pose* for Emilio's next humiliations.

But I go a step further and tell them about the Russos' proposal to me on Emilio's behalf and that Nero thinks Emilio is camping outside my apartment.

"He's *what!*" Ivy yelps as she lurches to her feet and shuts the curtains tight. "Friggen pervy fuck. You are absolutely not posing for him. Not without both of us and several bodyguards present."

"Not even then!" Cara yelps, her eyes wide with shock. "You have to quit, Lulu. Enough of this. You had a good run with them and I know you're...attached to them, but you told me for years that Troy wasn't good for me and I didn't listen and look how that turned out."

"Pretty great, if Mr. Green Eyes is any indicator," Ivy teases. That has become Ethan's nickname when we're on our own. "Although," she adds, turning to me. "It sounds like Lulu might have a Mr. Green Eyes of her own now, if Nero King's walkin' around calling himself your boyfriend and using his cyber-whatever company to save your reputation."

Cara must've told her what happened the other day.

But neither knows what happened when I went to dinner with him. I open my mouth to tell them, but Cara speaks first, diverting us to more serious topics.

"Honey, I think they're trying to punish you."

"Who?"

"The Russos," Cara says.

"I know. The whole posing thing—"

She cuts me off with a shake of her head. "You turned down their son. I know you think they were okay with it, but...I'd guess most families wouldn't be. Most relationships don't survive a rejected proposal."

"Not even one where his mommy proposed for him," Ivy adds.

"That's not fair!" I almost meow the words. "Why did they have to ruin what we had?"

"Who knows?" Cara offers. "Whatever the reason, it's not your fault. And I am so sorry they made it your problem."

"I'm fired the second they realize that painting's not coming back, so I'm...mourning that as I go." That's a polite way of saying I've taken to randomly bursting into tears at all hours of the day just thinking about it. "But...what do I do about the other paintings he's going to put up? And how do I save my relationships with the artists if the Russos try to blacklist me?"

"Well, the artists should be easy," Ivy says. "Get ahead of it, yeah? Go talk to every single one you can. Especially the ones who were there New Year's Eve and saw that painting. The Russos may know a lot of people, but I don't believe they'd all shun you just because that family told them to. These are *artists*, babe. And they're people who know and respect you. I'd bet a ton of them would stand by you if it came to it."

"At the very least, if you talk to them, you'll have a better idea of who's on your side," Cara adds.

I can't argue with them. Maybe facing that fear head-on is the only way to alleviate it. And I'd love to know if Sarah Stout was an outlier or not.

"Maybe hint that you're looking for work too when you talk to them," Ivy continues. "All it takes is one job offer and that's one massive weight off your shoulders."

Panic spikes through me like a sun flare. "I don't even know what I want to do."

"What do you mean?"

There's one thing I've never told my friends and it's the same thing I've withheld from every other person I've ever met...save Lorenzo and Carlo Russo. And the only reason those two are the exception is because I wouldn't be here if they didn't know.

All Cara and Ivy know about my childhood is that it was terrible, and that I left home early. They know I struggled for a while until I got a scholarship to RISD and they know the Russos recruited me as soon as I graduated. That's all I felt comfortable telling them, and they accepted the story for what it was—a sanitized blurb hiding all manner of other horrible things that happened.

By the time I trusted them enough to even *think* about telling them the truth, I didn't see the point. I'd finally made peace with what happened to me.

Or maybe I was just scared, since it's the sort of thing that can't help but forever alter how people see you.

Let's just say I didn't wake up as a twenty-three-year-old woman and decide to be an art advisor for one of the largest crime families in North America. It was the job they offered me to save me from a shit situation. It was a lifesaver they threw me. One I held onto for dear life for ten years. It gave me security, protection, a chance to build a life for myself.

And I got addicted to that safety.

I got addicted to the way they treated me as one of their own.

I *liked* belonging to a real family. Sue me.

The saddest truth is, if Carlo were still around and Mrs. Russo had asked me to marry *him* instead of Emilio, I would have seriously considered saying yes. Not because Carlo is spectacular—I never lusted after him or anything—but because I know he's a good and decent man down to his core, where it counts. I would never have reason to doubt he'd care for me or try to change the shape of me. Whereas I'd doubt that every day with Emilio.

"Art advising isn't exactly my calling," I tell them instead of all that. "I really love being in the world and helping people, so maybe a museum might hire me?"

"Or you could go back to painting." Ivy almost sings this against the rim of her wine glass before she takes a sip, but she stares at me pointedly the whole time.

"That's not what I'm supposed to do," I say, waving that away.

"Why?"

"Ivy, shh," Cara says.

"No, I want to hear her say the nonsensical thing again so we can tell her—*again*—that she's being nonsensical. Louise Rathbone—lover of art and life and love and sex, mini-powerhouse of creativity—dimmed her light because *some professor* back in college told her she wasn't any good."

It wasn't a professor, but the rest is true.

"That's *nuts*, girl," Ivy chides.

"Ivy!" Cara hisses again.

"Fuck that guy, whoever he was. Fuck him with a red-hot poker. *No one* should be telling a *student* that their work isn't any good. Certainly not a teacher. Art is the thing you love most in the world, Lulu, and you stopped expressing your own because of one dickhead ten years ago."

Dickhead is underselling it, but again…I just can't bring myself to tell them the truth of who he was, or how the Russos saved me from him. Maybe they would understand my situation better if I did, but fear nibbled holes in my courage long ago.

"Whatever you choose to do," Cara says, shifting the conversation, "Just don't sell yourself short, okay? Look at me. I…I'm doing all these incredible things now that I thought I couldn't."

I smile, gesturing to Ivy. "I think we both owe Ethan an edible arrangement for that."

But Cara shakes her head gently, "I owe you two, too. You and Ivy protected me for so long in my marriage. And you're a *huge* reason why

I didn't completely fall apart when it ended. You're both one of the best parts of my life, you know?"

That makes me want to cry. But I'm all cried out today, so I leave my half-eaten plate of food on the coffee table and dart around to give her a hug.

"Ivy and I will do everything we can to help you set up your new life away from that family, okay? The bigger issue, I think, is stopping him from humiliating you again."

"No," Ivy counters. "Not just stopping him. We need to give him a taste of his own medicine."

"Oh," I flinch at that. "I would if I could. But...these are powerful people, Ivy. We need to be careful—"

"I agree," she interrupts. "Careful, brutal, and precise."

A twinkle appears in Ivy's eye a second before Cara asks, "...what are you thinking?"

"I have an idea, but...you might need Nero King's help to pull it off."

CHAPTER 32

NERO

Today has been about as big a shitshow as I've ever had. I spent the morning at Star-King, sitting in on company meeting after company meeting in which Ethan ignored my existence as if one glance my way would turn him to stone or something. After that, it was a virtual board meeting with the heads from other branches of the business. He ignored me virtually too, and any time I posed him a question someone else had to chime in to answer.

It was funny the first three meetings I was on with them.

Now, anger is starting to creep in. Anger and resentment because it's better than acknowledging the real emotion I feel about his continued stonewalling. I've tried catching him at odd hours as he leaves his home or the office. I've even resorted to shoving little notes under his door hoping he'll read them.

I need him to talk to me.

I hate that he won't.

I hate it more that I watch his face constantly during those meetings and I never see anything resembling curiosity or interest. All I see is the anger I feel reflected back at me.

Fuck, I don't know how to fix this. But I won't fucking sell my forty percent of Star-King unless he talks to me.

Not one fucking percent of my shares.

The rest of the day I've been here, at Omnisight, dealing with a…situation…I really fucking hate. It's the worst part of this job. It's the worst part of being human, frankly.

And it's something I wish I could share with Ethan, because I think he'd understand a lot of who I am if I could show him this. If he just showed an interest in what I do.

He seems to think I'm some scummy hacker trying to rule the world from an alpine lair or something. He doesn't know that half my business is contracting to various agencies for humanitarian purposes.

Don't get me wrong, I do it for the money and data. Mostly. But it's also my way of guaranteeing I *don't* turn into the villain Ethan has made me out to be in his head.

A year and a half ago, I found out some shady shit about Ethan's former partner Vincent Star. He liked to frequent a certain warehouse in Jersey, one with a reputation for being a dark playground for human depravity. It's not a place that opens very often, but when it does, they pull out all the stops for their clientele.

Star's preferred fantasy was waterboarding women while he fucked them. The kink itself—if that's what he called it—isn't illegal, but it's rare enough he had to turn to a black-market entity to find women "willing" to do it. Let's just say the women they found weren't exactly free-range. Not to mention the kink is obviously very risky...and it eventually went sideways for him and his victim.

Had I been out of prison and free to do something about it, I would've called the cops, but my guys don't do that without my say-so and there was no contingency in place to make that call without me. It was an oversight I've spent the last fourteen months feeling guilty about.

I used the video footage to buy my share of Star-King and have been ruining Mr. Star's life in other ways ever since. But I've also continued filming the warehouse, recording faces, gathering intel.

Today was the day we sat down with one of our government contacts to discuss how to handle the warehouse and everything it stands for.

It took hours.

Hours of reviewing key pieces of footage.

Hours discussing ways to attack the problem, and the potential fallout of doing so.

The often-lamented truth about doing things the legal way—especially when they began by illegal means—is that it takes time. So much fucking time considering how quick a sting operation with AK47s would handle things.

And those hours of *talking* with our government contact resulted in us agreeing to help collect more evidence to build a bigger case against whoever's running the warehouse before doing anything about it.

As if watching women get brutalized isn't enough reason to intervene.

No, "catching the assholes at the top" matters more.

I fucking hate this world sometimes.

Doesn't mean I can't ruin the lives of the perpetrators I can identify in the video footage, which is what I told our team we're doing.

I've been sitting here for three hours going through old footage, collecting faces like a serial killer or some shit. One of them will lead to the "top asshole" eventually, but in the meantime, we can conduct a little target practice with the peons lower down on the totem pole.

It's *something to do*.

I know Lulu thinks I want to control people, but that's not it exactly. The real thing I want is more shadowy, even to me. It's right there in the darkness waiting for me, but I'm too much of a coward to step into the dark and find out what it is.

The footage isn't the only thing I'm watching on my screen. Half of it shows a live feed of Lulu's apartment, her living room where she's eating dinner with her friends. I'm sort of listening as I go. Apparently, they call Ethan "Mr. Green Eyes," and Ivy teases that I might be Lulu's Mr. Green Eyes.

I like the sound of that.

But then Ivy mentions "some dickhead professor" from Lulu's past who knocked the wind out of her sails. Pausing the warehouse footage, I turn my full attention to the women in Lulu's life. I can tell Lulu is hiding something about this guy from her past, something even her friends don't seem to know. He's a clue to her grander puzzle—one I will absolutely solve.

She doesn't indulge that part of the conversation, though, and it drops before I learn any more. Then the conversation moves to more fertile ground.

"I have an idea, but…you might need Nero King's help to pull it off."

"I'm listening," Lulu says.

"You need to *nuke* any attempt Emilio might make to ruin your reputation after you quit working for them," Ivy says.

"Yeah, which is impossible," Lulu replies. "He could paint me at any point."

"And then you could sue," Cara suggests.

But Lulu shakes her head. "With what money, you know? And I'd probably lose, so not only would I draw attention to the Russos *and* piss them off, it wouldn't even do anything. It'd probably only make him paint me *more* and *worse*, if that's even possible."

"No, babe." Ivy's eyes are so bright with excitement I can literally see the gleam on my screen. "Here's what you do. This exhibition is called "*Faces of Womanhood*" right?"

Lulu dry heaves playfully. "Gross. Yes. Continue."

I chuckle and so do the women.

"What if that face is…you?" Ivy says. "What if it's *only* you? Or mostly you. Mrs. Russo signs off on the artists, right?"

"Yeah."

"What if once she signed off, you went to every artist and told them what Emilio did, then asked them to paint you? What if Emilio showed up on the day and his paintings don't even stand out? They're just one of dozens—all respectful, all paying homage to the glory that is Lulu Rathbone."

Lulu's mouth opens and shuts in surprise as she mulls it over. "I…couldn't *make* them do it."

"No, but maybe you could incentivize them."

"Ooh," Cara says in realization. "And that's where Nero comes in."

"Exactly," Ivy says. "If he's willing, you could ask him to, like, *saturate* the web with the paintings of you and information about the artists, boosting their profiles in the process. That way, even if Emilio tries to retaliate or humiliate you, his pieces are just *other paintings* that come up when people google your name. *You* become the Great Muse who inspired a thousand artists."

"You'd get to control your own narrative," Cara says. "Ethan's teaching me about that. They try to get control of the narrative when clients have scandals."

That's brilliant. It would completely neuter the Russos' power over her.

Several hours later, on my walk home through Manhattan, I find myself anticipating her call. Lulu said yes to the plan. She said she'd call me, and I'm so fucking impatient to be her go-to guy, it feels like I have ants crawling around in my shoes. I'm just waiting for her to fire the starting pistol and I'll make her the most renowned and respected muse from here to Taiwan. There won't be an artist alive who isn't begging to paint her and add one more link to her armor against Emilio.

Hell, I have an idea for how to take their plan even farther.

But a runaway thought nearly ruins my anticipation.

Lulu and I left things on a sour note the other night.

I told her I wouldn't help her remake the painting.

What if she thinks I won't help now with this plan? What if she hesitates to call? Or decides not to call at all?

Fuck. She needs me. *She needs me.*

I can't stand the thought of not being the one she calls.

So, I do the only thing I can think to do. I take out my phone and send her a text, one I hope will at least make her less reluctant to reach out.

Lulu, I'm sorry I can't give you the photo you want, but I'm here if you ever need any other kind of help. I mean it.

I hit send and listen to the little *woosh* noise of the message zooming away into the void. Then I go to tuck my cell away in my pocket, but I never get that far. There is an immediate *ping*—a response.

The phone almost flies out of my hand as I bring it out again to check, but I almost wish I hadn't when I see her reply.

Do you have your eyes on me right now, Mr. King?

Fuck.

She knows I'm watching her.

CHAPTER 33

LULU

I'm laying in bed, staring at my phone screen, waiting on bated breath for Nero to text back.

Waiting to see if he'll admit he's spying on me.

He knew where I was meeting with the Russos.

He knew Emilio sat outside my apartment every other day.

And he said too many little things at dinner that left me wondering whether he takes his work home with him from time to time.

But the text he just sent me? He offered to help only hours after my friends and I came up with a possible way to save myself from ruin *with his help*. I don't believe in serendipity nearly as much as I believe that a man who spies on people for a living might be spying on me.

After all, he has the technology, the training, the inclination. It's too much of a temptation, I would bet, not to watch people. And it doesn't take a psychic to know Nero King wants me.

So, when he doesn't answer right away, I call him and wait.

Eventually, a click lets me know he's on the other end of the line, but he doesn't speak. I wonder where he is right now, if he's in front of a computer or if he has a spying app on his phone.

"Can you see me, Mr. King?"

I glance around my bedroom. Everything looks as it always has, not that I'd know what a hidden camera looks like. Every man who's ever watched me did it in person, when my old "professor" allowed it.

He said that "rarified" me. Made the experience of me more

interactive. Because he could tell me how to pose, tell me how to touch myself for them.

If that's what Nero is hoping for, I suppose I can give him what he wants. With a quick flick, I take hold of the corner of my duvet and send the whole thing fluttering to the floor. I'm in a simple black cropped shirt and purple hipster underwear to sleep tonight.

"I didn't know I'd have an audience," I say quietly. "If you had told me you were spying on me, I could have dressed up for you. Made this special."

Still, he doesn't speak and I wonder if I'm wrong that he's watching. I don't think I am; he would have corrected me by now.

It's a strange thing, the heady swirl of emotions I feel knowing he's watching. Knowing he violated my privacy to put cameras in *my* private, sacred space.

On the one hand, I'm curious to know what excuse he'll use to justify it. Protection? Lust?

On the other, indignation flames in my stomach as if I swallowed a hot coal. It wants me to yell at him, shame him, even though it knows there's probably no point. There's something about nudity that makes men think they own you...and our fucked-up world lets them think that. Enables that. Sometimes encourages it. There's something ironic about seeking help from one pervert against another.

"Is this what you want, Nero?" I ask, bending my knees a little and then parting them, flaring them wide like butterfly wings until they're flat against the mattress.

I slide my hand across my partially exposed stomach and tease the waistband of my underwear with my fingers before dipping within. On pure muscle memory, almost automatic now, I bring my fingertips to my clitoral hood and begin a gentle caress there, teasing, light, but exaggerated. Just enough so he'll see the movement through the fabric, if he's watching.

"Tell me the truth. Did you put cameras in here to watch me do this?"

CHAPTER 34

NERO

I'm frozen on the spot on some random Manhattan street when Lulu reaches for her panties. When her slender fingers disappear inside and begin to move.

I...can't look away. I want to.

No, I don't, but I should.

I know I should.

Fuck, I just don't. I opened the live feed on my phone the second our call began and now my eyes are glued to it like I'm watching a hostage video. Except the hostage is me. Me and the fucking monster between my legs trying to tear itself free of my pants. If I wasn't wearing a heavy coat, someone would probably have me arrested for public indecency.

"Is this what you want, Nero?" Lulu's voice is breathless and low; the sound caresses my brain and my balls simultaneously.

But then she says, "Did you put cameras in here to watch me do this?"

The reality of what a fucking creep I am comes crashing back down around me, times two when I remember I'm on a public fucking street watching this shit.

I can only thank God I had the wherewithal not to put the call on speaker. I pop in an airbud instead, almost tripping as Lulu's touch hastens and her voice mewls loudly in my ear.

"I can hear you there listening, you know," she says, which I know is a lie because I haven't taken a breath since this started. "Why don't you tell me what you want me to do?"

Fuck. Her words grip me low in my abdomen, tugging at the root, and a grunt of pure lust escapes before I can stop it, giving me away.

She coos, victorious. "Hey, Big Guy."

Still I can't respond. The second she knows I'm here, her hand leaves her panties and travels north, sliding slowly across the front of her shirt until she pinches the fabric and draws it up-up-up. One pink peak makes its debut, followed by the other.

There's a chill in her apartment.

It's incredible how fast the thought of being the warmth she needs gets my feet moving. I spot a taxi and I don't think I've ever hailed a cab harder in my life. Or navigated my mute button faster. As soon as my ass hits the back seat, I give him the only address that matters right now—the chilly apartment in Brooklyn where a siren calls out for my heat.

Then I turn my attention back to my phone.

"Can you see that?" Teasing herself, she tweaks her nipple in passing as she returns to touching between her legs. As she writhes for my pleasure, for me. "What do I look like to you?"

Fucking perfection, I restrain myself from saying.

"A painting perhaps?" she asks. "Is that what you want? To know whether Emilio painted me properly or not? No bruises on my chest, as you can see...You want me to take my panties off so you can decide how much I'm worth to you?"

And just like that, shame strikes my chest like a flaming arrow.

I don't want her thinking of Emilio and I in the same *breath* let alone the same category of perversion. My blood *boils* at the thought of her comparing me to that asshole.

I open my mouth to argue that I'm nothing like him—that I would *never* show this footage to anybody, that I'm watching for her protection—when she cuts me to the quick.

"Let me guess, this video is just for you. And it's different if *you* want a picture of me, right? *Your* intentions are pure. You'd never use this against me."

Fuck. I-I...I think I might be scum. How is what I've done any different than painting a picture of her without her permission? In the wrong hands, this footage would hurt her just as much.

"How does it feel to own me? Do you like it? Is it everything you dreamed it would be?"

Molten self-hatred pours through my body and I have half a mind to make some limp apology before disappearing from her life forever.

But then I realize I can't vanish from her life as a coward. I can handle a lot of things, but that's not one of them.

Pulling a wad of cash out of my wallet, I tap on the taxi's partition instead. "Hey guy, get me there in half the time and there's a thousand dollar tip in it for you."

CHAPTER 35

LULU

"Is it better than actually having me?" I whisper, still listening, still hearing nothing on his end. I haven't heard anything since he grunted, but that sound…mmm. I was just dry-rubbing myself before; now I'm so slick, I'll have to finish myself off when the call ends.

Which is a shame considering Nero could be here right now, doing this for me. Instead, he chose to watch. If I knew that was his fetish—if he included me, if he'd earned my trust—it would be different. I'd be giving him an even better show than I am now.

As it is, I don't know how to take this. What is it about me that makes men want to engage with some sort of prophylactic between us? It's becoming something of a pattern—Nero with his cameras, Kaden with his veils, even Emilio with his paintings.

I mean, I'm *right here*! I offered fun and friendship to Kaden *and* Nero. Even Emilio might have had a shot if he just came at me directly, offered me *a date, a conversation, anything normal*. Hell, I probably would've voluntarily posed for him, if he'd just asked.

Almost in response to my internal argument, my mind tosses out a tiny revelation that makes me laugh.

The men in my life are like clitorises—capable of making a woman happy if given a helpful fucking hand. I would happily tell them how to please me if they would *just ask*.

And actually listen to what I say.

"I'm right here, Nero," I continue after a long while of just pleasing myself with the phone pressed to my ear. "Why would you rather watch than actually be with me?"

Knock-Knock-Knock.

I jerk upright in bed like a spring-loaded toy. Phone to ear I whisper, "Is that you?"

Knock.

Knock.

Knock.

A flush of excitement washes through my body as I scramble to my feet. Almost skipping, I reach the door in seconds.

It *is* him. Nero barely fits in the viewing window of my peephole. His massive frame almost blocks out the hall light behind him, haloing him like some sort of dark angel.

I wonder how he got past the front door buzzer.

I wonder if he's watching me watch him right now.

I wonder if it'd be uncouth to just yank him in and have my way with him against the door.

Fuck, I know it's shameful, what he did. I want to yell at him.

But I also want to fuck his brains out. I want to self-medicate with a dick the size of the Titanic wielded by a captain worth the sinking.

Knock.

Just one knock this time tells me he knows I'm right here. My diaphragm tightens with anticipation as I yank open the door. My gaze finds his automatically, landing on the apologetic bent of his face and the gleam of something hungrier in his eye he's trying to tamp down. For a long moment, we just stare at each other, waiting to see what the other will do.

But it's not my turn. It's his.

"May I come in, Ms. Rathbone?"

"Yes."

Nero steps inside, a pillar of darkness that almost disappears into the shadows the second I close the door. He doesn't say anything else. He simply turns, walks down the hall, and disappears into my bedroom. I hear a squeak, see the edge of the bed move. For a second, the fantasy of walking in to find him arranged naked on the bed for me flashes in my mind. But that wouldn't match the expression on his face. And as sexy as the thought of him offering himself to me is, I don't want the humbled version of Nero in my bed tonight. I want the version who got hard watching me eat fried chicken, who looked like he wanted to eat *me*.

More noises lure me closer until I reach the open doorway to find his shoes set to the side and the giant man himself standing on my bed finagling with the smoke detector.

"What are you doing?"

The answer gleams at me from his hand. He reaches up with a pair of clippers and *snips* through a wire inside before tucking the pieces away and fitting the lid back on.

That's where the camera was. Right over my bed. He saw everything tonight and a lilt of excitement streaks through my center begging me to ask him if he liked what he saw.

But I know better than to let my clit talk for me. At least at first.

"You couldn't have just *asked* if I wanted cameras?"

In the pale light streaming through the window, I catch sight of a frown on his face. "When you left with Ethan that night and never answered my calls, I thought he'd told you things about me. Thought it might take weeks to earn your trust if you listened to him. I didn't want to leave you unprotected."

So 'protection' is his excuse. I roll my eyes lightly. "Uh-huh."

"I was going to wait until you invited me over and convince you that you needed to update your security measures. Then I would have replaced the cameras with other cameras so you never knew they were there all along."

I sort of stare at him for a moment. I admire the honesty, but my mind fritzes a little trying to decide how that would be any better.

Until he adds, "If I had known the real reason you weren't talking to me was because you were embarrassed, I would've been at your doorstep a lot sooner, Ms. Rathbone. I would've eaten you out like the homecooked meal I've craved for the last five years."

Fuck, what? I am...*way* too wet for that sort of talk. I don't even know what to say to that...because the only thing that comes to mind is *table for two, your order is hot and ready.*

Nero steps down off the bed. "There are two more outside the window watching the street. Can I leave those?"

"You put cameras watching the street?" Something about that cools some of my anger.

"Yes."

"You can leave them."

With a nod, he scoops up his shoes and passes by me, planting a soft sparkling peck of a kiss right on top of my head as his low voice rumbles, "I am sorry, Lulu."

He might as well have put a leash on me for how quickly I follow behind him into the main area of the apartment. Silent again, I watch him move around unplugging, unscrewing, and clipping little things here and there until a tiny pile of electronics accumulates in his hand, which he stuffs into his coat pocket.

And all I can think is *fuck, he's thorough. I wonder if that extends to other areas of his life.*

He does the smoke detector in here too.

And when he seems finished, he walks toward me and kisses my head again, unleashing another spark. I feel it all the way in my tailbone. It seems to nestle there, waiting for something. Waiting for me to ask the obvious question that shouldn't change how I feel about what he's done, but which I know will anyway.

"You didn't put any in the bathroom?" I ask.

In the low light, his emerald eyes twinkle faintly like gems in a darkened display case as he shakes his head, setting off the spark inside me. My hand grabs the lapel of his coat before he can even think about moving away.

"So it really was just for security?"

A guilty smirk darts across his gorgeous face. "Mostly."

I don't let go of his lapel while I study him. While he studies me. The anger I felt is long gone, replaced by something twisted and tangier.

I don't dislike the lengths Nero has gone to in order to be near me, to help me. In fact, it's a level of proactive interest I haven't seen from another man in years. Not even with Kaden.

Hard to describe how fucking sexy it is that Nero said he was sorry too. That he came here himself and let me watch him remove all the hardware he sneaked in here. I bet if I asked him how to spot this stuff, he would tell me.

I'd also bet he doesn't just want me, he likes me too.

But I don't want to be liked from afar.

"So what now?" I ask. "You're just going to leave me unprotected?"

A dark noise exits his mouth like the low warning growl of some great hunting beast. "I do offer in-person private security options, if those are more to your tastes."

"Options like what?"

I notice his lips curve right before he leans down into my space. His features materialize out of the darkness with each inch closer like some beautiful incubus. And a scent I think is sage and spice invades my system, demanding I cling to his coat tighter.

"There's the standard package—I go where you go, watch your every move, operate like a human shield, if necessary."

I shake my head. "That's a man's fantasy of what security is."

His smile grows. "Then you might like the gold package. I take you out on the town, hold your hand to ward off predators, live in your bed to scare off the cold."

I wish I was a more evolved person. I wish statements like that didn't work, and that they didn't get intercepted by my pussy on the way to my brain.

My eyes flutter shut of their own will, but even without seeing him I feel him move closer, until his lips land feather-light against my closed eyelid before pulling back and landing on the other. The sensation of this giant tattooed man, so strong I have no doubt he could literally break a man in half, being gentle with me sends my heart into a percussive panic.

Lips to cheek, he slides them back slowly until they're resting against my ear.

He purrs, "You tell me all your deepest fears, and I tell you mine. You let yourself need me and I make sure you never go without. And of course, I remember to apologize when I fuck up."

Well damn if that doesn't have my knees going out a little underneath me. I cling tighter to his coat, lean against his lips a little, for stability, just listening to his low, patient breaths.

"I'm sorry, Lulu," he says again, summoning a whimper out of the very depths of me. "It wasn't my place to make decisions for you. I should have told you my fears about giving you that photo and then let you make the final call. I'll give it to you now because it belongs to you and no one else should have it. Then I'll help you become the sexiest, most hypnotic muse this world has ever seen."

"Oh, fuck me," leaves my mouth like the accidental wish it is.

With a low chuckle right against my goose bumped, stimulated skin he says, "It would be my pleasure, Ms. Rathbone."

My heart does a loop-de-loop inside me at the promise. Then a second, when I open my eyes and turn toward him. We're so close, millimeters separate our lips, and he can't stop looking at mine and I can't stop looking at his. At any moment, a spark will leap between us and set us both to spontaneously combust.

But there's one last thing I need.

"And you promise you don't want to own me?" I ask.

It's a promise he can't know the full context or meaning of yet, and I know that's unfair. But I need to know how he'll respond to the question, at least. I need to see that look of disbelief, that look of irritation that suggests that never even occurred to him as a possibility in the first place.

And I do.

I do see it.

Even in the dark, Nero's emerald eyes blow wide with disgust before he declares "Oh, I promise."

But just as quickly, his eyes sharpen with mischief, and he adds, "The only place I want to own you is in the bedroom, Ms. Rathbone…and even there, I'd prefer if we take turns owning each other."

Jesus!

Sensation spikes through my body all at once, like someone spun the dial to switch me all the way on. But there must be a live wire loose in there somewhere because through my touch on his coat, through the graze of my knuckles against his rock-hard stomach, I can feel his own dial cranking sky high.

I'm shaking.

I'm literally shaking with impatient desire.

Barely a second of panting silence elapses between us before his massive hand sweeps forward and fists in my hair, yanking me right into his warm, full lips. It's not soft, this kiss. It's hungry like a starving animal, plundering and demanding on the tongue. His teeth nibble my bottom lip before they graze down to my jaw and lightly bite there before moving farther down.

And the second he clamps down on the side of my neck, just hard enough that I can feel every tooth in his mouth pressing against my skin before his tongue darts forward to lap and lick and soothe?

"Oh fuck!" escapes me in a bark.

My body tries to pull away from the teasing tickle of his teeth, but his hand in my hair won't let me get far. He only turns my head back to him and seals his lips to mine again. And his other hand curls around my waist, so commandingly, before my feet leave the ground completely. Even airborne, he doesn't stop his plundering assault on my mouth with his tongue. I don't think he can. *I* certainly can't. The taste of him and his scent, which pushes away all the other smells in my apartment, are like some sort of potent lust potion chemically engineered for my body. Together, they summon a flood; I think if he set me down now, I'd go slip-sliding all over the floor. So instead, I wrap my legs around his middle. And his free hand slides under my ass to hold me up.

Nero doesn't set me down. As if he's lived in this apartment his whole life, he turns on his heel and carries me to the bedroom, popping the door shut behind him with his foot.

"God, you're so fucking wet for me already, Ms. Rathbone."

He doesn't lower me to the bed, or make to put me down. In fact, he glances at the bed two feet away, then back at me, as if it's some distant place, impossible to reach.

"I'm not going to make it," he declares.

"What?" I ask.

"I need you right now."

"You have me," I almost squeak in confusion…right before his hands swoop under my ass. I hear a zipper, then I feel fingers and a brief chill as he yanks my panties out of the way before his cock is there against my entrance, tapping against my clit like it's ringing a doorbell.

So polite, his cock. So impatient. And paired with the gorgeous sharp smile that sprints across his chiseled, angular face? Fuuuuucccccckkkk.

"May I come in, Ms. Rathbone?"

"Yes—!"

Nero slams himself home like a knife into a juicy piece of fruit, and I scream before I can fully appreciate the sheer *impact* of him on my body. I guessed he was big by the way he carried himself, how unbothered he was by almost everything, but still. It's one thing to guess, another thing to know someone's being almost humble about their Big Dick Energy.

A battering ram of fullness sends a shockwave of pleasure rippling through my body from crown to toe, rattling my heart and brain in passing. And I cling tighter to him, because it's all I can do. All I can do as he pulls back and plunges in again before finding a stride that would make a jackrabbit blush.

Holy fuck.

I've always had good stamina—great stamina, if I'm honest—but something about where his perfect fucking cock hits inside me knocks the wind out of me, I swear. I can't catch my breath at the speed he's moving, while he's so desperate to be deep-deep-and-deeper inside me.

The speed isn't the desperate, uncomfortable, selfish kind. It's fucking mathematical. He watches my face and *adjusts his rhythm without breaking stride*—my god, it's fucking incredible! I don't know what he's seeing in my expression to know how to dial it back, but it takes only a few moments for him to find a rhythmic, relentless pace that has my entire body buzzing. Even my skin feels electrified.

But it's not just his size and speed; it's the fact that he's still wearing one of those dark suits he favors. From neck to ankle, he's clad in black armor like some sort of corporate knight... and it is *doing* it for me. It clashes so spectacularly with the tattoos that peek out of his sleeves and collar. The fact that I know he has more under his clothes and I haven't seen them yet? I just know he's covered in art.

Then there's the way he looks at me.

You'd think I was an actual goddess the way he stares at my face. And fuck if that doesn't have me tightening my hold on him in needy anticipation of every thrust, even though I'm kind of terrified this won't last long. How can it?

A streak of weird anger hits me at the thought.

"Nero, I swear to God, you better not tap out any time soon."

He only smiles. Leaving one hand on my ass, he brings the other to my hair, twisting his fingers through it for leverage, and somehow he deepens the thrust again, until I literally can't see him through the foggy haze of mind-numbing ecstasy clouding my eyes.

But I hear him loud and clear when he yanks me in and growls against my ear, "You think a man fresh outta prison has anything better to do than live inside your exquisite cunt?"

The words cut right to the core of me; they wrap a vice grip around my pleasure center and squeeze. That, paired with his unyielding grip, his brutal rhythm...

I'm suddenly whimpering.

Moaning.

Screaming as an orgasm tears through my body, leaving me temporarily blind and shivering and breathless. Until all I can do is melt against him.

All I can do is murmur, "One minute. Just gimme a minute."

Which he finds hilarious. Leaning in, he teases my bottom lip between his teeth and uses my own words against me, "I swear to God, Lulu, you better not tap out any time soon" right before his stride begins again.

Completely unphased.

Relentless.

And tucked against his chest, I have a front-row seat for his perfect cock as it thrusts into me from below.

Worse, he kisses my cheek so tenderly and growls, "If you didn't want me to own your pussy, you shouldn't have made it feel this good to fuck you."

This man. I raise my eyes to meet his, smirking.

"Fuck, Nero, now you've done it."

"Done what?" he goads playfully, trying to get a rise out of me.

I can't let a challenge like that go unanswered. Tightening my leg hold on his waist, I lean up and plant a teasing kiss on his beautiful full lips, rubbing mine against the stubble to either side of them.

"Don't drop me, Big Guy," is all I say before I begin.

CHAPTER 36

NERO

"Don't drop me, Big Guy," she purrs, and my grip tightens on her hot fucking body automatically, almost in offense. Pridefully. How dare she *ever* think I would drop her.

But I realize a second later that her words were a pure and simple warning. Like a pamphlet dropped out of the sky to inform the citizens below of an impending air raid.

Lulu shifts position in my arms like some sort of acrobat—that's how it looks to me anyway. She unlocks her legs from around me and shifts her feet into position against my belt, pressing for leverage, as she begins to bounce.

No, bounce would suggest she's not in control.

But she abso-fucking-lutely is.

She lifts herself to the very tip of my dick and *impales* herself on it. Again. And again. And again. But it's with a grace I didn't know was possible. She doesn't slam herself down into my hips. She sheaths me inside her to the base, then rises again, slow at first until she finds a comfortable stride.

And then...

Her smiling hazy eyes lock on mine, and she hums almost meditatively before she tightens her muscles around my cock. I can tell it's intentional—I literally watch the switch happen in her hazel gaze— and I'm trapped.

Honey trapped, love trapped, I have *no fucking idea!*

It doesn't matter. My arms cradle her beautiful fucking double-cherry of an ass, and all I can do is grip and support while she rides me. All I can do is *admire* the surprised smile on her face as she shifts her angle the tiniest bit and doubles down, like I'm scratching a fucking itch for her.

She's using me while satisfying me—and her moaned "oh my gods" are my reward. That and the tight desperate ache in my balls to fucking fill her and never stop filling her.

But we haven't discussed that. I don't want to presume.

Not that I have much time to argue the point—I'm about to go off like a fucking rocket. The way she's riding me, I have seconds to decide how to play this.

"Lulu-Lulu!" I almost beg.

"Mmm?" she hums so sensually, and I almost lose it on her then.

"Where do you want me?" I ask, clinging to some random baseball fact from 1996 I hope will buy me a few seconds.

Fucking Lulu has no idea what she's doing to me when she squeezes those muscles again and bites her lip with a smile. But just as quickly, she releases me, glances behind her toward the bed and *steps off* my body onto the mattress. Dropping to her knees before me, she whips her shirt off her body, exposing her beautiful bee-stung breasts to me.

Wrapping her soft hand around my shaft and beginning to stroke, she says, "Paint me with it, Big Guy."

There's nothing else I can do. I was lucky I held out this long with a knockout like her.

But fuck, I wish I was cooler about it. I sort of stagger forward a step when I feel the rush deep inside.

"God, I'm coming, I'm coming," I warn her.

Lulu bites her beautiful lip again and aims me at her chest and I unload like a fucking shampoo bottle opened after being in a pressurized tank for too long. And just like she said, she slides her fingers through the essence I've left on her skin, painting it across her nipples before she dips her fingers into the slick sliding down her belly and brings them to her mouth.

228

And fuck if I'm not hard again *instantly*.

"That was amazing, Nero. That was—ah!"

I don't have the mental clarity to *chat* about what she just did to me. Not when I'm locked and loaded and ready to go again.

Instead, I reach for her thighs and yank her legs out from under her, splaying her on her side. I tear her soaked panties from her body and kneel on the mattress before she can say any other word that sounds like goodbye. There is no fucking goodbye right now. She told me not to tap out, and I'm no quitter, so...

I slide inside her again where I fucking belong.

Our moans harmonize into my new favorite song as I lay a gripping claim on her gorgeous fucking thighs and begin to pound into her as if she was the home I couldn't wait to get back to all those years.

Because I think she might be.

"Fuck, Nero!" she squeals with pleasure, and I fucking lose myself in her voice.

Especially when she turns her head into the mattress and bites the comforter to muffle her screams of pleasure.

It's perfect.

She's perfect.

She's—

I stagger suddenly as something catches my eye. Her dark mass of hair slides away from her back, revealing...a scar.

I think it's just a trick of the light for a moment until she turns a little more and I see it for what it is. It's a brand of someone's initials —*JV*—that scarred long ago along her left shoulder blade. Barely the size of a quarter, but fuck if that matters—it's clearly from some sort of heated metal seal that was pressed to her back.

My hand slides across the silky expanse of her skin and my fingers glide across that old—

"What are you doing?"

I recoil as Lulu jerks slightly, turning onto her back to hide what I've already seen.

My stride flags as she stares up at me. Her eyes are wide with anger, at the intrusion, but also fear. Shame. As if she thinks those initials will change what I think of her.

"Who did that to you, Lulu?" I ask.

"Don't worry about it."

Don't worry about it?

"Lulu," I try again.

"Don't ruin this," she replies instead of answering. But it's in a pleading tone, as if she thinks the moment will be ruined for *me* if she answers…and her fingers curl around my hand where it grips her hip as if she's trying to keep me from pulling away.

Fuck, it must be something bad. I almost want to pull out of her, but I know if I do, she'll throw me out instead of telling me.

"Please," she says quietly. "I just need to feel good. Don't you want to feel good?"

Me? I need *her* to feel good. So, so good.

So I deepen my hold on her instead. She's on her side, and I tuck her into a slightly tighter ball before leaning down over her. I wrap one arm behind her knees, and seal my other hand to the back of her neck as I bring my face to inches above hers, listening to her heady groan of bliss as I bury myself as deeply as I can.

The rest of the world disappears. It's just us and these couple of inches between.

"Lulu, I'm not going anywhere," I tell her, kissing her cheek-jaw-neck, nipping with my teeth just to make her pant. "I'll be here when you're ready to tell me."

"Nero, please."

Her eyes widen and she shakes her head, begging, and all I want to do is push until she reveals the evil piece of shit who branded her…but I restrain myself. I force myself to let it go for now.

Instead, I tighten my grip on her body just a little, until I know it's nothing but my warmth and my cock she feels, and I begin to thrust again slowly. In and out and in again patiently, adjusting the angle until she whimpers and grips me tightly and I know I've hit her sweet spot.

I run my nose along her cheek, kissing her. "You're safe. I'm sorry for pushing. You're safe."

Again, she shakes her head softly. But this time, she sobs too, and I swallow the sound with a kiss, pulling her back into this moment with me. Pulling her back into a night of pure pleasure that only ends when *she* finally taps out on top of me, and falls asleep while I'm still inside her.

I don't think I've ever felt this sated. Or comfortable being used as a mattress. But as I gently maneuver her to the bed beside me, I know it isn't enough.

I need to know her.

And I need her to want to share with me.

She doesn't seem to understand I want something real with her, at least more than just some late-night hookup.

I get her situated under the covers and then I head to the kitchen where I figure out her coffee maker and set it to go off in the morning when she wakes up. I find a pad of paper and leave her a note, too, saying *Don't wait so long to call me this time*.

Then I walk over to that wall of framed photos and take a harder look at the smashed one of the guy ogling Lulu while she lays on the couch in front of him. Using my flashlight app for light, I find exactly what I expected to find—a fucking ring on his fucking finger carved with the initials *JV*.

I could claim I don't understand what it is about that woman that has men thinking they can hurt her without consequence...but I *do* understand. She's vibrant and mysterious and indefinable. But she's also tiny...and she's never fully embraced her own power. She's the sort of woman men don't just pedestalize; they burn her in effigy hoping "their sacrifice" will be rewarded.

She's the reflection of every single man's worst insecurities.

It's easier to dehumanize her than face the reality that you've *never*— not once—felt that alive.

But I know what that feels like—to be seen as a threat. My father once told me I could never measure up because I was a "splash of him that got into the wrong hole."

That wasn't the worst thing he ever told me, but he was still saying that sort of shit to me when we ended up in the same prison together.

No, the worst was something he said near the end, before he died. I'll never forget it. With a sneer on his miserable old face, he told me, "Your brother's ashamed of you. You're just a joke to him. Just like me. Probably tells people you're dead. Probably hopes you never come home."

I hate that that memory squats in the corner of my mind like some sort of demon I can't exorcise outta myself.

Knowing he just wanted to hurt me with those words—that he was just a small, mean little bastard—doesn't make them any more bearable.

The same goes for Lulu and this *JV* asshole.

Knowing she's safe and away from him doesn't make his injury against her bearable. If anything, it makes me want to know his name so I can destroy it. Just like I plan to destroy Emilio's.

CHAPTER 37

LULU

I wake up as a very happy blob of Jell-o. Relaxed to uselessness. Jiggly with joy as I roll over and stretch.

I've had my brains fucked out before, so I'm not sure why last night was as satiating as it was…but I don't care. I needed that. Way more than I thought I did.

Nero King was…is…someone I'll be thinking about for a good long while.

All I can hope is that he'll want to see me again.

Do me again, let's be honest.

I want an encore. Tonight. Tomorrow. However long he's up for it. In my experience, the second you sleep with a man some invisible countdown clock begins and there's no telling how long they'll stay interested before moving on. Could be days, could be weeks. Hell, Nero's could already have struck zero and I'll never see him again.

I mean, he left while I was sleeping, so…

At least, I think he did. A scent hits my nose and I inhale deeply—coffee. I wasn't planning on having any this morning so I never set the pot; he must have done it.

I pull myself out of bed and throw on my old shirt before making my way to the front of the apartment. Sure enough, the coffee pot is burbling away, but there's no Nero in sight.

Which is a shame, because my pussy's almost scratching at the door for him. If he'd been here when I woke up, honestly I would've probably called out sick to work and ridden him till I collapsed again.

Sometimes, you just need to feel good…and *damn*, was that a good night. Aside from that part between our first and second rounds, anyway. I'm glad he didn't push me too much for information about…all that. A nosey guy like that *not* prying for details is a miracle, and the fact that he just let it go and got back to boinking me senseless made the rest even more enjoyable.

Fuck was it good!

Made even better when I spot the note Nero left by the coffeemaker asking me to call him.

For seconds? To plot Emilio's demise? Perhaps both? I think he's still willing to help with Emilio, which is all that matters.

It puts a skip in my step as I head back to my room to grab clothes for the shower, but I find another message waiting for me back there. My phone lights up with a text and I accidentally do a cartoon skid when I realize it's from Kaden.

He has amazing timing, ha.

To be honest, when I use my thumb to flick open the message, I'm expecting some excuse from him about how busy he's been, or a limp apology for what he said.

But that's not what I find.

He's sent a video attachment.

I press play, again not expecting much.

And then I freeze. I freeze because Kaden's gorgeous, ridiculously fit stark-naked body appears on my screen, along with…my painting. The nearly finished painting I posed for.

It's so beautiful, I don't even notice what Kaden is doing at first. I'm fixated on all that blue. On the fact that there's no veil.

Maybe it's coming—the painting *is* unfinished, after all.

But something tells me there won't be one, and that startles me a little bit. He painted me without a veil. He put me on display proudly. *Reverentially.*

My heart flutters at the thought of it.

And then I hear Kaden's first deep growl of pleasure and I forget the painting is even in the video at all. No, I rewind that video so fast, the phone glitches for a few seconds before starting again.

Kaden's not just naked. He's at full mast. His beautiful cock is so hard it looks like the hilt of a knife sticking out of his body. Then he dips off screen for a second and returns with a handful of paint. His eyes latch onto the camera as if he can see me watching him and I can't tear my gaze away as he says, "With pleasure, Ms. Rathbone."

Fuck, he…

Kaden reaches for his cock with his paint-filled hand and begins to stroke himself off while staring right into my soul. It's…intense. Like peeping on someone, except they know you're there watching, giving them your full attention. I know I am. He made this for me and there's something so fucking intimate about that, I don't look away until the end.

Until his eyes start to roll back.

Until his chest hitches like a sail in a storm.

Until he moans so deliciously…and groans, "Fuck, Louise."

And then…well, there's no delicate way to say this. He spurts his cum into his cupped hand, like it's some precious resource he can't waste, and glances up at me again.

"I need you to come back to finish this painting with me, Louise."

Kaden walks to a table just at the edge of frame and picks up a paintbrush. Dips it into a can I realize is that shade of blue ruin that once hit me on the head, then lets it drizzle into his cum-filled hand. After a moment, he uses the brush to mix the color with himself before he walks right up to the painting of me…and begins laying down a base coat of blue along that unfinished final quarter of the canvas. Just a thin coat, and only the top corner; there's only enough paint for that.

Then with a sheepish blush-stained smile, he walks toward the phone, still gloriously naked and paint-slicked.

"Your move, Ms. Rathbone," he says as the video ends.

And I…realize I'm smiling when my cheeks begin to hurt from the stretch. I'd look insane to most normal people, I guess, but…*he did what he promised he would do*. Finally. Those weeks ago when he embarrassed me, this is all it took to erase it, but it's more than that. He put himself out there for me. He's still a reclusive weirdo, but I know he doesn't like most people. I know this took a lot for him to do.

And I promised that I'd go back and pose for him again if he went through with sending me this, so…

I'm not going to reply right now; I have work to do.

But later?

Oh, it is *on* Mr. Malbec.

Today, though, I have a meeting with Mrs. Russo to discuss artists for the upcoming exhibition, and a new mission to fill her final list with people I think will help me if I ask. Malbec will be right at the top of that list.

Knowing this is the last large community-wide event I'll ever plan for the Russos fills me with an emotion I never thought I could feel regarding them—relief. I know it's fear-laced relief, but still. I'm so *relieved* to think there's only one hurdle between me and being free of any attempt Emilio might make to paint me in a negative light ever again. The more I think about Ivy's idea, the more excited I am about it. The more excited I am about…everything. For the first time in weeks, I feel light as air and satisfied—emotionally as well as physically. The future seems as bright as dawn on an early spring day.

And I decide to celebrate the start of the rest of my life by giving myself an extra thirty minutes with my massaging shower head to wash Nero King's abstract art off my body.

CHAPTER 38

NERO

I step into the Star-King offices feeling like my namesake—a king. On top of the world. Untouchable. Cloud 9 ain't got shit on how I feel after being with Lulu last night. Hell, how I felt with her this morning, when she nestled down on my chest and hummed with satisfaction as she fell asleep—fuck I should've stayed. I should've just risked her being awkward in the morning when we woke up, but I didn't want to scare her away.

Doesn't mean I won't *absolutely annihilate her pussy* the second she asks me back.

And she will. I just know it.

The thought makes my stupid fucking heart leap.

Even Rita, the receptionist, seems to sense the change in me. Instead of greeting me with a nothing-smile as per usual, she does a soft double-take in my direction and smiles.

"Morning, Mr. King."

"Good morning, Rita," I reply, trying my damnedest not to just skip like a schoolgirl in front of her. "Is Ethan in yet?"

"In a meeting."

"Okay, thanks."

"There's someone waiting in your office for you."

"K."

Today's the day I've decided to confront him. He's got a new assistant, some toddler intern from NYU who looks like he'd have to give himself a hernia to pop out a chin hair. I've been buttering the kid up a little bit each time I come in by bringing donuts from the shop downstairs. I raise the little brown bag in my hand when I spot him walking in the hallway by my office.

"Morning, Mr. King," he says. "Donuts?"

"Here, saved one for you," I lie lightly, handing him what I bought specifically for him. A cursory glance through his socials told me he likes a certain type of custard monstrosity, the kind nobody should be eating for breakfast, but which a twenty-year-old would eat by the bag full.

"Oh man, my favorite!" he says a second later when he peeks inside.

"Enjoy. Hey, and can you set up a meeting between me and Ethan today—I don't care what time."

"Oh, but—"

"Thanks, man. Appreciate it."

Hate to trap the kid, but I don't give him the chance to make up some excuse. I just plod along to my office, step in, and shut the door before he can speak.

My brother *will* talk to me if I have to literally lock him in his office like I did sometimes when we were kids and he wouldn't tell me what was bothering him. He had a terrible habit of bottling things up until they caused problems for everyone, like his migraines. Little punk tried to hide those from me for months before they started affecting his schoolwork. Once they did, I shut that shit down immediately. Locked us both in a room together while Mom was out of the house until he admitted he *literally couldn't see sometimes*. Couldn't read. His head hurt so bad, he went to bed right after dinner some nights.

I still have no idea why he didn't just tell me.

I handled it as soon as I knew. Got him to a neurologist. Got him the meds he needed. I would've razed the city to dust to get him help.

I'd do that now too, if he'd get his head out of his ass long enough to see I saved Star-King from the inevitable fallout of Vincent Star's shitty behavior. Not only was Star a fucking *murderer*, but he'd been up to shit for months that would've killed Ethan once he found out.

"Nero King?"

I don't flinch at the voice I hear behind me in the antechamber of my office, but I totally forgot Rita said somebody was in here in the thirty seconds since I left her desk.

"Yes, hi," I say, turning to find…some guy in a suit sitting in a chair with a subtle smirk on his face. "Can I help you?"

"You already have," he says, rising to his feet. He walks toward me and taps an envelope against my chest before letting go, so I have no option but to grab it before it falls to the floor. "You've just been served."

He leaves the room half a second later, shutting the door behind him. And I sort of stand there like a chump for a full minute before I tear the envelope open and read over the first page of the document. It's a formal "demand for arbitration" from Ethan, regarding my purchase of the company.

A laugh escapes me as I sit down at my computer to read through the paperwork. The dude could have *just talked to me*, but I guess he wants a barricade of twenty suits between us instead. That's fine. We have to start somewhere.

But…that doesn't mean I'm going into this thing blind, and it's about time I shake up his perfect little hermetic world up here in the sky.

A few days ago, I stashed one of my surveillance kits in this office. I pull it out now, and reach for one of my favorite little bugs—a temporary audio transmitter that the public doesn't even know exists yet. It looks like a translucent band-aid, barely bigger than a dime, with a sticky side covered in parchment.

I remove the parchment and palm it before yanking open my office door dramatically and stalking to the bullpen, where I make sure everyone sees me as I make my way to Ethan's office.

His assistant lurches to his feet the second I tear open his door. "Mr. King's busy right now."

I ignore him and tear open Ethan's door next, expecting to see him at his desk.

But that's not where he is.

I hear a soft moan, then a gasp, as I turn and find him with his face and fingers buried in Cara's pussy where she's perched on the couch. Straight out of some comedy, I watch her legs snap together around his head in surprise when she sees me.

"Nero!" she yelps, reaching for Ethan's suit jacket to cover herself.

I use the distraction to my advantage and lean back against his desk, pressing the audio transmitter to the underside.

By the time I turn back, Ethan's found his feet again and I smirk in his red face.

"Little early for lunch, don't you think?" I ask.

"Get the fuck out, Nero!" Ethan yells, spinning me by my shoulders and shoving me toward the door.

"Good to know you're only selfish with your brother," I tease, dragging my feet. "Got your summons, bro. A little extreme if you ask me."

To my relief, a flash of confused surprise crosses his face, as if he didn't expect me to say that. But he's too flummoxed right now to think about it.

So instead, he counters, "More necessary than I ever imagined."

I smirk again, "Talk to me and this all goes away. After lunch?"

Again, Ethan's spastic energy hiccups for a moment, but he hears what I'm saying this time. I know he does.

"Fine, whatever, get out!" he barks, right before he slams the door in my face.

Ha, got him. Knowing a man his entire life entitles you to certain cheat codes—and one of Ethan's is that if you catch him in an awkward position, he'll agree to things before he's thought about them. At least, as far as me and our mom is concerned.

I don't care if I had to trick it out of him; that's the most he's said to me since I left prison. We're making some progress, at least.

With the bug planted, it takes little more than syncing it to an app on my phone once I return to my office to hear their voices through my airbud.

"Baby," Ethan says. "I'm sorry I didn't lock the door."

"I know, it's fine," Cara says. "Sorry, I'm just a little embarrassed."

"Too embarrassed to sit on my face?" I hear him growl, her yip with surprise, then moan with pleasure.

"Always too embarrassed for that," she laughs.

"Well, we need to fix that," Ethan says. "We have twenty minutes before our next meeting. Thirty five if we leave Winnie waiting."

Cara yelps again, this time in a way that tells me I need to mute this soon or I'll be the fucking creep listening to his little bro's sex noises.

But right before I end it, Cara says something that surprises me, "Ethan, you know he cares about you, right?"

I hear Ethan's muffled sigh. It sounds like the world is on his shoulders—or she is.

"I know. I just wish he didn't take it out on me."

CHAPTER 39

LULU

When I was a kid, long before things went wrong in ways I never knew they could, my mom used to tell me that a "smile made all the difference between a rainy day and a sunny one." I didn't understand what she meant for a long time. I mean, the difference between sun and rain was pretty black and white as far as nine-year-old me could see.

Then I got a little older and watched her life fall apart and realized she meant a figurative smile. Your emotional and mental mindset can make all the difference between a good and bad day. A good and bad life.

By the time I understood what she meant, though, not even a smile fortified by every happy thought in existence could salvage our relationship.

What she did to me?

What she let happen to me?

There's no smile in the world bright enough to outshine the rain she brought to my life.

And fuck her for expecting me to fake one.

I pretended for as long as I could, but eventually I couldn't anymore—and in the end, the pretending cost me so much precious time I'll *never* be able to get back. If I'd stopped "grinning and bearing" everything earlier, it would've saved me immeasurable suffering.

I might not have even needed the Russos to begin with.

Of course, it's always easy to look back in hindsight and wish everything had worked out differently. To wish you'd made different choices. And it's just as easy to fall back into old patterns without realizing it.

I am a "grin and bear it" pro when I want to be.

And I am today.

It's just Mrs. Russo and I, going through my extensive rolodex of artists, so it's much easier to fake a perpetual smile while we narrow down who we'll be extending invitations to. Although technically I don't have to fake it. I just keep thinking about my night with Nero, that video from Kaden, and my conversation with Cara and Ivy, and find something new to smile about each time.

Then Mrs. Russo starts "demanding" I reach out to certain artists for pieces, artists I *know* will help me, and my genuine smile only grows.

The problem with grinning and bearing things, of course, is that some people *want* you to be sad. They thrive on your discomfort. And a smile becomes a target at which to shoot their shot.

"You seem very happy today," Mrs. Russo says around lunchtime when we're designing the invitation I plan to hand deliver to every artist in the city. "Something to do with your new man?"

Your new man leaves her mouth like a slur. I can't tell from the inflection what exactly she doesn't like about Nero, only that his existence seems to bother her.

I know better than to give Mrs. Russo any ammunition to use against me, though.

So I placate her with, "I'm just excited to organize the exhibition for you."

It's not a lie, not really. Since this is the last event I'll ever run for them, I've decided to make it special—a calling card, of sorts. A showcase piece for myself that I can use to hopefully get hired elsewhere. If I have it my way, it'll be *the event of the year*. Especially if I can convince the artists to help me.

Her cool brown gaze flits to me before she murmurs, "Perhaps he is why you have been too distracted to make yourself available to my son. This *convict* you have chosen. Tut-tut-tut."

Her tongue clicks with disappointment, destabilizing me a little, as do the rest of her words. The tone she chooses—I can't decide if she's genuinely concerned or baffled or readying some future barbed attack. I half expect the next thing she says to be some sort of character assassination such as, *"Perhaps you aren't the good girl my husband thinks you are."* Or for her to toss out some tone-deaf accusation. *"How could you choose this criminal over my son."*

But she surprises me with something worse.

"Emilio is in the studio downstairs preparing so you can sit for him today, after we're done here."

As if it's my body's only possible response recently, one of those flinches of panic spears me clean through. I hate it, the claim it stakes. How fucking helpless I feel until it fades.

And it ruins my ability to 'grin and bear' anything.

"Mrs. Russo—"

"It is no trouble; we're almost done here."

"Mrs. Russo—"

"There are only a few weeks left for him to finish his work," she cuts me off again. "You know better than me how long the painting process can take. And if Mr. King does not return Emilio's painting in time, you will have to model again for that replacement as well, so, best you begin today."

Bile rushes up my throat. My head blanks. I can't think of anything to say. Nothing clever, at least.

Nothing except, "No."

It's a tiny word. It floats in the air between us like a spark from a fire until it lands before her and sets her alight.

"Excuse me?"

"No, *signora*. I won't be modeling for him."

"Why not?"

Dragging my gaze up to meet hers takes ages. My fear has my eyes on a string and keeps tugging at them to stay down, but some tiny sliver of courage finally cuts the thread.

"Because I never did before, and I never will. Especially now that I know what he thinks of me."

Her dark eyes tighten the tiniest bit, assessing me. "You humiliated him."

"Well, then we're even, aren't we."

Vomit. It's right there, rising in my throat. It tastes of sour anger on my tongue. But I bite it back and I stare her down, even as I clutch my hands and let my nails embed in my palms to keep them from shaking.

"I am happy to continue working for you in a professional capacity—as I have always done—but if you don't think that's possible anymore, then I can resign."

My body is eating itself. My mind is scrambling. I honestly don't know if she tells me to leave whether I'll be able to walk out on my own two feet.

And it cuts like razors across my skin when she replies, "Are you so ungrateful? After everything we've done for you? *This* is how you choose to end things."

"I don't *want* to stop working for you," I say sincerely, because she should *know* that. Doesn't she know that? "I've always enjoyed working for your family. But if you won't respect me, I must respect myself."

Shaking. My hands are shaking.

"Respect yourself?" she doubles down. "What is there to respect? Everything you are is a result of my husband's generosity. My *son's* generosity. If there's anything to respect *now*, it's what they made of you."

More panic surges through me when I realize she's not talking about this job.

I...think she knows the truth about what Lorenzo and Carlo did for me. The truth of how I met them when I was nineteen, not the story we came up with when I begged for their help at twenty-three.

She didn't need to know the truth—no one did. But maybe I was naïve for thinking Lorenzo wouldn't tell her eventually. He probably never thought she'd use it against me. I wonder if Emilio knows too. If Matteo and Bianca do.

But I don't want to presume.

So I decide to test her. "Emilio never—"

"I'm not talking about Emilio, you selfish girl. I'm talking about Carlo and Lorenzo saving you from that predator calling himself an artist. The one who paraded you around for other men to paint and touch. The one who tried to sell you when you got too old for him."

The panic inside me grows almost unbearable. He told her. He told her the truth.

I feel sick. Laid bare for dissection. Unsafe. So fucking unsafe.

"You were a scrawny nothing thing when they saved you. When we—*out of the graciousness of our hearts*—gave you your freedom. You were too busy starving to death back then to have any respect for yourself."

That sickens my heart. I try to hold back, but I can't let her hold the past against me. Especially because if she knows what really happened then she knows better than to demand that I model for her son.

I finally snap, "If you know what happened then why would you try to force me back into that place again?"

Mrs. Russo's eyes blow wide with some emotion I can't read and a mean chuckle escapes her. "Ah, so the dog that once laid with her tail between her legs has finally found her growl."

"I mean no disrespect—"

"Your choices would suggest otherwise! I thought you would understand how lucky you've been with us all these years."

"I do!"

"Well, Emilio is waiting for you, so make your choice. I'm done with you."

Everything pops in a single second. She raises her hand and flicks her fingers away, releasing me to make my choice. She doesn't even look at me when she does it. She simply pulls the computer monitor in her direction, and takes the keyboard back, before sitting down and ignoring me completely.

It's a smooth, cold dismissal.

And my fate is left up to me.

The stairs leading down to the studio and the stairs leading up to the exit exist beside each other, almost taunting me to make a choice.

Torture or straight execution.

A safety net made of razor wire or a freefall into a potentially bottomless pit.

I wobble to stand, slowly collecting my purse and the little pieces of me scattered across the desk surface. I feel lost. Lost and slow and unsure. I don't know who I can possibly be without this lifesaver that's kept me afloat for ten years.

Turning on my heel, I take several strides toward the two options laid before me. Then I pause to consider them. Behind me, the heavy silence and stillness suggests she's watching to see which I'll choose.

But…it's not really a choice.

She thinks this is one-sided. She thinks that she's the only one who has the right to be offended and hurt. But she's not.

I worked my ass off for them. Kept my mouth shut for them. I gave them *ten years of my life!* I'm *heartbroken* that this is how easily and quickly they could dismiss me.

Worse, Mrs. Russo knows the hell from which Lorenzo and Carlo rescued me. And she would happily send me right back.

That cruelty, more than the rest, makes the decision for me, and I force a brittle smile onto my face. It's the hardest grin I've ever had to fake—it slashes across my face rather than curling—but I manage it.

Taking one stair at a time, I walk up and into the sunshine of an uncertain future.

I choose my dignity.

I choose myself.

I choose to leave.

But life isn't and has never been kind. The moment I step out of the Russo house, my phone *pings* in my hand with an email addressed from Mrs. Russo.

> *Dear friends, patrons, and long-cherished collaborators,*

It is with a heavy heart that the Russo Trust announces that it is ending its professional relationship with its long-time art advisor Louise Rathbone. While we appreciate the contributions Louise made during her time with us, recent developments have led to a decision to part ways.

We value the trust and professionalism that underpin our work, and this decision reflects our ongoing commitment to upholding the highest standards within our organization.

We appreciate your understanding as we work to identify an individual whose skills and approach more closely align with the needs of the role.

Best Regards,
Giulietta Russo

It's…

So fast. It's so fast.

So vicious.

I'm bcc'd on the email, and there's no way to know how many people she sent it to.

And I…

I finally lose it; vomit surges like a torrent out of my throat right onto the Russo's welcome mat.

CHAPTER 40

NERO

I'm sitting in my Star-King office, swiveling in circles, waiting for my meeting with Ethan to begin when my cell phone buzzes in my hand.

It's Kenzo. He hates phone calls; the only calls I've ever received from him have been during level 5 emergencies. Even then, he usually texts.

"Hey, what's wrong?" I ask.

"It's bad, I think," he murmurs, sounding distracted. "The Russo Trust just sent out an email saying Louise Rathbone has been fired. It implies she was let go for inappropriate behavior."

Fuck.

"It was sent out too quick to stop the first wave, but I stopped the rest from being delivered as soon as I could."

"How many got it?" I ask.

"Thirty percent of their mailing list, which is…about twenty-five thousand people."

Fuck.

"Thanks for catching it," I say anyway. "Get me a list of who opened it, okay? Watch the Russos' accounts like a hawk for a while—*any* mention of her, you kill it."

"Will do."

"Got anything else for me?"

"No, her new identity at nineteen was a clean reset. Whoever got her new papers was a professional."

"I'm guessing the Russos had something to do with that," I say, and he grunts his agreement. "Look, she's from Philly, she went to RISD. And some asshole with the initials JV—an art professor, I think—did something to her. Hurt her. That's what I've got. Can you root around and see if you can figure out who he is?"

"I'll see what I can find."

"Thanks."

I end the call and open Louise's tracker on my phone. I know I should've deleted that last night too, but I was distracted, what can I say?

It says she's in her apartment, and that's all I need to know. I leap to my feet and reach for my coat just as I hear the doorknob open in the antechamber.

"Hey bro, we're gonna have to raincheck," I say. "Something's come...up..."

I step out of my office to find Ethan hasn't come alone. Four people in rectangular suits—*uck, lawyers*—stand to either side of him. I'm sure to anyone who wasn't nearly shanked in prison, they'd seem intimidating.

"Mr. King?" one of them says. "I'm your brother's attorney, Jon Webb. I hope you don't mind if we sit in on the chat between you boys."

I raise an eyebrow at Ethan, trying my damnedest not to smile, before turning to the suit. "Sure, Dad, but we're going to have to reschedule."

Ethan stiffens. "Are you serious, Nero? *You said* you wanted to talk."

"And you brought half a baseball team," I point out, before I rein myself in and remember why I have to press pause on our brotherly bullshit. "Look, Lulu got hit bad today."

"What do you mean?"

"The Russos fired her, and they made sure it hurt, okay?"

"Fuck," he says.

"Yeah, I'm going to go be with her. Tell Cara, all right?"

Ethan reaches for my bicep as I turn to the door. Out of the corner of my eye, I notice all four attorneys jerk their gaze away to stare up at the ceiling.

"Are you being real right now?" Ethan whispers. "You can't get to me through her. You know that, right?"

That makes me pause. Kinda stings actually. So does the confusion I see on his face. All that white-hat/black-hat stuff is between *us*, but he's acting like he genuinely believes I'm a real bad guy. Disappointment surges through me at the thought.

"Don't flatter yourself. The only thing I've done to you is save your precious company from social ruin, all right. The rest of it—everything Troy did, this villain story you've made up in your head—is bullshit. You know me better than that—or you *should*. Now if you'll excuse me, my girl needs me, and frankly your higher-than-thou act is pissing me off more than usual."

***

I ride that wave of anger for Ethan all the way to Brooklyn, but by the time I leave the subway station, the emotion has mutated into something like dread. It's…some sort of gut feeling, I guess. Like sensing rain before there are any clouds in the sky.

The second I have enough reception, I pull up the remaining cameras around Lulu's building, the ones I left outside. The street looks dead, until my eyes prick on a town car with tinted windows idling down the block with a driver loitering in the front seat.

The Russos, it's gotta be.

And I have a good fucking idea which one.

A couple minutes later when I reach her building, I bypass the door buzzer and beeline through the lobby to the stairs instead of waiting for the uselessly slow elevator. A few seconds later, I arrive at her floor to find three figures looming outside her door. All men, or at least pieces of shit dressed like them.

Just as I anticipated, Emilio's among them. His beady little eyes whip in my direction, assessing, and I smile darkly at him, just to set us on the right foot here.

"Can I help you, gentlemen?" I ask. "Lulu's not home right now."

He pounds on the door again instead of responding, and I text a quick message to her: *Don't answer the door, Emilio is outside*.

But I forget that most people have sounds enabled on their phone. Through her door, we hear the ping of the message go through.

"Lulu!" Emilio suddenly barks. "Open up, let's talk about this. I just want to talk."

"About what?" I ask.

"None of your fucking business."

"Hey," I say, raising my hands. "Just trying to help here. You want to talk to Lulu, I'm the guy who'll be there with her when you do."

He glances back at me as if I'm intruding on some sort of intimate moment between him and the door. I just wait. There's no version of this moment where I leave Lulu on her own. If anything, I want her surrounded by people who care about her.

So I send another text, this one to Cara: *Lulu needs you. Can you come now?*

"You can't just walk out, Lulu," Emilio says quietly as I text. "Not without talking to me. M-Maybe I upset you? I know the painting was a little out there, but I couldn't help myself, you know. You drive me wild. You're an inspiration. *My* inspiration. It was meant to be a gift."

"Some gift," I blurt, almost laughing.

"Lulu!" he barks louder, ignoring me. "You're family. Whatever my mom said, forget it, okay? She's fucking dramatic. Trust me, I'm on your side here."

"With friends like you, who needs enemies I guess," I say very calmly.

"Man, *fuck you!* Get the fuck outta here!" he snaps in my direction, and I catch sight of a glint in his eyes that raises my hackles in warning. It's a look I saw a lot on my dad growing up, in the moments before he lashed out at somebody. Whenever I could, whenever I was quick enough, I'd get myself between him and my mom, or him and Ethan. I was big, even back then. I could take it.

It's the most natural instinct I have to get between him and Lulu now.

But, with his buddies here, I can't be sure Lulu wouldn't catch some of the punishment if I lost the fight. So when I see a door down the hallway crack open with curiosity, I use it to my advantage.

"Look, she obviously doesn't want to answer the door, right? For any of us," I say, deescalating. "We're putting on a show for the neighbors now. Let's all leave, huh? Give her time."

"Who the fuck are you, guy?" Emilio sneers. "She's mine. *Mine*, understand? You're just her temporary fucking dildo, and you won't even have that going for you if you don't back the fuck up now. Now!"

His buddies pat their coats, suggesting they're armed, and I raise my hands again.

"If she's yours then you know what you gotta do, right?"

"I know what I have to do!" he shouts.

"Do you? Think real hard about how long you've known her. Is bringing guys here to yell at her gonna win you any favors?"

That gives him pause. Just long enough for something to cut through the anger. He blinks, considering, and his shoulders sag.

"Fuck!" Emilio barks. "Lulu, I-I'll go. I'm going. But I'm coming back. Alone, okay? We just gotta talk through this. Everything'll be fine then, you'll see."

Like a rabid dog, he shoves past me and spams the elevator button, eyes returning again and again to Lulu's door.

But I've barely turned back when his guys hem me in. "*Amunì.*"

I don't speak Italian, but I know what they want me to do. They form a wall across the hallway and corral me into the elevator with them.

It's fine. I go willingly. Them away from Lulu was the goal and it's working. But it only works until we reach the street and their town car moseys slowly toward us like a hearse. One of his guys opens the back door for him, then motions me in and that's about where I draw the line.

"Get in."

"Not today, thanks."

"It wasn't a request," Emilio says.

"I wouldn't have said yes even if it was. My ride's on its way," I lie. "You got more than a shitty email from your mother to make up for, Emilio."

I'm surprised by his reaction to the sound of his name. He smiles. "She told you about me?"

As if it's flattering.

As if it's a win for him.

And I know she won't be able to stay here tonight no matter what.

When I don't answer, his smile shifts. "You some sort of creep, or something?"

"What?" A laugh stirs in me but never makes it to my mouth.

"Maybe you thought a broken girl would go for a fuck-up like you. Maybe you thought you could take advantage of someone without a family. But she does have a family. We've given her everything she is, and we protected her when no one else would. So, play the hero all you want, just remember we saved her first. Eventually when she remembers she's bound to us in ways you'll never understand and owes us more than she can ever repay, she'll come back and do what we need her to do."

I keep my face neutral and my feet planted on the sidewalk when he finishes speaking, because it's that or I bash his pretty fucking teeth in and take two to the chest from his friends.

"Thanks, man," I say after a moment.

"Thanks for what?"

"For letting me know that woman doesn't need a hero, just a better fucking family."

His eyes flare and his hands reach to shove himself out of the car, when a voice cuts him off.

"Nero?"

It's Cara. She jumps out of Ethan's SUV like a bat out of hell. Ivy scrambles out after, wearing a flour-dusted apron. Ethan follows...and so does Valerian. It's like a clown car of surprises.

"She's upstairs," I say, keeping my eyes on Emilio as Cara and Ivy dart for the building door.

"Everything okay out here?" Ethan asks, coming to stand beside me. A second later Val joins us on my other side, evening the numbers enough to make me feel a little better.

"I think we're good, right Emilio?" I ask.

"You got some balls," he says before turning his cold gaze to Ethan. "I want my painting back, Mr. King."

"Wouldn't you know, it's still in transit," he says.

Emilio nods pointedly a second before the car door seals him in. Then, they're gone like some sort of localized plague carried away by a rat.

I don't wait with the guys; Ethan's still on my shit list and Val will find his way to the apartment in his own sweet time. Lulu is all that matters right now. I turn on my heel and break for the door.

"Nero, wait," I hear Ethan say. I don't stop.

I take the stairs again, quicker this time, and find the door to her apartment open when I get there. But when I step inside, I'm surprised by the...I don't know...lack of energy.

I can feel Lulu's not here two or three seconds before Ivy calls out, "She's not in the bedroom or bathroom."

"She left her phone," Cara says, emerging from the kitchen with the cell in hand. "There's a note, but it's not in her handwriting."

She holds up the note I left for her this morning. Seems so long ago now, and like no time at all. I should have stayed. I know it wouldn't have made a difference, but maybe if I had Lulu would have thought to call me the moment Mrs. Russo gutted her.

"That's mine," I mumble, feeling like shit.

Cara eyes me with that uncanny piercing understanding she has. As Ethan and Val finally step in and shut the apartment door, she asks, "What happened, Nero?"

I don't tell them everything. Obviously.

"My guys have been...intercepting the Russos' emails. They fired Lulu a couple hours ago. Let me grab the email."

I shoot off a quick text to Kenzo and it's in my inbox thirty seconds later.

When I'm done reading it aloud, Ivy seethes, "Goddamn that family. They've had her at their beck and call since before we met her. They didn't used to treat her like shit, but it's all they seem to do recently. At least that's done now."

"No," Cara says. "It's not. If Emilio was here, then they're still trying to mess with her."

"They definitely are," I say. "We need to see your idea through, Ivy. We can't let him hurt her again."

Ivy's lips part in surprise. "She already told you about that?"

It'd be too complicated to explain how I know, so I just go with, "Yeah." Then I add, "It's a great plan. One we need to get going *now* once we make sure Lulu's okay. Do you have any idea where she might go?"

"Without her phone?" Cara says, almost flustered. "She didn't take it for a reason. She probably wants to disconnect somewhere."

"Does she have any family to turn to?" Val asks.

"Us," Ivy says.

"Check if she messaged or called anyone," he suggests.

I step closer to Cara as she palms the cell between us all and flicks open Lulu's texts.

"Oh, there's something from Malbec," she says.

The name sticks in my mind. "Malbec. Why is that familiar?"

"He's an artist I represent," Ethan says. "Basically, a hermit who lives upstate. A couple months ago, I sent her to interview him for me."

Before he's finished speaking, a sound pours out of Lulu's phone, drawing our attention to...a video.

A video of some naked asshole with a hard-on the size of St. Louis standing in front of a painting...of Lulu.

Ethan's eyes dart to me, as do Cara's, I guess to gauge my reaction. But even *I* don't know my reaction.

Not even when the naked guy says, "With pleasure, Ms. Rathbone," before he begins to stroke himself off with blue paint.

I…

What the fuck am I supposed to do with that? Get mad? I guess anger is there, like a friction burn in my chest. Jealousy too, but there's only a lick of that. After all, we've been on *a date* and that ended badly. We've had one night of sensational fucking, but I left at the end of it like an idiot.

More than anything, I feel…a competitive itch. It's the weirdest thing. Whoever this Malbec guy is, he's going to have his work cut out for him if he wants to get between Lulu and me. I'll make sure it's the hardest fucking thing he's ever done.

So when he says, "I need you to come back to finish this painting with me, Louise," I kill the video and ask, "What's his address?"

"Why?" Ethan asks.

"Because if that's where Lulu is, I want to see her."

Ethan eyes me baldly. "Maybe she doesn't want to see you."

"She does," I say.

"I don't know that," Ethan counters. "Even if she does, I'm not just going to let you show up at my client's house and harass them if that's where she is."

I don't fault him for trying to protect his client, or even her, but his tone bugs me. Fucking self-righteous asshole. I'm still the bad guy in his mind.

Before anyone can react, I tap the Malbec contact on Lulu's phone and dial Kenzo's number.

I ignore Ethan when he asks, "What are you doing?"

"What-up, boss?" Kenzo asks a second later.

"Run this number—555-604-4402—text me the address."

"You got it."

I end the call and swipe Lulu's phone out of Cara's hand before Ethan even steps forward with, "Nero, what the fuck?"

"I have to go," I say. "Cara, I'll text you once I know she's okay."

"Nero—" Ethan tries again, stepping toward me, but I put my hand up this time and let him bounce off of it.

"E, I swear to fuck, I am being so patient with you, bro. I know you're ashamed of me. I know you probably wish I'd just died in prison like Dad. But I'm in your fucking life now, just like I'm in Lulu's. The fact that you think I'd hurt either one of you breaks my heart."

It was more than I meant to say, but at least he heard it.

"Just let me help her and then we can talk about your precious company, okay?"

I don't wait for a response. It wouldn't change what I'm going to do. The bug up Ethan's ass will still be there when I get back, but Lulu needs me now, it's as simple as that.

CHAPTER 41

KADEN

I haven't been able to stop painting since I started last night with *Blue Ruin*. It's still sitting on the big easel, where it will remain until Louise finally returns to me to finish it. Until then, I've pulled out one of my ancient standard easels to work on.

I had to.

My fingers were itching to paint so badly I could barely muster the executive function to take a shower and wash the blue off my dick. I almost left it...until the drying paint reminded me that "body safe" doesn't mean comfortable.

After, though, I couldn't tear myself away from the studio. The fire has died in the woodstove. Daylight is fading. None of it matters. I've finished the primary stages of three different paintings today, and I'm currently working on a fourth. I already have plans to start six more.

But those second-rounders will hold until I finish the ones I've already started. I have to finish them because they're...her. Louise. Her face is on all of them. Her body. Her mannerisms. That bright, blinding glint in her eye. Burning these isn't and will never be an option.

In one, she's floating just under the surface of a sea of stars.

In another, she's peering at herself in a bathroom mirror, applying a face mask.

In another, she's pulling a veil back to peek under a table where "we're" hiding, smiling at the viewer with that open, unbothered smile she has, beckoning us out.

In this fourth one, she's peeking out of bedsheets—*my* bedsheets—reaching for me with a look on her face I cannot wait to see.

Maybe it's obsession. Maybe it's fixation. Or maybe I'm finally waking up after hibernation. This house, which once felt like enough, is starting to feel empty. Dead like a tomb. Painting her feels like I'm finally rolling away the stone. There's no rhyme or reason yet to the settings I've placed her in; I'm just free painting, emphasis on free.

I forgot, you know?

I forgot that I make the rules of my own art. My own life.

Sometimes you get so caught up in the routine of how you think things should be, it takes something or someone else to remind you it's self-imposed. Especially for someone like me who's already won the game.

I mean, isn't the whole point of winning having the freedom to own your own life?

I'm just finishing the initial sketch of Louise in my bed when I hear the front door open and my lungs actually hitch inside me with excitement. It's too late for cleaners, too late for missionaries, and everyone seems to have caught on to the fact that I've signed with another agent by now. Which means there's only one person it's likely to be.

"Louise?" I'm already moving through my supplies toward the door, expecting her to say my name, *anticipating* the sound of it in her sweet soprano.

But there's no response. I round the corner into the hallway, and I stop to absorb what's actually waiting for me.

Louise.

She's stock-still kneeling at the center of the foyer rug with her hands resting on her thighs and her neck tilted all the way back so her head is perched on her shoulder blades. Eyes closed above a crescent frown, she looks like a religious pilgrim, forsaken and small.

A perfect painting, if I were soulless.

If I were the same man she met a couple months ago, I'd go get my camera.

But I'm not, and I know it the moment my diaphragm twists with pain at the sight of her. The moment my feet start moving without my permission, forcing me forward, slow at first, then quicker.

The floorboards squeak, giving me away, and her big round eyes open and swivel in my direction. She doesn't turn her head, only her eyes move, and with them come tears, spilling down her cheek like a waterfall.

Beautiful.

She whispers, "Can I stay?" and my mouth says, "Always," before I can think about it. Even when I do, the answer is the same.

My fingers reach for the zipper on her parka and peel it from her, sloughing it to the floor before I coax her shoes off too. Then my hand slides under her thighs, the other around her back, and I lift her into my arms.

She doesn't fight the intrusion. Her head lolls against my shoulder and lets it happen. Lets me carry her up the stairs.

There are six bedrooms up here, but I don't know when the cleaners last changed the bedding, so I take her to mine. Still holding her, I coax the covers back so I can feed her right into the cool, cotton sheets. She hisses at the chill.

"Sorry, I'll…"

Before I can say I'm going to go build the fire back up, she curls in on herself into a perfect little roly poly shape, dark against the white sheets, and it's another accidental painting in the making. She doesn't even know she's doing it.

I fetch the blanket and cover her with it, wondering what to ask…if I should ask anything.

But her amber eyes track my movements and by the time she's tucked in, the pillow is wet with her tears, adding texture to the painting I can imagine so clearly. I sit on the edge of the bed, just painting her in my mind.

"Thank you," she says after a moment.

"Of course. You're more than welcome—"

The soft shake of her head quiets me. "Thank you for painting me like that."

"Like what?"

"Like a person." Her voice lilts with pain and it hits me the way it should have when I first saw her that something must have happened. Maybe that Russo guy painted her again.

If he did, well. Guess I'll have to handle it.

"Sleep, okay?" I say, sweeping a tendril of hair out of her face.

Then I leave her to rest and go downstairs to grab my phone. I haven't looked at it all day, or the last few if I'm honest. I gave up my need-to-know doom scrolling when I came to live here. But I think to check the latest art forums for any gossip, maybe reach out to a couple of well-connected contacts I have, or even just email Mr. King to ask what happened.

I don't get that far.

There's an email notification on my unlock screen—from the Russo Trust. I signed up after her first visit, just to…I don't know…show my support for Louise. Or hear what she was up to. Guess it doesn't matter now.

I open it with a flick of my thumb and grimace fifteen words into it. It's…corporate character assassination, plain and simple. The sort of legalese that makes injustice seem polite.

Sure, they have the right to fire her for anything.

But they didn't just fire her. They lied by implication.

If people ever ask me why I hate people, I can just show them this email.

It lights a fire under my ass, and I'm back working in my studio before the anger begins to fester. I return to the painting of her in a sea of stars—it's the most encouraging, I think. Or it will be when I'm done with it.

I decide to adjust the sketch, so that her face is just cresting through the waves, so she's surfacing out of the dark rather than submerged, when I hear a sound like footsteps.

There's a hard, confident knock on the front door and I hear, "Kaden Allard? I need to speak with you about Lulu."

CHAPTER 42

NERO

Kaden Allard.

Allard, as in the family that owns *Chez Moi*, one of the largest and most successful multinational holding companies for luxury goods in the world.

Allard, as in one of two heirs to a thirty-billion-dollar fortune.

No, excuse me. His name is Malbec now.

That's the *nom de plume* he prefers for his art.

It's nuts that I was able to find out *his* name before I found out whatever Lulu's used to be. Maybe they bonded over that. Or their love of art. Or maybe he's just another pervert who sent her a thirst trap. Maybe it was a totally professional...video of him jerking off in front of a painting of her.

I spent the entire drive up here trying to decide how to play this with her. Trying to decide if I should downplay him, or hype myself up, or take her away before whatever charm he has can rub off on her. My apartment off Central Park could be just as cozy a hiding spot as this place...with the benefit of way more take-out options.

He can't be that special looped in my head like a catchy chorus until Kenzo sent me a text about who Malbec actually is, and I started to worry.

Then he opened the door of this ginormous chalet and I got a fucking look at his face and I almost threw in the towel right then and there. I mean, I saw the video on Lulu's phone, and he was hot in that, but it doesn't compare to what he looks like in person. The lucky bastard's a damned GQ model…who also has a talent.

Rich. Successful. Disgustingly handsome.

God really does play favorites. Fucking pretty boy.

I keep the bitterness out of my voice, though. "Hey. Malbec, right?"

His violently blue eyes narrow on me. "You have the wrong house, man."

I get my shoe in the door before he can close it. "Please. I don't give a shit who you are, all right? I know Lulu's here. I know what happened to her today."

His brow furrows. "And you are?"

"Nero King."

"Ethan's brother? He has no right giving out my address or personal information—"

"He didn't. I'm a big fucking snoop and I found you myself, okay?"

Kaden's face splits in an incredulous grin and my bitterness at his prettiness only deepens.

"How does that make it better?"

"It doesn't. I'm not here for you. I'm here for her. I need to be here for her." He hesitates, and I feel the need to add the obvious, "Ask her. She'll tell you. We're…friends. She knows me."

"She's sleeping right now—"

"No, she's not."

Her voice cuts through the depth of ours like a songbird from the top of the stairs. She slips down a few steps until she's in full view, then sits down like she's too tired to stand. The circles under her eyes are dark, the whites are red with tears. Her beautiful cheeks are puffy.

It's automatic, how quickly I step past Malbec. He doesn't even try to stop me.

But she does. I'm halfway across the foyer to her when she says, "You didn't need to come, Nero."

"I wanted to," I tell her. "I saw the email."

"Oh." Her lips curl down a second before she grits her teeth like she's in pain at the thought.

"So did I," Malbec echoes.

"But only a few people saw it," I add. "We stopped the email before it could reach everyone. And it doesn't change what we're going to do, Lulu. Cara, Ivy, Ethan—we're going to make sure they pay for it."

"I'm tired," she says to that. "I'm sorry you came all this way. I just needed to get away for a while. Mr. Malbec is low-tech out here. And he doesn't care what the Russos think."

I know why—he could erect a museum to himself without breaking any bank, least of all his own.

But that doesn't matter right now, so I say, "I understand. I can go low-tech too. And I definitely couldn't give two shits about that family."

Before somebody makes me state the obvious, I shuck off my coat and toss it over the banister. Then I walk up to where she's sitting and scoop her up. Her eyes dart to Malbec, curious to see how he'll react, but I don't care how strange this looks to him. Or if he's jealous. Follow or not, that's his call.

"In there," she says when we reach the second floor.

I carry her to the bed and nestle her into it before I sit down right beside her, leaning back against the headboard, getting comfortable. I flick on the end table light too, so I can see her.

"Nero," she says, a little in shock…but there's more relief. I can hear it in her voice. And feel it in her grip as she tucks two of her fingers through one of my belt loops, basically cementing me to the spot. "Kaden might not like this."

Kaden enters the room as if summoned, and his eyes dart across us, assessing. He's not the only one. I don't bother saying anything. I just wait for him to decide how he's going to play this because this is where I'm going to stay, unless he fights me for this spot.

CHAPTER 43

KADEN

Maybe seeing them in my bed—seeing the way she reaches for him, the territorial bent of his body over her, the way he stares me down as he runs his fingers through her hair waiting to see what I'll do—should make me angry, but…that's not the top emotion.

I mean, she came here on her own. He's obviously important to her somehow, but how remains to be seen. She didn't seek him out. She came here to be with me. Despite his intimidating size and the aura of 'fuck around and find out' his tattoos inspire, she thought of me first.

And joke's on him if he thinks he can 'out-awkward' me in my own home.

The joke's also on me, though. Fuck my brain's immediate instinct to focus on shapes and lines instead of the larger picture. Looking at the pair of them, all I see is another painting. A lopsided one.

Louise is right in the center of the bed with him on her left, leaving a massive negative space to her right. I want nothing more than to fill it.

So that's what I do. I round the bed and crawl in on her other side, adjusting the pillows to make leaning back against the headboard comfortable.

By the time I'm done, Louise shoots her free hand out behind her and pats until she finds mine and takes hold of it with hers. Until we're suddenly a little chain.

Until she whispers, "I'm sorry. Thank you."

"Don't worry, we've got you," Nero coos at her, still playing with her hair, and I feel her grip tighten on both of us.

Again, maybe there should be anger but…that's not what I feel. It's curiosity more than anything. I've been self-isolating so long, it feels nice not to be fucking alone here.

The little twitches that begin when Louise eventually drifts to sleep between us are nice too. Like Morse code, her fingers flex in mine in random little spurts. They do the same in Nero's belt loop, and he smiles every time they do.

That alone—the little connection she has on him—I want to paint. My hands are so itchy it's insane. It's as if I hibernated for so long that a thousand notifications spawned inside me by the time I woke up and now they're all demanding my attention.

But they're all notifications involving *her*. So where else am I going to go? I wanted her back here to paint. To model for me. To paint with me. To see her paint something herself.

Does he know that side of her? He doesn't seem like an artist. The tattoos on his hands are jailhouse amateur, probably done with a ballpoint pen. But the ones around his neck? Those were professionally done. One in particular catches my eye—of a battered mailbox with initials drawn on it. The perfect lines of everything else tell me the initials were done to mimic actual handwriting—NK, EK, MK. I'm guessing him and his brother and…their mom? The MK is in a more feminine cursive. The nostalgia of it is so strange juxtaposed against…the rest of him.

"Who did that one?" His voice yanks my attention away from his neck.

"Hmm?" Nero points at Louise's *Hourglass* painting, where it sits across the room, and I tell him, "It's hers."

His gaze jerks to mine, almost in suspicion. I shrug at him so he believes me.

"Where's *her* gallery?" Nero asks aside to himself.

"You're telling me. Just wait until you see it in the daylight."

At that, his gaze turns to me, assessing again. His attention is bald and unflappable, completely unbothered by me. "I'm not going to leave unless she tells me to."

He's not asking me to let him stay. He's telling me what's going to happen, and honestly, I admire the 'no fucks given' way he declares it, like he's trying to warn me away from a fight we both know I'd lose.

"What do you expect me to say to that?" I ask, almost laughing.

"I don't know," he admits, chuckling. "Maybe say you'll help me give her what she needs, whatever that is."

Fuck, that feels like a big ask—one I want to give, even if I'm not sure I can. Whatever moments Louise and I have shared, I only just made up for one big mistake; I'm bound to make more. But maybe he knows her better than I do. Whatever they are to each other, she clearly trusts him.

When I don't respond, he adds, "Maybe say you're going to help us destroy the Russos."

"Now *that* I can guarantee," I promise.

"Really."

"I already offered to poison them."

"No shit?" Off my nod, the corners of his lips curl down, seemingly impressed. "All right then."

His unaffected response makes my curiosity itch again in a different way.

"What did the painting actually look like, the one he did?"

"You haven't seen it?"

"She drew a sketch…"

Careful not to disturb his hand where it lays on her hair, gently stroking her temple with the pad of his thumb, or her hand where it holds his belt, Nero finagles his cell out of his pocket and quickly scrolls to something before turning the phone to me.

It's worse than the sketch, which I didn't think was possible. Shouldn't be possible.

"God, I've never hated anyone that much," I murmur.

Nero frowns again and tucks the phone away. Not that it matters; that image is seared into my mind now. A hate tattoo on the folds of my brain.

"Whatever she needs," I say, as a promise to myself, to her. "Just tell me the plan."

CHAPTER 44

NERO

I wake a couple hours later with my arms around Lulu, enveloped in her fruit-kissed scent. Kaden is gone; he turned off the light when he left. I'm not surprised. When I showed him the painting and told him Ivy's plan, he wrapped his other hand around Lulu's protectively and sort of retreated into his head. His eyes swiveled back and forth like he was trying to figure something out; maybe he did.

I can hear someone moving around downstairs. Working downstairs.

I roll out of bed and cover Lulu before I follow the noises to…a giant gabled room at the back of the house. His workshop, obviously, given the insane number of canvases *everywhere*.

And the smell—holy fucking paint fumes, Batman. A wall of sharp chemical tang smacks me in the face as I step in.

"Jesus, do you like being high all the time or did you forget how windows work?" I ask.

"Huh? Oh. Nah, just used to it, I guess."

Kaden's standing by an easel working on something, but my eyes sort of leap over him to take in everything else first. The paintings on the walls, sure, but…it's the paintings scattered around on the floor that catch my attention.

Those, and the giant unfinished painting of Lulu standing a few feet away.

They're all of her.

And they're fucking *nice*. Even unfinished, they're as good as anything I've ever seen in a museum.

Talented asshole. *Reverent* asshole. If Emilio had painted her like this, none of us would be here.

This must be why she came here. He was already painting her and she knew he could give her what she needed to enact Ivy's plan.

Insecurity curls around me in a death grip. The second she sees these? What the hell will she need me for?

In the biggest one—the blue one—she's stripping down. The expression on her face is peaceful, relieved, protected, as if she's returning to a safe place where she can be herself. If she modeled for him like that...if he knows her well enough to make her feel like that...they must have something going on, right? Maybe I am intruding. Maybe I was just a good lay to her and me showing up is only getting in the way of what she really wants.

"How long have you spent on these?" I ask as I near one where she's crouched on one knee pulling back a tablecloth, smiling at me as if we were playing hide and seek or something.

"Just a few hours."

Fucking what? I feel some part of me twist awkwardly. Maybe I'm neck and neck with him in terms of the emotional part of his relationship with Lulu, but...how am I supposed to compete with the *raw mastery* of his fucking trade?

I mean, I have skills but I used mine to spy on her like a creep.

"Unbelievable," is all I can say.

"Do you think she'll like them?" he asks with absolutely zero self-awareness.

"Fuck man, are you kidding? I lost the race before it even started, I think."

"Yeah right," he scoffs.

"I'm serious, I can't compete with this." Because I can't.

"What? A barely human weirdo in the woods high on paint fumes who hasn't left his house in three years?" Kaden jokes. "Oh yes, every woman's fantasy."

"Old money rich. Successful. Talented." I check them off on my fingers as I go.

Kaden turns to me at that, brow bent nervously. "She doesn't know about the family stuff. Don't tell her, okay?"

Fuck! She doesn't even know about the cherry on top of everything else he can offer her? Again, I'm struck by competing thoughts that make me want to run for the hills *and* fight harder for her simultaneously. But…the thoughts are more of my own insecurities, not anything to do with Lulu.

"Yeah, fine. I don't think she cares about that anyway."

"Don't act like you're not…who you are," Kaden adds.

"I'm nobody," is obvious.

Kaden laughs at that. "Yeah, just a self-made billionaire who looks like a Renaissance statue of Lucifer. Fuck off."

So he googled me after leaving the bedroom.

"A convict, too, don't forget that. With a fucking family that doesn't trust me."

"She trusts you."

That hits me square in the chest, when I realize he's right. Her little fingers holding onto me even in her sleep? Pride washes through me in waves just thinking about it. Pride…and promise never to take that for granted.

"She trusts you too," I point out. "She came here first."

"I hope she made the right choice," he murmurs, surprising me.

Some dark inkling encourages me to latch onto his insecurity and run with it, let him self-sabotage so I come out looking like the better choice to her, but…fuck, I can't bring myself to give him bad advice, or no advice. It might hurt her.

"Be the right choice," I say instead. "You like her, don't you?"

"Of course."

"Of course," I echo, because that's the only acceptable fucking answer. I won't fight over her for anything less than 'of course.' Anything less than 'of course' and he can go sit in the shed for however long it takes to get her to come home with me.

"I just…" There's genuine worry on his face. Not just insecurity but…nervousness. "I don't remember how to be around people."

And I laugh because he's like the flip side of me. "Yeah, well, I spent the last five years trapped in a tin can with hundreds of them. It's lonely as fuck either way."

Kaden smirks at that. "Sounds like you should've been painting."

"What do you mean?"

"It's something my art teacher used to say. Anytime I was bored, anytime I was scared or lonely or anxious. Anytime I felt…stuck, she'd listen to me complain and say, 'Sounds like you should've been painting.'"

"The answer for everything, eh?"

"I've never felt overwhelmed or alone when I'm making something. A good go-to distraction."

I shake my head at that. "I don't think that's what she meant. I mean I don't want to tell you your business, but I think she meant you should be *doing something* to get you outta your funk. Something to knock you out of whatever's got you in your head. It's too easy to spiral forever, right? But you can snap yourself out of it—save yourself—with something you love, like painting."

Kaden blinks at me, considering. "Fuck, now that you say it like that, it's pretty obvious, isn't it?"

"I don't know. When I was a kid, I accidentally figured out I could kill my panic attacks by crunching on an ice cube. Not exactly intuitive, but I feel like it's sort of the same thing. I mean, I don't love ice cubes, which is why I moved on to tattoos when I could afford 'em, but…ya know. Whatever gets the job done."

Same goes for Lulu. I want her to have whatever she needs to get over the Russos. Whatever distraction. Whatever passion. Whatever triumph.

Even if I'm not the one who gives her those things.

As I stand there studying Kaden's art, I realize every single piece is already a hundred times better than what Emilio did. Give Kaden a week and we could drown the Russo Exhibition in Lulus without my involvement.

Hell, give Kaden a week with a dick and face like his and she won't need me at all.

The thought stings. Stabs. Disembowels.

Fuck-Fuck-Fuck. I hate the thought of giving up. I hate the possibility that I could leave and she'd never think of me again. And I hate that that possibility makes me want to pre-reject her, to protect myself.

She needs to need me. If she doesn't, then I'll be nothing to her.

In a world of fickle fucking people who think they always have options when they don't, need is the thing that gets people to stick around, and keeps them coming back. You can take the things you *want* for granted—time, success, affection—but *need* lasts.

Need makes the difference.

My dad's entire fucking life is all the proof I need to know need makes the difference. Selfish bastard saw all of us as accessories—my mom, my brother, me. He always told us he didn't need us, and if we couldn't give him what he wanted, we were fucking worthless to him.

But in the end, I had a front-row seat to just how wrong he was. To how much he needed us, after it was too late. He called out for me, begged for me to help him and I just watched. I just watched as—

A hand lands on my shoulder, scaring the memory back into the darkness.

I find Kaden holding a paintbrush out to me.

"Distraction?"

He makes the offer without a single ounce of ego. I might as well be a stranger struggling on a street corner and he's offering me a cigarette. I feel like a kid trying to grip a fork for the first time, when I take the paintbrush from him.

"I don't know how," I warn him.

He shrugs. "I forget how all the time. So long as the paint hits the canvas, I think you got it."

CHAPTER 45

LULU

I'm warm when I wake up. So warm, I have to kick off the covers, even though neither Kaden nor Nero are there when I open my eyes. I'm alone in the center of the bed where I fell asleep and I wish I wasn't. Being alone with my brain is torture. She doesn't like me most of the time, and lately? She fucking hates me.

She fucking hates me, but likes to use my body to make herself feel better.

Bitch.

Something about the possibility of waking up sandwiched between two tall, dark, handsome men had her opening floodgates prematurely. *And* sending *nonstop* signals to my clit like some sort of broken S.O.S. telegram system. She's down there, so stimulated, she's got me doing accidental kegels.

Which is a level of delulu wish fulfillment I could almost admire, if it was just for fun and she didn't punish me for telling her to calm down. The moment the bitch in my head realizes I'm manually shutting off the happiness circuits, she reroutes to thoughts that make me hate myself.

Memories of that meeting with Mrs. Russo.

Memories of having to take a bus, then the subway, while covered in vomit.

The mean reminder that *I'm unemployed* slams down into my heart from above. Then I remember that I wasn't just fired, but punished too and the hurt ricochets into my throat. Splinters of pain lodge in the soft tissue there making it difficult to swallow, or even breathe, as I sit up in Kaden's bed.

And then I see *my painting* sitting in the eave across the room. It's a reminder of everything I thought I could be when I started my life over at nineteen. The dreams I had. The delusions of freedom I had.

Well, you're certainly free now, my mind taunts me until my eyes fill with tears.

I wish it was easier for me to keep my 'eyes on the prize,' and my mind on the plan, but the exhibition is months away. I'm still jumping from one board to the next across the collapsing bridge; I can't focus on an as-of-yet imaginary future. My tired brain is focusing on the boards as they disappear underneath my feet.

But I'm used to outrunning them, and the tears never actually fall down my face. My eyes just sort of…reabsorb them for later. After all, how can I outrun the collapse of my life if I'm blinded by tears?

How can I outrun it if I stay in bed?

That thought gets me to my feet. That, and the smells in the house—wood fire, bacon, and wet paint. I know it sounds nuts, but…*fucking divine*, that combination. I never knew that's how I wanted to wake up every morning, until now.

I feel famished as I slip silently down the stairs in my socks, chasing scents, then sounds when I hear the clang of cast iron, the sizzle of hot tasty things.

But I realize I'm famished for more than bacon when I enter the kitchen and find Nero at the stove, shirtless and splattered in paint.

It's…he's a vision. Or a mirage. He has to be. The muscled expanse of his back looms like a stretched canvas before me, bedighted with art. The tattoos are everywhere, intertwining, wrapping around his shoulders and down the backs of his arms, and around his waist on either side. It's not full-body in the traditional sense; I can tell he accrued new pieces of work over time, until they began to touch and intersect. Some pieces are in fine color, others are cruder in black, using the tan of his natural skin to differentiate the negative space.

Beautiful.

And none of the art disguises *the fucking body* on which it's painted. He's built of pure discipline, muscled without diving too extremely into bodybuilder territory. He looks like he joined a prison gang, basically…for all I know, he did.

But what I love most about the work of art in front of me is how stark the contrast is between his bare torso and the slacks on his lower half. He never took off his clothes when we had sex, so seeing him half-dressed feels a bit *risqué*. Naughtier than it ought to be.

Then he turns and spots me. His lips curl indecently, like he knew I was there the whole time and didn't want to interrupt my show.

"Hey gorgeous," he says.

"Morning," I manage through the flood of drool that comes rushing to my mouth the second I see the front of him. His chest is starkly different from the back. There are almost no tattoos, for one. The ones creeping around from his back hug the edges, his waist, his arms, his shoulders and neck, almost framing his physique. It's sort of like looking at an aerial landscape painting of a mountain range of ab muscles beneath the twin peaks of his pecs.

It makes the singular tattoo on his front look like it's on display, even though it's only a name. On the lower right side of his abdomen, in red, just beneath his lowest rib: *Prometheus.*

"It's okay to touch."

His voice snaps me out of my musings. I discover I somehow crossed the kitchen without being conscious of it. My hand hovers between us, a bare inch above that tattoo—damn, this is the second time I've reached out to touch a piece of art without thinking about it.

But I'm more immediately embarrassed. What the hell is wrong with me?

I pull back a little, tucking my hand in the sleeve of my sweater, and the word "Sorry" rushes to my lips, but never quite makes it.

Because Nero reaches for my hand before I can pull it away, and plants it on his abdomen, on that tattoo.

"You're always welcome to touch me, Ms. Rathbone," he says,

almost chiding.

"That's dangerous," I laugh, even as my fingers slide across his warm skin, across the red letters there. "Prometheus?"

"The man who stole fire from the gods," he says quietly.

I grin, considering. "I didn't think your ego was that big."

"Well, if you remember, his punishment was to have his liver eaten out by an eagle every night."

The words pull my attention to his face, to the patience and amusement I find there, the spark in his emerald eyes. It's breathtaking. So is the shy grin he gives me.

"*Forethought*," he says. "When you operate outside the bounds of proper society, you have to be careful. I got it as a reminder to cover my ass…and make sure the consequences are worth it."

I…don't know what to say to that, but I love that he thought about it. I love that it means something to him.

"Do all of your tattoos come with stories?"

"Maybe," he lies—they definitely do. Then he steps back toward the stove and adds, "Kaden has something to show you. Let me finish making us breakfast and then I'll come join you."

His casual tone throws me a little. So does the word 'us.' So do the three plates and sets of silverware I see sitting nearby. He seems comfortable already…as if he's staying, which…isn't his call, or mine, I have to remember.

Unless Kaden told him he could. That we could. Did he?

It's the question toddling at the edge of my mind as I leave the kitchen and make my way to the studio, but it falls into the abyss of lost thoughts when I see what awaits me.

When I see what they did while I was asleep.

Emotion wells in me like a geyser seconds from erupting. Joy and fear and something darker I don't know how to deal with yet rush and surge and roil.

They…rearranged the studio.

Before, it was clutter city. Canvases, paints, tools—great piles of them had sat on tables, and under them, alongside drop cloths and paint-stained water glasses. Drying racks had sat crowded with forgotten art. The overall landscape of the room had looked like a haunted attic, and Kaden had existed in it like a ghost.

Now?

The clutter's still there but organized. The drop cloths are missing, the tables are still crowded, but tidy. The haunted attic is gone, replaced by...space. At the center of the room, they cleared a great wide circle and placed easels there—three of them beside the oversized one still holding the unfinished *Blue Ruin* painting.

Kaden's working at one of the easels as I walk across the room. He, too, is shirtless...and my mind tosses out a joke—that they both decided to make today *Shirtless Saturday*.

The joke is armor. It has to be because my mouth waters at the sight of him. He's narrower at the shoulders and waist than Nero, but just as beautiful. It's the difference between a swimmer's body versus someone who plays football—*not important at all*!

I'd take both! If I could have both.

I suppose I could on *Shirtless Saturdays*, my brain teases me again.

But...a more nervous part of me points out that I've invaded his home. *We* have. We're probably making Kaden uncomfortable, which is the *last* thing I want to do.

I chose to come here because he was so far removed from everything. Even though the painting he'd once given me went into the Russo Trust, he was entirely separate from them. Still is, you know?

And *that painting*? Our *Blue Ruin*?

Seeing it in the video of him made me want to come back and finish it. It's so beautiful. Everything I want to be. *That* Lulu looks so content, peaceful in a way I've certainly never felt. I wish I could crawl right into the canvas with her, live in that blue room with its blue freedom and comfort.

But as I round a table and the full open circle of space comes into view, I realize she's not the only one anymore. There are four other paintings, all in various stages of being completed, scattered around the edge of the circle.

And they're all me.

Me peeking behind a veil. Me studying my own reflection. Me floating in a sea of stars.

Me buried in bedsheets with a *come hither* expression of heat and love and trust on my face.

That one is hard to look away from.

Until I take a closer look at the two in-progress pieces on the easels. Kaden's is just a sketch yet, a close-up of my face peering up at something.

The other…is also me, but so starkly different, it catches me off guard.

It's an impressionist piece, so the brush strokes are bold and the details have been ignored, but it's still obviously me. A "portrait" of me, in browns and taupes, as if a near-sighted person without glasses painted me from three or so feet away.

Fucking beautiful.

It's not clean or competent the way Malbec's are; it's raw and tentative, curious and experimental.

"Nero did that one last night."

I feel my brow arch in disbelief as I turn to Kaden. He nods, almost proudly.

"He needed the distraction," he says, answering my unspoken question. "Pretty good, isn't it."

It is.

More than that, *he* did it.

It seems like such an odd thing for him to do, even if he made it in solidarity with Ivy's plan to save me.

Because there is no way it's going in the exhibition. *I'm keeping it.*

My Big Guy's first painting.

Somehow it fits in with the *showcase of Lulus* currently on display around me. It's overwhelming. I turn in a tight little circle studying them all, hoping the movement will shake some of the insecurities loose in my body, so I can enjoy this.

"Do you like them?" he asks, and I laugh because that's an insane question.

"I feel like crying," I admit. "When did you do all of this?"

"Yesterday."

I laugh again, at the joke. "Yeah."

But Kaden only smirks as if to say he's never joked about art in his entire life, but he likes knowing the thought made me laugh.

"Nero told you the plan?" I ask to confirm.

"He has now, but I jumped the gun a little bit with these."

"What do you mean?"

Kaden's gaze jerks from mine and I catch a shy smile streak across his face before he turns back. "I haven't been able to stop thinking about you since you left, Louise. Couldn't paint for days because all I could think about was doing what I promised I would do for you. Then I sent you that video, and it unleashed something. I couldn't help myself."

It's flattering. He means it to be flattering. My brain knows that.

But my body takes it differently.

That phrasing *"I couldn't help myself."* My hackles rise instantly. Anxiety crawls up my spine like a spider, pressing different spots simultaneously on the path to my brain.

And it makes no sense at all—I've always wanted to be the art. I *have* to be the art for Ivy's plan to work. And yet...

Kaden's words dig and scratch at things long buried in me.

I feel...disoriented.

Unsafe.

Which is crazy, because I know Kaden wouldn't hurt me. Nero wouldn't hurt me.

Still, panic rises in me as swift as a tsunami.

"Louise, are you okay?"

"Yeah," I lie, trying not to let the panic leech into my voice.

Kaden seems to hear it anyway. His beautiful blue eyes widen. Tossing his palette and brush aside, he comes to me, cooing, "Hey, it's okay."

The second his hands land on my shoulders, my breath hitches. I can't catch it. Even though the expression on his face is so fucking *generous* and *reassuring*, I go to pieces in front of him.

"I'm fine," I pray, trying to convince myself.

"I'll burn them if you don't like them," he says, so quietly to me. "Just say the word."

"No!" I yelp, because I can't think of anything worse. I reach for his hips and cling, to make him understand. "They're wonderful. It's not them."

"Then what is it?"

"What's wrong?" Nero's voice barks suddenly from the doorway and I turn to find him walking in with glasses of orange juice in his hands.

"I'm fine," I pray again, as Kaden's arms envelope me and pull me against his warm, hard stomach. His hand goes to my hair, petting, and his scent of paint and some sort of body wash creeps up my nose. "I'm sorry, I'll be fine soon."

I hear a *clink*. Nero has the glasses on a side table, but as I watch, he plunks two fingers into one of them and retrieves an ice cube, then stalks toward us, brow furrowed to pain. For a second, I think he's going to throw a punch at Kaden, he's so wired. My hand goes up to hold him back...

But I don't have to. He's not angry at Kaden, or me for that matter. His arms wrap around me from the side, practically sandwiching me between them, and my hand reaches for his belt loop again.

"You're safe," Nero growls.

Fuck. My body wants to fight every time he says that. But I resist and cling to both of them and close my eyes instead. The warmth between them feels too good to give up.

Until he says, "Open your mouth."

My gaze jerks skyward to his, uncertain.

"Please," he adds.

I part my lips, more to ask why than to do what he says, but I don't get the chance. He raises the ice cube to my lips and slips it into my mouth, accidentally running his fingers over my lips as they pull away.

"Crunch on it," he says.

"But..."

"It's okay. You're safe," he says again. "Just try."

I don't like the cold, but I do it. And the second I do, I groan with discomfort. "Fuck, Nero, I hate this."

"Crunch," he says again.

So I make a show of it, baring my teeth a little for them as the ice goes to pieces between them.

"There, happy?"

"Very," he smirks. "How do you feel?"

"Cold, you dick!"

"How about the panic?"

I freeze, realizing…it's muted. Like someone took things from sixty down to three instantly, the anxiety is still there at the fringes of my mind, but it's bearable. I can think, I can breathe, my skin doesn't feel prickly and uncomfortable. And a pink admiration blossoms in me. He…tricked me out of a panic attack.

"Better?" he asks.

"Oh, damn you," I tease.

Before I even stop to think about it, I dart forward and lick his stomach with my ice-cold tongue. He hisses and laughs and doesn't pull away…

But I feel Kaden's hand still on the back of my head. Shame tiptoes into my heart for a second, before I decide that's not what I want to feel. They're both here and I don't want either one to feel excluded.

So I turn to him and lick his stomach just as quickly, splaying my frozen tongue across his abs for half a second before Kaden gasps and pulls back. But he doesn't step out of my grasp; he only recoils slightly before he comes right back and I feel his thumb trace a gentle line across the curve of my skull again.

"Thanks a lot, you two," I grumble. "Now I'm cold."

I say it because it's true. I have the temperature regulation of a reptile—blazing warmth or torpor, there's no in between.

But when I glance up at them, I'm surprised to see them both just watching me. It's like two giant statues have come to life and bent over a mouse. No, not statues; they're too warm to be that. They're two giant space heaters I *really wish* were heated blankets right now.

Fuck, that thought spawns other inappropriate ones.

Like, *lie on me*, damn it.

Crush me, daddies.

I-I've been with multiple guys at once before, but not voluntarily. Not when it felt good. The wish to know what that might feel like prances through my head.

But I know that's selfish. Just because they've offered to help me, it doesn't mean they've offered everything. They don't even know each other.

They seem to realize that a moment later, as they both take a step back, breaking the accidental connection between us. Even though it's selfish, I miss it the moment it's gone.

"Let me grab you a sweatshirt," Kaden says, hustling away.

"Breakfast will warm you up too," Nero adds before he also darts out.

Then it's just me, alone in the studio. Me, myself, and I, as I study their paintings of me again.

They're beautiful. I'll be honored by whichever Kaden offers to put in the exhibition.

And I realize quickly, the paintings by themselves don't trigger any feelings of panic in me. It was only the words Kaden said.

Words he couldn't have known were a trigger, because *I* didn't know until now.

Words the worst person I ever knew used to use all the time to explain away his terrible cruelty.

"*I couldn't help myself,*" JV used to say.

What a fucking lie, one he told my mom and I as often as the chiming of a clock tower bell.

"*I couldn't help noticing your daughter is quite beautiful,*" became, "*I couldn't help thinking she'd make an amazing model for my art. I can pay you for the sessions—$150 a day.*"

I was only thirteen; it sounded like a lot of money to me.

And to my mom who "needed it" and "asked" if I could "be a good girl and help her make ends meet" that way.

I didn't know a mother who loves you would never make you do something like that.

And like a frog sitting in hot water until she boiled to death, I didn't know until it was too late how many things he *"couldn't help"* doing.

"I couldn't help painting you in that position."

"I couldn't help touching you while you slept."

"I couldn't help inviting my colleagues over. They need a model for their work too. Now take off your clothes and lie back on the lounge."

I hate that that period of my life still holds such sway over the rest of it. I hate that that *man* still holds the power to make my body freak out.

JV.

Over a decade later, I have a hard time even *thinking* his full name.

Fuck him, he doesn't deserve a full name.

Or one iota more of my time.

Neither does Emilio. At least, not today. Today I need a *fucking break!*

So I go back over to the glasses of orange juice Nero set aside and pop another ice cube into my mouth, as a preemptive measure.

And when both men return—one with food, the other with a thick, fluffy, gazillion-dollar designer sweater—I make a point of saying, "I need to do something fun today. You up for that?"

"Hell yes," Nero says, as Kaden echoes, "What do you have in mind?"

CHAPTER 46

KADEN

"This is a *terrible* idea," I say because it is. "This place is a maze of tetanus and asthma attacks."

"Come on," Louise teases, crooking her finger at me to follow her. "This is your house. If you can't rummage around in your own house, then what's the point of having one?"

I don't want to tell her this is a family compound that was mostly used for storage before I sequestered myself up here, which is why I never bothered moving anything around or throwing anything out. I never thought I'd stay here this long. That, and my mother would kill me.

Also, it's just *stuff*, mostly.

But I also don't want Louise thinking I'm some sort of hoarder with a shopping addiction.

"I'm just saying there's *a century* of clutter in this building, *two* centuries in the barn—even if you find something worth pulling out of the junk heap, it'll probably give you bed bugs or something."

"Ew," she laughs, turning as Nero steps out of the bathroom wearing a pair of my jeans and a black undershirt. Her eyes bug a little at the sight of him and I watch as her gaze darts to his waist. "Hey. Comfortable?"

"Yeah, I just can't button them," Nero says, lifting his shirt to show her. "They fit otherwise."

Louise bites her lip and a needle of jealousy pricks my stomach.

"Good, okay." But then she skips to me and reaches for my hand and says, "I think we need gloves. Do you have any?"

We spend the morning on a scavenger hunt through the house, each of us darting off in our own directions on a mission to find the coolest piece of junk we can before returning to the front sitting room and judging our finds.

In our first round, I find a pair of old fire pokers made during the Revolutionary War.

Nero finds a baseball mitt signed by Babe Ruth.

Louise, of course, trounces both of us. She finds a Toulouse-Lautrec painting I've *never* seen before. And suddenly, I'm scrounging around for a hammer and nails so she can hang it in a place of honor in the hallway. My stomach twists with jealousy again when Nero thinks to hoist her off her feet so she can reach the height she wants for it.

Second round, I try to cheat. I go find a bridal quilt dating back to the early eighteen hundreds, hoping it'll tip things in my favor.

Nero finds a chaturanga board from India that my great-grandfather brought back to France with him.

But Louise...well, she screams so loudly she has both of us sprinting through the house thinking she's being attacked by a Babadook or something. When we find her, she's literally jumping for joy with a William Trost Richards painting in her hands.

"How do you not know these things are here!" she yelps playfully, with no clue how her words affect me. "This is like a two-hundred-*thousand*-dollar painting! Not that it matters, because you have to keep it! Please say you'll keep it!"

I have no idea why I didn't look around my own house. I don't know why I've lived like this, so cut off from everything and everyone for so long.

Especially her.

When she takes the bridal quilt out of my hands so delicately and lays it out so she can study the design, I loiter just to stay in her gravity. Then she asks me what I know about the piece and I end up telling her the entire history of the quilt, the story my grandmother told me.

While I speak, Louise's smile grows, and she creeps closer, until she's listening with rapt attention as if the story is the most fascinating thing she's ever heard.

And when I'm done, a secret second smile takes over her face. I can't help asking, "What?"

"Something occurred to me, but I don't think you'll like it. Or you won't take it the right way, even though I think it's lovely."

"You can tell me," I say, not sure whether it's a lie or not.

She slides her hand into mine, still wearing that smile, and says, "I thought you were a misanthrope when I first met you, but I don't think so anymore. I think you love people more than anything but loving them hurts, so you came out here thinking you could get away from them."

My hackles rise at the suggestion, how close she sort of is to the truth, but because of her disclaimer I'm able to sort of laugh it off. "Maybe."

"There's just one problem, my friend," she says, leaning into me. "In order to get away from them, you had to give up all the things they *make* too. The art. The music. The food. The love. What's a life without any of that?"

I find myself in a chair later, sipping a scotch, listening to the *sounds* they've brought into my space in a single day. The opening of cabinets. The *clunk-clunk-clunk* of feet moving up and down stairs. The sneezes and whistles and laughter.

Obnoxious is the right and wrong word for it; their noises rub against me like sandpaper, I'm so unused to them at first.

But at some point, Louise joins Nero when he goes to the kitchen to make a late lunch. He sets his phone to a music channel and plays Louise some of his favorite classical scores—the pieces that got him through his time in prison, he tells her. Apparently, he was allowed to buy an mp3 player from the commissary and loaded it up mostly with Max Richter, Hans Zimmer, and Hildur Guðnadóttir, and he's been trying to "catch up" on latest releases since his release. Things from Natalie Holt, Daniel Deuschle, and Jordan Critz.

Louise is right, about me missing out on all the good things people have to offer. I haven't listened to a single fucking song in *months*.

The first string of notes that floats out of his phone—Max Richter's recomposed version of Vivaldi's "Summer 2"—strike me with the force of a sledgehammer.

I was depressed, once upon a time. Big surprise; I knew that when I first came here. But at some point, the sadness became something else— something worse and passive and lazy. Maybe I shouldn't call it that because in the moment it was all I knew how to feel and be, but looking back now?

This place was meant to be a temporary safehouse, not a tomb.

I think because my art had color in it, I thought there was color in my life. Then she walked in out of the snow, and I realized I was fucking colorblind.

I'm not the only one who thinks so.

When I can't take the solitude of the chair for one more minute, I force myself up and toward the kitchen to join them.

But I pause in the hallway when I hear Nero say, "We could always head into town."

"No, we can find something else to do in the house, so Kaden's comfortable."

She doesn't say it as if she's already bored, but rather like she's being thoughtful of me. Because she thinks I'm some sort of sad-sack agoraphobe who's afraid to leave his house.

I can't decide if that's better or worse than the truth, which is that…I never bothered to. In this age of grocery delivery and wifi, it became more tempting to rot.

I have the sudden gut-check urge to tell her we can go anywhere she wants to; she just has to declare a destination. But just as quickly, I decide not to. Fear stops me. Not of *the world*, but of losing her to it so quickly.

Fuck, I'm already losing her to Nero.

God, that's so fucking selfish.

I don't care.

I want her here with me for a little longer. I want to touch her again. Worship her again.

So later, when we're winding down for the night and Nero strips off *my* jeans and crawls into *my* fucking bed like he owns it, and echoes the beautiful lines of her body by curling around her, I don't even fucking hesitate. I crawl in on her other side.

She's facing me. I mirror her body, so my knees are touching hers. Ignoring his entire existence, I tuck her hair behind her ear. His hands are busy gripping her waist, which leaves her hands free to hold mine.

Sliding my fingers into hers takes Louise by surprise. I can feel her tender body tense with uncertainty through my hand. But she doesn't pull away.

She doesn't pull away, so neither do I.

CHAPTER 47

NERO

With my hand on Lulu's waist, I know the exact moment some quiet excitement in her kicks into high gear. Kaden takes hold of her hands and her heart beats so fast I can feel it, skin-to-skin.

I can also feel her holding her breath, although I can't tell if it's with anticipation or discomfort or just raw surprise.

She seems frozen, unsure of what to do, but she doesn't pull away from him or me. If anything, she doubles down on both of us. After a moment, her freeze thaws and I feel her ass nuzzle a little deeper against me as her head scooches an inch closer to his.

"Goodnight, Louise," he whispers to her.

"Goodnight," she whispers back. "Thank you for letting us stay."

"Are you kidding?" he laughs. "*You* are always welcome."

A burst of some twisted frustration and admiration flares hot in my chest—*this fucking guy is clever*. I might have a grip on her body, but she's looking at him. There's nothing *to* look at on that side of the bed but him.

"Goodnight, Nero," she adds after a moment.

I refuse to let it be anything else after the good day we had. Testing the waters, I lean in softly and run my stubble gently across the back of her neck. When she gasps almost silently, I plant a tiny kiss there and her heartbeat spikes again.

It's almost enough.

Softly—so fucking softly—I slide my hand across the gentle plain of her stomach to her waist under the covers, then trail my fingers over the curve of her hip and halfway down her thigh. As if I'm readjusting for sleep.

That's all I'm doing. Mostly.

But she changed into a pair of cloth shorts Kaden found in a box for her before crawling into bed, so I let my fingers slide across the bare skin of her thigh *once, twice,* before I run my nails across the same spot and then press my fingers there.

It becomes a little loop—slide, soft scrape, press—one that keeps her heart pounding, and her mind racing. One that has me hard as fucking diamond and recoiling a little so she won't feel it.

She doesn't let me. Her hips sense mine as they start to move and she presses one more inch deeper against me, making it *very fucking obvious* she can feel my rock hard cock against the crease of her ass...and likes it.

I don't push it though. I can't. I can't ruin this place for her, this sanctuary she chose, without her express permission. I can't just claim her in another man's bed—especially not while that man is eye-fucking the shit out of her, I just know he is.

No. Lulu has to tell us which one of us she wants.

CHAPTER 48

LULU

"What's it like up there in the boonies with nothing but two gorgeous guys to keep you company? Lucky lady."

"Ivy, let her enjoy it. We can wait until she comes back to the city to pry."

"Boo, Cara. Lu, you gotta give us the CliffsNotes at least!"

"I can't, really. There's too much to say."

"Mmm," Ivy hums so provocatively. "I *cannot wait* to hear about it, girlie. The X-rated version and nothing less. Seriously, you should be keeping notes."

"Ooh," Cara echoes. "*Is* it X-rated? Now *I* can't wait."

I've spent a week in Kaden's lodge with them and trying to summarize the experience over a phone call with Ivy and Cara seems preposterous. And impossible.

It's...complicated.

It's...a situation I never imagined myself in.

It's...everything I've ever wanted.

And not enough.

That first day was a break I desperately needed. The lightness of it, the serenity, the playful disregard for anything and everything outside this house—the combo was a perfect cure for the heartbreak I'd felt before coming here. I'd spent the entire trip from the Russos' house on Long Island to this upstate compound thinking my life was over in any way that mattered, only to get blindsided with peace when I got here.

Peace and a fucking *man-smell* that wrapped around me like a fog of weaponized hormones. It had me wet and needy long before they curled around me to sleep again.

I woke up that next day raring to go with Ivy's plan. *Impatient* for it. I called all the artists from the New Year's auction. Most *leapt* at the chance to paint me, I couldn't believe it.

They all said some variation of, "After what Emilio painted? Oh fuck yeah."

Then I called the artists I more or less *knew* would help, and got the same response once I shared the story of what had happened with the Russos.

Even when I double-checked that they understood the risk they were taking by sticking it to the Russos, they answered in their own ways with "art is rebellion," and "art is truth," and "art is whatever the fuck I decide it is for me."

One of my favorite watercolor pastel artists laughed and told me, "I didn't get into painting to lick boots, Lulu. Unless you want me to paint Emilio licking *your* boots—now that I can do."

Maybe it wasn't fair, in a way. After all, I was instrumental in half of them making their first (and second and third) sales, but Kaden and Nero convinced me the artists weren't helping me out of pity or obligation, but out of solidarity. The fact that Nero offered to help their stars shine a little brighter seemed like a cherry on top for them.

And it lifted my spirits like nothing else to discover that Sara Stout was an outlier—someone Mrs. Russo brought up because she knew the woman already disliked me.

Halfway through the week, I had to stop calling people because I suddenly found myself with a full calendar of dates and times over the next few weeks when I would have to visit the artists' studios and pose for them.

At that point, I found myself waking up happier every day than the day before. And terrified of what was going to happen when this vacation from reality ended.

Because in between and after calls, it was just me and my guys.

Every day they've found new ways to make me smile. Watching Kaden paint. Watching Nero learn how to paint. Letting Nero teach us both how to play chess. Arguing over a grocery delivery order and watching them arm wrestle over whether we would buy the pre-made cookie dough Nero preferred or make cookies from scratch using a family recipe from Kaden's mom's side.

Every day, they let me know they both want me.

Kissing my head in passing.

Somehow *always* losing their shirts at some point in the day and never finding new ones.

"Accidentally" taking my towel out of the bathroom so they have to bring two to me while I'm in the shower…while they're both half dressed and primed to join me if I just ask.

I'm not blind or oblivious. I just don't want the bubble to burst. Because it's all competition. Subtle, hot, "cold war" competition, but that's what it is between them.

They're not complaining. They're not demanding. But they want me to choose.

Neither has said it but I can tell.

Every night, I crawl into bed and watch them lunge for their spot as quickly as they can so they can tug me into their embrace. "Winner" gets to touch and massage me until they fall asleep while the "loser" spends that time running his thumb over my lips or playing with my hair while whispering impossibly lovely things to me.

"Remember to tell me your dreams in the morning."

"I love being here with you."

"You're so easy to talk to."

"I'm so glad you let me in."

I've never slept more peacefully in my *life!*

But…I've also never felt more sexually frustrated either. Everything they do turns me on. Especially their little caresses right before bed. Nero likes to tease my thighs. Kaden likes to massage my waist.

And once, while Nero was curled around me, Kaden got so flustered by the things Nero was whispering to me that he just slid his hand right between my legs and left it to rest there, gripping my thigh.

It's torture. It's the worst and best part of being here.

Every night, I've waited until they've both fallen asleep, then slipped away to the bathroom to give myself the orgasm(s) my clit demands night and day. I stand clutching the sink, biting my lip to stay silent as I coax my pleasure out while imagining they're doing it.

But then I crawl back in between them and their warmth overwhelms me. Nero hums in his sleep and Kaden searches for my hand until he finds it and I push back against having the conversation I know they're both waiting for us to have.

I can feel it looming, like some invisible timer, over us all.

I'm more terrified of that now than I am of the exhibition, even though that scares me too.

I'm scared of hurting one of them. Or both, because I don't have an answer for them—I don't know how to pick. Both seem too good to be true. Too good for me.

And then there's that third option, the one that scares me the most. The one that seems too impossible to take seriously as anything other than a fantasy.

The one that scares me for other reasons, because if they said yes, it feels like I'd have to tell them things about myself that only the Russos know. Things that will change how they see me.

See? Way too much to tell my friends over the phone.

So instead I say, "I'm just enjoying every moment I get with them. Once the exhibition's over, this'll probably end too. And that's okay. It's good while it lasts."

"Babe," Ivy chides. "They care about you. It's okay to let them."

Easy for her to say—I'm scared of that too.

CHAPTER 49

KADEN

It only took seventy-two hours to get used to Louise and Nero's constant presence in my house. In my life. I'd deluded myself into thinking it was okay—maybe even ideal—that they'd eventually get tired of being here and head back to the city. But then I woke up alone in my bed on the fourth day and my body strained with panic wondering if they'd slipped away while I slept.

Staring at the fucking empty bed, my throat tore with pain, my lungs tightened. I felt like crying, and I haven't cried in *years*.

Then the floor creaked and the bathroom door opened, and Louise tiptoed out still rubbing the sleep from her gorgeous honey eyes. She smiled at me and said, "Good morning, K."

And I almost barked, "Come here."

She slid into bed like a stretching cat and I reached for her just to make sure she was real. Then I pulled her into my chest and intertwined my legs with hers and tucked her head under my chin.

"You're shaking," she'd said. "Are you cold?"

"Yeah, a little," I lied. "Keep me warm."

Every morning afterward, my body woke me the moment I felt her stirring, so I could capture a few extra minutes alone with her, so I could make her feel not just welcome but *integral*.

By the ninth morning, I was apologizing to her. "I want you to know, I'm so sorry for what I said to you that day you left. You're not a doormat. I hate myself for telling you that. It was a shitty thing to say."

"It's okay," she said, reaching up to play with my hair. "Turns out you were half right. I'm scared of a lot of things."

"I didn't mean that," I countered, but she shook her head gently.

"I was ready to give away my dignity just to keep a job I was scared to lose."

But I hated that she was underselling herself again. So, I cupped her face and held it hostage while I told her, "You quit, Louise. It's not any less brave because it took you a little while to get there."

"I'm sorry for what I said too," she whispered.

"Eh, you were right. I came up here because I convinced myself people were the problem rather than the solution."

Her lips curled at that. "Some people."

I still had my hand on her cheek. I was staring right into her eyes, watching them dart from mine to my mouth and back again. And I didn't kiss her. I wanted to. She was *right there*, looking exactly like the painting of her in the bedsheets I'd started, and I blew my chance.

Before long, the door opened and Nero was there. "Hey, anyone want coffee?"

Louise shot me one more wistful glance, then rolled away from me. Nero and his fucking green laser eyes studied me from the doorway before wrapping his arm around her shoulders and guiding her away.

After that, he never seemed to take his hands off her body. They were never gropey, but he took every chance he could to kiss her head or play with her hair or massage her shoulders. And she cooed with warm purring delight every time, until I was fucking rock hard whenever I heard that sound, no matter where they were in the house.

Nero wasn't ashamed either; he acted like he was doing this as a favor for all of us.

"She carries a lot of tension in her back and ass," he said in a moment alone with me, adding, "I'll stick to the shoulders while we're here."

While we're here because he's going to take her back to the city with him.

While we're here like I'm just a waypoint on *their* journey.

Fuck that. Like I said, no one can out-awkward me in my own home.

"Great," I told him. "Guess I'll volunteer for her ass then. Once I get the all clear from her, my hands'll be glued there."

Nero snorted. "If you have the stones."

Turned out I didn't, but not for the reason he thought. Louise came running into the room with news that another artist had heard about the plan and wanted to offer her talents. Louise threw her arms around me and Nero in celebration, wearing a smile as bright as the sun, and I couldn't wreck the moment for her.

But later, when Nero disappeared somewhere, Louise came to me to ask if she and Nero were overstaying their welcome and I took a chance. I pulled her into my lap in the living room, wrapped my arms around her hips, and told her the most honest thing I could.

"I can't imagine this place without you now. I don't want to."

She giggled shyly and countered, "You'd get bored of me eventually. Everybody does."

"Sounds kind of fun," I said.

"What?"

"Being bored together." But then I added the obvious, "Not that I could be with you."

"You just wanna paint me," she teased.

"In vermilion," I told her, delighting in the flinch along her body as I watched the memory of that day I slicked her body with paint in the kitchen light up her eyes. She tried to hide her sudden glowing smile by dropping her head onto my shoulder; I only pressed my cheek to hers and held her closer. "Do you ever think of that?"

"All the time," she whispered. "I think about you fucking me with a paintbrush."

Fuck.

"I'd rather use a different extension of me, if I'm honest."

"That might work too."

I tightened my hold on her until I could feel her raging heartbeat. "Did you keep the outfit we painted together?"

"Mmhmm," she cooed against my neck.

"You want to make another, you just say the word."

Her breath beat a hot, fast panic against my skin. Her hand slid up my forearm, pressing and teasing.

She was seconds—*seconds*—away from telling me what she wanted, I think, when Nero walked hard across the room and dropped onto the couch across from us. He didn't make a fuss, didn't shy away from staring either, but Louise sat up like a startled meerkat and met his unblinking gaze.

"Hey, Big Guy," she said. "Dinner time?"

"Almost."

"I'll go set the table." And she was gone, leaving me alone with her Big Guy, who I could already tell was planning his next move with her while watching me.

Maybe I should've kicked him out. Or let him have her. Both seemed extreme, dramatic.

Maybe I should just clear the air and demand we sit down like fucking adults to hash whatever this is out together.

But I can't. Nero's not a bad fucking dude. That's the problem. In between all the thigh massages he gives her that he thinks I can't feel under the covers, and the fucking way he constantly pulls her into easy conversation, he also talks to me like I'm a normal human being. A friend, even.

Especially during dinner. Every night since they settled in, we've taken turns cooking for each other. Then we sit around the farmhouse dining table with wine and beer for hours talking.

About his surveillance business.

About the art she favors, the fact that *La Femme Damnée* by Nicolas François Octave Tassaert is one of her favorite paintings.

About Nero's brother and my sister and how we both are and aren't close to them.

It's too much talking for me most nights, so I just listen to them, but I love just fucking listening. And when I *do* have something to say, they loop me right in as if I was talking the whole time.

We've fallen into this addictive routine I'm scared of getting attached to. Every day, Nero enters the studio while I'm painting to ask if he can watch, and paint something himself. Every day, he asks me if I want to play chess with him. I lose every time, but I'm getting better.

Louise doesn't join us for either, but she watches or sits by us reading or goes and does her own thing. She drifts in and out, sitting with both of us, or neither, or one. But she always makes a point to give us both attention, like we're neck-and-neck and neither of us has won the race yet.

And then there was a moment I don't think I'll ever forget.

One night we ended up on one of the big couches in the den together, just laughing about nothing. She was between us and Nero pulled her a little toward him to massage her shoulders, so I reached for her feet, and it was so fucking sensual and silent between us while she clung to him and stared at me, I wanted to *live* in that moment forever.

The next day, Nero was back to touching her any chance he could, eying me in challenge to see if I "had the stones" to do the same, and I realized any territorial shit I was supposed to feel just wasn't there.

Except when one of them mentions leaving. It's never a formal declaration; it's a quiet impending inevitability, like knowing the sun will eventually set.

"My first posing session is next Tuesday."

"I have to meet with my lawyers to talk over the whole arbitration thing with my brother."

"My friend Ivy is leaving for Paris soon and I need to throw her a going away party."

All innocent statements. Yet every single one hits my chest like a gunshot. It hurts so fucking much to think of them leaving, but not because I'll be alone again. It's her. Them.

I want to protect this. Us. I don't know if I can, but it's all I want to do.

If I can't, well, then there's something I need from them before they leave me behind.

CHAPTER 50

NERO

I never imagined I'd leave my six-by-eight cell at Otisburg and voluntarily choose another. Kaden's enormous lodge isn't a prison; I'm just shocked how effortless the last three weeks here with them have been, cut off from everything and everyone I dreamed about getting back to for five years.

I still have to make sure Emilio doesn't fuck anything else up for Lulu.

I still have a company to run. Two, technically, until my brother stops hating me.

I still have to fix this shit with Ethan once and for all.

But tomorrow, Lulu and I head back to the city and I woke up this morning feeling unprepared for the transition. I've never slept well or for very long, so I've been the last to go to bed here and the first to get up, but the last couple of days I've sort of *snapped* awake thrumming with anxiety. I've found myself waking up and studying Lulu and Kaden like some puzzle I haven't figured out yet.

I don't think I'm the only one who's struggling with it. Kaden's default expression is haunted. Wallflowerish. He doesn't feel the need to engage unless there's something to add, which is fine because he's actually got a pretty macabre sense of humor when he gets going. But these past couple of days, he's looked more like a hangdog than usual. Sadder. He reaches for Lulu like he's already saying goodbye.

And Lulu...fuck. She's just getting comfortable with the unspoken dynamic between us. She's not pulling away every time one of us enters the room anymore. She's talking more. Smiling more. Sharing more.

Last night when I was telling them some story about my mom, she admitted she was envious that we had such good relationships with our mothers. She said she hadn't spoken to hers since she was fifteen. She almost told us why before deflecting with, "It doesn't matter, it'd kill the mood."

And every night without fail, she slips out of bed when she thinks we're both asleep to go to the bathroom. Sometimes she's gone just for a few minutes, but at least twice it's been for an hour, and I can swear I hear her sobbing.

If she's crying in there, I want to know. I want to know so I can make her feel too good to cry.

I can't pry, though, can I?

Not now while we only have a few hours left here.

But I don't want to wait until the two of us get back to the city where we can't *settle* anything between the three of us. I don't want to "win" by default. And Kaden deserves better than that. He's a good guy.

He needs to *get out of the cell he's caged himself in*, but other than that, I have nothing against him.

I just want to give Lulu what she needs. It's been my guiding light since I got here. At first, I thought I was competing with Kaden for her, and maybe I am. But it feels like friendly competition, if anything. Motivation to find new ways to make her moan...because I'm pretty damn sure Kaden likes to watch when she does. I *know* I do.

It's fucking hot every time she coos for him.

Last week I caught him dabbing a bit of paint on her nose while whispering things to her in the studio. He smiled, she whimpered, and I almost reached into my pants on the spot, just to relieve some of the *throbbing need* in my neglected dick.

She's not neglecting me, don't get me wrong.

I just wish I knew if she needed us that way. There have been moments where the sexual tension filled the room like a thunderstorm, but Lulu has always backed off before anything can happen. I think it's because we didn't have that conversation right at the start, and she doesn't want to ruin anything now.

I admit I didn't outright encourage her to explore whatever she needed because I didn't want her to choose *not* to explore with me. Or for Kaden to demand a premature choice out of her.

Maybe I'm supposed to be some machismo gorilla he-man, beating his chest to scare away rival males. But the only male I want to do that with is Emilio. I want to rip Emilio's dick off and paint his humiliation in blood.

Kaden, on the other hand. He's good for her. He'd be good to her. So would I.

Fuck, I want to tell them both that, even if I don't know what that means.

Around lunch time, I try to start a conversation with them about it, but the second I mention the fact that we're leaving tomorrow, Kaden changes the subject and Lulu runs with it.

I try again when a spring drizzle begins to fall—the first of the year, Kaden says—and we find ourselves out on the porch, enjoying the chill mist and sound.

"I think we need to talk—"

"Yeah, we do," Kaden says, leaping on my words.

"Do we?" Lulu asks between us, staring out at the rain.

I arch a brow at Kaden and wait, enjoying his sudden discomfort at being put on the spot.

"You were saying, Nero?" he asks.

"You first, by all means," I tease. Dude needs some practice actually speaking up for himself, so I nod for him to go ahead.

"Okay, um, there's something I need to ask you."

"Okay…" Lulu whispers.

She doesn't look at either of us. It's like she can't risk it; her shoulders tense at the thought that he's going to ask her something uncomfortable. To this point, I've reached for her shoulders every time they're tight like this, to control some gut instinct in me to take care of her. To tamp down how badly I want to *need her openly*. I don't reach for her now. I let him hold center court.

"I want to finish *Blue Ruin* for the exhibition," he says. "While we still have the light today, would you pose for the last part?"

The tension in her pops like a bubble. Her entire body jerks in his direction, giving him her full attention.

"Of course!" she says, suddenly smiling. "I thought you'd never ask."

"Good, okay," Kaden says.

"Right now?"

"Yeah." But his body language is tight, tense, like there's something else he wants to say. "How about it, Nero?"

My brow arches again. "How about what? If Lulu says she's cool with—"

"I want you to pose too."

"For...that painting of Lulu?" I ask just to clarify.

"Yeah. I need both of you."

I don't know what to say to that, but Lulu's eyes light up and she reaches for both of our hands, chaining us together again as she waits for my answer. I'm relieved there's only one answer I want to give.

"Sure. Let's do it."

I'm not opposed to being painted, not that anybody's ever offered before. But I am absolutely out of my depth as Kaden leads us inside. We're a silent little chain moving through the quiet house and every step feels heavier than the one before. It's as if we all know something is coming. Some confrontation. Some revelation. But we can't decide if it'll save us or destroy us.

When we reach the giant easel in the studio, Kaden kisses Lulu's hand, then gives it to me so I'm holding both of hers, while he bounces around gathering the things he needs.

Despite her connection with me, she can't keep her eyes off him. Her breaths are quick and unsure and I have half a mind to release my hold on her so she can go to him if that's what she wants.

Loosening my grip does the opposite of what I intended, though; the tension in her body spikes more and she tightens her grip on me.

"Can we help?" she asks Kaden.

"No, just one second."

He pulls back from a cupboard nearby holding a paint can. From the heft, it looks full.

"Are we going to be covered in paint?" Lulu asks.

"Only if you're okay with that." The words skitter out of Kaden nervously. "No concussions this time, I promise."

Lulu smiles at me as if trying to include me in the inside joke, but then she says, "Should we strip?"

I freeze at the words, more out of curiosity than concern. She's undressing in the painting, shedding clothing as she moves from left to right across the canvas. In the progression, it would make sense.

What surprises me more is the way Kaden reacts to the question. He turns his eyes to me and I see challenge in them. Cheek. Humor. "You wouldn't mind, right?"

My eyes narrow playfully. "Not at all." But I add for Lulu's benefit, "Would *you* mind if I stripped for you?"

Lulu's eyes blow wide with thinly veiled anticipation and her bottom lip disappears between her teeth. I can almost feel the heat rushing off her body as she shakes her head.

"I don't have a pose in mind yet," Kaden says. "So, maybe we can play around until we find something."

I almost smile at that—so he *does* have the stones to touch her, using me as a proxy.

"Are you sure you don't just want to watch us touch each other?" I risk asking.

"Nero...!" Lulu whispers.

But Kaden smiles at that. "This is a painting about coming home. Imagine Lulu's just getting in from work, tearing off her work clothes on her way to find you, grab you, claim you. What do you do?"

"Mmm. Plenty of things," I admit, pulling Lulu toward me playfully.

She giggles like a chime, and all I want to do is hear that sound again.

All I want to do is everything I've been holding back for weeks. So I hold her gaze and smile down at her.

"May I take off your clothes, Ms. Rathbone?"

Her round eyes widen and dart in Kaden's direction, but I don't look that way. I let them have their private moment, deciding how this will go, and wait for her to turn back to me. I can tell by the light in her eyes what answer she'll give anyway.

Her voice trembles. "Yes."

I start with the buttons. She's wearing a beautiful red cardigan Kaden found for her; my fingers take their time undoing the abalone buttons down her front. Each release exposes more of her milky skin to me, that skin I once painted with myself. Fucking beautiful.

In the daylight, I can see freckles scattered too, and a small mole on her stomach I want to kiss.

Lulu takes the sweater off as the last button separates. She lobs it far across the room, as if she expects the entire area around us to be bombed with paint at any second. But by the time she turns back to me, I've already undone the button on her jeans, the zipper too.

Splaying my fingers wide, I dip them into her pants along her hips.

I trail my fingers down her skin and luscious curves slowly.

Torturously.

I nudge the pants down as I go, but my eyes are on her face as I get closer and closer.

Then I plant a tiny kiss on her eyelid like I did in her apartment all those weeks ago now.

She whimpers as I do the same to the other.

When the pants gather around her knees, she wiggles them the rest of the way off, then lobs them across the room too.

Until she's basically naked before me, save for her panties, kissed in the rainy light from the skylight overhead.

My God, what a view. No *wonder* Kaden painted her.

And fuck, Emilio's a stupid man.

The words "You're fucking gorgeous, Lulu," blow out of me on a hot, panted breath.

"Thank you." Her eyes frenzy between Kaden and I for another second before she adds, "May I take off *your* clothes, Mr. King? A-As much as I can reach, anyway?"

This time, I can't help but look Kaden's way, to see how the sight of her has changed him. And to pitch a fit if he says no. But he doesn't say no, and the thing he's pitching isn't a fit.

The hangdog expression is long gone, replaced by hyperfocus and ravenous hunger. He looks *alive* in a way I've only seen glimpses of since our arrival. His gaze darts between hers and mine in a metronomic pattern as he nods.

"Absolutely," I echo, drawing her attention back to me. "But let's make sure you can reach everything, shorty."

I spot an empty crate nearby and toe it toward us before flipping it and offering my hand to help her onto it. Then I guide her hands to my waist and wait, watching. Her touch is tentative, but not with uncertainty. Her caresses are slow, savoring. Intentional. Like I've done so many nights here, she slides her fingers under my shirt, then pulls them back dragging the nails a little, before pressing into my skin. I can feel a second little squeeze, a deeper one, in her in anticipation.

My chest heaves with desire too; it's hard to take a deep breath. And there's no hiding how fucking hard I am as she lifts the shirt, because that fucking appendage of mine is peeking out of my boxers, out of my pants, wagging for attention.

This time, Lulu doesn't look to Kaden for anything. A tiny, needy mewl escapes her as she studies my peek-a-boo cock like a ruinous temptation.

And my entire body celebrates realizing she *does* want that with me again.

Fuck, the thought only makes me harder.

This is going to be torture.

Exquisite torture.

These are Kaden's jeans, so the button's already undone for her. *So carefully*, she tucks her fingers inside my pants as she slowly unzips the zipper, as if she's worried she might catch on me if she goes too fast. Then she coaxes the jeans down, trailing her fingers a little along my thighs.

Fuck.

Nothing about this is fast, and that thought floods my system with hot impatience I can feel in my balls and sweet longing I can taste on my tongue.

And then she goes to step down off the crate to reach for the jeans—

"Stay up there," Kaden says, his voice deeper than I've ever heard it.

Lulu leaves the pants at my feet and one of her hands on my hip—I don't even think she knows it's there; the rest of her attention is on him. And mine is on her profile, how she looks from above when her chest begins to billow with need.

Until she says, "May I take off *your* clothes, Mr. Malbec?"

My eyes snap to him, and to my surprise he looks up at me, as if for permission. I don't know if he needs to ask, but the fact that he actually waits to see how I'll take it? I realize it's not us against each other, and I don't think it ever was.

I think…it's him and me against Lulu *for* Lulu. She wants us both.

And I want this moment to continue.

Need it to.

So I nod.

Kaden brings the paint can with him, and sets it on the floor at our feet before his eyes latch onto her between us. In the heavy, aching silence, her eyes bandy between us, trying to decide her next move. I think we're both too curious to interfere. At least, I am.

Her grip on my hip lightens for half a second before she plants it there firmly again, deciding-deciding.

And then, she takes my hand in hers and settles it on her shoulder before turning to face him, as if she couldn't stand the thought of excluding me. Fuck, it sends a ripple of delight through me.

Plus, it's somehow hotter to watch her take off his clothes while I'm still touching her. Especially because, well, there's no ignoring that his fucking cock is hard as granite too. Just like with me, she leaves his underwear in place, removing only his jeans and shirt.

"Happy?" he asks after a moment.

She nods and I can't help it, I begin massaging the column of her neck to *ensure* she is.

Or maybe just to hear her moan.

Which she does. Leaning back, she glances up at me with a smile on her face, all while her hands remain on his waist, connecting us in a little chain again.

I want to just bend down and kiss her. Seize her mouth with mine and see what she does, encourage her to use me—us—however she wants. But I can't do that without flat out asking Kaden if he wants this, and he seems to be in another headspace entirely.

Despite the dress-down—and her delicate fucking hands clutching his body—Kaden still seems to be in professional mode.

"Paint," he says…and I want to pour it down his stupid throat for ruining this moment. But I don't say anything. I just watch him bend down and pop the top on that can.

The moment the lid moves aside, Lulu gasps. In a tone that sounds scolding she whispers, "Kaden…"

"What?" I ask automatically. "What's wrong?"

"It's our color," Lulu tells me. "Vermilion is our color, Kaden."

I don't know what that means—it's some sort of orangey-red—but he seems to. He stands again and his hands cup her cheeks, like I'm not here. Through my grip on her body, I can feel her uncertainty. Her reluctance. Maybe a little bit of hurt too.

"It can be all of ours," he offers. "It's okay."

Lulu doesn't seem to know what to make of it, but she slides her hands up, one onto his forearm, the other onto mine, tightening our little chain.

"Then we all need to be in the painting," she demands.

"Okay," he offers.

She looks at me. I nod. Only then does she consent, "Okay."

"Let me set up the camera," Kaden says, darting away.

"Camera? What camera?"

Given how Lulu reacted to *my* cameras, I expect more of a reaction from her, she only squeezes my hand reassuringly.

"I need to be able to go through video later to find our pose," is all the explanation he gives as he sets up a camera on a tripod and hits record.

The second he steps away from it and begins the journey back to us, the energy in the room shifts; a crackle of static electrifies the air. Kaden stares at Lulu as he prowls slowly closer. She stares back, the sway of her chest accelerating the nearer he comes, setting her beautiful puffy nipples to dance. I want to touch them more than I've ever wanted anything in my life.

He goes for the paint can first, raising it above Lulu's head.

"Ready?" he asks.

"God yes," she whimpers back.

"Might be a little cold," he warns right before he tips the tin, setting off a vermilion waterfall. The second it hits the top of her head, beautiful goosebumps race across her skin. Her nipples peak and harden, and I can't help myself. I swoop under her arms and cup her breasts with my hands greedily, smothering their chill with my warmth.

But Lulu gasps and glances down, accidentally, spilling the paint on her head forward.

"Careful," I croon into her ear as I release her beautiful breasts and raise my hands to her forehead. Capturing the paint before it can reach her eyes, I coax it down along her cheekbones and neck instead.

She leans back against me, looking up, and her smile is so warm I hardly feel the cold of the paint where it hits my chest. No, who could care about that when I see what the vermilion has made of her. She looks like some sort of cartoon hero now, her dark hair stained red at the top. The paint drips and follows the curves of her shoulder blades down the back and the curves of her breasts on the front.

"Your turn," Kaden says right before I feel paint hit my head.

It's fucking chilly and thick, but again it barely registers in contrast to what the sight of it does to Lulu. She turns toward me and her hands leap up into my hair to gather paint before planting her hands on my shoulders and dragging the paint down-down-down across my chest.

"Beautiful!" she whispers, kissing my *Prometheus* tattoo before pressing her painted hand to the spot she kissed, marking me with her handprint.

"And last but not least," Kaden says, drawing our attention to him as he pours more on his own head.

"Oh wow!" Lulu says, almost in awe.

The paint catches differently in Kaden's curly hair; in some places it soaks, in others it almost naturally follows the curves of the curls, so their darkness looks cartoonishly highlighted.

She lets some of the paint drip onto his shoulders, then trails the paint down his arms with her splayed fingers until he looks like some sort of warrior preparing for battle.

Kaden replies the same. He waits until she pauses to grab some of the paint from Lulu's hair and then rakes it down her entire torso in a Y, tickling the gorge between her breasts in passing.

I can't let him have all the fun.

I reach around her to cup her breasts again, this time clutching them with paint, leaving proof of my desire on her skin. My hands are enormous in comparison to her soft hills, so the effect of my palmprints on her chest is staggering. Like cave paintings, it looks primal.

And Kaden groans at the sight of it, as we both pull back to admire it. Her.

She loves it too. Her heart rages inside her; the beat is so fast that through her skin it feels like there's a hummingbird trapped in there, fluttering against the bars of its cage.

When she looks up at us again, her eyes are darkened with a lust so sweet I bet I'd be able to taste it on her lips.

"How do you want us?" she asks.

Kaden's gaze shifts to me momentarily before returning to her. "Like I said, this is a painting about coming home. What is that to you?"

"You," Lulu says, surprising me. But it's not the word, it's the tone, the way it hitches in her throat as if she can barely get the word out, the need in her voice. Again, she reaches for us both, gaze darting between as she adds breathlessly, "Both of you."

CHAPTER 51

LULU

I won't be winning any awards for self-restraint any time soon. I'm just not that girl, I guess. I don't want to be. Not in a moment like this. Not sandwiched between two of the most gorgeous men I've ever seen, both inside and out, slicked in a color that turns me on by association, trembling with a need so strong it's like my pussy is *roaring* at me to do something about it before she makes the decision for me.

"You," escapes my mouth like a fucking prisoner, loosed from wherever I had it caged deep inside these past few weeks. "Both of you."

I've been avoiding this moment since Nero stepped inside this house three weeks ago, and now that I've spoken my brightest impossible wish into the space between us, I wish I could take it back.

Because they just stare at me.

They just stare!

Through our physical connections, I can feel the intense bass beat of their hearts, but also a freeze. Hesitation.

I must've said the wrong thing.

"I-I didn't mean that, I'm sorry," I squeak, wondering if I've ruined the mood. Wondering if this whole thing will devolve into some argument I'm not ready for.

"Don't you dare say you didn't mean that," Nero growls above me, right before I feel his hand curve around my jaw from above and yank my head back so I'm staring straight up at him moments before his lips barrel into mine.

The upside-down kiss steals my breath away, not that I had taken one beforehand.

It's all consuming, frenzied, and angry...at me. His tongue lashes across mine before retreating before he nips my lip and does it again.

And then suddenly, there's a hand in my hair, twisting before I'm pulled from Nero's lips and Kaden's are there to replace them. His kiss is softer, but only barely; even then, his grip on me and the purring growl I can feel in his throat—the kiss's power is unmatched.

I feel thrown off-balance and completely secure at the same time—a sensation I've never experienced before. Not just overstimulation but hyperstimulation, aware of everything everywhere. The back of my head is pressed to Nero's chest as Kaden kisses me, and my arms cling to Kaden as Nero runs his hands along my sides doing that little thing he loves to do with his fingers—slide, soft scrape, press.

Nero's mouth goes to my shoulder, nibbling, Kaden deepens his claim on my mouth and my pussy's still roaring—*fuck!* Then Kaden trails his lips across my skin until he reaches the other side of my neck and—

"*Oh my god!*" rips out of me in mumbled exaltation.

The touch of them.

The press of them.

Everywhere. All over me.

A hand slides onto my ass from behind.

And Kaden drops to one knee, glancing up at me as he dips his lips into paint in passing and patters vermilion kisses everywhere on my front where there's an open bit of skin.

My hands twine into their hair as I yield to this feeling of being surrounded, *cocooned* in their warmth.

"Is this what you want, Ms. Rathbone?" Nero rumbles into my ear.

I nod because words can't fight their way past the little sobs crowding my throat.

"Is this *all* you want?" Nero asks next, and I don't know how to answer that. It's not a one-person question.

But I try to make my mouth form the better question I need to ask them—

BEEP-BEEP-BEEP-BEEP.

The noise yanks me from the moment so fast I feel like I have whiplash. It's not loud, or jarring; but it's outside of this, and it pulls focus.

And then Kaden rises to stand and wipes the paint from his lips before saying, "It's the camera battery. Sorry."

Oh right, we were supposed to be modeling. Posing.

I blink at Kaden, trying to read his face. The professional gleam, his focused eyes—is he still thinking like an artist?

I...I'm wet and panting for him. Nero's still pressing his hands against my skin and I can feel how badly he wants...something...to keep happening here.

Does Kaden? The beeping continues and he rushes away to stop it. Chill breezes into the spot where he once stood, even though the room isn't cold.

In the silence, Kaden glances between Nero and me and adds, "B-But I think we got enough stuff."

Oh.

"Right, of course," I say, trying to hide the let down—the way the pressure caves my chest in. I'm so fucking turned on, I'm overheating. My pussy is melting. Every bit of skin that isn't being touched feels forsaken.

Embarrassment is there too, just a twinge of it.

And I can't just take Nero somewhere to let him give me what I need. *Even though I need it to the point of pain.*

I need...

I need...

"Excuse me," I say. "I-I'm going to go take a shower."

"Louise, wait," Kaden says.

"No, Lulu," Nero adds, but with his hands slicked in paint, he can't hold onto me as I flee the room.

I'm too embarrassed to tell them I just need to touch myself until I feel better, until it's out of my system and I can think clearly again.

Kaden got what he needed, and maybe tomorrow when Nero and I leave, I can ask him if he'll give me what I've needed these last three weeks.

CHAPTER 52

KADEN

The moment Louise disappears from the room, Nero's fiery gaze snaps to mine like he wants to burn my face off.

"Good going, dumbass," he says, perfectly summarizing how I feel.

"I'm sorry," I say, so lamely. "It was just the camera."

"Fuck the camera! She was giving herself to us, dipshit," he says, shoving past me. "If you don't want her that way, that's fine, but I do."

Panic bites at my heels and I rush after him. "I do want her that way."

"Yeah? Could've fooled me."

Giving herself to us, he'd said. The truth of it is an open-faced smack. No, it's a smack to the back of my head. I really am a dumbass.

"I know painting means a lot to you," Nero adds as he stomps up the stairs with me on his tail, "But come on, man. You're fucking hard as steel for her. Read the room and *let the damned camera beep!* She doesn't need another reason to cry right now."

That makes me stagger. "Louise has been crying?"

"Yeah. Every fucking night. She goes into the bathroom when she thinks we're asleep and she stays in there forever."

"You saw her crying?"

"No, but I heard her sobbing."

We reach my bedroom in record time, but the shower's already running and I can't hear anything like sobbing as we close in on the bathroom door.

"Wait, Nero, wait," I whisper. "Let's talk for a sec."

"Fuck off, man. She needs me. Don't come in for an hour at least. We're gonna use your bed too, so fair warning."

"Just listen!" I ask, grabbing his arm to stop him. "I'm not the most socially intelligent person. I'm awkward as fuck sometimes."

"I'm aware."

"And this whole thing with the three of us is complicated, all right? I've experimented before but not with something this important. And Louise is...She's..."

Nero jerks his head sarcastically. "She's what?"

"She's fucking confused! She's vulnerable and looking for comfort wherever she can find it. I am flattered that she felt safe coming here, but what if this month has been, like, a mental reset. I don't think I can survive what happens tomorrow if I get any deeper into this and find out I'm just a temporary escape for her."

I don't know what I was expecting, but Nero's eyes darken to the point of contempt. "Do you love her, Kaden?"

The words lance panic through me from head to toe. "I don't think it matters."

"Yes, it does. Cuz I love her. I fucking *love* her. And downstairs just now, she was telling us she loves us too."

Fuck, panic spears through me again. "How could she?!" I try to calm down, try to leash my voice when I add, "She must be confused because she wouldn't pick me if she wasn't."

The contempt on Nero's face melts faster than late winter slush. His hand is suddenly on my shoulder, pulling me slightly away from the door.

"That's not how this works, K. If you want her and she wants you, you don't push her away. You count your lucky stars she's giving you a shot and you don't fuck it up. You match her fucking vulnerability, you don't decide there must be something wrong with her, ya idiot."

"Fuck," I say instead of "that's terrifying."

Nero seems to understand anyway.

"Some people are friends, some are lovers, and if you get *real fucking lucky* and don't ruin it for yourself, some are both. As for the three of us, we'll just have to hash out the details, all right?"

"You mean you're open to…complicated? Cuz I don't want to be the third wheel on the bike you two ride off on."

Nero snorts at that. "Nobody's a third wheel in this thing. I mean, I'm not into dudes, but frankly I like watching, I *love* knowing we could fucking rock Lulu's world together, and I'm okay when I know she's with you. You're a chill guy and we get along pretty damn well, don't we?"

His words are magic; all the bottled-up fear I've had in me since his arrival feels like it bursts as he pats my shoulder again.

"If I'm being honest," he adds, "I thought if anybody was gonna be odd-man-out, it was me, coming into your house like that. I kept waiting for you to knock my teeth in."

I chuckle. "No third wheels, then. We'll make sure of that."

"Yeah. Right now," he warns. "After that bonehead move downstairs, I'm going in there to make sure the woman I love gets whatever she needs. The woman you love needs you too, so…let's fucking *go*."

Relief and something freer trickles into me as he throws open the bathroom door and steam billows out thick enough to blind. It's like a weight has been lifted, like I know what to shoot for, at least. Like I don't have to fear letting myself have this.

It feels great.

It feels good.

It feels like I have things to look forward to.

Especially when Nero suddenly shouts, "What the hell is this?"

CHAPTER 53

NERO

"What the hell is this?"

I don't mean to bark it at Lulu as I open the bathroom door and the steam dissipates enough to see her in the shower, but I'm fucking *shook* when I realize what she's doing.

My woman—

Our woman is cheating on us...with her own goddamn hand.

Lulu is naked under the hot shower spray, furiously rubbing that little bundle of nerves between her thighs like she's trying to start a campfire.

There's not a damned tear in sight. Only a flurry of hot, desperate caresses against her clit, and her other hand pressed to the wall as if she's pleasuring herself so well she's losing her balance in there.

"Lulu!" I bark when I realize she didn't hear me.

Her gaze snaps to us as we step into the room. Her hand freezes between her legs, but she doesn't pull it away. She looks like someone who got caught trying to steal a cookie out of the cookie jar. Embarrassment stains her cheeks a cherry red pretty enough to eat.

Oh, I'll be eating something tonight, all right.

Kaden's gaze drops to her hand, too, and he grumbles, "Welp, there's another painting."

My boxers are off in seconds. I don't stick around to watch, but Kaden chucks his off too. I tear open the shower door and step in to find Lulu backing up against the far stone wall. Her deer-in-headlights expression is glorious, especially when Kaden steps in with us and her eyes dart between our faces…then drop to other parts of us she might be more interested in at the moment.

"Something we can help you with?" I tease, motioning to her hand, which is still poised over that bundle of nerves like a merkin.

Her beautiful lips part, then close, before the bottom one gets tugged between her teeth.

Fucking beautiful.

I step closer until she has to arch her neck back to peer up at me, at us as Kaden closes in too.

"I asked you a question, Lulu," I say quietly. "What do you think you're doing?"

"I'm just making myself feel good," she says.

I tut-tut-tut with my tongue. "That's our job."

Lighting a single finger on her collarbone, I smile as Kaden does the same on her other side. Lulu's eyes blow wide with desire at the accidental synchronization, watching with rapt attention as we both trail our finger down over the swell of her breast to her nipples.

I flick, he tweaks, and she squeaks.

Fucking sensational.

But Kaden beats me to the progression down her body. All five of his fingers slide across her stomach until they reach her hand…and dive underneath to her clit.

Her lips part again, this time to moan, and I dive for her mouth, uniting us. Fusing us. Making it *crystal fucking clear* we're both here for her. In the connection, I taste the tang of paint and the sweetness of her.

She's shaking when I pull back to stare into her amber eyes. There's a question in them.

"Both?" she asks.

"Both what?" I tease. Swooping my hands down, I cup her breasts and roll the pads of my thumbs across her nipples. "Both breasts? Both tongues?"

I dive down and nip the very tip of each with my teeth. Kaden dives for her clit with his tongue and Lulu squeals.

I'm having too much fun, so I lean into her ear, but growl loud enough for Kaden to hear when I add, "Or do you mean both of our cocks pumping inside you until you're screaming?"

"Fuck," she groans as I pull back. That isn't an answer, so I tweak both her nipples suddenly. "Fuck!"

"I think she wants a double fuck, Kaden," I croon playfully.

"It would be our pleasure, Ms. Rathbone."

Lulu's soft concern morphs into a grin so happy it summons one on my face...and Kaden's too. And Lulu cups his face and kisses him gently before turning to me. She crooks her finger to call me closer and plants a lovely little kiss on my lips too.

"Are you both okay with this?" she asks. "You *want* this? You're not just doing it for me?"

"We want more than this." Kaden smirks and adds, "But the rest can wait, my beautiful *cursed woman*."

Lulu almost swoons at the words, but Kaden rises to his feet, picking her up in his arms before she can fall.

The Cursed Woman—La Femme Damnée—a painting I had to look up after Lulu mentioned it was her favorite. Very apropos. In it, three figures pleasure a woman while they all float in the air. One takes succor from her lips, another from her breast, and the last feasts on her pussy.

I call dibs on the last.

Kaden seals his lips to hers and I reach for her legs, raising her glorious wet pink pussy to my mouth, ready to devour her.

CHAPTER 54

LULU

I'm light as a feather in the air, lifted aloft by my two gentlemen. Kaden's beautiful lips find mine and part them, plunging his tongue inside…

…at the exact same moment Nero's tongue plunges deep inside somewhere else.

The intrusion, it's everywhere. Their tongues, their hands, their breath against my skin. *My God*, I can't escape. I don't want to, but that's not the point. I'm higher in the air than I am tall, forming a bridge between tongue and tongue, spasming with a pleasure so bright and joyous I know for certain that the creator of my favorite painting meant the title *The Cursed Woman* as a condemnation…of all those who would look upon her and judge.

Those people *never* knew a feeling like this.

To be exalted.

To be cherished.

To be shared by a ghost and a dark angel who would never drop me.

Kaden tears his lips from mine and curls his tongue around my nipple, suckling lightly, and a spiral of ecstasy through my heart is my reward. So too is the *joy* and *hunger* in his beautiful eyes as they dart across my chest to the other nipple; he releases the first and drags his tongue across my slick warm skin to the other, to give it proper attention.

And Nero licks and laps and sups from me, twirling his tongue around my clit, setting my legs to shake. His stubble rubs my inner thighs, his fingernails graze the curves of my ass. He holds me up, and the spiral of ecstasy leaves my heart, traveling down-down-down.

I can't help but reach for them both. Run my fingers so softly across their hands on me.

"Nero, hold me up, okay?" I whisper, and I know he heard me from the glint in his eye.

Not breaking the brutal assault of his tongue on my clit for even a second, his hands curl around my waist, one in front, one in back. I let my top half drop until I'm upside down…and my mouth is at the perfect height to have fun.

The vermilion paint is mostly gone from their skin, but little trickles of it from their hair flows down along the gorgeous ridges of their bodies, and along their sides in red waterfalls.

But their cocks? Those are paint free. And mine.

Kaden's cock is beautiful. It was when he pleased himself with my tights in his kitchen, and it is now, unveiled and dangling a few inches from my face. Nero's perfect cock is like a dark angel on my shoulder, wagging for me to go ahead and taste Kaden while it watches.

I turn and give the head of Nero's cock a little lick and kiss—he'll get his soon enough—and then I turn my attention to the new masterpiece ahead of me. Taking hold of my new friend, I pull him gently toward me, into position.

The tip is a beautiful rosy pink, too beautiful not to kiss and lick-lick-lick before I wrap my lips around him and swirl a little. Like someone trying to feel their way in the dark, my tongue darts ahead of me along his velvet-smooth shaft. I open my mouth as wide as my jaw allows to fit as much of him as I can.

From above me, a roar from some primordial earth monster escapes Kaden's mouth.

Almost in competition, Nero buries his face deeper against my sex, kissing and flicking and tasting.

And then—like the most beautiful harmony I've ever heard—both men bark, "Fuck, Lu!"

Delicious.

Kaden's hands slide behind my head to assist in the movement, and my hands wrap around his beautiful toned ass, and we're connected again, lost in a pleasure haze that erases the rest of the world from existence. There's only the movement of the three of us, together as one, and the sounds of my breath as Kaden cuts it off in little bursts, pursuing his own pleasure.

Until Kaden's trembling voice begs, "Put her down. Put her down!"

I mewl in protest as my feet return to solid ground. My eyes dart to Kaden. "What's wrong?"

"It's my turn," he says darkly.

His hands swoop around my ass and lift me off the ground again. It's only three feet to the nearby bench, where he splays me like some heathen sacrifice before kissing me deeply and making his way down my body. His kisses feel like promises, he takes such time placing them.

And when he reaches my sex, he kisses that too, lifting his dark gaze to my face.

"Are you going to disappoint me now?" I tease, making him chuckle.

"In all the best ways," he purrs. "Take him in your mouth, Louise."

Well, if he insists. Nero's perfect cock is there just above me, dark against the light behind it. So is the rest of his mountainous body; from this angle, he looks like a giant come to claim a maiden. He bends over me, lining his cock up with my mouth and I open for him, expecting him to plunge it in.

He doesn't.

I glance up to find the sweetest look of wonder on Nero's gorgeous face.

"What?" leaves my mouth, tender and curious.

"You're not just his muse, you know," he whispers, running his thumb over my lips. "Savor me."

I can't say why those words hit me so hard, but they do. And he means them. He positions himself comfortably and lets his perfect cock rest just above my lips, waiting to see what I'll do.

It makes me want to worship him. Please him. Love him.

So I kiss the tip reverently, and wrap my hands gently around him, coaxing his beautiful length past my mouth so I can reach his taint. I lick slowly from his taint, between his balls, up the shaft, flicking the frenulum in passing before I tip the head down and push up, swallowing as much of him as I can when he's least expecting it.

Nero inhales sharply with aching pleasure and it's so fucking hot, I can hardly stand it.

But the sound doesn't just affect me. It's like a dinner bell for Kaden. The flat of his tongue lands on my clit and begins a slow, torturously wonderful writhe. The pace, the patience—it has me moaning like a cat in heat.

It's impossible, the balance of attention. My mind's on Nero's cock while my pussy's mind is on Kaden's coaxing teasing exploration of me. The split is exquisite.

So is the pleasure. It feels *so good*, but divided. Parts of me are screaming while others enjoy the show. I don't mind—I could last forever like this—especially while listening to their serenade; their overlapping moans tug at some secret pleasure center inside me. They make me want to tease more sounds out of both of them, which I do by tugging on Kaden's luscious locks, and by puckering my lips and pattering Nero's cock with sucking little kisses that have him squeezing his hands into fists.

Nero begins to overload when I worship the head of his cock, though. Teasing licks and kisses and sucks, paired with my fingers on the underside of his shaft where he'd hold it if he was pleasing himself. His body mutinies. His strong hand swoops under my head and hastens my tempo, desperate to be deeper inside me. I want him there too, so I tilt my head back a little to line up my throat. And when he's least expecting it, I swallow him all the way down. His chest hitches, his groans become breathless graveled gasps, and he keels.

"Fuck!" he barks suddenly, but not at me. "Kaden, get her off, man. I can't come until she does."

Kaden smirks, "You got it, boss," and spears me deep with two thick fingers before I can even yelp, "What?!"

What does he mean he can't get off before me? I want to tell him that's not necessary—his pleasure is mine too—but Kaden's fingers begin a rhythmic, relentless massage of my internal wall and his eye contact burns me from below and the only words I can manage are, "*Oh my god!*"

Nero's cock pulls from my fingers and he's suddenly there, kneeling by me. His hand slides around my throat and turns my head to him, pinning my gaze to his. I try reaching for his cock, but he intertwines his fingers in mine and holds my hand hostage as Kaden—

As Kaden's relentless licking and rubbing—

Fuck! It intensifies! It all intensifies! My mind scrambles against the barrage of *pleasure-pleasure-PLEASURE-PLEASURE!*

"That's it, Lulu," Nero purrs, licking my lips. "Come for us."

"But…"

"Right now, baby, I need to see it."

Mumbling. It's all I can do.

Nero trails his hand down from my throat, dragging his nails, and growls, "Show us, baby. Show us how good you feel. How good we make you feel."

Fuck!

I can't fight the onslaught. It builds and builds and builds as he coos more encouragement at me, until I explode. Until some part of me trembles and erupts. My back arches off the bench like I'm possessed. My hand grips Kaden's curls, the other strains against Nero's hold on me, all while Kaden pins my hips where he wants them. Where he continues his frenzied lapping and licking and plumbing.

I feel wetness between my legs, and it isn't from the shower.

"Whoa," I hear Kaden say, right before Nero beams, "Fucking gorgeous."

I don't know what's gorgeous about it. I'm shaking. Boneless and completely out of control of my body in the sweltering steamy heat of the shower. The thought makes me giggle.

So does the sudden excitement I have that it isn't over. It's their turn. Leaning up, I smile at them, watching Kaden patter my inner thigh with kisses and Nero suckle and tease my breast, patiently waiting for me. It's such a beautiful sight.

"How do you want me now?" I ask.

Nero only laughs; I feel his husky breath around my nipple as he continues his slow savoring.

Kaden, though, studies me earnestly, like he's unsure how I'll take whatever he wants to say.

"You can tell me," I reassure him, running my fingers along his beautiful jaw.

"I want to fill you—us to fill you," he says, motioning to Nero.

The shiver that runs through me would break an iceberg in half. "Show me."

"Nero, pick her up. I'll be right back."

Kaden leaves the shower and I giggle as Nero hoists me up, because it already seems second-nature for him to do it. And second nature to be in this position with him, my legs around his waist, my arms around his neck, and his hands under my ass.

"Hello again," I tease.

"I love you like this," he says, kissing me so sweetly.

Some fleeting feeling passes through me, though. Things are different now than they were in my apartment. It's not just us anymore. Gently, I nod my head toward Kaden where he is in the bathroom.

"What about like this?" I ask, tamping down the fear I feel that this scenario is a wish-shaped bubble that will burst at any second.

Nero's warm smile surprises me. "I misspoke. I just love you."

"What?"

"How you are today, how you might be tomorrow. I want to know you. I want to be with you. With him or without him."

"You can't mean that."

His brow arches boldly, daring me to argue. "I've never said anything to you I didn't mean."

This time, the shiver rattles me on its way through my body. A dozen people in my life have claimed they loved me. Until this moment, the only people I believed were Cara and Ivy…and it took *years* to accept what they were saying.

But staring into Nero's eyes, there's no denying how sincerely he believes the words he just said. And it breaks my heart with fear to realize he's the first man who's ever meant them.

CHAPTER 55

KADEN

The unspoken truth of being celibate for three years is that it required certain…subscriptions and bulk orders of certain substances. I grab the coconut oil-based lube from my cabinet and make my way back to the shower, genuinely fucking terrified of what's going to happen when I find myself inside that beautiful woman. She makes my heart feel like it's being torn out every time I look at her.

In all likelihood, I'll last three seconds and just have to watch.

Which…sounds fucking great too, honestly. Watching her play with Nero's cock got me so close to the edge, I had to literally pinch myself while I was going down on her to keep from coming.

But when *she* came? Fuck, I've never made a woman squirt before. It was like proof of God, the way her body shook, the way her pussy clutched my fingers, the way she cooed as the aftershocks tore through her.

It was another painting, one that may just have to live rent-free in my mind forever.

I cannot wait to feel what her orgasms feel like when we're both buried in her to the hilt.

But it's the strangest thing. That's not what I'm most looking forward to.

It's her expressions.

Louise has a thousand and one soul-shattering expressions—when she's happy, when she's nervous, even when she's curious. She didn't smile the first time we fooled around in my kitchen, but the divine ecstasy on her face as she orgasmed was so beautiful I could've painted it a thousand times over. The smile on her face only a few moments ago was just as breathtaking.

The thought of seeing another has me rushing back to the shower, lube in hand.

But when I step back in, something has happened between them. He's holding her, she's clinging to him, but Louise looks at me with a weird expression I've never seen before. Like fear and hope all in one.

"What happened?" I ask, closing the distance between us.

"I told Lulu how I feel about her." There's a smile on Nero's face and he watches her as closely as I do.

Does that mean he told her he loves her? I can't tell from their expressions—his adoring, hers rapturously terrified. She glances at me like I'll offer an escape from her feelings.

"I need you inside me," she says breathlessly to both of us.

"With pleasure, Ms. Rathbone," Nero says before he lifts her ass and slides his dick into the gorgeous depths of her.

She squeals with relief...but it's a relief I can't match when she releases one of her hands from Nero's neck and reaches for me.

I don't want to be the escape from her feelings. I don't want her to hide them from us either.

I take a bit of lube and coat my cock with it, but I decide her ass can wait—if I have my way, we'll have plenty of time for that later. Instead, I line myself up right alongside Nero's cock. Gripping her hips, I thrust slowly up into her perfect pussy.

"OH FUCK!" she shouts, but not in pain. Surprise and ecstasy limn her voice. *"Ohmygod, ohmygod!"*

"Careful, Kaden," Nero huffs.

"She can take it," I counter. "If you need a break, Louise, just grab one of our ears, okay?"

"Okay-Okay," she whimpers. "It's good, it feels so good."

Despite the lube and how soaked she still is from her orgasm, I go slow. I push an inch, and let her adjust, listening to her chirps of bliss and Nero's shuddering grunts, before pushing in again.

Only once I'm deep inside her do I lean in and kiss her shoulder-her neck-her spine.

"Louise, I adore you," I whisper, ignoring the flinch I can feel in Nero's grip on her.

"Kaden, don't," she yelps, turning back to look at me.

She's not asking us to back off—that's not what her plea is. Her eyes are saran wrapped in tears because she's avoiding an uncomfortable truth. So I swallow that plea with a kiss as I begin to move inside her...and Nero does the same.

Slow at first.

Then faster, alternating thrusts.

Then I add my hands, gliding my nails across her skin in little bursts; she glitches every time.

"Oh no," she moans after a moment, her eyes rolling back. "Oh God, please!"

It's heaven. Fucking *heaven*. I've only been in one threesome before, when I was in college and it was good. Mechanically good, anyway. I could feel the other guy's dick through the thin tissue between the girl's channels and it both spurred me on *and* took me out of the moment a little.

This just hits different. Because of them.

The way she clutches me. The way he clutches her. Her eyes can barely stay focused but every time her gaze lands on either of us, it seems to drive us wild. Nero's face slackens with ecstatic disbelief and he doubles his speed and it feels like I'm fucking her even if I'm not moving. She gazes into my eyes, and I speed up too.

It's torture trying to make this last, because I want to give them all I've got.

Especially when Louise's head falls against Nero's chest, and her eyes roll back, and he presses his head to hers.

Especially when he says, "We love you, don't you ever forget that."

"Nero, please," she begs again, reaching for me to be her anchor—her downer, her pessimist or some shit.

But I don't fucking want to be that to her.

Instead, I press myself to her back, press my mouth to her ear. "He's right, Louise."

"Please," she begs.

"This is your life now. You and us and this," I double down. "We love you so fucking much."

I thought the rogue wave we coaxed from her pussy a few minutes ago was intense, but it was *nothing* compared to this. Louise screams suddenly—bedighting her face with an expression so glorious it's like she's singing directly to God—and a dam bursts inside her. Her body *quakes*, and her pussy grips us both, demanding our satisfaction.

I feel Nero's cock twitch and blow and I can't stop my own orgasm from tearing through me like a cannonball through tissue paper.

Fuck!

Her body milks and milks and milks us until I'm pretty sure there's not a single drop left to give. Even then, we don't pull out; we stay right where we fucking are inside her. Nero and I hold her up, support her, as the orgasm continues pulsing through her body again and again and again. *For minutes.*

"Fuck, I can't," she yelps when it doesn't stop.

"Yes you fucking can," Nero croons with pride, watching her tremble.

"Your body loves us," I tease, trailing kisses down the nape of her neck, and across the hair-slicked expanse of her back—at least as far as I can reach while staying inside her. "You just have to admit…"

My voice dies, though, as my lips trace something slightly hard but organic along her left shoulder blade. My brain leaps to the possibility that it's a piece of dried paint—although *nothing* has been dry around us for hours now. I think it might even be a bit of leaf from the porch, maybe…

Until I slide the mass of her dark hair aside looking for it.

It's not a leaf.

It's not dried paint either.

It's a brand—*JV*—burned into her skin long ago and hardened with scar tissue now.

Maybe if I weren't still lightheaded with pleasure, I might have thought about it for more than half a second, but I didn't.

"Who the fuck is JV?" I ask before I can catch myself.

CHAPTER 56

NERO

"Who the fuck is JV?"

I'd forgotten about those initials on Lulu's back. In the weeks since coming here, my mind simply deleted them to make room for better memories.

But the second that sentence leaves Kaden's clueless mouth, it all comes flooding back in. *JV*. The brand on her beautiful fucking back. That smashed photo in her apartment.

Lulu flinches in my arms like she's been bitten. Her breath catches. I wrap my arms around her more tightly while she's too weak to hold onto my neck.

"I-It's nothing," she tries, shifting her gaze to the floor so she doesn't have to look either of us in the eye.

"It's not nothing—there's a fucking *brand* on your *back*, Louise—"

"Kaden!" I snap, even though I want to know too. I grit my teeth at him in warning, nodding to her fucking downtrodden face hoping he can fucking read the room here.

"Did you know about this?" he asks instead.

"I've...seen it before," I admit. "Let's just let it be—"

"No. No-No. Louise? What is that? Who's JV?"

Kaden reaches for her, as if he's going to take her from me. I'm half a second from literally pulling her away like a kid with a ball they don't want to share when Lulu's legs jerk out of my grasp and close, expelling both of us from her body.

"Put me down, Nero," she says, so I do gently, trying to hold onto her.

She doesn't let me. Her hands cross her bare chest the moment her feet hit the floor. She rushes for the door and throws it open, leaping the few inches to the bath mat and grabbing a towel. Still she doesn't look at us.

"Louise. Louise, you can't run from everything!"

She turns and walks out the bathroom door, and I grab Kaden's arm to stop him from following.

"Let her go, man, she doesn't want to talk about it."

"Who is it?" He wrenches his arm out of my grasp, but doesn't walk away. "Who did that to her? What are you doing about it?"

"I don't know yet," I admit. "I'm looking into it."

"Look *harder*!" he scolds. "That's obviously not an accident. Someone gave her a fucking third degree burn on purpose."

"I know that!" I snap.

"You fucking said you love her."

I freeze at the implied accusation that I don't.

"You want to be very careful about what you say next," I warn him. "I do love her, that's why I'm letting her come to me about it."

It's a half-lie. My fingers are already itching to call Kenzo the second I can to check if he found out anything.

But Kaden doesn't like my answer. His eyes shrink with some emotion I can't read and then he's gone, stomping after Louise faster than I've ever seen him move in his life. I almost slip as I rush to shut off the shower and race after him.

By the time I reach the bathroom door and step into the bedroom, however, the chase is already over. Lulu's sitting on the bed in her towel-dress, staring at her lap. Kaden's down on his knee beside her, touching her leg, pushing her wet hair behind her ear.

"Please, Louise," he begs quietly. "I meant what I said in there. I love you. Nero loves you. We can't help if we don't know what's wrong."

"I've already *been* helped," she sniffles. "And you're already helping."

Her phrasing gets my feet going. I cross the room to their side in seconds. Dropping on the bed beside her, I do the only thing I can think to do, which is rub her back and kiss her head.

"Can't we just chalk it up to my villain origin story and leave it at that?" she asks.

I raise a brow at that. "Whoever's villain you are, you aren't ours. And if *you* have another villain, you need to tell us so we can put him in the fucking ground, right next to Emilio."

"Don't joke about that," she says.

"Oh, it's barely a joke."

"Come on," Kaden adds, rising to his feet. "Let's get into bed. Just get into bed and we'll listen."

CHAPTER 57

LULU

When you grow up like I did—when you escape what I did—you cement the cracked parts of yourself as they are, so you don't risk them shattering completely. Then you don't talk about it, don't look at it, in the hope that not acknowledging the damage will keep the cement seal in place for as long as possible.

Settling back against the headboard between Nero and Kaden like this, letting them crawl under the covers with me, and sandwich me with their giant warm bodies, I can already feel once-hard mortar beginning to melt.

But…it's not fair to them to keep this from them. Not if whatever this is between us is real. God I can't even entertain the possibility that it's real! It's too good! Too good for someone like me. And they'll know that the second I open my mouth and puke a whole bunch of ancient history at them.

But for fuck's sake, I *want* to believe I've reached the end of the collapsing bridge that is my life! I want to believe they actually care…

More than that, I want to *know* if they don't, so I don't let myself get more attached to them than I already am. It would be better to lose this now at the start than risk total annihilation later.

So, when Nero and Kaden both slide their hands into mine and wait so patiently, I begin.

"I don't know how much you want, but I'm warning you now, I'm not ready to talk details, or anything. I might never be."

"That's okay," Nero claims. "We're just going to listen."

I glance up then, because his tone is chiding, but not at me...at Kaden.

"Right, Kaden?" Nero adds.

Kaden pouts a little, but finally says, "Yes."

"I don't know where to start, really," I admit. "But I feel like you won't understand unless you know what my mom was like. She c-couldn't afford much of anything, and never tried to. She relied on the men she dated to foot our bills, and she always found a new one before she ditched the old one, but it didn't matter. Even though she knew she wasn't going to keep them, she changed for all of them. It was like living with an actress who switched roles every six months."

I giggle at myself because I never verbalized that analogy before, but it fits so well.

My smile dies quickly, though.

"The boyfriend she had *before* JV was...vile. Stank of chemicals and always brought more than food with him when he visited our house. He got her hooked on something—I think maybe meth, looking back now—and she changed overnight. She wasn't the best mom *before*, but after..."

I shrug, unsure if more needs to be said about that.

"Eventually he got arrested and my mom's supply disappeared and...so did she, sort of. She went hunting. JV was worlds different than the previous guy. Polished. Sophisticated. *European* from the Netherlands—so fancy. He had his own business—where he and a group of artists moved from place-to-place teaching newbies technique and craft, you know. *Wildly* successful—in a way that would have been suspicious to me, if I'd been older and knew any better.

"I met him through my mom. Sort of. There was no food in the house and she hadn't been there in a week and so I went out looking for her. When I found her, she was modeling for one of his classes. I cringe now thinking about what he claimed the inspiration was for that week because she did *not* look healthy.

"I told him I was taking her home and he offered to drive us. Bought us groceries too, and I thought he was nice because he asked me what I wanted to eat.

"But the next day he came back. Then again. And again. I didn't know what he saw in her, but there was food again, so I didn't question it. Or why he never tried to get her help for her addiction. He would just tell me to "help her any way I could" because she needed me.

"And then one day, he told her he needed a young model for one of his paintings. It paid $150 a day and I thought that was a lot of money, so when my mom begged me to do it, I did. I thought I was helping us survive."

Strange, the things our brains remember. I remember the smell of the studio because it didn't smell like paint and I thought it would. I remember the "choice" he gave me between two outfits for the modeling session, and how he said, *"I want to make sure you're comfortable, so this has to be your choice, petal."* I thought it was considerate of him, even though neither outfit covered much of my body.

I remember the actual sketches he produced during our first couple of sessions. They were good, so I thought *he must really be an artist*.

"Lulu?" Nero says softly, drawing me from my thoughts.

"Sorry," I whisper.

"You have *nothing* to be sorry for," Kaden almost growls, but not at me. His hands are tight around mine, thrumming with discomfort. It hurts to know I'm making him uncomfortable, but he asked for this.

"I fell in love with art when I was thirteen…because he introduced me to it," I tell them. "After one of our early sessions, he took me to the Philadelphia Museum of Art. He offered to pay for my ticket. Acted like it was a gift to me for everything I'd done for him and I was so grateful, promising I'd pay him back one day. There was this grand, magnanimous smile on his face that I don't think I'll ever forget."

Pain tugs at the back of my throat as I add, "I didn't know until later that it's free for minors under the age of eighteen."

Then I chuckle the sadness and embarrassment out because that's probably TMI even in the midst of all this.

"Anyway, after a few weeks, JV and his art classes moved on and I thought that was the end of it, which terrified me because my mom wasn't getting any better. I had to lie to her about where the money went because every time I gave her any she used it to feed her habit. But that meant I couldn't bring food home because she'd demand to know where I got the money for it, if I didn't have any. I didn't know about food banks then. If I had, I could have told her that's where I got it, but I didn't know and so I just had to eat without her. I felt so guilty not being able to feed her!"

Fuck, it hurts to think about. Tears bully their way out of my eyes no matter how hard I try to shut them.

They get worse when Nero leans against me and whispers, "You're safe, I promise."

I cry because I believe him and I don't know what to do with that.

"I ran out of money eventually," I tell them. "And then I hated myself more because I kept thinking that the hunger I felt was what she must have felt that whole time."

"It's okay. I promise, it's okay," Nero says.

"Sorry," I say again, and Kaden leans in, peppering my head with frantic kisses.

When I get control of myself, I continue.

"I ate out of dumpsters for a few weeks until I got really sick. After that, I did the only thing I could think to do…"

"You called JV," Nero fills in.

I nod. "He started sending money every week and told me he'd find a way for me to make it up to him when he came back to Philadelphia, which he eventually did when I was fifteen. By then, I'd "matured." He showed up at the house, took one look at me, and everything changed.

"I don't know exactly what he offered my mom, but the next thing I knew she had a bag packed for me and told me I was going to live with him. He promised that he would take care of my mom and make sure I finished school, and in exchange I would model for him."

"When you were *fifteen*?" Kaden asks.

"I thought he saved me," I whisper. "We drove straight to his house in Rhode Island. He began introducing me as his goddaughter and I started homeschooling. I thought everything was finally going to be okay…but…

"Two months later, I woke up to his hand up my night gown. He told me he "couldn't help himself." A month after that, he started having me 'model' for an all-men's painting class he hosted at home. Let's just say no actual painting was done."

This time, it's Nero who flinches. When I glance his way, his eyes are closed, but a muscle is feathered in his clenched jaw.

"Don't grind your teeth, Big Guy."

"I'm not," he lies, wiggling his jaw for me.

"Do you want any more?" I ask, to check.

"I want his name and address," Nero says.

"He's too powerful," I counter.

Nero's dark gaze lands on me like a shadow. "So am I."

I shake my head at that. "I like to leave it at JV. He doesn't deserve a full name anymore."

Nero opens his mouth to say something but Kaden beats him to it, "What happened after that, Louise?"

"Three years of that," I say, shrugging. "By the time I was eighteen, I could sort of sense he wasn't as interested in me as he was before. I wasn't happy, I couldn't eat very much or *do* very much, and he was getting bored. I think he didn't like that I knew more about art than he did at that point, either. Painting was my escape, and he had the supplies for it, so he let me do it at first to keep me busy when he didn't want to be bothered.

"I started selling little paintings online, trying to make some money so I wouldn't be completely screwed when he threw me away. And one of those led me to the Russos."

"What do you mean?" Nero asks.

"I sold one to Carlo Russo—five thousand dollars, my first big sale. It was a total fluke. He heard about me somehow and bought the painting and I couldn't help emailing him to thank him. We exchanged messages for a little while before he revealed that he knew someone at

RISD and was willing to put in a good word for me. I didn't know who he was then. All I knew was that he was a patron of the arts and helped me get a full scholarship to art school.

"Just in time, too, because I woke up one day and JV was done with me. Said I had to move out and wouldn't tell me anything else. My home for three years, gone like that. Along with most of my paintings—all the ones I couldn't carry as I left."

I glance at Kaden and add, "He told me later that he burned them."

Then I motion to the *Hourglass* painting he put across the room. "That was one of my thesis paintings."

"It's phenomenal, Louise," he lies so sweetly, but I like the lie, so I don't bring it up.

"Yeah, well..." Clearing my throat, I move on to the least interesting part of the whole story. "I went to school, did okay, but eventually JV came back. He saw that I was getting a bit of attention for my work and he showed up on campus one day demanding that I give him one of my paintings to pay him back for taking care of me."

"The fuck he did," Nero snaps, eyes wild with some emotion that seems too big, considering.

"It's okay," I say. "It was a long time ago. And he didn't get it, in the end. Carlo would occasionally message me to ask how I was doing at school, and I told him about the visit. I didn't see JV for a while after that, not until my thesis showcase where I sold a painting for about twenty grand and *ArtForum* mentioned it. I was really proud, you know, but JV showed up and nearly ruined the celebration for me. I had to leave early with him just to stop him from making a scene and of course all he cared about was the money. When I wouldn't give it to him, he...did some not nice things. Broke my arm. Branded me. Told me I owed him my life and if I wasn't willing to pay him back he'd have to take it from me a different way.

"I waited until he left, and then I called Carlo."

Those last three words sum up the beginning of the end for me.

"I told him I was scared, and he promised to take care of me. I didn't know who his family was then, but JV never came back and after I graduated, the Russos offered me this crazy-cushy job and treated me more or less like family, and the rest is…what it is."

"Do you keep tabs on JV now?" Kaden asks and I shake my head.

"I googled him a couple of times—there've been mentions of sales of his art abroad, but the Russos told me they scared the fear of God into him and it seems like they did."

I blow out a breath and offer a nothing-smile to Kaden. "The End."

"Not the end," Nero counters. He grips my chin and turns me toward him. "Not even fucking close."

CHAPTER 58

KADEN

Last night was…perfection.

The shower. Louise's story. They were just appetizers to what came after. Nero and I whispered sweet and silly nothings to her until she was laughing again. Until she was lifting our hands in hers to kiss them. And then Nero spread her legs between us and ate her out like he was trying to draw poison from a wound. And I watched because I couldn't look away, from the pointed desire in his eyes, the pleasure in hers. She clung to me as if I could save her from him. But I couldn't. He was desperate. Immoveable. A force to be reckoned with.

And when she came so hard we had to massage the cramps out of her curled feet, Nero grinned at me and goaded, "You're up, champ."

I accepted that challenge.

So did Louise afterward, when she showed us just what a skilled multitasker she is. I don't think I've ever been with a woman who worshipped me the way she did. She was so *alive* again, drawing our cocks into her mouth one after the other and back again as if they were free samples of ice cream she couldn't choose between.

And when we came like fountains, she beamed triumphantly up at us and watched the show we put on just for her with her lip tugged between her teeth.

Maybe we slept a couple of hours after that, curled around Louise in our normal configuration. But that's all we could manage before I sensed Nero's hand moving along her thigh under the covers and my hand went to my familiar clutch between her legs, and Louise kissed me and Nero kissed her.

Suddenly, we were a writhing ball of bodies under the covers, her between us, whimpering with a need I could taste on my tongue. The intimacy swallowed us like a stormy sea, and I could barely breathe unless it was her breath, and I could barely see, except when she stared at me, her face twisted in a way I had to memorize to paint later.

The entire experience hit me the way seeing Van Gogh's *Starry Night* in person did all those years ago—I realized this was a pivotal moment for me.

I knew that if I didn't make some tough decisions for myself, this night we shared would be one-of-a-kind, never to be repeated. It would fuel my inspiration for a long time—maybe forever—but it would fade to fantasy and cost me *the more beautiful reality* I could have with them. I knew when she fell asleep afterward that there was no remaining in the house. Not without them.

And yet, I also knew I needed one more confirmation before I let them change my life forever. I stole from the bed and filled a bag with clothes, then I hid it in the foyer closet just in case they woke up different this morning. Just in case they claimed last night was just one crazy night.

Maybe it was immature.

Maybe it was silly.

But I needed to know.

It terrified me a couple of hours later when Nero came down dressed in the outfit he'd originally worn here and clapped a hand on my shoulder in passing before heading to the coffee maker. The small talk was excruciating. I couldn't tell if we were just pretending everything yesterday never happened or not.

But then I heard sprinting footsteps down the stairs, and Louise appeared, her round eyes bulging with hurt. She came right to me with her hands tucked in her sweater and said, "You weren't there when I woke up."

I reached for her and admitted, "I couldn't sleep."

Louise curled into my arms right there in the kitchen. "You don't regret last night, do you?"

"No, of course not. Of course not. Do you?"

"No." She ran her fingers through my hair and said, "I don't like waking up without you."

"Me neither," I whispered.

"You know...my apartment isn't as big as this place, but it's big enough for three."

Most of my fears evaporated the moment she said that. And the rest disappeared when Nero leaned on the kitchen island and added, "So's mine. Why don't we spend the drive down to the city talking all this over?"

"I-If you think you can leave?" Louise was quick to add for my sake. "If you want to?"

I smiled at that and rose from my seat. Hand in hers, I led them both into the hallway and showed them the bag I'd stashed. Let me tell you, I don't know that I've seen anything more beautiful than the smiles that spread across their faces, as wide as the sea is vast.

And I knew everything would be okay.

"When do we leave?" I teased.

"In a couple of hours, maybe?" With a quick reach and fling, Louise pulled off her sweater and tossed it for Nero to catch before bolting up the stairs. "Come find me!"

CHAPTER 59

NERO

The moment Kaden stepped out onto his porch with that bag in hand and climbed into my car, I knew something had shifted for us all. More than the sex, I thought that moment cemented the possibility that we were trying for something real here.

I decided the best thing for us was to get the most uncomfortable questions out of the way up front...but I discovered quickly that I was wrong about what the most difficult question really was.

For me, I thought the toughies would be, *"Will we all move into your apartment or mine or somewhere else entirely?"* or *"Is there anything you want with Kaden that I can't have with you?"*

But Lulu taught me the true meaning of 'uncomfortable' with her first question. She asked us both, "Would you want to have other relationships outside the one you have with me?"

I think you could've heard a pin drop. Neither Kaden nor I knew how to respond to that...mostly because I'd never considered it—or the opposite, that *we* might not be enough for her.

And honestly, it terrified me. I literally didn't know what to say.

Lulu took our silence head on. She scooched forward in the middle back seat and kissed each of our shoulders.

"I understand if you do," she said. "It's probably not fair that I get both of you to myself."

Kaden jerked dramatically at that. "What?"

"You're wonderful," she said. "I don't want anybody else, but if you do, I don't want to stop you."

The words made me want to slam on the brakes in panic. Instead, I pulled the car onto a side road and parked it because my hands were shaking a little.

"But you're selfish," I countered.

"Dude, no she's not," Kaden said.

I waved away his confusion and turned to Lulu. "When we went to dinner at Amy Ruth's you said you were existentially selfish."

"Yeah, I'm a little broken," she shrugged. "But I'm trying to be better."

"No, I mean…"

How could I say this? Her generous offer had struck a nerve I never expected. It made me *so uncomfortable*. To my core. It felt as if she'd accidentally nicked some artery full of acidic discomfort and I was now bleeding internally.

But it was more than that. I'd felt this type of discomfort before—in prison, when my father told me Ethan probably wished I would never come home. The suggestion almost destroyed me. I couldn't sleep for days, and the only thing that helped in the end was summoning Darius to the prison and telling him to find a way to buy Star-King by any means necessary.

Only once I had dirt on Vincent Star…Only once I made the deal with Troy Singer to work as my proxy until I got out of jail…did the anxiety go away.

Because I was terrified that my dad was right. I thought Ethan was ashamed of me. I thought I'd get out of prison and find out he didn't need me anymore and I'd be completely alone without anyone who gave a shit about me.

Given Ethan's stonewalling, I'm still not sure if my dad was right.

But Lulu cares about me. Even Kaden does, in his way.

Just to kill the acidic discomfort roiling in my gut, I told them the truth.

"I'm going to be very honest with you two right now—I *want* you to be selfish with me because I want to be selfish with you. You're both mine, and I'm yours. I need you to need this with me. I need to know you see a future with me. I want to see where this goes and give it a real shot."

"My Big Guy," Lulu said, wrapping her tender hand around the back of my neck. "You can't be replaced."

"This is special," I pushed. "What we have feels special—the three of us. Be with him on your own, be with me on our own, be with us together and sleep between us every night. I don't need anybody else."

"Neither do I," Kaden leapt to add.

Lulu's gaze jerked to him in surprise. "Really?"

I forced the words "Are we enough for you?" out of my mouth, even though I thought the answer would destroy me.

"More than enough," Lulu swore, shooting us both a smile that I could feel in the root of my cock. Kaden felt the same, I learned a second later.

"Let's make sure of that," Kaden said to me, before we tore open our doors and got into the back seat with her.

Maybe having this conversation while driving in a car wasn't the best idea. Then again, that hour we spent in the back seat buried inside her was fucking incredible.

But with that big brutally uncomfortable question answered and the overall idea of our connection established, the rest of the conversation was a breeze.

What are we all looking for with each other?

Will we be open with friends and family?

How will the scheduling work?

What will we do if one of us wants something more (or less) in the future?

It felt miraculous and insane how comfortable we were talking about all of it, once we just admitted our trio was the thing to protect. It felt fucking real. Reliable.

It felt like I finally had some sort of axis around which to manage everything else going on in my life. The stuff with my company, Omnisight, the stuff with Ethan's company, and Emilio—it was all tangential to this Central Thing we were building.

Hearing Lulu and Kaden say they felt the same way put everything else into perspective.

And it's probably the only reason we didn't fall to pieces the second we saw what was waiting for us at Lulu's apartment.

CHAPTER 60

LULU

"What...happened?"

I spent a month away from this apartment, so I expected to come back to dead plants and a notice on the mailbox saying there was too much mail to leave any more.

I *didn't* expect this.

It's trashed. My home is destroyed. The lamps are toppled, the glass coffee table is shattered, the artwork once on the walls is in a giant torn heap on the floor. Someone scattered coffee grounds across the kitchen. They left the patio door wide open, too; the wood floor is warped with water damage from whatever rain and snow hit the city while I was gone.

My bedroom is worse, somehow. All of my clothing is missing, my jewelry too. My shoes all have broken heels, as if someone took the time to break each one by hand. My bed is covered in trash—like actual compostable trash. Banana peels and eggshells.

I left in a hurry, so I expected to come back to a smell, but...

Someone took things a step further and wrote the word *schulden* on the wall using one of my red lipsticks.

"Let me check in there first," Nero says, kissing my head in passing as he dips into the bedroom to open the closets fully and look under the bed.

"Lulu, I'm so sorry," Kaden says, taking my hand.

I don't really know what to say, but it feels apropos to joke, "Here I was thinking I'd finally get a fresh change of my own clothes."

"We'll replace all of it, I promise," he says, which is sweet even if I don't really care about the clothes.

It's a violation of my private space. Again. And this time, I don't think I'm going to get an apology for it. I outfitted this apartment with love, care, my own sweat equity. It hurts my heart to see so many cherished pieces taken from me. To see the lovely patterned wallpaper I *made by hand* torn in certain places. To mourn the loss of several first printings of paintings I'd received as gifts from artist friends.

In the end, though, it's all *stuff*, and I've lost stuff before.

The bigger violation is that word scrawled across my wall in big red serial killer letters: *schulden*.

"Do you know what that means?" Nero asks as he leaves my bedroom.

I do. And I hate it.

I have to force the words out. "*Schulden* is the Dutch word for debt...JV—*Johan Ververs*—is Dutch. But I haven't seen or heard from him in a decade..."

My words die as Nero's gaze catches on something. He stomps past us and his hand swipes something off the little end table by the front door.

"Fuck," he says under his breath.

"What is it?" I ask.

When he doesn't answer, Kaden barks, "Nero!"

Nero's hand opens toward us holding something I hoped I'd never see again—the silver ring with JV's initials on it that he used to brand my back.

The sight of it...

The implication of it...

A painful flinch of panic wracks my body.

"No," I say, trying to deny it. "I'm not listed here. The only people who know I live here are Cara and Ivy and the..."

My stomach twists as Kaden finishes for me, "The Russos."

"They wouldn't tell him where I live, would they?" I hate how scared

I sound, but I am. I am scared. "Are they punishing me again?"

Kaden wraps his arms around me before I can collapse. "Don't worry, we'll deal with this. But do you really think it's him, Nero? After so long?"

Nero's eyes flare at that, but the spark shifts a second later and I can't tell why.

"I don't know." Turning to me, he adds, "But we're going to find out. Come on, let's get you settled at my apartment. Call your friends, see if they can come be with you, and then Kaden and I have places to be."

I scoff at that. "Yeah, no. Please don't tell me you're trying to leave me behind because I'm a woman."

Nero's laugh matches mine. "Lulu you're a survivor. You survived him once and I think you'd do it again. But you're connected to him, to this entire mess. It's your apartment, your feud with the Russos, your history with this JV guy. You're going to stay as far away as possible from all of it for plausible deniability's sake. I want you fucking *untouchable*."

"Oh." Honestly, the man has a point. "Okay…but what are you two going to do?"

***

"It's not much, but please come in. Make yourselves at home."

I spent the entire ride to Nero's Fifth Avenue apartment listening to him make calls to his contacts and watching Kaden discreetly google Johan Ververs while I texted Cara and Ivy. There were a lot of quick words, quick turns, and frustrating pauses in traffic.

In contrast, the second we step into Nero's apartment, I shuck off all that tension like an ill-fitting winter coat. I can't help but smile at how…nondescript…Nero's flat is. Outdated furniture, drab colors, nothing but the electronics made after 1980.

"You live in an old lady's apartment?" I tease.

Kaden chuckles. "They come like this."

"Cut me some slack, I haven't exactly had time to redecorate," Nero smirks, kissing me in passing. "Besides, I think that's your job now."

"I don't know that you can afford me," I snark.

But Nero doesn't rise to that bait. He spreads his arms wide, gesturing to…all the boringness around him. "I thought you'd find the lack of zebra stripes disturbing, but if you're fine living in a post-World-War-2 museum, I suppose we can keep it this way."

"No," I grunt playfully. "I'd have this place gutted in a week."

"You say that as if you're joking," he says. "I'm not. One week, Lulu—I expect results."

Despite our conversation in the car on the way here, his words and tone still surprise me. He really isn't joking.

Neither is Kaden when we follow Nero to the master suite, and he gestures to the bed. "We need a king."

"Agreed," Nero replies. "The mattress at your place was fucking incredible. You want to order it, or should I?"

"I got it," Kaden says.

"Make sure our *new interior designer* picks out the frame," he teases, clearly talking about me. "And let me know which room is best for an art studio. I can hire movers to clear it out, along with whatever Lulu doesn't want to keep."

Despite everything, watching them talk with each other and move around the room as if we're already sharing it, makes my heart swell with joy. Nero makes room for Kaden's clothes in the dresser and then shoves his stuff aside in the walk-in closet, promising they'll fill the space with everything I've ever wanted to wear. Then Kaden pops into the en-suite bathroom and sets up his electric toothbrush to charge and Nero pulls two more towels out of a closet and…

I think it's a moment I'll remember for the rest of my life—this normalcy.

Another core memory forms a few minutes later when the doorbell rings and Cara and Ivy arrive. I rush to open the door for them and give them both big welcome hugs while they eye my guys over my shoulders with lascivious curiosity.

"Hey Nero," Cara says before her gaze flits to Kaden and his paint-speckled shirt. "Hey...paint guy."

"Looks like *someone's* been busy," Ivy teases.

Nero, Kaden, and I discussed how to handle family and friends on the way down here, so I smile, step back between them, and reach for both of their hands proudly. A trill of joy shoots through me as they both intertwine their fingers with mine.

My gals already know what's up when I say, "Cara, you know Nero King, but this is Kaden Malbec. Kaden, Nero, these are my best friends, Cara and Ivy."

"Nice to meet you," Kaden says.

"Thanks for coming," Nero adds.

Ivy grins. "Oh, the pleasure seems to be entirely Lulu's."

"Hush you," I say.

Ivy only grins wider. "I brought pastries."

"I brought wine and dinner," Cara adds. "Nero, Ethan and Val are downstairs waiting for you guys."

That takes us all by surprise, Nero more than anyone. A full-body flinch rolls through him and into me through our connected hands.

He pins his worried eyes to me. "Did you ask her to ask him?"

"No," I swear, because it's true.

"He wanted to come," Cara says. "Seriously, I couldn't keep him away. Go on, we've got Lulu now."

I admit the joy from moments ago fizzles to worry as my men pull me in for kisses and hugs, whispering things like "We'll see you soon" and "Call us if you need anything."

In the car ride over here, they told me what they're going to do, but I still hate it. I hate the risk of it. I hate that I don't feel worthy of their concern either. JV and Emilio are dangerous, I know that, but I'd rather think of them as nuisances. They're not worth *any* potential harm to Nero or Kaden. I'd rather lose a thousand apartments worth of mementos and suffer the humiliation of a thousand of Emilio's paintings than lose a single second with them.

But they already told me they had to do this for their own peace of mind as much as mine.

Nero said, "Men like this only understand one thing—actual consequences. It's time they faced a few."

And Kaden added, "They've been protected way too long."

So, I do the only thing I can do. I kiss them both goodbye and see them to the door with a hopeful, "I don't care how late it is. Wake me when you get home."

After they leave, I turn to the two most important women in my life. "Come on, let's find a corkscrew. You'll need a *large* glass of wine to deal with everything I'm going to tell you."

CHAPTER 61

NERO

I feel like a damned liar as I walk toward my brother's SUV with Kaden on my heels. A liar because I'm hiding my shaking hands in my coat pockets, and the fear on my face with a mask of indifference. There's a part of me that's *convinced* I'll open the car door and see nobody inside. But I'm more scared that Ethan is actually in there.

Kaden seems to see right through my façade. "Are you okay?"

"You got any brothers?" I ask.

"No."

"It's like having a sworn enemy you'd die to protect."

"This should be fun then." He claps a hand on my shoulder, completely unaware just how much I need the reassurance. But then he adds, "I'm here if you need anything," and the mask of indifference completely crumbles.

When I open my door, Ethan's face is the first one I see and I feel that acidic discomfort sloshing inside me again.

"Nero."

I have no idea what to say, so I just nod at him, feeling like a jackass as I climb in. Then Kaden climbs in and Ethan doesn't know what to say.

Kaden does, though. "Hey Ethan, good to see you."

Ethan blusters a little, studying him. "You too, although it's weird to see you outside your house."

"Sorry I was such a dick to you the last time you visited," Kaden says, and I remember that Ethan is Kaden's agent.

"Sorry I couldn't keep my brother from finding out where you live," Ethan grumbles.

"Hey, if you had, I wouldn't be here," Kaden says with a smile. "You must be Val."

Val's perceptive gaze peers back at us in the rearview mirror. "At your service."

"I'm Kaden Malbec."

"The painter?" Val asks, knocking me out of my silence.

A strange streak of protectiveness seizes me. "Yeah, keep that between us, okay? Kaden's pretty private."

"For now," Kaden says, surprising me.

"What do you mean?" I ask.

"I think it's time I stop hiding, you know?"

"Seriously?"

He shrugs with a smile. "Something to discuss with Louise later."

There's no doubt on Kaden's face, no fear...and that surprises me too. So does the heavy silence in the front seat. Val's eyes are on me, but so are Ethan's, watching and listening to both of us.

I realize how...intimate this conversation might sound, and the discomfort riles inside me again. Not because I'm ashamed of what Lulu, Kaden, and I are doing, but because I haven't spoken with my brother about stuff like this in a long, *long* time.

And that makes me feel fucking awful.

But it's not the time for this shit, so I push us on and turn to Val and my brother. "Do you two really want to help us with Lulu's situation?"

"You don't want our help?" Ethan asks.

I'm quick to say, "You're welcome, it's just I didn't think you would want to."

"Well, we do, all right?" Ethan says, turning to face the road ahead. "Lead on, king."

I guess today is full of surprises. With that directive, I pull out my phone and call Kenzo.

"Yo, what-up boss."

"Anything on the photo in Louise Rathbone's apartment. The guy with the initials JV?"

"Sorry, I couldn't find any matches. There's no professor with the initials JV and there's nothing connecting Louise Rathbone to anyone with those initials."

"The Russos must've paid someone to scrub their connection. His name is Johan Ververs—a transplant from the Netherlands. I was wrong about him being a professor. He owned a traveling art studio based out of Rhode Island about ten years ago. He's a sexual predator who may or may not have a rap sheet and it looks like he just broke into Louise's apartment and trashed the place."

Ethan and Val's eyes whip back to me again before looking to Kaden, as if they don't believe me and need confirmation from an outside source. Fury rushes through me like a backdraft—fury and disappointment.

But Kaden nods beside me and it dampens some of the heat.

"Tell Tony to go through the footage from the security cameras and our cameras outside her building, identify everyone who entered and exited, cross-reference against her neighbors, and send me a list of the people who don't belong. Remind him to watch the building across the street too."

"While he's doing that, you want me to look into Ververs?" Kenzo says to confirm.

"Don't look—find. I want Ververs tagged as soon as possible. Send me his current location when you have it and put everything else aside until you do. In the meantime, tell me where I can find Emilio Russo."

"It looks like he's having an early dinner at The Pompadour."

"Alone?"

"I can't say. That restaurant doesn't have security cameras."

"Okay, thanks Kenzo."

I almost end the call, but Kenzo has more to say. "Is the war finally starting, boss?"

Again, Ethan's gaze collides with mine. I'm expecting judgment, self-righteousness, and disappointment to color his face...but I don't find that. He's just curious, as if it's my call and he's still willing to help either way. It surprises me, considering how dangerous it would be.

But it also reminds me that everything that's happened—with Ethan, with Louise and the Russos—is a game of chess, not of war.

I would always rather win a game than lose a fight.

"Taking down an organized crime family doesn't happen overnight, Kenzo," I say lightly. "Priority goes to destroying the two dumb motherfuckers who pose the greatest threat to the woman I love."

CHAPTER 62

LULU

Telling the story of my childhood *twice* in the same 24-hour period after keeping it locked away inside me for over a decade feels like some sort of therapy technique I accidentally stumbled upon.

It comes out so much easier the second time too.

And I realize holding it in all my life was like ignoring an infected wound hoping it would go away on its own instead of just cleaning the fucking thing so it could heal properly.

The pity I expected to see on their faces isn't there either.

Only anger for me. Ivy's natural mama bear energy has her fuming on my behalf. Even normally meek Cara slices through her steak like she's decapitating an enemy and wants to make sure it hurts. Each new revelation I give them is punctuated by the squeak of her metal knife against the ceramic plate.

Especially when I tell them about what happened at my thesis showcase at RISD and I dip deeper into details I didn't tell my guys.

"When JV showed up, I thought he'd heard about it and wanted to congratulate me, but he ended up telling me my work was shit. Accused me of fucking the teachers to get favors, said it was unfair for someone like me to get attention when there were so many better artists who deserved it more. Caused a big scene, I was so embarrassed. The only way I could get him to stop was literally taking him out of the building, but once we were alone, he got scary. Started rambling about how I owed everything to him—*belonged* to him—and if I wasn't going to admit that, he'd make it permanent. He had this…ring with his initials. He used a lighter to heat it until it was fucking red as a coal and I tried to fight him off, but I couldn't, and he pressed it to my back. The pain was awful. I tried to pull away and he accidentally twisted my arm until it snapped—"

"There was no *accidentally* about it, Lulu," Cara says. "That piece of shit attacked you. Everything that happened as a result of that choice is *his fucking fault*."

Ivy literally growls. "You said this prick's name is Johan Ververs?"

She pulls her phone out like she's about to call the manager of life and I chuckle in disbelief.

"Ivy, I love you, but don't worry about it. Nero has an actual army of cyber-people helping them look for him."

Ivy smirks at that. "I love a challenge. Come on, Cara, let's see if we can find this asshole first."

CHAPTER 63

KADEN

I forgot how fucking *intense* the city can be. Going from zero people to two was hard enough, but driving through the hustle and bustle of this town feels like we're inside a hive of buzzing-beeping-*sneezing* insects.

It's annoying and overwhelming, and fucking fascinating.

I used to live here. I used to be around people all the time at parties and showcases, back when everyone knew me as Kaden Allard and I could walk around listening to people talk about this "up and coming Malbec guy" with a bemused smile on my face, proud that I'd done something without my family name paving the way for me.

Of course that also meant I had to weather the heartbreak alone when I overheard people talking shit about my work.

Then I started to sense how superficial the art scene could be and low-grade panic became my constant companion. It didn't matter that nobody knew I was Malbec. Or rather, *because* nobody knew, the artificiality of it all was much easier to pick up on.

I let it get to me.

But driving through the rabble now, I think I did myself a disservice by focusing on the negative. There's an organic rhythm to a city that's unlike anything else—horrible if you decide it is, and beautiful if you let it be.

I want to let it be beautiful, because I think Louise was right—people inspire me. This drive alone has given me a dozen ideas for scenes to paint. And knowing I have two real people to spend time with in the midst of this artificial jungle makes all the difference.

I'm still going to talk to Nero and Louise about spending the weekends upstate until I'm used to this again, but for a few moments I find myself luxuriating in the chaos.

Until the chaos invades our car.

"You can't confront Emilio at The Pompadour," Ethan says.

"I'm not going to merc the guy in public, dipshit," Nero snipes. "I'm just going to talk to him."

"No, asshole. I mean, it's as close to ultra-exclusive as you can get without being members-only."

That's a little cryptic, so I cut in. "The Pompadour is the kind of place where you either own a table or you have to make a reservation eight months out."

Nero grunts.

"On top of that, *you* would be an idiot to confront him yourself," Ethan says.

"Well, we both know I'm not an idiot," Nero replies.

"Do we?"

Val cuts in with a quiet, "Easy, gentlemen…"

Neither brother hears him.

Nero continues, "Which one of us had his head so far up his own ass he didn't know his own partner was a *murderous creep* planning to sell half his company to a fucking tool?"

Ethan laughs. "Do you mean *you*?"

"I've never killed anybody!" Nero barks.

"I *meant* you're the fucking tool Vince sold it to."

"You know what, man? I saved your fucking company for you."

"Oh yeah?" Ethan twists in his seat. "So you're gonna give it to me? You're gonna save me again, bro, and hold it over my head *forever*?"

I expect Nero to snap back, but the light goes out of his eyes suddenly, as if Ethan threw a physical punch at him and knocked him to the ground.

"You only ever do anything for yourself," Ethan pushes. His words seem to wound Nero again.

And Val mumbles, "Chill out, mate."

"No, you know what, Nero?" Ethan adds. "You go in there and cause a scene with Emilio, you're either going to end up dead or in prison forever, which would make 'giving' my company back to me that much harder to do. So *I'm* going to save *you* today. I'll call around to see if anyone I know has a table there, then I'll—"

"I do." Their eyes turn to me, so I explain, "My family 'owns a table' at The Pompadour. I could call right now, if you want? Table for four?"

"No," Ethan says. "Make it for three. *Lulu's boyfriend* will wait outside. The second Emilio sees Nero, this is going to devolve into a dick-measuring contest."

"Ethan, just shut up," Nero says. "You don't even know what you're going in there to do."

"Then tell me," Ethan challenges. "If you actually care about Lulu and this isn't just some bizarro way of living rent-free in my head, tell me what you want to know and trust me to get the information for you."

"Pfft, sure," Nero laughs.

But despite everything Ethan's thrown at Nero since we got in the SUV, he seems sincere about this. He turns a little more and unfurls his hand, revealing a weird round transparent band-aid-looking thing sitting in his palm.

"What's that?" I ask.

"My brother didn't tell you? He likes to bug people's offices and listen in on their conversations," Ethan explains. "I'll put this on my phone so you can hear us. How about that?"

I glance at Nero—to gauge his reaction and to confirm the truth of it.

Nero's sheepish shrug speaks volumes. "How'd you find it?"

"Let's just say Cara noticed it under my desk." His eyebrow rises, daring us to let our imaginations run away with us at the implication. "Now do you trust me to help or not?"

CHAPTER 64

NERO

Little brothers are over-fucking-rated, I swear to God.

Ethan wears that self-righteous grin on his face like he has the upper hand here because he found the bug I put in his office. But he didn't, did he. Cara did. Worse he thinks I don't have enough restraint to go in there and get the information I want out of Emilio without starting a fight.

Jackass forgot Emilio doesn't like him either.

But…

Fuck, he's right that Emilio *really* doesn't like me…and it'd be easier to get Emilio to talk openly if he feels comfortable.

"Nero, just tell us what you're thinking," Kaden adds when the silence stales. "Let us handle it. For Louise."

Who the hell does he think I'm doing this for?

"Fuck, fine," I say. "Look, Lulu's unlisted in her building and she pays everything through a P.O. Box. The only people who knew she lived there were Cara, Ivy, and the Russos, and we all know it'd be wild fucking timing for Ververs to separately find her now after so long."

"He might have heard she was fired and gone looking," Ethan says.

"Sure, but it's way more likely that either the Russos told him *or* he isn't the one who broke in."

Kaden's quick to say, "But the word he wrote on the wall? The ring."

"Remember what Lulu said—Ververs was getting bored with her because she aged out. He came back to her later for money, but she hasn't painted in a decade so her paintings aren't well known anymore. Why would he care about her now?"

Then there's the thing Emilio said to me when I confronted him at Lulu's apartment.

"Before I drove upstate to be with you guys, Emilio told me the Russos 'protected her when no one else would' and 'saved her first.'"

"She told us the Russos made Ververs go away," Kaden points out.

"Exactly. It's easy to take a ring off a corpse," I tell them.

Val grunts and I know he's picking up what I'm putting down before he says, "You think it was Emilio."

I nod. "But, in case I'm wrong and it *is* Ververs, I want to confirm it."

"How?" Ethan asks.

"Mention it to Emilio. He doesn't know she's back in the city yet, otherwise he'd already be at her door. I'm thinking that one of two things'll happen when he hears about the break-in. If Ververs *did* do it, he'll call Lulu, promise to 'save her' again, and then go after the prick and we can follow him right to the disgusting piece of filth who abused her for years. But if Emilio did it, well. I'm guessing his reaction will be pretty different."

"All right," Ethan says after a moment. "Let's go find out which it is."

"You're either gonna have to get him drunk or let him talk your ear off, you know?" I warn them.

"Why not both?" Ethan teases.

"Whatever it takes. I'll call Lulu."

I've already pulled out my phone when Ethan asks, "Why?"

"I'm going to warn her just in case. So she's not blindsided by a call from that prick."

I hate the expression I catch on Ethan's face before he glances away—it's surprise. It's fucking *surprise* that I care about her. It riles my resentment.

I want to remind him he's wrong about me—*again*—but I don't bother. He'll understand soon enough.

CHAPTER 65

LULU

"No, look at that, it's a BurgerBun sign."

"You can't possibly know that's a BurgerBun sign from a tiny bit of red in the corner of that photo."

"I'm telling you, it is."

We've been *on the hunt* for JV for nearly an hour, searching through the handful of photos we've been able to find of him online. His business used to have a website, but that's gone. The house we used to live in in Rhode Island belongs to a real estate company now. And none of those scammy "find this person" websites have recent information about him. Cara even tried calling his old number that I still had stored on my phone—it's disconnected.

"How is knowing he took a picture by a fast food restaurant going to help us locate him?" I ask as my friends bicker.

"They only have twenty locations, which might narrow down our search region," Ivy insists. "Look, text Nero and ask if we can use his computer. He must have one in here."

I open my mouth to tell them it *really would be okay* if we never located the monster from my childhood when my phone goes off—it's Nero. "His ears must've been ringing...Hey Big Guy, I was just about to call you."

"Is everything okay?"

"Of course—"

"No," Cara pipes in. "Can we use your computer?"

"I'm gonna go find it!" Ivy echoes before she leaps up from the couch and disappears down the hallway.

"Sure," Nero chuckles. "It's in the far north office. I'll text you my passwords."

"Thank you!" Cara sings as she darts away after Ivy.

"Are *you* okay?" I ask Nero when she's gone.

"Oh yeah," he says. "Just imagining you three running amok in my apartment."

"We're here, Nero," I hear Val say in the background. "I'll leave the keys with you."

I hear three doors open and close before I ask, "Where are you?"

"Childlocked in the car," he grumbles. "They're going to talk to Emilio."

My face folds with concern automatically, but Nero's quick to add, "Don't make that face."

His gentle laughing tone knocks the fear out of me a little. Turning in a circle, I look for cameras. "Are you watching me again, Mr. King?"

"I wish," he says. "No, I just know the look you get whenever he comes up."

Warmth flutters in my stomach at the admission.

But then he adds, "Listen, I need to talk to you about something, Lulu," and concern comes rushing back in.

CHAPTER 66

KADEN

I'm walking into The Pompadour with Ethan and Val fueled by rage and disgust—and honestly, I like these emotions on me. Before Louise, I hadn't felt them in a very long time, but every time I'm reminded of what she went through, my body revs to life with purpose.

Maybe it's not healthy, but neither is being numb for years.

And using this new palette of emotions makes me feel human again. Capable. I want to be those things for her.

"Mr. Allard!" Even after three years, the host knows me on sight. "It is such a pleasure to see you and your guests. Welcome. Please, follow me."

My family didn't *directly* invest in The Pompadour, but we own the companies that supply the napkins, silverware, place mats, menus, and dishes, the seat cushion fabric, the bespoke lights, and waitstaff's uniforms, among other things.

Half a dozen heads turn as we enter the dark, smoky restaurant and, as I was taught to do long ago by etiquette coaches my mother hired for me, I don't make eye contact with any of them. I follow the host to our table and sit down facing the room so everyone and their business partner can ogle me from afar.

Me and *Mr. King*, because they all know him too.

To them, this probably looks like a power dinner, and that works in our favor. It'll keep most of the people who recognize us from trying to strike up a conversation. There's only one person we've come to engage with tonight.

Ethan puts his phone with Nero's listening device on the corner of the table, and Val sits down with a quick, "Eleven o'clock."

Sure enough, Emilio Russo is seated at a booth nearby. It's just him, two bodyguards, and several whiskeys tonight.

I start to ask, "Are we going to—"

Ethan cuts me off, "We'll wait for him to come to us."

"What if he doesn't?"

"He will."

Ethan is a consummate "own the room" type, and as useful as it is for being an agent, I can kind of see why it annoys the hell out of Nero. Ethan acts so confident and stalwart, it'd be easy to mistake it for arrogance. Or worse, entitlement.

But while we were at my place, Nero told Louise and I dozens of stories of their time together as kids—about their shitty dad, their struggling mom, and the things they used to do to help each other cope. So I know Ethan's confidence is the end result of succeeding against something I've never faced—actual struggle.

So is Nero's.

Crazy that neither brother knows how much the other loves them.

Or maybe they haven't figured out yet that fighting's their love language.

It's not my place either way to tell my agent how to talk to his brother.

But…maybe it *is* my place to tell the other guy in my fucking throuple to stop pussyfooting around the only family he has left.

In fact, while we're waiting, I send Nero that very text: *Not my business, I know, but your brother fucking loves you*.

Three dots populate on my phone screen but disappear just as quickly, offering no response. I didn't expect one, but I find myself hoping Ethan's help tonight will bridge some of that weirdness. After all, at the drop of a hat, Ethan showed up to help us trick the son of an organized crime boss into revealing his secrets—if that isn't love, I don't know what is.

"Mr. King, what a surprise."

My gaze jerks up to see Ethan was right; Emilio came to us, and in record time.

"Mr. Russo," Ethan says.

Emilio turns his gaze to me, gesturing to Ethan. "Be careful around this one, his brother might just steal your girl."

We all smirk at that, keeping things friendly.

Ethan plays along. "Hey, I am *not* my brother's keeper."

"Well, you come to his rescue enough," Emilio replies, his voice still light, but insinuating, and my eyes dart to Ethan to see how he'll react.

"Not that *he'd* ever fucking appreciate it, amiright?" Ethan jokes.

"Is he here tonight?"

"Nah, his girl's apartment got broken into, so he's handling that."

I'm kinda awed at how casually he delivers the line.

Doubly when he adds, "Some guy wrote words on her wall or something. She thinks it's an old creep from her past, it's a whole thing."

I can't help it – I watch Emilio's reaction baldly, expecting...well...I don't know what I was expecting. Nero said he'd either freak out, or he wouldn't.

And he definitely *isn't* freaking out.

"Is that so?" he says. "Rotten luck, I guess."

It isn't enough of a reaction. It isn't proof of anything, except that he's drunk and distracted. By me. Emilio's eyes dance over me again and again, and I can't tell if he knows me or not.

"I'm being rude here," he says, turning to me and Val. "Emilio Russo."

"Valerian Fox," Val says introducing himself.

Ethan jumps in with, "And this is my client—"

"Malbec," I finish for him, just in case he intended to use my birth name. "Kaden Malbec."

"*Malbec the artist?*" Emilio's eyes light up and his hand darts forward to shake mine. "Holy shit, I'm in the presence of a legend."

"I don't know about that," I laugh.

"I'm an artist too," Emilio says, grabbing the fourth chair and pulling it out for himself. "You gotta let me buy you a drink. You like whiskey?"

CHAPTER 67

NERO

Emilio thinks he's untouchable. He's wrong.

He also thinks he's smart. Wrong again.

I listen to him invite himself to Ethan's table. There's a faint sound of snapped fingers as Emilio summons a waiter and orders a bottle of whiskey.

Prick.

I wish I was there to glare at him, but I'll admit—at least to myself—that Ethan was probably right. If I'd gone in there, my resting bitch face would've given the whole game away.

My surprised face would have too—Kaden just outed himself. I know he mentioned that he might, but it hits different that he did it to help Lulu.

"I hope I'm not interrupting," Emilio lies.

"Well, you know, Kaden's pretty private. Rarely comes to the city, so we gotta make time when he's here," Ethan says. "Obviously, keep that between us."

"No, yeah-yeah," Emilio replies. "Makes total sense. Your secret's safe with me. But…I gotta ask. Why the hell would you hide yourself away, man? Do you know how much pussy *Malbec* could be getting?"

I smirk when Kaden croons, "Oh, I get plenty."

"You have more restraint that I do. I'd be shouting it from the rooftops if I was as famous as you."

"I mean you're halfway there already, right?" Kaden says. "You're

Emilio Russo—I've heard that name around. Seen a couple of your pieces too."

I hear the sound of liquid being poured, as Emilio beams, "Fuck yeah, you have. I *am* getting there."

"You'll definitely be there in April," Kaden pushes. "The *Faces of Womanhood* Exhibition. That'll be huge for you."

"Huge for us, right?" Emilio says and I can hear the slight undertone of desperation in his voice. "You're coming. We got your RSVP."

Kaden's silent for a long beat, and I'd pay anything to be in that room right now and see Emilio's stupid little nervous face. The invitation for the exhibition landed on Kaden's doorstep a few days after Lulu and I arrived, and he RSVPed a couple days later.

"I'll definitely send my pieces," Kaden says.

Ethan echoes quietly, "This friggen guy. Too shy. I keep telling him he should make his debut this year, but…"

"You should!" Emilio almost blows out the audio transmitter.

"Nah, I don't want to pull focus from you," Kaden replies.

Not to mention it's called the *Faces of Womanhood* Exhibition. Leave it to Emilio to promote a dude at an event like that.

"Fuck that! The Russo Trust would *love* to help with your debut. Shit, we could put your pieces right next to mine, it could be a whole thing—I could introduce you, if you want."

"You'd do that?" Ethan asks, hamming it up.

"For *Malbec*? Everybody'd be talking about it."

"Well, what kind of pieces are you planning for it?" Kaden asks.

"Brother, let me tell you…"

And Emilio is gone, lost in a monologue about the symbolism of his own work. Waxing poetic about the Russo Trust's commitment to championing women and their allies…which he apparently considers himself to be.

How many allies trash women's apartments regularly, I wonder? How many of them paint revenge porn of them?

Too many probably.

But it's the first time since meeting that dumb fuck that I'm enjoying the sound of his voice. The more he talks, the more Kaden nudges him on, the more I can hear Emilio getting too comfortable with him.

Until I realize that with a little push, they'll be bosom buddies in no time.

I rattle off a text to Val: *Let's get this going. Leave Emilio and Kaden alone for a little while.*

CHAPTER 68

KADEN

"No-No, she wasn't invited," Emilio tells me when I start pulling the names of artists out of my ass, trying to generate more questions to ask him. "But we don't need her. Her work has always been derivative."

I forgot how exhausting conversations can be, especially when the person you're speaking to doesn't ask you anything in return. I ran out of actual questions for Emilio a while ago. No joke, if Louise and Nero hadn't invaded my home and given me some much-needed practice, I would have fumbled this mission twenty minutes in.

But Emilio's drinking. He hasn't *stopped* drinking since he sat down. And the drunker he gets, the more fascinated he becomes with me. That's a good thing, I think.

The problem is I have no idea how to transition from questions about which artists have been invited to anything related to Louise's break-in. I keep waiting for Val or Ethan to help.

Instead, about an hour in Val suddenly pulls his phone out of his pocket and says, "Ah damn. I need to make a call. Ethan you might want to hear this."

"Okay."

I blink at how fast he agrees, how fast they're on their feet. I scream internally for *one* of them to *fucking stay put!*

But they don't. They leave the table in *seconds*, and then it's just me and *this fucking guy*.

And because my social battery is running on fumes at this point, I reach for the whiskey and fill both of our cups.

Emilio grins wide. "I was wondering why you weren't drinking. Best behavior for the rep?"

I smile back, rolling with it. "Something like that."

"I can imagine. I mean, I can't. I'm not repped yet—because I want a *real* rep, someone who believes in my work, not just my name. I thought he might offer at some point, but it's probably for the best that he hasn't."

I gave up believing in God a long time ago, but...it feels like he finally showed up for me as those words leave Emilio's mouth. He's implying something; he wants me to ask.

And I see my way in to more personal topics.

"Why? Because of the thing with his brother? Did he *really* steal your girl or something?"

Emilio peeks over his shoulder, checking that Ethan hasn't returned before he leans forward and says, "*Twice*, the fuckers."

I furrow my brow. "How'd he steal her twice?"

"Eh, I don't want to get into all that," he says, and for a second, I think he's going to shut down. But he doesn't. He leans in again. "King bought one of my paintings—of the woman I've been crazy about for years. My *muse*, you know? She let me down in a big way and I got all that frustration outta my system by painting her. One of my most provocative pieces. It generated a ton of buzz. I shouldn't have put it up for sale, but I got excited. You know how that is."

"Sure."

"Anyway, I went to get it back from him. I offered to refund him the whole ten million he paid for it, but no dice. He won't fucking hand it over—*my work*! It's mine. I realized after it sold that I wanted to turn it into a triptych, my first real statement piece."

A triptych? Fuck, Louise never mentioned that. Does she even know?

"So what? You just going to paint something else?"

"And let the King brothers win? Fuck no. I've already finished the other two panels since the first sold and I'm doing the elevated version of the original painting for the third."

Fuck.

I don't know why it's the first thing I think of, but I say, "Can I see them?"

Louise's apartment can be fixed. Ververs will be found eventually. I just want to know what we're up against here. How he's going to hit her next.

"They sound amazing," I tell him. "Seriously, you got any progress pics?"

Emilio grins. "I'll do you one better. I'll show 'em to you. Come on."

He lunges to his feet before I can blink, sending his chair flying backward into the one behind him.

"Right now?"

Where the hell is Ethan?

"Yeah, we'll take my car."

I don't know what to do. We don't have the info Nero needs yet, so I rise to my feet. With the half of a percent mental battery I have left, my mind catches on Ethan's phone still on the table, and I swipe it into my pocket a second before Emilio wraps his arm around my shoulder and guides me away.

CHAPTER 69

NERO

Oh shit. Kaden was doing so well until those last few seconds.

The audio transmitter rubs against something and their voices distort a little, muffled.

"Is it far?" Kaden asks.

"No, twenty minutes, come on."

At least I can still hear them. He must have grabbed Ethan's phone before leaving. Clever man. Not that he should be *going anywhere with Emilio Russo*, friggen idiot! But in Kaden's own words, he's "not the most socially intelligent person," he's "awkward as fuck sometimes."

Well, congrats to him, he just won the awkward Olympics. *And* he's landed on my shit list because I can't go home to Louise without him.

The only saving grace here is that I cloned Ethan's GPS tracker ages ago. I text Val about what happened and a few minutes later, he and Ethan leap into the front seat.

"Can you see where he's headed?" Val asks.

"Yeah, two lights then take a left."

Despite being drunk as a skunk, Emilio was right on the money. It *is* only a twenty-minute drive to his studio, which is in an ugly little stretch of industrial warehouses. Unfortunately, it's halfway down an alley of units behind a privacy gate, so Val drives by, spotting cameras, before he finds a place just out of view to park the SUV.

My stomach sinks watching Emilio loop his sloppy arm around Kaden's shoulders and guide him inside. I start to feel sick when

Emilio's guards follow them in. And I start craving an ice cube half a second after the light from inside the building winks out when they shut the door.

"What do we do?" I ask.

"We just wait," Ethan says.

"Emilio's dangerous," I counter. "Maybe I should call my guys? Val you know people who could—"

"Relax, Nero," Val urges. "He'll be okay. He was holding his own in the restaurant just fine."

His lulling tone is the only thing that soothes me. He glances back at me in the rearview with a knowing look on his face that sets me at ease too. He's always been perceptive; it's why we got along so well when we were kids. We used to do those "solve a mystery" puzzles together all the time before we transitioned to watching people for money.

Now he's watching me, and I wonder what he's seeing. I doubt he'd guess the truth, or maybe he would.

Fuck, I don't care; Kaden's voice cuts in a second later, glueing my attention to my phone.

"Oh wow," Kaden says, still muffled. "Some setup you've got here."

"Yeah-Yeah," Emilio quips. "I needed a space of my own for this. My parents didn't get the whole 'painting' thing when I was younger. But buying storage space they understood no problem."

The sound of a heavy metal door squealing open sets my nerves on edge.

So does the sound Kaden makes next.

"Uh…" Like someone fucking stabbed him in the back.

"You like it?" Emilio preens.

Kaden's silent a long beat and then: "…Wow again."

"Damn right, wow again. Come on, get closer. Take a good long look at it."

CHAPTER 70

KADEN

Art isn't about punching down; I told Louise that when she came to me after Emilio painted her the first time. It shouldn't be used for eviscerating the character of a private citizen either. Public figures? Symbolic figures? Sure. Go for it. They've made themselves available to scrutiny and we have every responsibility to humble them when they've done something wrong.

But this isn't that.

Louise isn't a politician or some rich asshole who chose the Villainy archetype. She didn't *do* anything to anyone; it wouldn't matter if she had. And "letting Emilio down in a big way" isn't justification for what he's done to her.

Two paintings, and one in progress, sit on large easels at the center of his rusty, dusty studio. They stand out as much for the bright lights that dangle overhead and cause an accidental halo effect around them as they do for what they contain.

The first—the in-progress one—is the painting Nero showed me, that Louise sketched for me. I don't know how Emilio thinks he's "elevated" it, but it looks just as awful as the original version.

The second is meant to be shocking. He's painted her as the Madonna. The Virgin Mary. Except that she's giving birth to him—to Emilio—with her robes hiked up, exposing her "secret" fishnet tights and the baby's head ripping her open, blood trickling all the way down the canvas.

The third is less shocking but laughably un-self-aware. It's a wedding scene in which Louise is marrying Emilio. Their hands are outstretched and the priest is shackling wedding bands around their ring fingers with a chain linking between them.

Honestly, they're all so…distasteful…he's killing his career before it even begins. And that would be great—to let the trash take itself out—except that he's hurting Louise in the process.

The faces. He's put so much detail into capturing her face in each painting, they're almost photographic and I'm at a loss as to why he'd waste his time ruining himself and her instead of just *using his fucking talent properly*.

And that, as much as his slander of Louise, exorcises my lingering social awkwardness. I know *exactly* how to get him to talk about her now.

When Emilio steps up beside me, expecting praise, I give him exactly that.

"Fantastic, man, really. I'm shocked by the detail. The color. I love how you did this section right here—that texture is *killer*."

Emilio's drunken head swivels to his men. "Malbec likes my work, you hear that?"

"You really captured her likeness too," I say. Then I wait for him to realize…

"Her likeness?"

"Louise Rathbone. That's who that is, right? Is she your girl?"

"Yeah. How do you know her?"

"She bought a piece from me a while back—*Morning Fog*. It was a woman in a foggy bathroom—"

"Yeah-Yeah-Yeah! My family loved that piece. My ma wanted to keep it for herself, but you know… nothing draws people to an auction like a Malbec."

"So…one of the Kings stole her from you?" I redirect.

"Dumb fuck got her all confused just cuz he's handsome or whatever," Emilio grumbles. "*I'm* handsome. *I* have just as much money as he does. And my family's done things for her no one else would, fucking bitch."

I can hear it in his voice—he's primed for oversharing.

So I push, "So what's happening? You just giving up on her? You gonna get her back?"

A sloppy smile seeps across his face. He leans in, all fire breath and gross charm.

"Already working on it."

"Yeah? How?"

"I don't want to get into her whole thing, but let's just say a woman like that would do anything to feel safe and protected."

Discomfort tightens the back of my throat. "Is she in danger?"

A sneer splits his face. "No, what? I'd wreck anyone's shit who tried to hurt her." But then he smiles, "I'd wreck anyone's shit who tried to *help* her too, but... Nah, I just know who scares her and I made her think he was still after her."

I twist my face a little and lean in, whispering, "So that whole break-in thing at her apartment?"

Emilio winks at me. "Sooner or later, she'll remember my family's always protected her and she'll come back. I won't have to chase her at all."

Well...there it is. Nero was right.

I'd hoped knowing would set me more at ease, not less, but...these paintings are worse than a destroyed apartment. Far worse. So is his plan to trick her into returning to him—not that it'll ever work now.

I find myself wishing Nero was here to wipe the floor with him and end all of this without the need for a show. I also wish I could see Nero's reaction to this conversation...if he's hearing it.

But, I'm in no position to do anything right now other than go along with Emilio. And he's far from done with me. His hand clamps onto my shoulder like a vice.

"Come on, let me show you the rest of my work. I'd love your take on it."

CHAPTER 71

NERO

I'm proud of Kaden. The guy did it. He got Emilio to admit that he broke into Lulu's apartment, which should reassure her that she doesn't have to worry about Ververs *and* that Emilio deserves every single awful thing that's coming to him at the exhibition.

I feel bad, though, that Kaden's stuck in there with Emilio, on a long, *long* tour of his studio.

We can't leave him here, not that I want to. But it means the SUV has fallen into an empty silence over the last two hours, listening to Emilio's rambling voice as he talks Kaden through every. single. painting in his private portfolio.

Thank fuck Kaden's socially awkward; anyone with any social skills would've probably gone insane an hour ago.

At least they're talking about art and technique, something Kaden knows intimately.

But that leaves the rest of us with nothing to do but sit here and wait for Emilio to *hopefully* let Kaden go without issue.

"All right, gents," Val says after a while. "I can't do it. There's a café down the block. I need a flat white or I'm going to go mad. You want anything?"

"Nah."

"No thanks."

He's out the door in seconds, maneuvering down the street and staring at his feet to avoid being identifiable on camera. Even like that,

Val oozes charisma, lucky punk.

But then it's just Ethan and I trapped in this car together...and the silence *intensifies*. Anyone with a sibling will understand; it's like the charge in the air before a thunderstorm. He can tell. And I can tell. And the rain and thunder and lightning are just waiting for the silence to break.

To my surprise, I'm not the first one to speak.

"Don't do it," Ethan warns.

"Do what?"

"Don't use this time alone to talk with me like you've claimed you've wanted to for months. No, the silence is much better."

I can't help but smirk and murmur, "Fucking chump."

But he's right. It's time. The problem is...I don't know how to start this conversation. Even when I tried to talk to him before, I wasn't sure what I'd actually say to him when I had my chance. Earlier tonight, though, he accused me of trying to save him so I could "hold it over him forever" and that shit *hurt* to hear. Because he was right; I realized it the moment he said it. His reasoning as to why I did it is wrong, although I'm not sure it'll matter now.

But I have to say something, so I go with, "I *was* trying to help you by buying your company. Sort of."

Ethan chuckles. "Sort of."

"Vincent Star killed someone, and he was involved in human trafficking. It would've wrecked the company's reputation when it got out and it *was* going to get out. My group just agreed to work with the FBI on that situation and his name is on the list of people they're going after. Part of that deal protects you—they agreed to shield Star-King from further investigation."

"Is that true?"

"Yes."

"And that thing with Sam?" Ethan asks.

"The poisoning thing? Do you really believe I'm capable of that?" I want to yell it at him, but I try my best not to. I fucking try. "How the fuck would I have even known she was pregnant? Or Cara? I didn't know Cara existed until you reached for her hand at that auction."

Then I add just in case, "I like her for you, by the way."

He hums instead of answering, but it doesn't grate on me like it normally does and he doesn't seem as prickly as usual. I think I finally got through to him. But there's one more piece he's really concerned about, I know.

"I'll sell you most of my Star-King shares," I add, and that surprises him.

His body shifts in the front seat, and he peers back at me with disbelief; I wish I could enjoy subverting his expectations of me more.

"Most," he says. "Why not all?"

"Because."

"Oh, fuck off with the vagueness," he scolds.

"You fuck off with being unreasonable," I snap back. "You'll still be king of the castle like you always wanted. The majority of the company will be yours."

"Jesus Nero. *What do you want?* It's not to sit in on fucking company calls all day. You've got your own company, your own life. Why do you need mine?"

This time, I can't stop myself from shouting, "Why do *you* want me out of it? Am I *that big* a disappointment to you? Do you fucking hate me?"

"No!" His offended tone surprises me, reassures me.

"Then…why the fuck are you pushing me away?"

"Because!"

I smirk at that and throw his own words back at him. "Fuck off with the vagueness."

His eyes spark in defiance and amusement, but not hatred, and it cools my jets instantly.

Carefully, I say, "I'm in your life, okay?"

And something happens then which changes everything. Ethan gets flustered. He rolls his eyes like he did when we were kids and huffs out a breath like I'm just *so annoying*.

"Of course you are, dipshit," he says. "You're my brother. I fucking love to hate you and I fucking hate to love you, all right?"

Well shit…

My chest twists almost to pain with relief. Who knew twenty-three words could fix years of sleep-stealing, mind-fucking worry?

"Yeah?" I ask.

"Just try fucking communicating with me next time. You could have just *told me* about Vince. You could have *warned me* about Sam. You've had my back my whole life; you think I'd suddenly decide you didn't?"

Fuck, I'm an idiot.

"I spent *five years* of my life worried you weren't going to make it out of prison, numbnuts. So if you want to keep ten percent of Star-King, I just want to know what fucking scared you into acting like this."

Shit, I did all of this *because* I was scared to tell him.

"Fifteen percent."

"Twelve."

"Twenty."

Ethan smirks at that. "Fifteen."

But there's one more thing I need. Leaning forward I hold out my hand to him. He stares at it like it's a fucking tentacle, but I leave it there. "Shake on fifteen percent, and give me your word you won't change your mind once I tell you."

"Nero—"

"No. Your word."

Ethan rolls his eyes again and shakes my hand with a breathy, "Yes, fine, you dramatic fuck," and I let it be what it is.

I also don't beat around the bush. "I let Dad die."

Pain streaks across Ethan's face, and surprise; he wasn't expecting that.

"It was free time, we didn't sit together or anything. Barely spoke near the end because he was as big a piece of shit on the inside as he was back when we lived with him. A few days before he was killed, he told me you were ashamed of me, that you hoped I'd never come home, and it fucking broke me, man. Didn't sleep for days. I kept thinking he was right and I'd get out and you wouldn't need me anymore.

"We were in the day room when it happened, he was playing cards with some guys. A riot broke out and he went down. I could see him from where I was across the room, but I didn't go to him. He reached his hand out to me and I didn't go. I just left him there. I figured maybe he was having a heart attack—not that that's an excuse, but I thought they'd get to him eventually if he was. I didn't know he'd been stabbed until he was already dead."

It's sort of burned into my brain, the memory of his face as he was laying on the floor. People were everywhere and I just...kneeled where I was and put my hands on my head and let the riot sort itself out.

"Fuck, Nero," Ethan says. My eyes snap to his face, to read his expression, but I can't tell if he's judging me or pitying me.

"If it's any consolation, I hated myself. Still do."

"Nero," Ethan says. "I got the autopsy report. It was one stab. They hit his aorta. Unless they'd gotten him to a doctor in a couple of minutes, there was nothing you could've done."

That helps a little. A lot, really.

"But I didn't forgive him," I shrug. "And if I couldn't forgive him when he was dying, I thought you wouldn't forgive me for messing up. So I...started looking for ways in at Star-King. I just wanted to make sure you couldn't throw me away."

"You overreacted," Ethan says.

"Yeah. Sorry."

"Eh, you rarely do, so I knew it had to be something big. Look, I had a *long* time to make peace with a lot of shit, and our dad was shit. Do I think you need therapy? You bet your ass I do. But...all this?" He motions toward Emilio's studio, toward Kaden. "I'm sorry I said you only do things for yourself. You seem to actually care about that guy and Lulu and I *know* you care about me, so...just gimme back my company and let's do better than we used to do."

He grins as he says the last few words, and the weight I've been carrying since our dad died, finally lifts.

The silence after is...nice. Light.

And Val is the cherry on top. He finally reappears with four coffees and Ethan reaches for one to hand to me. Val glances between us and groans, "Finally. You absolute bellends have been taking the piss for way too long. I'm losing hair over you."

"Who's the fourth coffee for?" I ask instead of replying.

"Him."

As if he's psychic, he motions to Kaden, who I didn't even notice speed-walking toward the SUV.

"Did neither of you notice you couldn't hear him anymore?" Val tuts, waving my phone at us both. "Didn't even notice I nicked it. For shame."

The door wrenches open and Kaden leaps into the car. "Go!"

"How did you—"

"He finally fell asleep! For the love of God, go."

CHAPTER 72

LULU

It's nearly dawn when I hear the lock turn in the door, but none of us are asleep. We never went to bed. Wine gave way to coffee, which gave way to espresso, until Cara, Ivy, and I were so wired we couldn't have slept even if we tried.

Tracking JV down became too intense. Too fun, sort of. Like hunting your own boogeyman.

Something about the search helped a lot. It might seem silly to say, but it feels like it healed a bit of my inner child. The kid who was scared of him; she's not anymore. Not as much, anyway.

Reverse searching photos gave way to old county records and business receipts and a web of albums on social media. Eventually, in the edge of a townhall meeting photo in Vermont, I noticed JV…and Carlo…six months after I went to work for the Russos.

I took a chance.

Carlo left the family, but he always left an open line for me. An emergency number to text if I ever needed him.

So I texted asking for the truth—whether JV was in that Vermont town, and if so, what his address was.

I'd expected a response later, or maybe a warning from Carlo not to ask, but after only a few seconds he replied, *Are you sure you want to know?*

One '*Yes*' later, and I had the address in the palm of my hand.

Triumph isn't a strong enough word for what I felt. It was

overwhelming. Terrifying.

And Ivy could sense that. "We brought stuff to make French toast, hon. Want some?"

"Yeah."

They gave me a hug, guided me into Nero's kitchen, and that's where I've been ever since, letting the information ruminate.

It's well settled when I hear the lock turn in the door. I leave my seat like a cartoon character; I literally hear the chair rattle behind me and skid a little when I hit the doorway and try to angle for the foyer.

"Hey gorgeous," Nero says.

"Come here," Kaden commands.

I guess maybe I shouldn't have *launched* myself at them—they didn't sleep either—but…they don't seem to mind. They wrap their arms around me and take turns kissing me. Over their shoulders, I watch Cara greet Ethan with a foot-popping kiss, and Ivy and Val give each other a warm hug, and I'm home again.

Or finally.

I don't think I've ever felt like this before. Especially not when Nero opens his home to all of us and everyone settles in like they've come for a holiday or something. Ethan's the first to accept the offer to stay.

It's almost too good to ruin.

But hours later when everyone's rested, the guys tell us what happened last night. They tell me about Emilio's scheme to bring me back to him…and his awful paintings. For the first time in forever, the thought doesn't scare me. It motivates me.

Emilio wants me scared.

JV wanted me scared.

I don't want to be anymore. Not of them, and not of being myself.

So, I tell them about our search for JV. And I ask them all to go with me to confront him.

A few hours later, we arrive in the middle of nowhere, Vermont, and turn onto an ordinary, everyday neighborhood street where the houses are spaced just far enough apart that no one's gabbing on front porches to one another. The house is small, forgettable, and I think that's on purpose as I approach the front door with my army of friends. It doesn't look *lived in* so much as *maintained*.

Nero and Kaden's hands slide onto my shoulders when I knock, and they stay there when a nurse in scrubs answers the door.

"Louise?" she asks.

"You…know me?"

"Carlo let me know you might come. Please, come in."

The first thing I notice as I step in is the smell. Cleaning chemicals, but also shit, as if no amount of scrubbing could erase it.

The second thing I notice…are my paintings. All the art I made when I lived with JV. The art that saved me. The art JV claimed he burned. Someone framed and hung the pieces high on the walls, as if to stop someone short from tearing them down. Among and between these, someone cut out and hung articles about me. About my successes as an art advisor. The exhibitions, the gallery showings, the auctions. The latest one is about the auction on New Year's Day.

"What…is…all of this?" I ask softly, not expecting an explanation.

"Karma," the nurse replies.

I don't understand what she means until a buzzing sound fills the room, and an electronic wheelchair rolls down the hallway toward us…carrying my boogeyman.

Johan Ververs is a broken man. There's a tube sticking out of his throat, and I can tell from the thinness of his legs that he hasn't used them in a long time. The only parts of him that seem to be able to move, in fact, are his eyes, and a hand, which he uses to steer the chair.

It's hard to look at. *He's* hard to look at…because his eyes haven't changed. He's older, sure, but those eyes are the ones who used to appear at my bedroom door in the middle of the night. They're the ones that used to decide outfits for me. Positions for me, when his "friends" came to visit.

And they haven't softened at all. He stares at me as if this is *my* fault.

"Are you okay?" Kaden asks.

"You're safe," Nero echoes.

I know that. I believe that.

"What happened to him?" I ask.

"Karma," the nurse says again.

Hard to know if I should even pry deeper, but I need to know. So, I pull out my phone and text Carlo again: *Did you do this to him?*

And just like when I texted him before, he answers almost immediately: *Yes. I'm not sorry.*

I reply with the obvious: *You shouldn't have.*

Carlo replies with a picture—of a wall in an Italian villa where one of my paintings hangs, lit by the evening sun.

He doesn't deserve another second of your consideration, Lulu. Be happy, okay? Be free.

"You sure you're okay, honey?" Ivy asks.

"These are my paintings," I say. "Can you help me take them back?"

"Would love to, darlin'," Val says, stepping right past me headed for the far wall.

A second later, the rest of my friends join him. They dart around grabbing the paintings and walking away. The nurse only smiles and lets us do it.

Kaden and Nero help, until the walls are mostly bare and JV turns and disappears back down the hallway.

"What'll happen to him now?" I ask the nurse.

"Well, this is his life—Carlo hoped you'd take the paintings back. Now all he'll have to look at are the bare walls...and any new announcements of your success I hang up."

On that note, I turn to Ethan just as he's reaching for the last painting still left on the wall—it's a pair of horrible eyes in the darkness, glaring at me from across the room.

"Leave that one, please, Ethan. I painted that one for him."

One Month Later

CHAPTER 73

KADEN

"Louise, you're gonna have to show me eventually."

"Oh I will. At the exhibition."

"Not even a peek?"

"You won't let me see yours."

"Yeah, but you've already seen three-quarters of mine."

"Nope! You'll just have to be patient, baby."

"Will you let *me* see it?"

"Sorry, Big Guy."

We relocated to Nero's apartment a month ago and already Louise is hiding things from us, sneaky girl. I've explained to her several times that I'm not *hiding* the *Blue Ruin* painting, merely preserving the big reveal because I know she'll love it. She, on the other hand, is torturing Nero and me by hiding what she's going to present at the *Faces of Womanhood* Exhibition in a few days.

This apartment has six bedrooms, two of which we've converted into individual studios because she *insisted* on keeping her work a secret…which is *fucking frustrating* since she's been painting almost continuously since we returned from Vermont.

We came back here, and she couldn't stop herself. Couldn't wait. We took her to all my favorite suppliers, got her loaded up with her preferred oil paints and charcoals. Then we made a day of clearing out two rooms and letting her claim one before she kicked us out with a kiss and sealed herself away for a few hours. When she emerged, paint-splattered and glowing, she was like a leveled-up version of herself. So happy (and horny) we could barely keep up with her.

Eventually, during a post-orgasm coma, she explained that she hadn't painted since college. Hadn't allowed herself to because "JV always crawled outta the woodwork after she finished things" and the last time he did, he broke her arm and branded her.

Knowing he can never do that again, made her feel free to paint. Unleashed her.

Unleashed is one word for it.

In between traveling across the city to pose for paintings, and painting for herself, she's redecorating Nero's apartment, planning a kick-ass going away party for Ivy, and finding excuses to jump our bones every chance she gets.

It's like living with an energizer bunny.

A respectful energizer bunny, of course. One who hums and squeaks and coos so often, I feel like I'm always at half-mast now.

She says I'm just happy to be alive. And I knew she was right the moment she hugged my shoulders from behind and whispered, "So am I," into my ear.

But she still won't show me her painting—her response to Emilio's—and I've taken to hiding just outside her studio door now when I know she's coming out for the day. Not to peek but just to keep her on her toes.

Nero caught on to my game a few days ago, so he's joined me too…which has led to two incidents where Louise stepped into the hallway, saw us waiting, and climbed us like trees right then and there.

It was a tad awkward the second time, since Ethan and Cara were over for dinner, but Louise wasn't embarrassed at all. She claimed the seat between us like she'd always belonged there.

Then after they left, she sat on my and Nero's faces as if she'd always belonged there too.

CHAPTER 74

NERO

"Honey, I'm home."

Never in a million years did I ever think I'd be the sort of man who said that walking through the door of his own home. Well, to be clear, I never thought I'd have a home *or* someone waiting for me when I got there. Two somebodies.

Two freaky weirdos who have made it their personal mission to get paint on *everything* in this apartment.

I usually hear Lulu coming before I see her, the *pound-pound-pound* of her feet as she runs down the hall to greet me is fast becoming one of my favorite sounds. So is Kaden's slower, more measured step.

But as I close the door behind me today, I don't hear anybody coming and I'm not going to lie...I miss that welcome *immediately*.

Until Lulu's soprano rings out, "Come find us, Big Guy."

I spoke too soon—*that* is fast becoming one of my favorite sounds. And I chase it down the hallway until I come to their corner of the apartment, where their studios are. I find Kaden and Lulu in their painting overalls waiting for me, and the smile slides off my face. Kaden looks...upset. Lulu looks consoling.

"What happened?" I ask.

Lulu reaches for my hand immediately, enfolding her other one in Kaden's, turning us into a little chain again. "Kaden wants to show us something."

"What?" I ask.

"I realized that I probably *shouldn't* spring the *Blue Ruin* painting on you two at the exhibition tomorrow."

"Why not?"

"Yeah, we trust you," Lulu says.

Kaden shakes his head. "It might be too intimate. I want to make sure neither of you are embarrassed to be seen like this in public. If you are, tell me. We can keep this between us. Keep it here. I have other paintings I can show off."

He might as well have given Lulu her equivalent of catnip. "Now I gotta see it! Come on!"

I've been curious about which pose he'd choose from that day in his studio too, but nothing quite prepares me for the one he went with.

The right quarter of the painting is an explosion of vermilion, purple, and blue erupting away from our three figures. I'm standing behind Lulu, framing her, with my hands covering her breasts and my head tilted down to whisper in her ear. Kaden is in front of her, kneeling, feasting on her pussy with her leg over his shoulder while she stares down at him. All while Lulu's hands reach up and down to lovingly run her fingers through our hair. Our painted kisses and handprints are everywhere across each other's bodies.

From left to right, it's a moving blur of color as Lulu comes home, removes the uniform the world *out there* requires her to wear, and lets her men worship her as she truly is.

And it *is* worship. Despite the intimate nature of the painting, there's nothing lewd about it. It's our very own version of *La Femme Damnée*, modernized.

Lulu's voice is tight and high when she turns to smile at us, silver tears shining in her eyes. "Are you going to put a veil?"

Kaden smiles. "No."

I've heard them talk about his veil before, but never really understood until now what that meant. The other three paintings he's taking with him to the exhibition all have them, but this one doesn't and its absence is unignorable. And yet, there's no denying the painting is his—it's in the details on the bodies themselves; those are the same as in his other pieces.

Aside from being one of the most beautiful things I've ever seen, the fact that it's him showing off in a new way? Fuck it gets to me. This is a gift to us.

"You can show it off, but you can't sell it," I say, turning to them. "Is that okay?"

"Are you sure?" he asks.

"Oh yeah," Lulu replies. "It's us. After tomorrow, we're hanging it over our bed."

My stomach tightens at the thought, and I start to take off my shirt. "Well, in that case."

Lulu teases her lip with her teeth, and Kaden takes it as a challenge, stripping off his shirt too. I reach for my pants next.

"Ooh, is the art turning us on, Big Guy?" Lulu coos.

"Always, but…if I recall, Kaden painted part of this canvas with himself?"

Kaden smirks and Lulu's cheeks flush red with the memory and I add the obvious, "I think it's time for my contribution, don't you think?"

CHAPTER 75

LULU

Today is the first day of the rest of my life.

Today is the *Faces of Womanhood* Exhibition.

Eighteen artists. Twenty-two paintings of me—*not* including the ones I know Emilio is unveiling. Twenty-three, if we include my painting; I had to paint myself to truly humiliate Emilio, although I tried to make the female figure as general as possible.

All of the artists had to lie to the Russos about the pieces they would be exhibiting. All of them have to sneak their paintings of me in. But every single one has assured me they're going through with it. Even if they don't, with Kaden's and my work standing side by side with Emilio's, the point should still be made.

And when it is, I'm ready to confront that family once and for all.

Doesn't mean I'm not scared shitless! I'm shaking in my little booties when Ethan's SUV and a white moving van roll up outside Nero's apartment at a quarter to eleven. Kaden's four paintings, and mine, are wrapped and loaded into the van. Then my friends and my guys—my family—climb into the SUV like it's a clown car. I'm too nervous to speak, but they're here for me.

They, and we, are here for Kaden too. He's decided to disclose his identity today. To stand by his paintings proudly. And to make room for me, when my moment comes. After all, I wasn't invited to the exhibition. I'm not allowed, technically.

Fortunately, I knew a couple of rich guys who were willing to throw money at the problem. And one talented artist willing to give up one of his five spots for my painting.

That's how I find myself hiding in a retrofitted meat packing plant hall closet—I finally grew a spine and decided to stop avoiding conflict. I don't know if the Russos will ruin me for doing this, but considering all the perks I've gained since deciding to stand up for myself...

I'm willing to risk it.

CHAPTER 76

KADEN

I honestly can't believe I'm here.

My knees are weak. My throat's squidgy, like it's trying its hardest to hold back my puke from spewing across the concrete floor. There are so many people milling around it's claustrophobic, made worse by the fact that all of my friends are hiding amidst the crowd so Emilio doesn't suspect anything until Louise's moment comes.

The thought of that is the only thing that buoys me while I wait; if she's brave enough to face the Russos, then I'm brave enough to hold space for her. Frankly, "coming out" as Malbec feels more meaningful since it's actually *for* something, not just because I want the attention. I don't. It only means Ethan will receive a thousand and one more phone calls from people asking me for stuff. And my entire family will know what I've been up to. That should be fun.

Louise said I didn't have to do this, but I want to, for her.

Due to the nature of the five paintings we brought with us, they're all hanging on the wall behind me covered. They'll remain so until the right time comes. Which means *I* am currently the attraction on display. It's like a brutal form of exposure therapy.

But it also seems to be helping our cause in an unexpected way. Across the room, I can see other artists in on our plan standing in front of covered paintings of their own...and all of them have crowds forming. The hidden paintings are little lures, drawing people in.

Including Emilio.

"Hey, buddy! Long time no see!" I haven't heard Emilio's voice since I escaped his studio last month, and boy does it trigger some latent PTSD.

"Hey Emilio."

"I could not get ahold of you to save my life, man! King wouldn't give me your number," he says, swinging an arm around my shoulder. "Where have you been?"

"Hiding," I admit. "Had to get these pieces done. It's what I always do."

"Man, I do *not* get you. But! I admire you," he says, glancing at my covered wall. "You gonna unwrap everything?"

"I'm going to wait until you introduce me," I say. "I'm looking forward to it."

"Me too! This thing's kicking off soon, I'll be right back."

He rushes off to rejoin his family, almost prancing. He seems to be the only one of them excited to be here today. The other Russos look stranded on the dais with the microphone. There are no spotlights, no banners proudly declaring this to be a Russo Trust event. Louise mentioned that she usually organized these things; is that why it all looks...rustic today?

Emilio seems frustrated by the lack of support. I can't hear what's said, but Emilio sort of stomps his foot as his parents glance away.

I'd almost feel sorry for the guy...except...

Like a broken clock that's wrong all hours of the day save two, he pulls off a curtain hanging across the wall beside my section to reveal his contributions to the exhibition—two paintings that would honestly be pretty decent if he put the same amount of effort into them as he did into his triptych.

As for that three-paneled abomination...cameras begin flashing *immediately* the moment those irreverent paintings of Louise are revealed. A crowd gathers, gossip begins to spread. Emilio has definitely adopted the mindset that even bad publicity is better than none. And he eats it up, winking at me as if this is *his moment*.

Again, if he'd earned it without punching down in the process, I'd never dream of taking this from him.

As it is, I cannot wait to hit him exactly where he deserves—right where it'll hurt him the worst.

CHAPTER 77

NERO

I have Tallest Man in the Room syndrome, but literally. There are only so many spots in this building where I can loiter and not stand out like a wild hair in a field of trimmed ones. It works in our favor a little, though; one of those spots is right by the hallway where Lulu is hiding, so I'm on door duty to let her out.

I should be in there with her, but…today isn't about me.

It isn't about Emilio either, no matter how much he thinks it is.

I hear the crowd gasp and Ethan nods to me from where he's standing—the first nod is a warning. Emilio has shown his hand; those fucking insults to Lulu are on display and the crowd surges in that direction. It's probably a good thing I can't see them from here; even now I have the urge to knock his fucking lights out.

Especially as "Emilio's peacocking hour" goes on for some time. Long enough, it feels as if the entire crowd has surged in that direction, then retreated again after taking in his work.

And then, like narration from my nightmares, Emilio's twerpy voice booms over the speakers.

"Welcome! Welcome! Thank you so much for coming to the Russo Trust's *Faces of Womanhood* Exhibition. Thank you for supporting this celebration of beauty, resilience, strength, and the diverse stories that shape the essence of womanhood."

Emilio doesn't have the gravitas of his father…and it strikes me then how odd it is that Lorenzo Russo *isn't* speaking. Or at the very least, his wife. I suppose it doesn't matter.

"Today, we are honored to host some of the most incredible artists of our time—Youko Asahi, Pooja Indrani, Edin Nest."

Applause roars with each name, and he waits until the crowd falls silent again to do the tone-deaf thing I know is coming.

"They are wonderful. Fabulous artists in their own right. And they also happen to be sharing the exhibition today with art royalty. The Russo Trust is honored to have been entrusted with the true identity of a living legend, and he's chosen this event today to reveal himself to the world for the first time. He's received the prestigious Leonardo da Vinci World Award of Arts, and been shortlisted for the Praemium Imperiale. His art has been featured at The Met and Tate Modern. Please welcome, Kaden Malbec!"

More yips and gasps and roars of surprise from the crowd, more hushed conversation and flashes of light from cameras. And Ethan nods to me again.

It's Lulu's time to shine.

CHAPTER 78

KADEN

Like a kid trying to be seen in the back of a live television segment, Emilio abandons his raised spot on the dais the second the crowd turns to face me.

Fuck it makes my skin crawl, all that attention.

Even more so when Emilio appears beside me, soaking up as much notice by association as he can.

"Go ahead and unveil your work, K."

Well, if he insists…

I start with the farthest from him, ignoring the flashing lights and recording phones as I peel the brown paper off. It's the painting most like the ones I've done before—the painting of Louise pulling back the veil and peeking at us.

I don't look at him as I move to the next—Louise floating in that sea of stars.

He doesn't catch onto the pattern until I peel the cover off the third painting and I hear a soft "The fuck?" being picked up by his microphone.

I didn't bring the painting I did of Louise in my bedsheets; *Blue Ruin* is sensual enough. No, I painted something new. It's Louise as a pagan goddess, in a temple of her own, visible behind a billowing curtain, and invisible without. It's light and lofty and intentionally reverent—such a stark contrast to Emilio's paintings of her, there's no ignoring how vulgar his truly are.

And then, just to really push home the fact that everything he painted was a *choice*, and he could have *always* chosen to elevate her sexuality rather than denigrating it, I unveil *Blue Ruin*.

I knew it would cause a stir, especially hanging only a few feet away from his.

But I wasn't expecting this reaction. The crowd...whimpers. Coos? Squeals with delight.

Especially once they realize I'm in the painting.

Especially once Nero steps out of the crowd to join me, and they realize he's in it too.

Emilio isn't as thrilled to see him. He takes half a step forward as if he wants to clock the huge dude beside me, and honestly, I'd love to see him try and fail. But I know we're on borrowed time.

So instead, I pull focus as I stride across to the final painting and carefully strip away the cover to reveal...

Fuck. It's...

She...

Louise painted something even I wouldn't have the stones to do. It's a painting within a painting. An easel sits on the right side of the canvas holding Emilio's painting of her—the first vile one he did of her splayed and sexualized with a dog collar around her throat. The woman's features are a little more vague, but it's *very obviously* the first panel of the triptych sitting not three feet away.

Beside it, she painted the artist himself. Emilio. Except she turned him into...a monster. It "wears" Emilio's body and face like a mask along its front while his true grotesque nature spills out of the back.

It's beautiful.

It's hideous.

It's fucking *competent*.

And it pisses off its intended target immediately. Emilio bursts forward, red in the face, before I can even back away. I steel myself for the punch I think is coming...but it never arrives because Nero is there right behind me like a dark fucking threat.

"What the fuck, man?" Emilio whines instead. "Why would you

paint something like that?"

"He didn't," Louise's voice rings out. "I did."

CHAPTER 79

LULU

The tough thing about being small is that people think they can take advantage of you.

The nice thing about being small is that people rarely see you coming.

The crowd parts for me the moment they hear my voice, almost drawing aside the veil of humanity to reveal the bog beast himself. The bog beast and his "art," which is just as bad as Kaden warned me it was.

Especially when compared to Kaden's work.

The contrast has the exact effect Ivy thought it would—no one with half a brain could look at those paintings side by side and think Emilio's were done with genuine artistic integrity or thoughtfulness.

Knowing our plan worked steels my soul as I step forward to have the chat that's been a long time coming. So does the appearance of my friends. Cara and Ivy step to one side, Val and Ethan to another, making sure no one can interrupt what's coming.

Because I don't stop at Emilio.

I couldn't give a flying fuck about him anymore.

No, I walk right past him and up the dais stairs…to join the Russos. The guards around them seem unsure whether to hold me back or let me through, but they don't move and Lorenzo doesn't tell them to engage, and so I find myself standing face to face with the most powerful man in the city, and his awful wife.

"Hello, *signore, signora,*" I say. "May I speak with you a moment?"

The bog beast tries to interrupt, "Pops—!"

But Lorenzo's hand rises in his son's direction and the bog beast falls silent. His mother—who I have to this point avoided looking at—doesn't say anything either, which surprises me more.

"Of course, *passerotta*," Lorenzo says, shooting his son a deadly amount of side eye.

"Thank you." Setting my shoulders back a little, I tell him, "*Signore, signora*, your son lied to you. I *never* posed for his paintings. I never consented and never would have considering what he made of me. I know he's your son and I was just one of your employees but he insulted me deeply, which is why I chose to resign when I was told he was going to paint me again. I loved working for your family, *signore*, and I took that job very seriously for many years. I deserved better than how I was treated in the end. And the only reason my life isn't ruined today is because other people were willing to stand up for me."

At that, I turn and wave my hand across the gallery space.

Like a beautiful little wave, canvas covers fall away from paintings all over the room, revealing *me* twenty times over. The crowd catches on quickly, and so does Emilio. The work of the other artists only alienates his pieces more, until they're nothing more than self-indulgent pornography.

And as the crowd roars behind me, moving around to look at the other pieces, I turn back to face Lorenzo.

"I was lucky. Someone else without the sort of support I have might not have been. Emilio mispainted me, he destroyed my apartment, and he tried to use Johan Ververs to scare me into coming back to you."

At that, Lorenzo's mouth drops open and his head whips sideways to find his son, as if he didn't know…and Emilio definitely didn't tell him.

"So what would you ask of me?" Lorenzo asks after a moment.

"*Signore*, I have nothing but respect for you, but he does not have respect for me. Please help him find some."

Although I keep my eyes on Lorenzo, I catch a smile on Matteo's lips out of the corner of my eye. And then, Lorenzo steps toward me with a smile of his own. It's softer, caught between the side-eye he's giving his son and the warmth he has for me, but...

"I will see it is done," he says, before bending forward and laying a tiny blessing kiss on my forehead. "Fly free, *passerotta*."

Then, like a turning storm, he steps past me down the dais stairs toward his son.

"Pops, I—"

"No! *Va eccati!*" His hand lands on Emilio's collar and shoves him forward through the crowd and away. For another ten seconds, trickles of Italian insults of shame and disappointment echo through the building until they're gone.

It was more than I hoped for. Warmth pools in my belly, or maybe it's relief. Until—

"Is it too late to tell you I'm proud of you?"

It's not Matteo who says that to me...it's Mrs. Russo. She steps forward with an enigmatic frown-smile on her face.

"Excuse me?"

"I warned Emilio that the little bitch who found her growl would eventually discover her bite," she says, her voice ringing with shame and admiration in equal measure.

I don't know what to say to that, but she seems to. Mrs. Russo steps closer again and leans in whispering, "I am forced to keep the peace in my family; that is my duty. But you are not part of the family, so it is not yours. When Emilio began his chase of you, I tried to act as unpleasant as possible, hoping you would stand up for yourself. I forgot that your tolerance for cruelty is abnormally high. I should have been brave and spoken with you rather than scaring you away. I'm sorry for that, and my son's behavior. But...I'm not sorry that you aren't afraid to stand up for yourself anymore."

"I'm not."

"Good."

And then she steps around me and walks away. Just like that. I'm not sure I believe she really *was* trying to help me all that time. Then again, she let Lorenzo drive her precious son away, so...

Matteo steps into her place beside me. "Well done, kid."

"Thank you."

"You already have two blessings. Will you accept a third?"

"From you? Of course."

"You never needed us. Don't get me wrong, we were happy to have you, but...you deserve your own life." With a twinkle and a smile, he motions to my friends, who are all standing by Kaden's wall of art, watching us. "I'm glad to see you living it."

***

You know, I think some of the darkest moments in our lives are attempts by God to show us the light. To remind us where it is so we can walk toward it and leave the darkness behind.

Our little stunt does more than just flood the image search for 'Louise Rathbone' with artwork of myself. It earns me a profile in *ArtForum*—about my comeback as an artist after so many years away—and a legend that surges ahead of me across the art world. Just like Nero suspected I would, I start getting calls from artists all over the world asking to paint me, which is...humbling to say the least.

And daunting, because Nero seems to make it his personal mission to become my shadow PR agent. I show up on websites and private art grids that would be inaccessible otherwise. It's very sweet, but ultimately makes me feel a little bad considering it's something most artists would kill for and I earned it accidentally through a publicity stunt. So, I tell him we'll have to find another way for him to support the arts.

I also get calls from private collectors and curators asking me to contribute to various shows and galleries, and to submit for consideration for several insane art awards.

I'm just flattered anyone cares at all.

And flattered again when the guy who originally owned my *Hourglass* piece calls Kaden begging to buy it back for ten times the price.

Instead, Ethan calls in his favor with the Director of MoMa and Kaden lends my painting to them to put on display.

As for Kaden, his debut goes as well as anyone would expect, considering he looks like a Roman god and paints like a master. It's funny, though, because he becomes even *more* reclusive, as far as publicity goes. Knowing who he is and being denied information about him seems to throw the art world into a tizzy. Suddenly *everyone* has an opinion about the "Allard heir" turned artist.

But nothing quite compares to his family who suddenly start messaging him about opening a subsidiary under their *Chez Moi* brand "fueled by his creative vision."

That's all outside stuff, though. It's the frosting on an already very lovely cake.

Nero, Kaden, and I...we...well, we're pretty damn happy. I *never in a million years* thought we would last, so the fact that each day seems better than the one before? That's worth protecting.

The warmth.

The love.

The most peaceful sleep of my life sandwiched between two literal and figurative hotties.

Oh yeah, I'm a lucky girl.

Although, let's be honest, sleep isn't exactly a priority for any of us...

EPILOGUE

LULU

This is my second favorite view in the entire world.

Nero's beautiful body rests against the headboard, his powerful thighs spread in a wide V that allows me to kneel between while I take his perfect cock in my mouth, and Kaden takes my pussy from behind.

Their frenzied breathy groans speak the language my pussy is most familiar with, and she responds by squeezing and milking and begging for more.

"Fuck, Louise," Kaden says, bending over my body to kiss my spine, my scar, my shoulder. "I could live inside you."

"You do," Nero jokes in between mouthwatering hisses.

My dark angel sweeps his massive hand across my cheek, gathering the sweaty hair there, so he can see me worshiping his cock. I've discovered his favorite thing is having me tease the underside of his head with my tongue and lick his shaft and deny him as long as I can before he gets impatient. Then he uses my hair to pull me away from his dick while I try to hold onto the tip by sheer suction.

And I can tell he's gearing up for that when both his hands go to my hair. So I make a show of trailing my wet tongue over his balls and up his beautiful shaft, lingering at his frenulum. Lapping and kissing.

"Savor me," he begs, and I know it's coming. *He's* not. I won't let him yet, but...

"You want me to go *slower?*" I tease, beginning to suck his head and twirl my tongue so slowly his cock might as well be an ice cream cone.

"Fuck, don't tease me."

I don't listen, I just stare him down, smiling and daring him to do something about it as his chest begins to billow and his eyes blow wide and I know I *actually* have to back off or he'll come too quickly.

Not that it matters, really. The sight of Kaden having his way with me without him always has Nero coming back for seconds. It's some competitive thing between them—and it's *fucking hot*.

But the moment I unseal my lips from the tip of Nero's cock, he does his favorite thing. His hands fist desperately in my hair and try to pull me away to scold me. I wrap my hands around his shaft and seal my lips back, sucking and sucking and sucking in tiny little desperate bursts—like he couldn't tear me away from my favorite thing in the world if he tried!

"Oh my fucking God!" his voice gravels, watching me need him.

And his face, that beautiful ecstasy? It summons a quake in me that Kaden can feel, and he seals himself to my back thrusting and thrusting and thrusting through the orgasm, until I'm so fucking *out of it* with pleasure, I gobble Nero down all the way to the base and let him come down my throat as Kaden comes inside me.

Fuck, their moans are so beautiful. Best sound in the world.

I listen to it for ages as we allow ourselves the smallest break we can.

And then it's time for Kaden's favorite thing. I discovered it accidentally one day and now I pull it out of my little bag of tricks whenever the moment is right.

While Nero's still hard, I shimmy forward and impale myself on his beautiful dick, then reach back for Kaden. His eyes light up with a gratitude and excitement I don't know how to properly qualify. But he loves it. He loves this, me including him.

Especially when I whisper, "I love you," against his lips, then I turn to Nero and do the same.

Glorious cock coated with both of us, Kaden slides into my ass slowly, already hard again but taking his time for me, so I can adjust to the sheer *intensity* of having them both inside me. Their pressing hands. Their tongues and teeth. Their sensational cocks. It's overwhelming, being surrounded by them. My men.

Kaden seals his lips to mine and Nero suckles at one of my breasts while pulling me down onto his cock again and again until there's nothing left in him, and we all collapse together.

Then it's time for *my* favorite thing.

They've started worshipping me, when they're happy and sated. I lay between them on my back, and they take their time kissing and massaging their way up and down my body.

And the sight of them? The heavy-lidded love in their eyes?

That is my favorite view in the world.

THE END

Read the first chapter of Book 3
of the *Revenge & Riches Billionaire* series

At Your Service, Ms. Montclair

CHAPTER 1

"A little too sweet, no?"

It's amazing how fast five little words can ruin your entire day, especially in Paris.

The customer motions to a half-eaten tarte au citron sitting on their plate with the sort of concern an American would reserve for a neighbor's dog shitting on their lawn.

For shame, the look says.

More accurately it says, *I'm doing you a favor, fix this before anyone else finds out.*

Too sweet. She could've slapped me and hurt me less.

Or maybe I'm too sensitive. Back home, those would've been fighting words.

In Brooklyn, I might've said, "You want to come around the counter and say that to my face?"

But here? Spoken so gently by a customer who comes into the shop every single week? They're a humility bomb.

"Thank you," I say, offering the softest of smiles. *"I can adjust for the next batch."*

It's the answer she wants. She responds with a furrowed brow of concern and a small wave before she wanders out into the city, while I swallow the discomfort squatting on the back of my tongue and reach for the tray of now-unservable tarts.

I avoid the sideways gaze of one of our shop clerks as well, and dip back into the kitchen so I don't have to listen to their gossip about the exchange.

It's normal here. It's cultural.

That doesn't mean I want to hear it.

"Tarts?" Alex, one of my pastry cooks, asks the second he sees the tray.

"Too sweet."

"*Impossible*," he almost growls, swiping one up and biting into it. "Ridiculous. This is so sour, my balls are puckering."

Like a little chain, he hands the pastry off to my sous cheffe, Sunny, to try, and she breaks it in half, handing part to me.

My soul sinks the second lemon touches my tongue. Any non-French person would gobble that treat down like sour manna from heaven, but here? It might as well be caked in sugar.

"I like it," Sunny says with a shrug. "But my palette's still adjusting."

"Mine is not," Alex sniffs. "This is divine, and Ivy has grown too French."

Sunny and I smirk at each other.

"Is that possible?" I ask.

"A New York chef would kick somebody's ass for insulting her food in this way—we need more of that here."

"You always give the worst advice, Alex, thank you," I tease.

"*You want me to start on a new batch anyway, so we don't run out?*" he asks.

"*You're working on the order of flan pâtissier?*"

"*Oui.*"

"*Finish that. I'll do the citron.*"

Alex doesn't say anything, but every French person I've ever met knows how to say volumes without speaking at all. The subtle judgy look he gives me is one I've grown used to since I opened here in Paris—it says *that isn't what a Cheffe Pâtissière should be doing.*

Normally I'd agree with him, but one of my other pastry cooks, Myla, caught a stomach bug and we're understaffed today. And Alex has lost his damned mind if he thinks I'm going to "run out" of tarte au citron before closing time. I might be new to Paris, but I absolutely know that is a huge *faux pas* here.

I swipe a tarte au citron from a different batch to taste. It's good, and I hand the fresh tray off to one of the counter staff already waiting by the kitchen door for it. Thankfully, we're efficient enough as a kitchen now to handle mistakes like this in stride, but...

Too sweet—if that doesn't describe my whole damned life as a pastry chef.

Too naïve until I wasn't. Too inexperienced until I wasn't. Too nice for my own good.

And too sweet for an industry that routinely sanctions chefs for "knife fights in the kitchen." No, that is not a euphemism. And no, we don't do that here. It's part of why I chose pastry in the first place—the cutthroat culture of restaurant kitchens turned me all the way off before my first year of culinary school even ended.

"You okay?" Sunny asks me when I get set up at a station and start rolling out dough.

"Of course I am," I lie. "Wore my big girl pants today."

"I think you were born in those," she teases gently, before getting back to her own work glazing a fresh batch of chocolate éclairs.

Sunny's been with me a long time and she knows I'm lying, but she lets it go like she always does, and as always, I find myself grateful that I brought her with me when I left Brooklyn. It's nice to know you have a hug of home available whenever you need it.

I don't grab that hug now, of course. It was just five little words...even if those five words mean hours of unexpected work. No, I need to save those hugs for the moments that *really* hurt.

Instead, I hip bump her gently in appreciation and commiseration. She knows, like I do, that it's not *just* the fact that our tarte au citron was too sweet. It's what that means in a bigger sense that bothers me.

But that conversation isn't for Sunny; it'd be like talking to a mirror. No, I want to bitch and moan about it with people who *don't* understand. Two people in particular who love me and my sweet-ass lemon tarts exactly the way we are.

Continue reading in At Your Service, Ms. Montclair, now available on Amazon.

GRAB A <u>FREE</u> BONUS EPILOGUE FOR THIS SERIES...

As a thank you for following this series so far, I've written a bonus epilogue containing juicy updates for all five of our lovebirds so far—Ethan, Cara, Lulu, Nero, and Kaden. This epilogue also works as a fun little teaser-prologue for *At Your Service, Ms. Montclair*, the series' third book, which follows Ivy's story.

You can read that now by visiting the **Bonus Chapters** page at sierraprynne.com.

A GIANT THANK YOU TO MY PATRONS

Antonia Martin, Melanie Ansley, Jenni Appleseed, Donald and Cristy Trippeer, Allison Buckmelter, Liz Luu, Xian Xian, Naman Gupta, Tarek Tohme, Alice G, Mercedes Quiñones, Poppy Burke, Camden Ryce, Max Karyna, Lori F, Stella Forde-Fox, the Bird Trio, Olive West.

If you would like to become a patron or name a future character, please visit my website www.sierraprynne.com to learn more.

IF YOU ENJOYED *WITH PLEASURE, MS. RATHBONE…*

Reviews are insanely powerful for a self-publishing author like me because they help me draw attention to my stories. Someday, I might be lucky enough to have the financial might of a big wig publisher on my side, but for the moment it's just me.

If you've enjoyed this book, I would be eternally grateful if you could spend just five minutes leaving a review (it can be as short as you like) on whichever platform you purchased this book.

And, if social media's your style, please support me with a follow on Facebook, Instagram, and Pinterest.

ABOUT THE AUTHOR

Sierra Prynne is a cheeky little pen name inspired by a run-in with a lovely drunk lady who told me: "You can wake up ten years from now living the life you have or the life you want."

The women in my family have a tradition of using their middle names and Sierra is mine. Prynne is a gift to a certain complex and self-possessed literary character who deserved better. I'm learning about who I want to be as I write these stories and I think she'd respect that.

As for who I am, well, I'm a hopeful romantic who believes you can find true love if you're brave enough not to settle for less than extraordinary. Also, I probably like fantasy a little too much for my own good and when I'm not writing, I can be found wandering through theme parks, national parks, and book parks…those are a thing, right?

You can check out more of what I'm up to at www.sierraprynne.com or email me at sierra@sierraprynne.com.

COPYRIGHT

LURING PRESS

A LURING PRESS book.

First published in the United States in 2025 by LURING PRESS
LLC
Copyright © 2025